Praise for Jacey Bedford's *Winterwood* and *Silverwolf*

"Swashbuckling action, fol[...] about: this is an authentic E[...] tasy, magic, and class."
—Kari Sperring, author o[...]

"A fabulous and fun action-packed story, with an engaging heroine." —Liz Williams, author of *The Ghost Sister*

"I should read outside my comfort zone more often: this book proves it. *Winterwood* is an easy, compelling read which ticks loads of boxes—pirates, Fae, adventure, angst, ghosts, wild magic—whilst managing to surprise you with unexpected plot developments and delight you with its beautifully paced story and believably strange world. A delicious page-turner."
—Jaine Fenn, author of the Hidden Empire novels

"Bedford crafts emotionally complex relationships and interesting secondary characters while carefully building an innovative yet familiar world." —RT Reviews

"Bedford skillfully evokes both the society and the high seas of 1801 England as the story takes her heroes across the British Isles and into the realm of the Fae. She mixes action, intrigue, and romance in a satisfying fantasy-of-manners; Ross and Corwen make a formidable team as they fight monsters and zealots alike. This is a worthy continuation of the series." —*Publishers Weekly*

"It's like an irresistible smorgasbord of all my favorite themes and fantasy elements all in one place, and a strong, compelling female protagonist was the cherry on top."
—Bibliosanctum

"A finely crafted and well-researched plunge into swashbuckling, sorcery shape-shifting, and the Fae! Highly entertaining."
—Elizabeth Ann Scarborough, Nebula Award-winning author of *The Healer's War*

**DAW Books proudly presents
the novels of Jacey Bedford:**

Rowankind

WINTERWOOD
SILVERWOLF
ROWANKIND

The Psi-Tech Universe

EMPIRE OF DUST
CROSSWAYS
NIMBUS

ROWANKIND

Rowankind: Book Three

JACEY BEDFORD

DAW BOOKS, INC.

DONALD A. WOLLHEIM, FOUNDER

375 Hudson Street, New York NY 10014

ELIZABETH R. WOLLHEIM
SHEILA E. GILBERT
PUBLISHERS

www.dawbooks.com

First Printing, November 2018
1 2 3 4 5 6 7 8 9

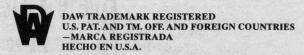

ACKNOWLEDGMENTS

My family: husband, mom, and kids for understanding and support way beyond the call of duty.

My editor: Sheila Gilbert and all at DAW, including Josh Starr. My new agent: Don Maass and my previous one, Amy Boggs, both of Donald Maass Literary Agency.

Beta readers: John and Sara Moran, Terry Jackman, Gus Smith, Tina Anghelatos, Tony Ballantyne and Sue Oke. Most of those are from the Northwrite SF writers; group. And all the Beta readers from the previous two *Rowankind* books.

My good friend and singing partner in Artisan, Hilary Spencer, who takes it as a challenge to find my typos before I make too much of a fool of myself.

Larry Rostant for his superb cover images for this and all of the *Rowankind* trilogy.

And lastly BBC Radio4 for their timely reminder that females were not allowed to observe debates in Parliament in 1802. I heard that just in time to make the alteration and avoid an egg-on-face moment.

Any other mistakes are all my own work. You can let me know when you find them via my web page at www.jaceybedford.co.uk.

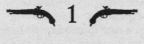

1

Trial

3rd January 1802

The Okewood, somewhere in Devon.

FREDDIE WAS ON trial for his life.

Corwen sat beside me, sick with dread. He owed his life and his allegiance to the Lady of the Forests, but he didn't owe her his brother. And he was sure that she would demand the highest price.

It was no secret that Freddie and I were not friends. For Corwen's sake, however, I hoped that some accommodation could be found for the troubled wolf and the even more troubled man sharing the same mind.

Freddie had killed one of the Lady's sprites. The matter wasn't in doubt. We had all heard the death shriek. To hear such a sound from one of the usually silent creatures had brought the whole camp running to its aid, but it was too late. The sprite was a mangled mess on the ground beneath the stark branches of a winter beech tree, and Freddie had sprite blood all over his maw.

The Lady of the Forests ruled over Britain's magical creatures—shapechangers, pixies, sprites, trolls, hobs, and even a kelpie or two. She had deep magic, but though she had acted swiftly, her sprite was beyond help.

I knew the Lady felt things deeply, but I'd never seen her weep.

Her sprites were perfectly proportioned, humanlike creatures, no more than three feet tall and of no particular gender. They carried out the Lady's bidding in silence. They were her eyes and ears, agents of healing and nourishment, silent helpers, but so much more than servants.

I had never seen one injured or ill before, never mind dead. They didn't age, unless there was a home for retired sprites somewhere deep in the Okewood that none of us knew about.

I couldn't weep for the sprite. I hadn't known it, but the Lady's grief caused my own eyes to leak saltwater.

The Lady called, and her sprites answered, emerging from between the trees, more of them than I'd ever seen in one place or at one time before. They were almost indistinguishable from one another, but when you saw them together, you could pick out slight differences. They gathered around the small corpse, covered it in a silken cloth, and four of them carried away their fallen comrade without a second look at the miscreant who had done the deed.

Freddie, still in wolf form, lay with his nose between his paws, his ears flattened to his skull. He knew what he'd done.

Corwen knelt beside his brother. I wanted to tell him not to, that Freddie was dangerous, even to his own kin. The sprite wasn't Freddie's first kill.

"What were you thinking, Freddie boy?" Corwen asked softly.

Freddie whined in the back of his throat.

"I don't know what's to be done with you."

"That is for me to decide." The Lady loomed over both of them. I don't think I'd ever heard her voice so cold before.

Corwen rocked back on his heels.

"Change!" the Lady commanded Freddie.

"You can do it," Corwen encouraged him.

Freddie's wolf-change had never been easy. Both Corwen and his sister Lily had changed as children and their changes were fluid and fast, but Freddie's was a bone-wrenching, gut-churning change. You could hear his joints popping and his tendons twisting.

"Change!" This time the Lady wasn't taking no for an answer. She was going to force him to change, here in full view of everyone.

Freddie yowled, possibly in protest—it was hard to tell, but the Lady simply folded her arms across her chest and said once more, "Change!"

Freddie's fur began to shrink back from his front paws and his fingers extended. It was a start.

He flung himself sideways, his tongue lolling out of his mouth. As we watched, it began to shrink back, and his snout shortened perceptibly. He whined again, but this time the whine had a more human sound to it, more like a groan. He arched his back, and his whole rib cage began to snap and pop as it changed shape.

I couldn't watch anymore. All I could think of was that I was thankful Corwen's change wasn't like that or—if it was—it was all over in an instant.

"Does it hurt when you change?" I asked Corwen. "I mean, do you go through all that but faster?"

"You've never asked me that before."

"Your change seems almost instantaneous. If I thought that was what you went through—"

"You'd what? Walk away from me? Smother me with pity?"

I shook my head.

"There is a moment . . . but the pain is fleeting, and I've learned to ignore it, knowing it won't last."

"You never said."

He shrugged. "It is what it is."

Freddie's change was advanced now. He was almost human again, though covered in wolf hair which only retracted gradually. By the look on Freddie's face, even that hurt.

Charlotte, our rowankind friend, one of the magical refugees under the Lady's protection, walked forward and dropped a blanket over Freddie to cover his nakedness.

He clutched it around himself as he became fully human once more.

There was still sprite blood on his chin.

He sat on the ground, shivering but not, I thought, from the cold. Everything about the way he held himself, his arms wrapped around his chest defensively, said that he was miserable and ashamed. He knew that the Lady had ordered magicals killed for the kind of transgressions he'd committed at least twice. He looked directly at the floor, not even glancing up when Corwen said, "Welcome back, brother."

The Lady contemplated Freddie.

I don't know exactly what or who the Lady of the Forests is. She's not one of the Fae and she's not a goddess, not quite, though her powers are extensive. She is the consort of the Green Man, who may have been worshipped as a god once, long ago, by the number of carvings of foliate heads on many of our ancient churches. The nearest I can reconcile is that they are, between them, the spirit of the land given form. He is the earth and slow-growing things; she is the skittering woodland creature, the half-seen doe in the deep woods, and the lark in the clear sky.

He appears in leather, crowned by horns, skin like tree bark, eyes unfathomable. In the spring when the sap rises, he's the May King and Jack in the Green. In the summer he's the Oak King, Herne the Hunter, the Green Knight, and Robin Hood. In the autumn he's John Barleycorn, and when the snow falls, he's the Holly King and the Lord of Misrule.

His consort, his queen, however, shuns all names. She simply is. Sometimes she appears as a fresh-faced virgin, at other times she carries her pregnant belly high and with pride. She may also appear as a mature woman, wise and powerful. She is the nameless maiden, the mother, and the crone: three in one.

Even the Fae recognize that the couple are to be respected in all things.

"Frederick Deverell." The Lady spoke and then left the air empty of sound until, inch by inch, Freddie was compelled to look up and meet her eyes. I don't know what she saw when she looked at him, and I don't know what Freddie saw when he looked at her, but their eye contact continued without words until Freddie looked away again.

"A sprite lies dead," the Lady said. "What do you have to say for yourself?"

Freddie shook his head. "I killed it."

"That much is obvious. Why?"

He shook his head. "I don't know. It . . . annoyed me."

"If I killed every creature that annoyed me, half of England would be covered with graves. I don't accept your reason."

"It came . . . too close to me."

"That is not normally an excuse to commit murder. Have you anything to say before I pass judgment?"

Freddie didn't answer. I could see where this was going. The wolf wasn't helping his own case.

"May I speak?" Corwen asked.

The Lady nodded. "Someone had better speak for him. He's not speaking well for himself."

"Freddie hates his wolf," Corwen said. "And that might be my fault. For many years I was the only shapechanger in our family. My father never understood that I had no choice in what I was, and he gave me hell for it. Freddie thought himself safe when time passed and he didn't change. He spent too many years sneering at me, so his metamorphosis came as a terrible shock. He felt that his own body had betrayed him and was angry and resentful. He tried to hold back the changes, so when they eventually forced themselves on him, they were violent and uncontrollable. His wolf terrifies him, and he lashes out."

"You make me sound like a coward, brother."

"It's not cowardice, Freddie. This is not something that most men ever have to face. I left you to face it alone, and for that I'm sorry."

"I wasn't alone. I was at university. A friend stayed by me, but he's gone now. I drove him away."

"You try to drive everyone away, but that's not who

you really are, Freddie. You have family. They want you back home. Since Father died, it all belongs to you."

Freddie bared his teeth as if he were still a wolf. "You don't understand, do you? I don't want to go home. I don't want to be a country gentleman. I can't be what Mother wants me to be." He turned to the Lady. "Pronounce sentence. I won't fight it."

"I'll fight it." Charlotte stepped forward. "The Mysterium took my daughter, Olivia, and imprisoned her at sea on the *Guillaume Tell*. Freddie was there, in wolf form, tortured every day to make him change to human. They turned him savage, but when they threw my child into his cage, he protected her. The way he behaves is not his fault. I'm sure there's a good man trapped inside the wolf. My daughter loves him and with good reason. I will always be grateful to him."

It was my turn. I tried to be as concise as I could, though the story could have been much longer if I'd told it all. "I don't know about the sprite, and I make no excuses for Freddie's actions today, but the first time he killed, he did it to save my life. He killed the man who'd tortured him for weeks and who would have murdered me with dark magic. If Freddie hadn't intervened, I wouldn't be here."

"Two lives saved. Two lives lost," Corwen said. "Balance of a sort."

The Lady remained silent. Her face gave nothing away. Finally, she nodded.

I heard Corwen release a pent-up breath. "If we take him to our cottage in the Old Maizy Forest, far from where he can hurt anyone, we can let his spirit heal."

The Lady looked around. "Does anyone have anything else to say before I pass judgment?" She looked at a group of sprites. "You?"

They shook their heads.

"All right, Freddie. I will give you one more chance, but you need to learn to control your wolf. To that end you will stay a wolf until you learn. Do you understand?"

"I do." He lifted his head. "I'm truly sorry about the sprite."

"If you are, then you will do everything in your power to make sure it never happens again. If it does, I will end you as I would end a mad dog. You have been warned."

"Thank you, my lady."

"You may change to wolf now and stay that way until I give permission to change back."

Freddie's change began again. It was no easier than his change from wolf to man. I winced and tried not to feel too much sympathy. We were going into self-imposed exile to keep Freddie safe . . . or to keep the world safe from Freddie.

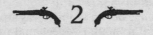

2

Letter

I'M A WITCH.

I have very good hearing. Magically good. I can hear someone sneaking up on me a mile away.

This time it wasn't the clip-clop of hooves, nor the soft tread of boots, but the rustle of a small animal running through winter-wet grass followed by the snick of claws on the flagstones of our front path.

"We have a visitor," I said.

Corwen pushed his dish away and sat back in his chair, nostrils flaring. "Relax, it's Aileen."

Corwen's nose is a thing of beauty. All I could smell was the rabbit stew in my bowl.

A snarl and a frightened yelp brought Corwen to his feet so fast that the crockery on the table rattled and his chair crashed onto the hard earthen floor.

"That's Freddie!" he said.

I grabbed the latch and yanked the door back on its hinges, sucking a great gust of chill air into the cottage. Corwen raced into the yard ahead of me. A ginger fox bolted down the path, Freddie snapping at her heels. The fox hurled herself at Corwen. He scooped her up into his arms and whirled around to shelter her with his own body. Freddie skidded to a halt, but not fast enough to prevent him from slithering sideways and hitting Corwen in the back of the knees.

Wolf, man, and fox landed in a tangle on the damp path.

"Freddie, no!" I grabbed the broom by the door, fending the wolf away from his prey. "Leave the fox! Leave her. Leave!"

Freddie suffered from selective deafness when he was in wolf form. Anything more complicated than a few basic words didn't get through to any part of his brain that understood language.

He was on his last warning. We couldn't allow him to attack anyone else.

The fox twisted free and fled into the cottage. She leaped onto the table and dropped flat between the remains of our dinner. It was then I noticed she carried a letter in her jaws.

Corwen had rolled onto all fours and was staring Freddie down, eye to eye. "That's no way to treat a visitor," he said.

I didn't know how Corwen managed to keep his temper with Freddie. Surely, he could only take brotherly love so far. Freddie was a danger to himself and to all those around him.

Freddie retreated, ears back, head down, looking repentant, though it was probably just for show. I didn't trust him to stay that way. He'd shown signs of improving since the sprite incident. Then something like this happened, and we were back to the beginning again.

"I should think so." Corwen took it as an apology and stood, brushing off the backside of his breeches.

They often had these one-sided conversations, Corwen inferring answers from Freddie's stance or expression.

Freddie's long sojourn in wolf form worried Corwen half to death. Corwen rarely stayed a wolf for more than a few hours. It was too easy to get lost inside the beast.

But we still hadn't seen enough improvement in Freddie to seek dispensation from the Lady for him to turn back.

I was beginning to think Freddie had already surrendered himself to the wolf. For Corwen's sake, I hoped not. In the space of just over a year, Corwen had already lost an older brother and his father; he didn't want to lose Freddie, too, troublesome as Freddie was.

"Are you coming in or going out?" he said to Freddie, holding the door wide. "If you come in, you have to be polite to our visitor."

"Hurry up, one way or the other," I said. "It's freezing."

Freddie turned and slunk back down the path toward his favorite willow tree. He had a thick pelt to keep him warm, so Corwen shrugged and closed the door.

The fox, whose name was Aileen Reynard when she was in human form, had dropped the letter on the table. She sat amidst the debris of our meal with her tail wrapped around her feet, trembling slightly.

I pulled a blanket off our bed and held it up between her and Corwen. He looked the other way while she jumped down from the table and transformed into a skinny, ginger-haired girl, naked except for a small pouch tied around her neck. I draped the blanket over her shoulders and she drew it closer, shivering from the sudden loss of her fur coat.

"Thank 'ee kindly, Missis. Yon wolf is in a bad mood today. He nearly had me."

"Sorry about Freddie," Corwen said. "His manners are abominable. Come to the fire and warm yourself. Are you all right?"

Aileen stuck her chin out and took a deep breath but made no move toward the hearth. "Aye. He only had a few hairs out of the end of my tail. Do you want me to wait for a reply?" She nodded to the letter lying on the table, crumpled and damp.

Corwen tore it open and skimmed it.

"Thank you, Aileen. No reply." He gave her a coin which she dropped into the pouch with evident pleasure.

I saw the glint of gold, a solid apology for Freddie's behavior.

"Right, then. I'll be going, sir, if you'll see me safe past the gate."

Corwen opened the door and shepherded Aileen past the willow tree where Freddie lay, curled nose to tail beneath its branches. He didn't even flick one ear in Corwen's direction. At the gate Aileen dropped to all fours beneath the blanket. A fox shot out and disappeared into the forest's undergrowth.

Corwen glanced at Freddie again. "No following, brother. Leave the fox-girl alone. She's hardly more than a child. If you want some exercise, I'll give you a run you won't soon forget."

Freddie whimpered in the back of his throat.

"Good. As long as we understand each other."

Corwen returned to the cottage and sat down at the table. Our meal was cold and congealed. He read the letter as I cleared away the bowls. He took a deep breath, put it down, and picked it up again. I recognized the handwriting. It was from Lily, his younger sister.

I wanted to snatch the letter from him, but I could only wait until he was ready to tell me the contents.

"Bad news from home?" I asked. "Your mother?"

Corwen's father had died in early December. He'd slipped away peacefully in his sleep after spending a year immobile and uncommunicative following an apoplectic attack. His death had hit Corwen's mother hard, but my one-time maid Poppy had stepped up into the role of housekeeper and was doing a splendid job of looking after domestic arrangements at Denby House. Stephen Yeardley, her husband, was acting as estate steward until Freddie chose to reclaim his inheritance.

If he ever did.

"Not Mother. If there was a problem, Lily would have told me." Corwen stared at the letter again. "It's the rowankind at the mill. The Mysterium has accused two of them of practicing magic."

"Who?"

"Jem Richards and Sam Hardcastle. I know them both. They're good men. The Mysterium has had them arrested and taken to Sheffield."

"Did the Mysterium have grounds? Were they practicing magic?"

"Not according to Lily, at least, not that she knows."

"God's ballocks!" My command of the English language vanished, and I could only manage an obscenity from my seafaring days.

"I couldn't have put it better myself," Corwen said.

He ran a hand through his hair and read the letter again. He may have been more restrained in his language, but I was under no illusions; he felt this injustice as deeply as I did. All Great Britain's magicals, ourselves included, were in danger from the Mysterium, but the rowankind were innocents, their magic newly awakened. They didn't deserve to be dragged away and hanged.

It was less than two years ago that I'd first become involved in efforts to free the rowankind from two centuries of bondage. We'd succeeded, and thousands of rowankind had gained their birthright, the use of natural magic. They'd shrugged off their masters. Some had gone to Iaru, to live with the Fae. Others had chosen to remain and make their own lives in Britain. It had been, for the most part, a peaceful revolution. I'm not even sure that the Mysterium, so focused on prosecuting human witches, realized that the rowankind had magic—not at first anyway.

Rowankind have weather magic. They can calm a storm, or call a wind, or cause water to flow uphill. They can bring gentle rain or whip up a gale.

When the authorities noticed, I suppose their first reaction was fear, and that makes men either courageous or cowardly. The courageous reaction would have been to talk to the rowankind, find out their capabilities, ask what accommodations could be made for them to live peacefully alongside humanity. Unfortunately, the cowardly way prevailed. The Mysterium must have decided to strike first at what it perceived to be a threat.

The rowankind were not, in fact, a threat. They hadn't used their magical power against humanity. I was amazed and impressed. After two hundred years of bondage, they could be forgiven for a little righteous anger.

Corwen turned the letter over. "Lily sent this on the sixteenth of January. It's taken five days to reach us, but there may be something we can do if we act quickly."

"We're going to Yorkshire, then." I stood. "I'll pack. But we can't take Freddie. Dare we leave him here without supervision?"

"One of us should stay with him," Corwen said.

"If you mean me, that won't work." I scowled. "You know Freddie would sooner tear out my throat than obey me."

"Could we ask David?"

"To wolf-mind?"

Corwen shrugged. "Will he?"

"He might have a solution or a suggestion," I said. "The Fae keep him busy, but they want a favor from us, so they might be willing to let him help."

"Can you call him?"

I nodded.

I have some wind and weather empathy, and can perform a few small magics, but my large talent is that of a summoner. I can call things and people to me as long as I have a connection with them. I can also summon spirits of the dead, something I don't do lightly, at least, not anymore.

I concentrated my thoughts and invited David to visit.

Our cottage was in that liminal space, halfway between the real world and Iaru, the realm of the Fae. A glamour protected it from all but the most determined.

Iaru and our world coexist in the same space, though maybe not the same time, since in Iaru it's always summer. There are gates that link the two. A Fae like David could open new gates. Corwen and I, with permission from the Fae Council of Seven, could only pass through existing ones.

I heard David coming and opened the cottage door as

he walked up the garden path, glancing sideways at Freddie, still lying under the willow tree. Freddie's ears and eyes tracked David's approach, but otherwise he didn't move.

It was drizzling, but the dampness didn't touch David—one of the benefits of being Fae.

"David!" I hugged my little brother. He was now taller than me by a handspan. At sixteen he was no longer a gangling youth. Though we shared a mother, David was all Fae due to his father's heritage. Fae matured quickly and then stayed young for centuries. They aged so slowly that I thought the elders I'd seen might have already been middle-aged when Jesus walked the earth.

David hugged me back. He was warm and dry and smelled of summer.

The rest of the Fae never hugged. They were too icy in their dealings with mere humans. David had grown up among humans, though, so I hoped he would never lose his warmth.

David and Corwen shook hands. They were about the same height now, but Corwen had more muscle. David had a lithe elegance, however, emphasized by the immaculate calf-length robe he wore over soft trousers. The colors were all greens, from the shimmering emerald of the robe to a darker forest green for the trousers. He looked every inch the Fae prince that he was.

"You wanted me," he said.

"Come into the cottage. Close the door. I'll put the kettle on."

"Ah, tea. I miss that."

Food and drink in Iaru is magical, but they don't have tea, and they don't understand the ritual of tea-making and its social importance.

"Well, we don't have a china tea service, but we do have tea."

"Are you coming in, Freddie?" Corwen opened the door and called, but the brown wolf never moved.

"Still sulking?" David asked.

"I'm afraid it's beyond sulking now." Corwen closed

the door. "I made the Lady a promise, but I admit I don't know how to deal with him, and time is passing. We have things to do and promises to keep, as well you know. We hoped you could help us with Freddie."

David pressed his lips together. There was no magical solution to Freddie's ailment.

"We need to go back to Yorkshire right now," Corwen said. "The Mysterium has taken two of the rowankind workers from Deverell's Mill."

I passed Lily's letter over to David.

"Does my father know?" David asked.

"I don't know. I hope not," I said. "The consequences could be dire if the Fae react. Please don't say anything until we've had the opportunity to find out what's happened and why."

"I won't say anything unless I'm asked a direct question."

The Fae had given us a task. They demanded we deliver their warning to King George: *look after the rowankind and treat them with respect or suffer the consequences.* It was a ridiculous task for a pair of commoners with no access to the court. Unfortunately, when the Fae asked for something, they wouldn't accept a refusal, even for the best of reasons.

"We can't take Freddie to Yorkshire," Corwen said. "Can you look after him for us?"

There was a low growl outside the door. Corwen opened it. Freddie stood on the threshold.

"Yes, you do need looking after," Corwen told him. "If only to protect others."

The growl subsided.

"Come in if you're coming, Freddie," I said, reaching for my shawl. "You might have a fur coat on, but I don't, and you're letting the heat out."

But Freddie didn't move.

David looked at Freddie. "What if I put a barrier around the cottage and its environs?" He turned back to us. "Freddie won't be able to leave, but more importantly, no one will be able to stumble into Freddie's territory by accident. It won't be a fence, simply an invisible barrier no outsider will be able to cross in either direction. There will still be game for Freddie to hunt."

"Can we cross it?" I asked.

He nodded. "I'll show you how to unpick the working at the edges and then how to remove it completely when you're done with it."

Corwen nodded. "If that's all right with Freddie. I won't cage him unless he agrees."

Freddie had been looking from Corwen to David and back again as they spoke, following the conversation.

David looked directly at Freddie. "What do you think?"

Freddie yipped once, turned, and padded back to the willow.

"It looks like he agrees," I said. "At least he's not snarling at any of us. That's probably as good as we'll get."

I pushed the door closed again.

❦

My own magic works when I concentrate my thoughts and will something to happen. Back when I'd thought David was my half-rowankind little brother, I'd helped him to tame his powerful fire magic by teaching him the way I did things. He'd obviously learned a lot from the Fae since Larien had taken him into Iaru, so I was curious to watch David's magic at work now. Insulated from the January weather by my heavy woolen cloak, I followed him down the path. He collected his horse, grazing outside the garden fence, and with a light touch on the rein led him toward the path which ran through the Old Maizy Forest, entirely in the real world. Travelers could pass by within half a mile of our cottage and never know we were here, protected as we were by a glamour.

Safely cottage-side of the path, David mounted his horse and pointed a finger at the ground. A flame sprang up. Startled, I gasped and stepped back, bumping into Corwen who steadied me and whispered, "There's no heat."

He was right. The flame was an illusion.

"Wait here," David said, and touched his heels lightly to his horse's sides. The animal leaped forward from a standing start into a gallop. Wherever they passed, a ten-foot-tall wall of cold flame blazed up. I watched David's path through the winter-bare trees as he sped away from us, enclosing a sizable hunting ground for Freddie, and coming back to us from the opposite direction. He closed the circle with us inside it, whispered a word, and the flames died down, not even leaving scorch marks.

He drew Corwen and me into the middle of the barrier. My head swam, and my skin itched all over as if a million ants were crawling across my body. He put his index finger first to my forehead and then to Corwen's. I suddenly saw the shape of the spell and understood its working.

Corwen nodded. "Got it."

David smiled and led us back out. "A normal human can't push through the invisible barrier from the outside, and Freddie can't push through from the inside. Since you two know what it is, and how to cross it, it should hardly disturb you. You might feel dizzy as you pass through, but the effect will quickly fade."

It was a small price to pay for knowing Freddie would be safe, and the world would be safe from Freddie.

3

Rowankind

DAVID LEFT US to our packing. Corwen put on his coat and went outside to talk to Freddie. I opened the window a crack to listen. He explained why we had to go back to Yorkshire. I thought Freddie wasn't paying attention, but when Corwen got to the part about the Mysterium taking the two rowankind, I heard a low growl.

"Yes, the Mysterium," Corwen continued. "That's why we have to go quickly and take the shortest route through Iaru. If we're not back within a few days, David will check on you, but in the meantime, take it easy."

As usual, Freddie's reply was silence, but he'd understood enough.

Corwen called our horses from where they were grazing. Corwen's gray, Timpani, stood sixteen hands high, and my bay, Dancer, was a couple of inches shorter. Both had elegant heads and intelligent eyes. They were beautiful creatures, a gift from the Fae, and far wiser than normal horses. I was sure they were sentient in some way, but Corwen assured me they weren't shapeshifters, which was a great relief. That would have been so embarrassing to discover.

I tied our valise onto the back of Timpani's saddle. Though small, it held all our clothes and belongings. Like the horses, it was a gift from the Fae, but we'd never asked how it worked. No matter how much you put in it, it never got full and it never got any heavier.

"Ready?" Corwen asked.

I nodded. He held his hand out for my left ankle and boosted me into Dancer's saddle, then handed me my warm cloak as an outer layer over my riding habit. It seemed prudent to dress properly for a visit to Denby House. Corwen's mama had seen me in man's attire, but she didn't really approve. Besides, I would scandalize the neighbors if we arrived during a social visit. Regardless of convention, however, I refused to use a sidesaddle. Riding astride in a dress was awkward, so I'd had my riding habit made with a split skirt.

We rode deeper into the forest. The gate into Iaru is barely a mile from the cottage. It doesn't look like a gate. In fact, it doesn't really look like anything, but pass through it in the right direction and suddenly it's summer without you actually noticing a transition. Corwen is much better at locating the gates to Iaru than I am, but I can feel the transition in my bones. Dancer knew it, too, and he tossed his head in appreciation.

It didn't take long for me to shrug off the cloak and drape it across the pommel of my saddle. Iaru is always the same balmy temperature of late spring, early summer. It must rain there sometimes, or the grass wouldn't be so green and the forests so verdant, but I've never been caught in a rainstorm. Maybe it only ever rains at night, or maybe the Fae keep moisture in the ground by magic. Their connection with the earth runs very deep if they can control the weather to such a degree.

Iaru occupies another dimension alongside ours. Imagine two sheets of loosely rolled paper existing in the same space, sometimes touching, sometimes not. There are places where they touch, and if you know how, and

have permission, you can pass through from one to the
other, and then out again miles from where you started.

Iaru is not simply summer, it's the best summer can be.
Tall and stately broad-leaved trees rustle their branches
gently, though down at ground level whatever breeze
blows up above is muted to a gentle breath. I felt the
breeze kiss my cheek in welcome and heard the splash of
a swiftly running stream close by. I breathed in the summer scents of the forest, redolent with ripe vegetation.
Bushes I couldn't identify flowered profusely along the
side of the track where dappled light filtered in through
the gap in the forest's crown. There was no sign of habita-
tion. That didn't mean the Fae were far away, but I
doubted they would approach us.

Corwen knew where he was going, so I followed him
through Iaru, half recognizing some landmarks. We had
a choice of routes. There was a gate which David had
created for us near the mill, or we could emerge from
Iaru south of Sheffield and pass through the city. The
rowankind had been taken to Sheffield, so that's where we
would go first. Corwen knew the Mysterium office was
close to the market on what had once been the site of a
castle, at the confluence of two rivers, the Sheaf and
the Don.

The effects of Sheffield's industrialization—the grime,
the noxious effluent, and the smoke-filled air—were bleeding through into Iaru to the consternation of the Fae. It
made the gate to Sheffield easy to spot, even for me.

We emerged south of the town close to the Baslow
road and rode down the hill into the pall of smoke from
the steel mills and iron foundries. Sheffield was sub-
merged in a constant sooty haze, day in and day out.
Heaven knew what it did to the lungs of the people who
lived here.

The streets were full of traffic, heavy carts rumbling
over cobbles on iron-shod wheels, packhorses and por-
ters, as well as people going about their business. Rows of
brick houses stepped down to the steel mills, crowding in
on themselves. The center of the town, though devoid of

large foundries, was tightly packed with shops and businesses. Yards nestled between buildings with workshops run by little mesters, craftsmen of high repute finishing the blades and fitting the handles of cutlery, small pocket knives, and edge-tools. Today it seemed as if the whole world was crammed into Sheffield's streets.

"We seem to be going in the wrong direction," Corwen said as we pressed through the crush, Timpani and Dancer shoulder to shoulder, eyeing the crowd warily.

"Where are they all going?" I asked, and then realized the awful truth as we reached the market square.

"They're coming from, not going to," Corwen said through clenched teeth.

In the market square, six bodies, all in white hoods, dangled from a triangular gallows, two to each side. The crowd had lost interest, and most of them had already drifted away.

I closed my eyes and concentrated on breathing to quell the sick feeling in the pit of my stomach.

"Are they . . . ?"

"Ours? I can't tell." Corwen almost choked on his words. "If they are, we're too late to do anything. It must be recent. They only leave them hanging for an hour before taking them down. You, there!" he positioned Timpani in front of a stout fellow leaving the marketplace. "What's going on here?"

"Not from around here, are you?" the man said. "You missed it. Witches. Hanged."

"Are they rowankind?"

"Dunno. Does it matter? Witches."

"What were they accused of?"

"Dunno. Witch stuff."

Corwen eased Timpani to the side and let the man past. He swore under his breath and turned away.

We left Sheffield at a fast clip, following the River Don for a while then climbing up to Oughtibridge and over the moor top by Snowden Hill toward Denby.

"Do you think our men were among the hanged?" I asked as we trotted through Ingbirchworth Village.

"I hope not, but whoever they were, it's six more lives lost to the Mysterium."

The Mysterium had targeted a group of Lily's mill workers as magic users last year. They'd fled to Iaru. It was a pity Richards and Hardcastle hadn't gone, too. Had they actually been using magic, or were they victims of some informer with a grudge?

The darkening afternoon washed all color out of the Yorkshire countryside. At this time of year dusk arrived early with a little over seven hours of weak daylight between sunrise and sunset.

Dancer snorted and lived up to his name by jiggling sideways. He pricked up his ears and stepped out eagerly as we turned for Denby House, Corwen's family home.

It was a grand house, elegantly proportioned, with origins going back centuries. Corwen's grandfather had rebuilt it in the modern, classical style, and Corwen's father had added a wing at either side of the main house to accommodate his growing family.

The stable courtyard, close to the house, was the province of Thomas Bridge, who'd been with the Deverell family since before Corwen was born and who knew the family secret and guarded it well.

"Mr. Corwen, sir, and Mrs. Rossalinde." Thomas came scurrying out from under the arched gateway as we halted in front of the house. "Good to see you both, but a sad day."

"How goes it, Thomas?" Corwen asked as we handed over the horses.

Thomas didn't have time to answer before Lily yanked open the front door and ran to meet us.

"Where have you been?" Lily's face flushed with anger, her eyes were red-rimmed with tears. "Why couldn't you have come yesterday?"

"Hello, Lily. Nice to see you, too," Corwen said. "We only got your letter this morning. We came through Sheffield."

As Thomas took charge of Timpani and Dancer, Lily grabbed each of us by the wrist and almost dragged us into the hallway.

"You saw, then? They hanged them. This morning. Without even a trial or proof or anything." She dropped our hands. "George came to let me know."

George?

I looked up. Behind Lily, hovering as if unsure of his welcome, stood George Pomeroy, the Mysterium agent.

I stepped back so quickly that I trod on Corwen's foot, but he hardly seemed to notice. He inserted himself protectively between me and Pomeroy. I sensed his wolf coming to the fore, but he didn't change.

The moment was charged with intent.

"Corwen, stand down! It's all right."

It may have been the second or third time of Lily saying it that finally got through to Corwen's wolf-brain. I felt the tension ease.

"He's a friend," Lily said, keeping it simple. "Friend."

Corwen took a deep breath.

Pomeroy had proved an ally when the redcoats had come to the mill intent on taking the rowankind magic users. He'd given us time to send the rowankind away, though I'm sure he'd never expected us to call David to take them to safety in Iaru. I knew he was sweet on Lily, but I didn't realize she was sweet on him until she turned and took him by the elbow, drawing him into our circle.

More than sweet. I recognized the signs.

I put my hand on Corwen's forearm to prevent him from saying anything rash until we'd heard what Pomeroy and Lily had to say.

"Mr. Pomeroy." Anyone who knew Corwen well would have heard the tension in his voice, but I doubted Pomeroy noticed.

"Your servant, sir." Pomeroy inclined his head enough to be polite, but not enough to appear subservient, then he turned to me and did the same.

I dipped a curtsey in return, thankful I'd not dressed in breeches. "Mr. Pomeroy, how . . . unexpected."

"Mrs. Deverell, ma'am. I'm pleased to see you took no injury after the circumstances of our last meeting."

"None whatsoever, thank you."

"A strange occurrence, was it not? To see the mill's rowankind create magic like that and then disappear."

He was fishing. He'd recognized David as Fae, I was sure of it. Had he played it down and attributed all the magic that happened to the rowankind themselves?

"I've never seen anything like that before," I said with all honesty.

"Quite." He almost sounded as if he believed me. "I reported all the magical rowankind gone from Deverell's Mill," he said. "I'm so very sorry these two—"

"You can say their names, George," Lily said, a shiver of anger in her voice.

Pomeroy inclined his head. "Jem Richards and Sam Hardcastle. I'm sorry for what's happened. Believe me, I had nothing to do with the accusation or the arrest. If I'd known it was going to happen, I would have warned—"

"I know you would." Lily patted his hand and turned to Corwen. "George is a friend. It bears repeating, brother."

How much of a friend? Had Lily told him anything about the family secrets? I could see Corwen wanted to ask, but the very action of asking might do damage if she hadn't told him anything. I saw Lily shake her head slightly as if answering Corwen's unspoken question.

"Let's take tea," Lily said. "Mother is resting. There's no need to disturb her." That was a euphemistic way of saying that Mama was in bed with her head under the blankets. She had bouts where she refused to come downstairs for days on end. She'd always been a strong woman, but her strength seemed to have evaporated when her husband died. She'd always had to be strong for her children, but they were now grown and independent. Then she'd had to be strong for Corwen's father while he was so ill. Now she only had to be strong for herself, but she didn't seem to be able to find the will.

Lily led the way into the parlor. In daylight it had a magnificent view across the grounds to the lake at the bottom of the gentle slope, but now the shutters were closed against the oncoming darkness. "Please, sit. I'll ring for tea."

Corwen and I sat side by side on the sofa with Pomeroy across from us. A fire burned merrily in the grate. Were it not for the underlying tension, it could have been any cozy family scene.

Mary appeared from belowstairs, took the order for tea, and disappeared again.

"So," Corwen said. "Jem Richards and Sam Hardcastle. I know Sam had family. What about Jem?"

"A widower with no children," Lily said, seating herself next to Pomeroy. "He lodged with Sam and his family."

"We must see Sam's widow and children taken care of, of course. Is she rowankind?"

"No, a local woman. That's what saved her, I believe. And the children look more like their mother, all except for the oldest boy—nine years old—who took off like a rabbit when the redcoats came. He's the one who raised the alarm. By the time neighbors arrived, the redcoats had both men trussed like Christmas geese."

Though rowankind were not allowed to marry officially, if a couple jumped the broom together, they were considered respectably married by the community, even without an entry in the parish register.

"Did the redcoats read out any charges?" I asked.

Lily shook her head. "I don't know. Mrs. Hardcastle doesn't remember. There was a scuffle. They pushed her aside. She knows both men were accused of witchcraft, but she doesn't recall how formal the accusation was or whether the redcoats had any papers."

George Pomeroy cleared his throat. "If I may continue the story."

We all turned our attention on him.

"When I heard what had happened, I rode straight to Sheffield with a writ of *habeas corpus*, but I was too late. Five men and one woman were hanged at noon, two from here, one from Penistone, and three from Sheffield, all of them rowankind. I'm so sorry. The Mysterium exceeded its authority."

"How did they come to accuse Richards and Hardcastle?" Corwen asked.

"There was an anonymous tip from someone in Denby Dike Side."

"Someone from Kaye's Mill, do you think?" Corwen asked. Mr. Kaye had once masqueraded as a friend but had proved to be a scheming rival.

Pomeroy shook his head. "I don't know. I suspect my superiors kept me ignorant because of the sergeant's report following the escape of your rowankind. It was obvious my hesitation gave the rowankind the opportunity to get away."

"And why exactly did you do that?" Corwen's voice had knives in it.

"I've studied the statutes, and as far as I am aware, the rowankind are, in law, non-persons, and therefore not required to register their magic with the Mysterium."

"That's exactly what I told W—" I stopped myself from saying the name, Walsingham.

"The problem is that as non-persons, they have no rights enshrined in law either," Pomeroy said. "They're in a strange position. It's as if they don't exist. Do you know how many rowankind were living in this country on Tuesday, the tenth of March, 1801?"

I shook my head.

"I was curious, so I asked my grandfather to request the census figures for me. The figures were recorded by parish and township. Added all together, in England alone there were fifty-two thousand rowankind employed in agriculture, domestic service, and in trade. That's not counting the ones who disappeared eighteen months ago. No one knows where they went."

We did, but we weren't saying.

Mary's arrival with a tray of tea cut short Pomeroy's response. She placed an elegant silver pot on the side table with a matching milk jug and sugar bowl. James, the footman, carried in a hot water urn and set it on a small burner to keep the water hot enough for tea. Sarah brought a tray of teacups, saucers, and plates, together with a platter of thinly sliced bread and butter.

I saw Corwen's lips twitch into a smile as Lily did the duty normally reserved for her mother. She did it exactly as her mother had taught her, drawing hot water to warm the pot and tipping it into the waste bowl before measuring out leaves from the caddy on the sideboard, and adding hot water to brew the tea.

As she poured the first cup and handed it to me, she glanced sideways at her brother and said, "He did it for me, Corwen. George is a true friend."

"He's Mysterium," Corwen said, as though Pomeroy were not there.

Pomeroy cleared his throat to draw attention. "I see I must explain."

"You need not, George. My brother should take my word."

"Ah, but I should." He turned to us. "You know I was a second lieutenant in His Majesty's Navy?"

We nodded. He'd told us that last year on our first meeting.

"After I was shipwrecked, I could have gone back, taken a place aboard another ship, under another captain."

"But you left the sea." I knew how that felt.

"I did. My grandfather is Robert Winter, Earl of Stratford. I'm the younger son of a younger daughter. I don't have a title, nor do I aspire to one, but my grandfather is very dear to me. He takes his duties in the Upper House very seriously. He's a great supporter of Mr. Pitt, but he doesn't favor the policies of Mr. Addington whose pursuance of peace with France—peace at any cost—is, in his opinion, doomed to failure."

Pomeroy placed his cup and saucer carefully on the table. "Grandfather has lately become disturbed by the power of the Mysterium, a power that, for all practical purposes, is above the law. The situation was brought home forcibly when his nephew was accused of being an unregistered witch. My grandfather employed an army of lawyers and brought his own considerable influence to bear, so my second cousin didn't suffer the consequences he might have had he not had a rich and influential family. All the same, the unfortunate has now been packed off to India for the good of his health."

I sat forward, my cup of tea forgotten.

Pomeroy continued. "Though I am an officer of the Mysterium and will do my best to prevent dangerous use of magic, I also report back to my grandfather on the state of magic in the country."

Corwen gave a low whistle.

"See?" Lily said. "George is an ally."

"Not so fast, Lily," Corwen said. "Because Mr. Pomeroy is reporting back to his grandfather doesn't mean he's sympathetic to magic users." He turned to Pomeroy. "I am, of course, referring to the rowankind."

Pomeroy picked up his teacup and almost spoke to the tea rather than looking directly at us. "I'm aware this household has secrets, and I'm not seeking to either learn or expose them. On this I give you my word." He took a considered sip; when no one offered any denials, he continued. "I'm very fond of Li—Miss Deverell—so I will simply say that if there's anything I can do to help this family—anything—I would be happy to render assistance." He took another sip of tea and waited for a response.

"And you should know, Corwen, that I'm very fond of Mr. Pomeroy." Lily reached across and squeezed Pomeroy's fingers.

"I see," said Corwen, not seeing at all.

"I must leave you now." Pomeroy returned Lily's finger squeeze and stood. "Please remember what I said."

"Mr. Pomeroy, there is one thing you may be able to offer advice on." I jumped to my feet. "Your grandfather is a peer of the realm. If a person needed to ask for an audience with the king or send a letter for His Majesty's personal attention, how would he do it?"

Corwen looked at me sharply, but I merely shrugged.

"I've seen His Majesty, of course," Pomeroy said, "but never had cause to speak to him or do more than bow when once my grandfather and I came upon him unexpectedly strolling in Green Park with the queen. I believe he likes to pretend to be ordinary on occasions, and since it's only a minor eccentricity, his staff and his ministers play along."

If only we could catch him when he was being ordinary.

Pomeroy frowned. "You might send a letter via the Clerk to the Privy Council—one of them, anyway—I believe there are four at the moment. My grandfather did once say Sir Stephen Cotterell was a good man to know." He tipped his head to one side. "I don't suppose there's any point in asking why you need to send a message to the king?"

"It's on behalf of some friends. In view of what's happened today, it's suddenly become more urgent."

He nodded, content to take my word for it or, if not content, at least resigned.

If the Fae heard the Mysterium had hanged six rowankind, there would be trouble.

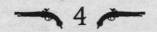

Plain Speaking

"**T**ELL ME ABOUT George Pomeroy," Corwen demanded of Lily after the Mysterium officer had retrieved his horse from the stable yard and clattered off down the driveway. If he was going all the way back to Barnsley tonight, he would likely not arrive back until after full dark, but he could always put up at the inn in Cawthorne if clouds obscured the moon.

"You were unnecessarily harsh, I thought." She rattled our teacups as she put them back on the tray. "George is trying his best to be fair."

"He's Mysterium. He doesn't have to be fair. He doesn't even have to be truthful. Didn't you hear what he said about his grandfather being worried about the amount of power the Mysterium has?"

"It's precisely why he wouldn't abuse the power."

"That's what he says."

"He has a good heart. I know it."

"Don't get too close, Lily. Don't lose your heart to that good heart."

Looking from one to the other, I knew Corwen's warning was too late. I interrupted Corwen's tirade. "Has he made an offer yet, Lily?"

"An offer of marriage?" Corwen's voice rose.

"What other kind of offer could there be?" I asked. "Well, Lily, has he?"

"He might have."

"Might have!" Corwen was on his feet and pacing the room now. "Make up your mind. Has he, or hasn't he?"

"He hasn't spoken to Mother yet, but she likes him."

"Mother's idea of suitable marriage partners isn't always the best. Look how she tried to talk Freddie into proposing to Dorothea Kaye."

"Well, that was never going to work, was it? For more reasons than one. But as soon as he turned into a wolf, she saw sense."

"And what about you, little sister? Supposing you marry your Mysterium man, what do you think he'll do when he discovers you're the black wolf that lopes across the moor in the moonlight? Or are you presuming to keep him ignorant for the rest of your lives together? And what about the children?"

Lily's mouth had developed a pout. She knew all this, but she obviously didn't want to think about it. "Then I shall have to tell him beforehand."

Corwen's face drained of blood. "Lily, if you tell him and he doesn't accept it, he's a danger not only to this family but to magicals everywhere. He could go running to the Mysterium and tell them everything, and then there would be such changes as you never want to see happen. The rowankind would be the least of our worries. If you tell him and he rejects you, I'll have to kill him."

Now Lily's face was as pale as Corwen's. "You wouldn't. You couldn't."

"I could, and I would before I saw magicals hunted down. That would certainly attract the Fae's attention. They could easily decide humans weren't worth the trouble they caused."

I touched Lily's arm, and she jumped visibly. "Although our dealings with the Fae have been civilized so far, they have the power to destroy every last human on these islands."

"And might even spark off the same in other lands," Corwen said. "Before I'd let that happen, I would kill Pomeroy, though I wouldn't enjoy it."

"Well, that's no consolation!" Lily gave a strangled sob, turned, and fled from the room. I heard her feet on the stairs and her bedroom door slam.

"Was I too harsh?" Corwen asked.

I shook my head. "You told her the truth. If only there was some way to test Pomeroy's reaction. After all, it's not as if we're sure he would go running off to the Mysterium. Your father didn't when you changed."

"That's true, but whether that was out of consideration for me, fear of what Mother might do, or a desire to protect the rest of his family—his normal family—from scandal or investigation, I really can't say."

"All of those things." Corwen's mother stood in the doorway, her dress creased and her hair softly mussed as if she'd been sleeping and hadn't had time to let her maid see to her toilet. "Lily sounds upset. What did you say to her?"

"How are you, Mother?" Corwen's voice was full of concern as he jumped up to lead her to a chair. She looked fragile. She'd been broken by the loss of her husband, even though she'd had a year to get used to the idea that he was never going to recover from his apoplectic fit.

"I'm all right, Corwen, don't fuss. Tell me what you said to Lily to upset her so."

"A few truths about what might happen if she told Pomeroy about herself and about magicals and he decided to take it all to the Mysterium."

"Ah, I thought it might be something like that. He's been a regular visitor here since your father passed. I have to say I like the young man. He seems very decent and quite besotted with Lily."

"And she with him," Corwen said.

"Indeed."

"I can't see a solution, Mother. She can't enter into a marriage without telling him, and she can't risk telling him because if he reacts the wrong way, it will end in either disaster for this family or his death." He pressed his lips together and then said. "If I didn't do it myself, the Fae might send someone, or, for that matter, the Lady. Neither can afford to have their secret revealed, not as the law currently stands."

"There are people who share and guard the family secret," I said. "Maybe all is not lost. We simply have to find the right way to introduce George Pomeroy to the wider magic world—maybe in a small way to see how he reacts. When Freddie revealed himself, the servants hardly acted surprised."

"And speaking of Freddie, Mother, how are your hands?"

She held them out. "They're fine. The scars are fading."

The worst of the scars on her right hand were still red. However, the smaller ones were already fading to thin white lines, though the flesh around the base of her right thumb was uneven. Considering the size of Freddie's fangs, the damage could have been a lot worse. I shuddered to think what might have happened if he'd gone for her throat. He would definitely not have survived. I think Corwen might have killed him himself.

"How is my wayward son?"

"Physically, he's fine," Corwen said, "but he's still in some turmoil."

"Tell him I forgive him."

"I will, but, frankly, I'm at a loss."

"May I see him?"

"It wouldn't be wise to bring him back here."

"Then can you take me to him? Is it allowed?"

"Allowed? Yes, of course, but you might be better waiting a while. Let him think about his life as a wolf and see if time helps."

Corwen didn't say that Freddie didn't want to resume

his life in Yorkshire. That was a discussion for another time.

◆————◆

That night we took the opportunity to begin drafting a letter to the king. The Fae had given us the task of contacting him on their behalf, but we had little chance of success. The king was both protected and isolated by his court, and though we could petition for an audience, our request might never get further than one of his undersecretaries.

The Fae had a distorted idea of how government worked. It had been many years—centuries, in fact—since they had dealt directly with a monarch. Things had changed. The Fae still had the idea that a king was omnipotent and accessible to his subjects, just as the Fae Council could be approached by any Fae or rowankind, regardless of their place in the hierarchy.

So though both of us regarded the letter as a forlorn hope, we were determined to try our best. It almost broke our marriage apart. I wanted to explain matters, Corwen wanted to keep it terse and to the point. We argued about whether we should both offer to meet with the king or whether it should be one of us alone. I said it should be me. Corwen said it should be him. We did agree, however, that the king would likely not be willing to meet with two people if we were asking him to come alone.

I wanted to inform the king that six rowankind had been hanged in Sheffield for their magic, but Corwen said if the rowankind in general were not already under suspicion, then it might tip the balance against them. The last thing he wanted to do was to stir up more trouble.

Reluctantly, I agreed.

In the end this is what we came up with.

To His Majesty George the Third, by the Grace of God, of the United Kingdom of Great Britain and Ireland King, Defender of the Faith.

Greetings.

With all due respect to Your Majesty, Your Majesty's Government, the country and the people of Great Britain and Ireland, an urgent matter regarding the safety of the realm has come to our attention. As this matter concerns magic, I cannot, for fear of my life, give you my name or abode. However, I will undertake to explain everything in person if Your Majesty will agree to meet with me.

I will come alone and unarmed and trust Your Majesty will do the same. Should Your Majesty wish for observers at a distance, please let them stay one hundred paces back. When Your Majesty hears the nature of this matter, I'm sure you will understand. The information is sensitive and of a similar nature to the information which used to be reported to you in private by a succession of gentlemen referred to by the name of Walsingham.

If Your Majesty is willing to meet with me on the last day of February at noon, please come to one hundred paces east of the White Lodge in Richmond Park. I will be waiting.

From A Loyal Subject

It wasn't the best letter either of us had ever written. It was difficult to know where to start and how to end. We couldn't put in details because it might be read by a secretary, or an underling to the secretary. We needed enough content to intrigue His Majesty without giving away any details, so I hoped the name of Walsingham would tickle the king's curiosity and help to impress on him that there was serious news to impart and we had information based on sound knowledge.

Also, the White Lodge was currently the home of Mr. Addington, the first minister. I hoped the location would give the king confidence to meet us there.

We couldn't entrust the fox-girl with such a letter. She would be in as much danger as we were if apprehended.

We thought of sending it to the Deverells' man of business in London and asking him to place it anonymously in the hands of a reliable courier to deliver it to Sir Stephen Cotterell, Clerk to the Privy Council, but that would have to be handed over at the palace gate and might end up on the wrong desk altogether.

"Pomeroy's grandfather," I suggested to Corwen. He gave me one of those looks that asked if I was off my head.

"No, listen. Pomeroy said he was gathering information on magic and the Mysterium and passing it on to his grandfather, the Earl of Stratford."

"And . . . "

"If the Earl of Stratford delivered a letter, surely it would reach the king."

"But how do we persuade Pomeroy and the Earl of Stratford to act as go-betweens in this matter?"

"We'll take Lily to talk to Pomeroy in the morning."

"You're putting a lot of trust in someone who is, essentially, the enemy."

"Can you think of any better way?"

He admitted he could not and went off to find Lily to make the arrangements.

◆━━━◆

I fell asleep in Corwen's arms, worrying about Lily, Pomeroy, and the Mysterium. I can only think that was why my dream took me through several encounters with Walsingham. It seemed he'd been dogging my footsteps ever since I'd become aware of my family obligation to free the rowankind. He'd inserted himself into Philip's life and won over his loyalty to the cause of keeping the rowankind subservient and ignorant, turning my own brother against me. That wasn't entirely surprising, of course; Philip was never one for family loyalty.

My dream skipped over the incident on board James Mayo's flagship when I'd blown up the ship in an attempt to kill Walsingham. I'd thought him dead until that awful moment on board the *Guillaume Tell* when I discovered that, even maimed and blind, he'd been instrumental in imprisoning a variety of magicals, rowankind, goblins, witches, trolls, hobs, and even a kelpie. And chief among these, Corwen and his brother, Freddie.

I shuddered to think of Walsingham, even in his maimed state, having the power of life or death over any magical creature, but Corwen and therefore his brother were special to me, and I knew what Walsingham was capable of. My dream went where reality had not. I saw scenes of torture and death. Walsingham had Philip, my traitorous brother, with him, even though I knew that Philip was dead. Walsingham was the brain and Philip his eyes and hands.

In my dream, Philip was about to put out Corwen's eyes with a hot iron. He'd already lopped off Corwen's left arm at the elbow to make Corwen as maimed as Walsingham. That was the point at which, Freddie, in wolf form, leaped and tore out my brother's throat.

It was the surge of joy that woke me, and the guilt that immediately followed it. I'd killed Philip to save David and Corwen, but I'd felt nothing but guilt ever since. I didn't want to think I could find joy, or even relief, in my own brother's death.

I must have been restless. Corwen was awake at my side.

"Bad dream?"

"I'm sorry. Did I wake you?"

"You know I sleep with one eye open, like a wolf."

I chuckled. Corwen was certainly a light sleeper.

"Were you worrying about Pomeroy?" he asked.

"Not so much. I know you won't do anything drastic unless it's absolutely the last alternative. It was Walsingham. I couldn't get the bastard out of my dream. Philip was there, too."

"Philip's never going to trouble us again."

"I know."

"And Walsingham's somewhere in a French prison. With his state of health, and what I've heard about the treatment of French prisoners of war, I would be surprised if he isn't dead by now."

"I don't know. He's tough. Surviving the explosion on James Mayo's ship proved that. I was stupid. I should have put a bullet in his brain when I had the chance instead of leaving him to the French."

"You didn't have it in you to kill a cripple in cold blood. I respect that. Come here."

He pulled me closer and nuzzled the sensitive spot just below my ear. Pretty soon I wasn't thinking about anything but Corwen.

Mysterium

THE FOLLOWING MORNING, as soon as the weak
winter sun had crept over the horizon, we set off for
Barnsley in the family coach with the reliable John Mallinson up on the box. Lily had sent word to the mill not to
expect her until the afternoon. As we were preparing to
leave, Corwen's mother had appeared in her winter redingote and said she wanted to pay a visit to the milliner on
Market Hill. It was encouraging to see her taking an interest in something, even if was only hats, so we made
room for a fourth person and Mallinson produced an extra rug for Mama's knees.

I have a great respect for Mama. I wasn't sure she liked
me at first, but I soon came to realize her feelings for me
were all about protecting her son. Once she realized I
wasn't a danger to Corwen, she accepted me into the family. She hid a great deal behind her formal façade, and her
position in local society kept her well-informed.

"I hear Dorothea Kaye is engaged to be married."
Mama delivered the news with one eyebrow raised. She
had, at one time or another, pushed each one of her sons

toward the divine Miss Kaye whose looks were incomparable. Sadly, her intellect didn't match them.

"I wish her very happy," Corwen said. "Who's the lucky fellow?"

"Joshua Stanhope."

"The magistrate?" Corwen asked.

Mama nodded.

"He's twice her age," Lily said. "But I begin to see how our two rowankind came under suspicion. It would only take a word in the right ear."

"Or wrong ear in this case," I said.

"Quite," Mama said.

That small amount of conversation seemed to have used up her supply of news, and she lapsed into silence for the rest of the journey. We pondered the likelihood of more of the mill's rowankind being targeted as the coach rumbled its way into Barnsley via twisty, narrow roads and through the villages of Cawthorne and Barugh. The Fae were right; unless the law changed, the rowankind would never be safe.

From Redbrook, we climbed the long hill to the outskirts of town and from there down past St. Mary's Church to Market Hill. It being a Friday there were a few market stalls, but the main market day was Wednesday, so the town was less busy than on my previous visit. A pall of smoke hung in the air from the wire-drawing workshops, and the stone buildings were black with sooty deposits.

The Mysterium office was little more than a single room above a draper's shop at the bottom of New Street. It being a pleasantly dry, crisp morning, Corwen, Lily, and I alighted at the bottom of Market Hill and left Mallinson to see Mama safely to and from the milliner in the coach while we walked to New Street, a distance of less than a quarter mile. When we arrived, the office was empty except for a young clerk who invited us to wait.

There was little of interest in there: a desk, a bookcase in want of books, and four chairs.

The boy scratched away at a ledger with a quill, keeping his head down and not looking at us.

After a few minutes the silence got to him. "Have you heard the news from Sheffield?"

"About the hangings yesterday?" Corwen asked.

"Indirectly. The gallows was set afire in the middle of the night, but the wood was not consumed. This morning the fire still burns as high as ever." He lowered his voice. "They say it's witchcraft, but no one knows who to blame."

It seemed likely the Fae had heard about the hangings. If so, they were damned lucky that the whole of Sheffield hadn't gone up in flames.

We waited another ten minutes.

"Could you tell us how long Mr. Pomeroy will be?" Lily asked.

The young clerk cleared his throat, then admitted that Mr. Pomeroy was partaking of a beefsteak breakfast at the Market Tavern, but since we had been waiting long enough, he would run and inform him he had visitors.

The Market Tavern was not a salubrious hostelry, so Corwen tipped the boy two shillings to fetch Mr. Pomeroy at his earliest convenience and then to stay and have breakfast himself because our business was for Mr. Pomeroy alone. The lad didn't need telling twice.

We shuffled uncomfortably on our hard wooden chairs.

I got up, paced the office, and then stopped by the desk, opening one of the ledgers. It was a list of cases handled by the Barnsley office going back five years, so mostly before Mr. Pomeroy's appointment. Lying loose in the front of the ledger was a letter, or rather a printed circular which must have been sent to every Mysterium office in the land instructing officers to be vigilant not only for regular witchcraft, but for magics of another and possibly more subtle kind in respect of those folk commonly referred to as rowankind. It was signed beneath the print in blue ink by J. H. Leigh, Director.

"So the Mysterium has appointed a new director, and he's not called Walsingham," I said.

"Is that a good thing?" Lily asked.

"It's good there isn't a Walsingham involved in Mysterium business," I said, "but it doesn't tell us if another Walsingham has been appointed as an agent reporting directly to the king."

I glanced at the ledger, checking the more recent incidents written in a neat hand. These I presumed were Pomeroy's entries. I checked back to last year, to see what he'd written about the report of rowankind using magic at the mill. He'd noted the warrant issued in Sheffield, the name of the sergeant in charge of the redcoats, and a list of the rowankind so charged, but on the incident itself, all he'd reported was that the rowankind concerned had run off into the woods close to the mill and had left no tracks to follow. He hadn't noted the involvement of the Fae or the screen of fire, an illusion David had created to protect the fleeing rowankind from pursuit. No wonder it hadn't caused a stir. I closed the ledger quietly when I heard footsteps on the stairs, and by the time Pomeroy arrived, I was back in my chair looking bored.

"Miss Deverell!" Pomeroy only had eyes for Lily. "If I'd realized it was you, I wouldn't have insisted on finishing my breakfast." He bowed over her hand and then, in turn, to us.

"Don't blame your clerk," Corwen said. "We didn't give him our names. I trust you left him behind to enjoy his breakfast."

"I did. What can I do for you?"

Corwen took the letter from his pocket and tapped the paper onto the palm of his free hand as if still in two minds whether to entrust it to Pomeroy.

Lily stood and slipped her hand through the crook of Pomeroy's elbow. The gesture wasn't lost on Corwen. "George, we need a favor and we need you not to ask why."

"Oh, now you have me thoroughly intrigued."

Corwen made up his mind. "Yesterday you advised us

that for a letter to reach the king, we should address it via Sir Stephen Cotterell, the Clerk to the Privy Council."

"As far as I'm aware."

"It's vital the information in this letter reaches His Majesty personally, so we hope to prevail upon you to send it to Sir Stephen via your grandfather. Who would deny an earl access to the king?"

I saw a frown knit itself briefly across Pomeroy's forehead.

"We can promise you that what it contains will not harm His Majesty in any way," I said. "Nor will it harm your grandfather as the bearer. However, if you can contrive to keep our name out of it, we would be very grateful. I'm sure you would not wish any questions concerning the use of magic, rowankind magic that is, to be directed to Lily's family."

"Indeed, I would not, but I'm not sure that will convince my grandfather."

I could see Corwen was thinking about how much to tell him.

"It's a chance to protect the rowankind," Lily said. "The six rowankind who were hanged yesterday may only be the start of it. Do we know how many rowankind have been condemned throughout the rest of the country?"

Pomeroy shook his head.

"Your grandfather is interested in the extent of magic, I presume?" I asked.

"He is."

"You can promise him that when it is safe to do so, we'll give him testimony and answer any questions he might have. In the meantime, for the sake of the realm, this letter must reach the king."

"Only on condition I get an explanation."

"Oh, George," Lily squeezed his arm. "To know what we know and not to tell the Mysterium might put you in danger."

"And to tell the Mysterium would put all of us, including Lily, in danger," I added.

"In fact, Lily would be in the most danger," Corwen

said. "Ross and I can retreat to a place where we can't be found, but unless Lily were to leave her family and the mill, she would be here for the Mysterium to find and question." He put extra emphasis on the word, question, so Pomeroy was in no doubt Lily might be in physical danger from such a process.

"The Mysterium wouldn't—" Pomeroy began.

"I'm afraid they would," I said.

"If your grandfather is collecting information on how the Mysterium conducts its business," Corwen said, "tell him to ask the Mysterium about a ship called the *Guillaume Tell* and the prisoners taken to sea."

"The *Guillaume Tell*?"

Corwen nodded. "Captured from the French and intended to be refitted for Navy use, but before she was commissioned, the Admiralty lent her to the Mysterium as a prison ship. Ask yourself what kind of prisoners the Mysterium might have."

George Pomeroy held out his hand. "I'll see your letter gets to my grandfather with your request for delivery."

"It might be better if you didn't commit what we told you to writing," Corwen said.

"I have some business in the capital, and I have to report in person to the Mysterium headquarters every three months. I'll deliver your letter to Grandfather myself, and if he's interested, I'll pay a visit to the Admiralty to inquire about the *Guillaume Tell*."

Corwen nodded and shook his hand.

"Oh, George, I told them they could trust you. Thank you." Lily gave his arm one final squeeze and then let go.

I had one more thought as we were leaving the office. "Mr. Pomeroy, does the name Walsingham mean anything to you?"

"He was the head of the Mysterium when I was appointed."

"Did you meet him?"

"I did. He was younger than I expected, close to my own age. He died suddenly. I haven't met Mr. Leigh yet. He was only appointed at the beginning of January."

"You haven't heard of anyone else called Walsingham, an older man?"

"No, I don't believe so."

"If you do, would you mind telling Lily, so she can get word to us?"

"Certainly, as long as it doesn't conflict with my duties."

"Of course, we wouldn't expect that."

We took polite leave and nodded to the young clerk as we passed him on the stairs.

"I hope we did the right thing," Corwen muttered to me as we walked back from New Street toward Market Hill.

I sighed. So did I.

❦

On the way back to Denby House we asked Mallinson to take the steep route down Miller Hill to Denby Dike Side to the house of Sam Hardcastle. Jem Richards having been a lodger, the hanging represented a double tragedy visited on one household.

Mallinson pulled up the coach a hundred yards short of the stone terrace where the Hardcastle family lived. It was easy to see which house it was; shutters had been nailed closed across the windows, but the front door stood ajar as if there might be a visitor.

"Should we all go?" Mama said. "We don't want to overwhelm the poor woman. Losing a husband is so . . . "

"I think she would like to know that the whole family is here to pay respects," Lily said. "We don't have to stay long. We must tell her we'll look after her and the children and arrange for the bodies to be brought back."

"Can we?" Mama asked. "Get the bodies, I mean."

"George has requested it," Lily said. "At least they'll get a proper burial."

"Not in the churchyard, though."

Rowankind couldn't be buried in the hallowed ground of any churchyard, just as they could neither be christened nor married in the sight of God, but on the hill above the village was a small walled cemetery, always kept neatly, where the rowankind buried their own.

Mrs. Hardcastle had company. I was pleased to see the villagers had rallied round. The children, four of them, all under five years old, Lily had said, were nowhere to be seen, so probably another neighbor had taken them out of the doom-laden atmosphere. Three mature ladies attended Mrs. Hardcastle. One looked like an older version, and I took her to be Mrs. Hardcastle's mother or older sister. Mrs. Hardcastle herself sat in a chair by the fire, her hair covered by a modest mourning cap made of muslin with a yellowing lace trim. Around her shoulders she had a black shawl. I doubted anyone could afford mourning clothes on a millworker's wage, but the neighbors had probably helped.

The new-made widow started to rise as we entered, but Mama waved her back into her seat and we let the senior one among us say what was necessary to pay our respects. Lily pushed a small purse into Mrs. Hardcastle's hands. As we left, the older lady who, indeed, proved to be Mrs. Hardcastle's mother followed us to the door.

"Sam and Jem . . . " she said. "They were good men even if they were rowankind. How could this have happened?"

Corwen took her hand. "It shouldn't have happened. It's a great injustice. We mustn't let it happen again."

◆―――◆

Corwen and I didn't stay for the funerals, returning to the Old Maizy Forest the following morning to our little cottage and to Corwen's troubled brother. David's boundary had held. Though we felt its presence, we could cross it.

Freddie listened to our news from home, though whether he understood it all was doubtful. He whined when Corwen told him Lily was enamored of a Mysterium officer, so at least something got through to his lupine mind.

Corwen hoped a quiet winter would ease Freddie's troubled soul and help him to work toward reclaiming his humanity, but I was beginning to think he preferred wolf form.

February came in wet but unseasonably mild, with rain spiking down from gray skies. Freddie slunk into the cottage and stretched himself in front of the fire in such a way that I almost tripped over him twice. He snarled at me, and I snarled back.

Damn wolf.

We'd sent our letter to the king, and a fortnight later we had a note from Lily, this time delivered by Mr. Reynard who doubtless wanted to check on Freddie before he let his daughter come anywhere near the cottage again. A big, old, scarred dog fox in his animal form, Mr. Reynard shouted his business from outside the barrier and, when I let him through, sauntered up to our door as if trying to tempt Freddie to chase him. Despite the provocation, Freddie, for once, behaved himself.

The letter said George Pomeroy had confirmed that his grandfather would deliver our letter into the hands of Sir Stephen Cotterell, with a special request that the letter was for the king's eyes only.

"Do you think he read it himself?" I asked Corwen.

"I would have in his place, wouldn't you?"

"Absolutely. I wouldn't want to deliver anything seditious."

"I don't think the letter gave anything away except for Walsingham's name. All we have to do now is hope the king acts on it."

"How likely is that?"

He shook his head. "Not very. I'm expecting a trap, but we should go through the motions if only to prove to the Fae it's a futile task."

Until then we could only hope that not too many rowankind suffered the same fate as poor Sam and Jem. Lily's note said she'd asked George Pomeroy to let her know if he heard of any other summary hangings.

 6

Aunt Rosie

THE MIDDLE OF February brought a touch of frost and a welcome visit from Aunt Rosie and Leo. Our home had been Rosie's, but she'd left it to us when she'd married Leo and moved to Summoner's Well.

Rosie and Leo didn't arrive via the Fae gate. They came along the deeply rutted forest road, riding two sturdy cobs, one skewbald and the other a flea-bitten gray. Rosie, one of the most powerful witches of her generation, though she'd never brag, had no trouble in recognizing David's barrier for what it was and finding a way through.

I heard them approach, their ponies crunching across frost-crisp grass, and ran down the path to meet them, hugging Rosie and being hugged in turn. Corwen drew Leo into the cottage.

"You've made a few changes," Rosie said, looking round our one room which was bedroom at one end and living area at the other.

I swung the kettle over the fire to boil water for tea. "Corwen's pretty good at basic carpentry," I said. "He fixed up your old chairs and built cupboard siding on the bed. Very useful when you share a home with your brother."

"Yes, I never had the privacy problem, though I did once take in a crow who might have been more than he seemed. He was a little too interested in my undergarments." She laughed. "I was glad when his wing healed, and I sent him on his way."

The kettle boiled. I made tea in our willow-pattern teapot with the chip out of the spout and offered it in two almost matching china cups complete with saucers, while Corwen and I had a plain white mug and a floral cup without a saucer.

"Sorry. We don't get many visitors," I said as I poured.

"You don't need to impress me. I've come to see you, not the state of your china, which, by the way, is all I left you." She grinned, her eyes crinkling in a most becoming way.

Rosie, my mother's twin sister, was as round and as full of fun as my mother had been gaunt and embittered. I sometimes wondered what might have happened if they'd stayed together and my mother had not rejected the practice of magic. My life would have been very different. Best not to go down that line of thought.

When the Mysterium found them, my mother, Marjorie, had fled to Plymouth, married a sea captain, Teague Goodliffe, and started a family: first me, named for my Aunt Rosie; then my brother Philip; and finally David, her third, unacknowledged child. She'd hidden her little bastard away with a Kentish family for the first ten years of his life until, as a lonely widow, she'd brought him home to be her servant, never telling him he was her son. Long before that happened, she and I had quarreled one time too many, and I'd run away to sea with Will Tremayne.

In the meantime, Aunt Rosie had fled to the Fae where she'd raised a child, Margann, fathered by Dantin. I still had a hard time imagining Dantin as someone my jolly aunt would take to her bed, but I supposed there must be another side to him.

Reuniting with Leo, her childhood sweetheart, had changed Rosie's life again. He was a blacksmith, tall and white-haired, but still vigorous. She'd become the village midwife and wisewoman. Indeed, during her years in this cottage, Rosie had grown into the use of magic, while my mother had been busy rejecting hers. Rosie had lent me some of her notebooks so that I could learn more.

"Have you finished with the notebooks I left you?" Rosie dropped a small package wrapped in brown paper onto the table. "I sense darkness gathering. I don't know what or where, but there's something. I've been dreaming."

Aunt Rosie's dreams were much more reliable than mine. "Anything we should know about?"

She shrugged. "Are you sure Walsingham ended up in a French prison?"

I shuddered. "As sure as I can be without actually being there. The French took the *Guillaume Tell,* and he was on board."

I wondered whether to tell her about my Walsingham dream, but I was pretty sure that it had simply been the result of what had passed earlier in the day with Pomeroy. Aunt Rosie had a degree of prescience which I'd never aspired to.

"Ah, it's probably nothing, but you shouldn't let up on your studies. Read the notebooks. Make your own." She patted the package. "Here are the next ones." She untied the string and slid one notebook out, then thumbed through it to one of the middle pages. "And here's a spell you need to learn."

I looked at the page. "A protection spell."

"It's difficult to put a protection spell on anything animate. People and creatures are too fluid in their movements. Besides, a protection spell might protect them from certain kinds of intimate contact they don't want to be protected from, or from useful magic, such as a glamour. This spell is really for things like the roof over your head, or the carriage you are driving in, or maybe that ship of yours. It won't necessarily save you from a cannonball or a gunshot, but it will help protect against magical attack."

I nodded, already absorbed in reading the spell until Aunt Rosie tapped the book again and turned to Corwen. "It wouldn't hurt for you to study these, too."

"Me? I'm a shapechanger, not a witch."

"The Lady gave you some power over illusion, didn't she?"

"Well, yes, but—"

"If you mastered that, you can master some of these. You have the potential." She didn't give him the opportunity to contradict, instead turning back to me. "I think you might be interested in some of the passages about magical creatures, too."

The Fae, together with the Lady's trusted agents from the Okewood, had been hurrying hither and thither trying to round up some of the magical creatures, both dangerous and benign, who had escaped Iaru and the woodland realm. Corwen and I had dealt with a particularly nasty kelpie last year.

"Is there anything in particular I should study?" I asked.

"You might take a look at the passage on hobs."

"They're not dangerous, are they? I thought hobs were helpful to humans."

"Not dangerous in themselves, but if a human were to bind them, they could defend themselves."

"Is there such a thing happening?"

"I heard a rumor of a hob near Radstock, a village called Vobster. Things have gone quiet, now, but I have an uncomfortable feeling about it."

Aunt Rosie's feelings, like her dreams, were not to be taken lightly. If she thought I should study the next set of notebooks, then I would.

"Vobster?" Corwen asked. "You think someone should take a look?"

"Would you? Oh, yes, please."

Her relief was so evident that even though I guessed Corwen hadn't been intending to volunteer personally, he immediately relented. He looked at me.

"Why not?" he said. "We can't do anything much until the last day of February. Let's take a trip to Vobster."

7

The Vobster Hob

I READ AUNT Rosie's notes on hobs before we set off for Vobster. Then I read them out loud to Corwen. "Hobs are smaller than the average human, and largely benign. They often use their magical abilities to help humans, usually around the house or farm. Though they don't expect payment, putting out a bowl of milk and even a cake now and then, keeps them sweet and encourages them to stay. They are excellent at persuading crops to grow and yield, but also good with cattle in the dairy."

Corwen absorbed that and then held out his hand for the book, reading the passage again. Good, he was taking Aunt Rosie's encouragement to heart.

We'd met a pair of hobs when we'd rescued the magicals from the *Guillaume Tell* and found them to be strange-looking, but pleasant-natured.

We made our peace with Freddie again before leaving him within David's enclosure. He didn't seem to mind, but since he couldn't change and talk to us, we really had no idea how he felt about things.

The nearest Fae gate to Vobster was a patch of woodland south of Radstock. Mining had encroached into the trees, and I wondered how long it would be before the gate itself was exposed.

"Do they ever close gates?" I asked Corwen.

"I believe they do if the gate is compromised," he said. "I understand there used to be several gates in the Sheffield area, but the industrial blight spread too far and too fast. There's only one left now."

On this February day, it didn't so much rain as drizzle water over us until we were clammy and damp. We each wore an oiled cotton cape that slicked the rain off, but it still chapped my cheeks and a persistent rivulet trickled down my neck and inside my shirt.

We asked directions from a passing pack man leading four scrawny horses, each carrying a sack of coal that looked to be approximately the weight of a man. He pointed out the way but warned us the road was particularly bad at this time of year, full of ruts and mud.

And so it proved. Timpani and Dancer, being Fae bred, managed to avoid the worst of it, but twice we passed small carts mired in the mud, the second one with a donkey collapsed between the shafts, and the owner smacking its back with a stick to get it on its feet again.

"Ho, there," Corwen called. "Give Jack a chance, man."

I dismounted from Dancer, glad I'd chosen to wear breeches and boots. Dancer followed me to the donkey's head and nuzzled its ears. The donkey raised its head from the ground, gave a groan, and dropped back into the mud. By the gray around its eyes and muzzle this was an old beast, and the burden was too much for him.

"He's lazy. Allus has been, allus will be. Just needs a crack or two to get him moving again." The man thwacked his stick across the donkey's rump.

"That's no way to treat him," I said.

"Mind yer own business and I'll mind mine."

I looked into the donkey's eyes and saw hopelessness. Right then and there I wanted to free him and take him with us, even if Corwen called me soft for it. I glanced up.

Corwen hadn't dismounted, but he'd ridden Timpani closer to the man, hampering the movement of the stick.

"Poor Jack." I stroked the donkey's furry cheek. What should have been soft was matted with wet mud. The donkey flicked an ear, but otherwise didn't react. I sensed life hanging by no more than a thread.

I'm a summoner. I can call a spirit to me. Sometimes, if that spirit is still in its body, I can call it out. On occasions like this, it was a mercy. I latched onto the donkey's spirit and gently invited it out of the wrecked body. It came gladly. As the donkey's ear stopped twitching, I had the ghost of a pretty, brown-eyed jack donkey standing by my side. The owner couldn't see it, but Corwen could. He touched fingertips to temple in salute while I gave the donkey permission to move on. I saw the apparition wobble forward like a new colt on unsteady legs, then he began to trot. As he faded, the ghost-donkey kicked up his heels in a joyous buck and brayed loudly. Dancer whickered in reply.

"You're not going to be able to beat any life into the poor thing," I stood. "He's gone, and you're on your own with the cart. I suggest you pull it yourself."

I mounted Dancer as the man began to ask for assistance, but neither Corwen nor I had any inclination to help, so we left him alternately cursing the dead donkey and shouting after us.

"That was well done," Corwen said.

"The poor thing was a whisker away from death anyway. He certainly couldn't have drawn that cart any farther."

"It's a bad husbandman who uses up his animals instead of treating them well. Setting all kindness aside, he'd get more out of his beasts if he looked after them better. It's common sense."

"Sometimes I think we live in sad times."

We rode on in silence.

Vobster was a few miles south of Radstock on the River Mells, a haphazard collection of houses with an inn and a bridge. The village was surrounded by outlying farms and the whole area was pitted with small coal mines and the occasional stone quarry. The bridge over the River Mells had four stone arches which carried the road over the swollen river. The date on the bridge was 1794, so it was recently built, probably to replace an older structure. Right then I wasn't so much interested in the bridge as the inn, tempted by the idea of a hot meal and a roof over my head.

The inn's ostler came out at the sound of our arrival and offered to take our horses, but we asked him to show us the stable and led Timpani and Dancer there ourselves. The building was dry and smelled sweet, with fresh straw in the stalls and hay in the racks.

"This will do nicely," Corwen said as we unsaddled the horses and arranged for a feed of oats.

"Do you know a carter with an elderly jack donkey?" I asked.

"Oh, aye, that'd be Clem Weatherall." The ostler's expression told me what I wanted to know.

"We passed him on the road. Looked as though he'd worked the poor beast to death."

"Aye, I've been waiting for that to 'appen."

"So you'll not be sending out anyone to help him, then?"

"I reckon he can fend for hisself. He's always the last to offer when anyone needs a hand."

We left the horses in the capable care of the ostler and ran across the yard into the inn to get out of the drizzle which was steadily turning to something more closely akin to actual rain.

The landlady was a jovial, round-faced woman who kept a clean house. Her ale was good, and she quickly served us with a pork pie still warm from the oven, together with pickles and crusty bread and butter.

We couldn't ask after a hob, but we did engage her in conversation. Like many landlords, she was an inveterate gossip. We soon discovered who'd said what to whom, and which lady in the village was no better than she should be. One tale which caught my attention was about a farmer named Hingston whose wife came from Cheddar, and who had had sudden success with his cheeses, producing creamy pale cheese that quite matched the best Cheddar could offer.

I raised my eyebrow at Corwen. He was obviously thinking there might be some hob involvement.

"Do you think he might sell us a wheel of cheese?" Corwen asked. "We're on our way to see an old friend in Holcombe who likes his cheese. He thinks he's a bit of an expert, and I'd like to surprise him with something new."

"You'll pass Hingston's place on the way to Holcombe. Nutbush Farm."

❖———❖

By the time we finished our meal, the rain had cleared. Nutbush Farm on the Holcombe Road was not difficult to find. The farmyard was neat with the cottage, painted a creamy yellow, and the barn and a range of buildings forming three sides of a square. A black-and-white dog barked twice as we turned in off the road, but quieted as the farmer, a tall and big-boned man, emerged from the barn to see who'd come. Corwen gave him the story about visiting a friend who fancied himself an expert cheese taster. Hingston's chest puffed up like a pigeon when we told him his cheese had been recommended as being better than anything from Cheddar.

"My missis will be right proud. She comes from Cheddar, and her folks were cheesemakers, though she don't take after either of 'em."

"It's not your wife who makes the cheese, then?" Corwen asked.

"Lord love yer, no, it ain't. She bakes a fair loaf, and her pastry is as good as any, but she doesn't have the hands for dairy, or the heart. No patience, you know. Butter and cheese need loving patience."

"Do you make it yourself, or have you got a dairy maid?"

I didn't catch the farmer's reply because I dismounted and looked around for anything out of the ordinary while

Corwen engaged him in affable conversation. If anything, the yard was too tidy. I doubted the farmer could afford an army of servants, so perhaps that was an indication that there was a hob about the place.

I saw a shadow move inside the lean-to at the end of a range of buildings, and for a moment a strange face looked out at me. It was a small person the height of a nine or ten-year-old child, but that was no child's face. The eyebrows didn't so much meet in the middle as combine to make one heavy ridged eyebrow covered in dark tufted hair. The eyes wcre heavily shaded, and the nose turned up way beyond retroussé. I'd found my hob.

"Is that your dairy?" I cut across the conversation that Corwen was conducting and glanced at him briefly. He got my meaning straight away.

"I'd be fascinated to see where this perfect cheese is made," Corwen said, "and to hear any secrets you deem able to share."

The farmer seemed reluctant to move, but Corwen dismounted and began to walk toward the door I'd pointed out.

Farmer Hingston scurried to get ahead of us and made a great fuss about opening the door, but he also did it extremely slowly, which might give any hob the opportunity to either find a hiding place or, more likely, turn invisible.

The walls were thick and the window small, keeping the inside cool in hot weather, but protected from frosts in the winter. The walls were covered in blue-and-white Dutch tiles and the floor with plain glazed tiles.

Corwen's nose twitched as we followed Hingston inside. I raised one eyebrow, and he nodded imperceptibly. Yes, he could smell that there was a hob in residence. It wasn't a large dairy, but it was as clean and neat as any I'd seen, with a good-sized stone table in the center and a watertight ledge all around it. Water surrounded wide, shallow milk dishes, cooling the contents. A butter churn stood ready. Shelves held terra-cotta bowls and jugs of varying sizes and shapes.

A door led through to a second room, and when

Hingston opened it up, we could see a third room beyond that. Corwen distracted Hingston with more conversation while I hung back.

"I know you're here," I said. "How can I help?"

I didn't get an answer, but I felt the hob stir.

"The Lady of the Forests can offer sanctuary," I said. I hoped her name would help.

I heard a fast chittering kind of sound and could have sworn there were two voices rather than one. They were talking to each other faster than would have been humanly possible.

"Are there two of you? Are you being held here against your will?"

I wondered whether Aunt Rosie had been mistaken and the hob, or maybe hobs, were here voluntarily. Farmer Hingston seemed a jovial fellow, not at all the kind to imprison hobs.

"Why don't you simply leave?" I asked.

I heard a shuddering sound and a hob began to appear from the crown of his head downward. It was disconcerting to have hair appear first and then the fearsome brow ridge, eyes, turned-up nose, and then mouth and chin.

A second hob appeared in a similar manner, but this one I thought might be female.

"Baby," she said and pointed upward.

The ceiling, made of close-fitting boards, painted white, had a small trapdoor in it next to the far wall. An access ladder, also painted white, fastened to the wall below it.

"Is your baby up there?" I asked.

They both nodded.

"Mr. Hingston!" I followed Corwen into the next room and crashed into the conversation. "Is it true you have hobs on the premises?"

He tried to look surprised. "What are hobs?"

"Dear, sweet, gentle people who like to help, but they don't like being forced to help."

"Come now, they're not like people."

"So you do know what hobs are, or you think you do.

Corwen, there are two of them, and they say Farmer Hingston is keeping their baby in the loft." I jerked my head toward the ladder. "Up there. I'll let you do the honors."

There was a large padlock holding the trapdoor closed. It wasn't difficult to pick, or even to smash, but I surmised the problem was that the lock was made of cold iron. It was a myth that all magical creatures were afraid of iron and running water, but some were, and it seemed the hobs fell into that category.

"The key, please, Mr. Hingston." Corwen held his hand out.

"You can't come up here and set my cattle free. Or do you intend to take them for yourself? This farm has always had hobs, as far back as I can recall in my father's time, and my grandfather's, too."

"I bet your father and grandfather didn't have to lock up the hobs' children to keep them here."

Corwen's hand was still out. He gave Hingston a look which had something of the wolf about it.

Hingston stepped back, turned, and ran to the door, yelling loudly as he dashed into the yard. I didn't know whether he was calling out for his dogs or his farmhands, or both.

Corwen raced after him and tackled him to the floor. They both landed in a puddle from the earlier rain, Hingston facedown. Corwen rolled away and leaped to his feet. Hingston was no slouch in the fisticuffs department, and he came up swinging. His fist clonked on the point of Corwen's jaw, causing Corwen to reel back. I saw the wolf looking out from behind Corwen's eyes as he surged forward.

Oh, no. Please don't change. Not here, not now.

A shriek from the farmhouse door drew my attention. A woman—Mrs. Hingston, I guessed—rushed at the pair of them, broom in hand. She got in a couple of good whacks before I reached her and shoved her away, wrapping my arms around her and pinning her arms to her sides to keep her from swinging the broom.

"Leave them to it," I said as she wriggled in my grip.

She tried to kick backward, so I swept her feet from under her, pushed her to the ground, twisted one arm up behind her back, and knelt with one knee across her spine. The other hand, still clutching the broom, was beneath her.

By the time I had the opportunity to look, Corwen and Farmer Hingston were slugging it out. They looked pretty evenly matched. The farmer's outdoor work had built muscles and stamina, but Corwen was fit and determined. I had my pistols in my pocket, but I hoped it wouldn't come down to needing them.

Hingston almost got away from Corwen, but Timpani stepped forward and the farmer, half-blind from a bleeding cut over one eye, cannoned into the horse's shoulder. Corwen caught him on the rebound and, with a fist to his nose, punched his lights out.

"You can get up." I eased my weight off Mrs. Hingston's back.

"Arthur? What have you done to him? Is he dead?"

"No, he's not dead." Corwen wiped away blood from his split lip. "Only finishing what he started." Corwen bent over the unconscious farmer and checked his pockets for keys, coming up with a bunch that looked likely.

"What's all this about? We've got no money." Mrs. Hingston said, kneeling at her husband's head.

"We don't want your money," I said. "Just giving your hobs a choice of whether to stay or go."

"You leave 'em be."

Corwen went into the dairy. I heard him climbing the ladder to the loft and the scrape of metal on metal as he tried a couple of keys. There was a clang as he found the right one and dropped the lock to the floor.

"They asked about the road to Bristol. We couldn't risk it." Mrs. Hingston whined. "Their cheese making is good, and we're starting to get known for it."

"What do the hobs get out of it?"

"We keep 'em in comfort. What have they got to grumble about?"

"She's right about the comfort," Corwen shouted down. "They've got chairs, a table, and a box bed, all hob-sized, though their window has a broken pane."

"What about the baby?" I asked.

"Safe and sound in his crib."

I heard both hobs clamber up the ladder, and soon there were cooing noises coming from above.

"We never hurt 'em, only made sure they didn't leave."

"That's hurt enough," I said.

"The hobs are coming with us," said Corwen as he climbed down with a bundle in one arm.

"You can't take them. They're ours."

"They belong entirely to themselves," I said. "You can't own a person. Slavery is illegal in this country, even though, God help us, we allow the Africa trade to continue."

Mrs. Hingston's eyes widened. "But they are hobs. They aren't people," she said with all sincerity.

"I'm sure those who trade in dark-skinned men and women think they aren't people, either," I said. "Let the hobs go, Mrs. Hingston."

"You really don't have much choice," Corwen said, as he emerged from the dairy with a baby hob in his arms. "We'd rather have settled this amicably, without anyone getting hurt, but whatever you say or do, we're not leaving without the hobs—all of them."

The hobs followed him, each with a small bundle of possessions. Corwen handed the baby to the female hob, and turned to where Farmer Hingston, still on the floor, was starting to groan as he came to his senses. Mrs. Hingston knelt and dabbed the cut above his eye with the corner of her apron.

"Well? How is it to be?" Corwen loomed over the pair of them.

The female hob tugged at my sleeve and beckoned. I bent so she could whisper in my ear. I came back upright, smiling at what she said.

"Mrs. Hingston. Your cheese may not be so popular when people discover there's ground glass in it. Remember that broken windowpane in the loft?"

"What?" Her face fell. "All of it?"

The hobs both nodded.

"But hobs are helpers," Mr. Hingston said. "It's not in their nature to—"

"You credit them with human kindness and industry, but deny them their rights as people," I said. "I suggest you throw away all the cheese you have maturing and start to make your own. Who knows, you may have learned something."

We left them there, in the farmyard.

Corwen boosted me into Dancer's saddle and handed me the child to carry in my arms. Looking at his tiny sleeping face, I wondered how I would feel carrying my own children. We took one hob up behind each of us, where they quickly faded to invisibility for the duration of the journey.

As we rode back down the lane toward Vobster, I asked the hob whether she really had put ground glass into the cheese.

"No-no-no," she said, "Would never."

"But they will never know one way or the other," I said. "They're not going to try it to find out, are they?"

She chuckled. It served the Hingstons right.

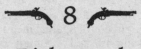

8

Richmond

ON THE TWENTIETH of February we had another letter from Lily. This time Corwen let Aileen Reynard through the barrier, and Freddie let her pass unhindered apart from a low growl, which was a marked improvement. I know Corwen took it as a good sign.

I wasn't convinced.

Lily's letter, however, brought bad news. Mysterium hangings had taken place in eight towns with a total of thirty-one more rowankind dead, so far, on little or no pretext. Apparently, the Earl of Stratford, George Pomeroy's grandfather, had raised questions in the Upper House but had received little support, and an inquiry sent to Mysterium headquarters received a reply which contained a list of names of the dead, but no charges or reasons for the summary executions.

We could only wait for the twenty-eighth day of February. Our letter had said the sender would meet the king alone and unarmed, and he would, but there was no reason to be stupid about this. The king, or any of his underlings, could easily decide we meant harm, so the whole place could be crawling with redcoats, Mysterium officers, and militia.

And there was the question of which of us would meet the king. Corwen and I argued back and forth over this. I argued that a woman meeting the king would not be seen as threatening. He said a woman would not be as credible, and I might not be taken seriously. Sadly, I agreed that my gender might count against me in this, but I could easily meet the king dressed as a man. Besides, Corwen would make a much better watcher because, in wolf form, he could sniff out a trap in seconds.

In the end I prevailed. I would meet the king in my man's clothing—presuming the king kept the appointment.

We'd chosen that spot in Richmond Park because it was close to a Fae gate which could provide a fast escape for us if anything went wrong. If the king did as we asked and left his followers a hundred paces away, we could easily reach the gate before any of them could reach us. This presumed they didn't have a good marksman with a rifle. One hundred paces was no distance for a sharpshooter, and the new rifles were much more accurate than muskets.

Early in the morning of the last day of February I dressed as a young gentleman in my breeches, linen shirt, and cutaway jacket. I pulled on my boots and wriggled my toes. I loved the familiar feel of this outfit. It brought back the days I'd spent as a privateer captain on my ship, the *Heart of Oak*. After Will, my first husband, died, it had taken me a while to slip into the role, but my crew, who might easily have taken the ship for themselves, left without a captain, stood by me. I'd led the men in skirmishes many times, and we'd done well chasing down French merchantmen for the king. This king whom I was about to meet.

I felt a little naked without my sword at my hip and my sash with three loaded pistols, but old habits die hard, so I did have a knife concealed in my boot.

We rode through the Fae gate into Richmond Park's trees; from Iaru's warm summer night to Britain's dank dampness, barely above freezing. It was still dark, but dawn came late in February. By my pocket watch it was close to six in the morning. It had been raining, but beneath the trees it was relatively dry. The leaf bed under our feet felt soft, but not wet enough to mire us down. Corwen's eyesight was much better than mine in the dark, so I left it up to him to do an initial assessment. I could have put up a witchlight to illuminate the area, but it would be too easy to spot.

"The ground isn't disturbed," he said. "But the wet weather isn't good for my nose. The scents are all mixed up. I might have to strip and go wolf to reconnoiter thoroughly."

"Let me listen."

My witch hearing is very acute. I picked up the sounds of an owl hunting, a badger grumbling quietly to itself as it waddled sleepily toward its sett, and crows cawing to the coming morning.

"Hear anything?" he asked.

"Nothing unusual. Smell anything?"

"Nothing unusual."

"I think we're in the clear."

We settled down to wait, confident that we'd spot a trap. We'd done all we could to prepare for the worst; now we had to hope for the best.

Dawn arrived reluctantly, the leaden sky slow to admit the possibility of day. As soon as there was light enough to see, a steward came and paced out the distance from the White Lodge, but he was a short-legged man and the meeting point was closer to the house and farther from the gate to Iaru than we had hoped. The man drove a stake into the ground and returned to the lodge. Four footmen arrived next and set up a canopy with a chair beneath it.

"The king must have his throne," Corwen muttered.

"If it makes him feel better, I don't mind kneeling in front of it."

"See how it's placed. If you stand in front of the throne, you are between the king and the White Lodge with your back a ready target for a sharpshooter."

Corwen was right. Damn.

For the next hour nothing happened. The sun clawed its way into the sky, appearing as nothing more than an occasional lighter patch of cloud.

"I'm going to check the rest of the park," Corwen said. "It looks as though they're doing as we ask, but if I were the king, even if I intended to keep this appointment, I would have a plan, and that plan would involve a perimeter guard at the very least. They don't know we have our own way into and out of the park. They are likely to be watching for us on the approach roads."

Corwen slipped out of his clothes and shoved them into the little bag that held them all despite appearing far too small. He slung it across one shoulder, shivering in the February air. "I'll be back as soon as I can. If you need to get out quickly, take both horses with you and I'll follow on foot."

"Be careful."

"I always am."

That wasn't strictly true. Corwen often put others before himself.

"I love you."

He smiled. "And I love you."

With that, he changed from naked man to wolf, his silver mane tipped with black and his eyes a clear luminous gray. There was beauty in both his forms. I blew a kiss as he streaked between the trees, nose to the ground.

I checked my pocket watch as the hands ticked toward noon and still no sign of Corwen. Four retainers came out of the house carrying a canopy, the king walking beneath it. He wasn't a young man. Compared to the retainers, he was portly around the middle though he walked with reasonable vigor. I'd brought a small spyglass, not as powerful as the one I used to have aboard the *Heart of Oak*, but good enough to help me pick out details. The king had a fleshy face with full lips. His hair was hidden beneath a white periwig and a hat. His suit was a fine cut, but light, and I wondered that he was not wearing a coat in this weather.

I straightened my hair and resettled my tricorn hat firmly upon my head. I was ready to step out of the trees, when I heard Corwen approaching at a flat-out run. He flowed smoothly from wolf to man, though his breath came in gasps.

"It's a trap. There are redcoats on the roads, and more in the park, closing in."

"But I can see the king down there already."

Corwen screwed up his eyes to focus on the man beneath the canopy. "Do you have your spyglass?"

I handed it to him.

"I saw the king once, and that's not him," he said. "Let's get out of here."

He boosted me into Dancer's saddle and slapped Timpani on the rump before dropping to all fours and running alongside in wolf form.

I heard horses behind us, the Blues, the king's bodyguard, no doubt.

Someone shouted, "Stop them," as we raced toward the Fae gate.

There was a moment of disorientation as we crashed through into the green of Iaru's summer. The sounds of pursuit fell away. I screwed up my eyes against the sun and eased Dancer to a stop. Timpani slowed with us and snorted as the silver wolf became human again.

Corwen dressed quickly. "Are you all right?"

"Yes, fine though disappointed. I hoped the mention of Walsingham in the letter would work."

"Ah, who knows why it didn't, but the direct approach was worth a try. Let's go and tell the Fae their plan is nonsensical."

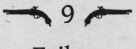

9

Failure

"ROSSALINDE."

"And."

"Corwen."

"You."

"Have."

"Failed."

"Us."

The Fae Council of Seven, who sat in judgment upon us, delivered their verdict, one word each as though they shared a brain. Then, Larien, David's father, with whom I had a somewhat strange and strained relationship, stood as if ready to mete out a sentence.

This wasn't a trial. We'd not been allowed to say anything yet, and I sure as all hell was not going to stand here meekly and take what they were saying without a spirited response even though we were in Iaru, their heartland.

I looked along the line of Fae, sitting on their throne-like chairs. I knew them all by sight, but the only ones I'd ever had direct dealings with were Larien and his brother Dantin. Larien was imperious but fair-minded. Dantin didn't like humanity and made no effort to hide the fact. The oldest Fae on the council, Lord Dax, looked ancient in the same way as a stately tree shows its age. His skin drooped down his face, and his eyes were almost lost in folds. His white hair, fluffy as swansdown, exploded from beneath a close-fitting headdress of what appeared to be flexible gold. Fae were not immortal, but since they aged so slowly, I thought he might be thousands of years old. I couldn't even begin to guess the ages of the others. They looked to range from their sixties down to a youthful thirty, which meant they were centuries old, not decades.

Out of the seven, only two of them were female, the elderly Lady Iphransia and the middle-aged Lady Coralie. I didn't know much about Lord Tarius except he seemed inclined to agree with Dantin, and I knew even less about Lord Eduran, who listened a lot but said little.

I knew some of the youthful Fae who stood behind their parents' chairs as cupbearers were two centuries old, and had the appearance of being barely twenty. David was the youngest. He stood behind Larien's chair, his face impassive. He was the only one I knew to be genuinely the age he appeared to be.

"You asked us to do the impossible, and you gave us no help to do it." Corwen stood close by my side, the back of his hand brushing the back of mine.

"This country doesn't work the way it did the last time you came out of your hallowed halls and spoke with a monarch." I directed my reply to Larien who, in my opinion, had been responsible for causing the whole problem in the first place—over two hundred years ago. "If you had given your help against the Armada when Good Queen Bess first requested it, the rowankind would never have been summoned to do your job for you and would never have been trapped as bondservants waiting for someone from my family to free them. Also, it's likely that without the knowledge you gave to the Crown, the queen would never have created the Mysterium to limit the use of magic and would never have appointed the first Walsingham to hunt down my ancestors."

I knew I was oversimplifying, but—broadly speaking—I was right.

Larien went frighteningly still. Maybe he was sharing thoughts with the rest of the council. "May I remind you, Rossalinde, it was your ancestor who had the idea of summoning the rowankind to use their weather magic."

"But he wouldn't have had to if you hadn't been so damned standoffish." I glared at him. "You, Larien, in person. You spoke for the Fae, then as now."

Larien's decision to keep the Fae out of the Spanish war had prompted my many-times great-grandfather, Martyn the Summoner, to do what he did. I wasn't sure how it had been achieved. I believe Martyn had some help initially from Dr. John Dee who thereafter kept out of the whole mess and, when Martyn had begged his help to send the rowankind home, had skipped off to Europe on a mission for the queen. Very useful.

Martyn had summoned the rowankind, the Fae's servants, out of Iaru with a complex magical working, binding them to our world. He'd sucked the weather magic right out of them and into himself, then used it against Spain's ships. But defeating the Armada broke the old man, and he'd been unable to send the rowankind back. Even the Fae hadn't been able to undo Martyn's working, so they'd done the next best thing, they thought, stealing away the rowankind's memories of Iaru and magic to enable them to live in the mundane world without yearning for something they could no longer have. Unfortunately, within a few generations, the rowankind had become little more than bondservants in the households where they had been placed.

The ability to free them had passed through the Sumner family, firstborn to firstborn, until it rested with me. With my firstborn dead before he'd had a chance to live, it would end with me.

Therefore, I had done it, returning knowledge and magic to the rowankind so they could go home.

Unfortunately, it wasn't as simple as that. The rowankind, descendants of the original ones, had made homes and places for themselves in our world. Some had intermarried with humans and felt that leaving the world they knew for what seemed like a fairy kingdom, was too large a step. Some went happily to Iaru, but others declared their wish to stay and make their own place in the world, free of obligations.

And that's where the trouble lay.

When the Mysterium began to persecute the rowankind, the Fae decided to send the king a warning. It was, they said, a matter of honor. In a time before time they had created the rowankind from the trees in the forest. Now they had a duty to protect them. We were supposed to tell the king to protect the Fae.

If only it had been that simple.

We'd already tried to tell them the king—even if we could find a way to speak with him, which, so far, had proved impossible—could not simply make laws. It all had to be done through Parliament.

And now the Fae said it was our fault the king had not yet changed the law.

Well, I wasn't having it.

"We didn't volunteer. You gave us this task without a by-your-leave, Larien. We told you that commoners couldn't simply march up to the palace and demand a private audience with the king. And the king can't change the law without Parliament."

"Then we shall have to make Parliament want to change the law." Dantin, Larien's brother, was always ready with a harsh solution.

The meaning in his words made me shudder.

I felt the hair on the back of my neck rise. What were they planning? The Fae had largely ignored the world of men because they simply were not interested. If they chose to, they could wipe us out in a heartbeat.

"How will you do that?" I dreaded his response, but I should have known the Fae never gave straight answers.

"You'll find out in time—or not," Dantin said. The threat was implicit in his tone of voice. Dantin had always been the hotheaded one on the council.

"What does that mean?" I asked. "Is it a threat?"

Larien gave Dantin a sideways look. "Be less hasty, brother." He turned to us. "Try again. Persuade the king, and Parliament, too, if that's what it takes, to make the changes necessary."

Corwen slipped a protective arm around my waist. "Why us, Larien?"

Larien stepped forward and bent his head as if he were addressing us alone.

"You, Ross, are sister to my son. You, Corwen, are husband to my son's sister. You are the nearest to family I have who are wholly human. I know you'll not play me false. Besides, I also know it's your dearest wish to be rid of the threat of the Mysterium for the sake of your own kin."

He looked down at my belly, still flat. How did he know? I was barely sure myself yet.

"I won't let you put her at risk, Larien," Corwen said. "Especially not now. Why have the Fae not kept up diplomatic relations with the Crown? Surely you could have had a representative at court any time you wished."

Larien shook his head. "Our ambassador to the king deemed it prudent to return home when the king was beheaded. We never formed a relationship with Cromwell the usurper. It seemed to us things had changed too much, and we were better off sealing ourselves away."

I thought I understood. Cromwell wasn't the rightful king, so anything lower than a monarch was beneath their dignity. I wondered why they hadn't made advances to the court after the restoration of the monarchy.

"You could simply go yourselves," I said. "Resume diplomatic relations."

"That would not be appropriate. We'll give your king and his Parliament the opportunity to correct their own mistakes first. If they don't take it . . . "

He left that sentence dangling. A threat, but not directly to us, not yet, anyway.

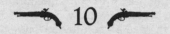

10

The Mad King

Maundy Thursday, 18th March 1802,

Outside the Chapel Royal, Whitehall, London

THEY SAID THE king was mad, but I had my own ideas. It seemed to me he was neither mad nor incapacitated in any physical way, but he had a whiff of magic about him. In a realm where unlicensed magic led to a merciless death at the end of a rope, the monarch would never have been able to reveal himself as magic-touched. Yet suppressing any kind of talent was dangerous.

Magic had killed my mother. Repressing it had eaten her from the inside. The medical profession might have diagnosed a tumor, but I had seen her on her deathbed and pieced her story together.

I knew.

For the last ten days, Corwen and I had been dodging the Mysterium and observing King George, third of his name, from a distance fitting for commoners. We'd seen him ride past in his carriage, and then a day later had seen him out walking with his family in Green Park, his retinue following behind at a discreet distance.

In the time we'd been observing him, we'd changed lodgings six times, only avoiding a check by militia troops by a very narrow margin. They weren't looking for us in particular, but if we'd drawn attention to ourselves, our descriptions were probably still on their wanted sheets. I was fairly unremarkable: brown hair, middling height, no distinguishing features. However, Corwen's silver hair and his piercing gray eyes were memorable, which was why he pulled his hat down low.

The silver showed his color as a wolf.

Neither of us liked being here, but we needed a way to get to the king, and the king was in the capital.

King George wasn't a young man. His sixty-four years, the loss of the Americas, the war against revolutionary France, and the exploits of his notorious elder son sat heavily upon him. As did his illness. If we succeeded in passing on the Fae's ultimatum, we would make his life infinitely more complicated.

London was a risk, but Larien was right. If we could make a difference to the way magical folk were treated in this great nation, we owed it to our future family to try. I was pretty sure now that there would be a future family. The discovery had come as something of a surprise, since I'd thought myself barren after my only child, Will's son, had been born early and had not lingered beyond a few days.

When Corwen had asked me to marry him, I had told him the possibility of children was vanishingly small, yet here we were. Of course, there was a long way to go yet and every possibility that I wouldn't carry the child to term, so, much as I hoped, I didn't let myself get too involved with the tiny being inside me. I would carry on as normal, I resolved. And what would be, would be.

The Fae's threat against the mundane world was real, too real.

They hadn't interfered with humanity for over two thousand years, but that didn't mean they couldn't; it simply meant they hadn't cared to. The rowankind were under Fae protection now, and the Fae took their responsibility seriously. I didn't know how far the Fae would go, but I was sure that if they wanted to, they could reduce London to a smoking hole in the ground.

So here we were, standing in the crowd at Whitehall, outside the Chapel Royal, waiting for a glimpse of the king on his way to distribute Maundy money to the poor. Though it was an ancient custom, no kings had actually participated in the service for over a hundred years until King George had taken it upon himself to distribute the Maundy gifts this year, possibly to prove to his people he had recovered from his most recent attack of melancholy and was entirely fit to rule.

I shivered beneath my woolen cloak and pulled my hood closer. Easter was early this year. It was still the middle of March. A cold dampness rose from the Thames, bringing with it the scents of fish, mud, and ordure in equal measure. I felt slightly queasy, but I didn't know if it was my condition or the stench.

"Cold?" Corwen put one arm around me and drew me close. "You're sure we need to be here? I could take you back to our lodgings and warm your bones."

I didn't think he was contemplating extra blankets and a warm mustard bath for my feet.

"You can warm me later. Right now I want to get a closer look at His Majesty," I said. "There was an air about him when we saw him in the park last week, but we were so far away that I wasn't sure."

"You think he's affected by—" Corwen wasn't going to say the word *magic* in public. That kind of talk could attract unwelcome attention, and here, close to Westminster, where the first of the Mysterium's militia companies had been deployed, everyone was watching out for magic users. Even talking about it could draw the interest of concerned citizens all too ready to claim the offered reward.

I nodded. "I think it's possible."

"Will it make our job easier or harder?"

I shrugged and heard him sigh.

The crowd stirred. The king and his retinue were emerging from the chapel.

"God bless Your Majesty," someone in the crowd shouted, and the rest of the crowd took up the cry.

"The people love him," Corwen said softly in my ear. "Even though the poor have been struggling for bread."

"They blame Bonaparte and the French, not the king. He presents a good face to them. Farmer George."

The king was closer now. He'd stopped to shake hands with someone, and the crowd had surged in his direction. This was my chance. Emboldened, I shrugged off Corwen's arm, squeezed between two men, and pushed my way to the front. I doubt the king had intended to shake the hand of a random female, but as he held out a hand to the man on my right, I snatched off my glove, reached out, and took it.

The reaction was instantaneous. I felt a shock run up my arm, and it was obvious the king did, too. For barely a heartbeat the king's gaze met my own, his eyes wide, and then he was past, being hurried away.

"Did you get what you wanted?" Corwen was right behind me.

"Oh, yes." I turned to him, grinning. "Now all we have to do is find a way to talk to him."

❖────────────❖

Corwen and I walked back to our lodging at the Golden Lion, where we'd taken a room under the name of Parker. Since our direct approach had failed, we had to come up with a more creative plan. Finding a way to talk to the king was easier said than done, but I had an idea. The king was, if not fond of, perhaps inured to being dipped in the sea. I'd read about it in the *Gentleman's Magazine*. In fact, I still had the copy in my valise. This started to spark an idea.

"You can swim, Corwen, can't you?" I asked him as we walked.

"Yes, why? You aren't planning any more terrifying trips along the Thames, are you?"

"I didn't plan that one; it just happened."

We'd shot the rapids beneath London Bridge, chased by Walsingham's hellhounds while trying to rescue my brother Philip, who turned out to be not worth rescuing, though we didn't discover our mistake until he tried to kill us.

"I'm thinking of a way we might be able to get to the king," I said. "You saw how many retainers surrounded him today."

"Well, he is the king, and not well by all accounts. And I expect our letter alerted those around him whose job it is to keep him safe."

"Did you read the article in the *Gentleman's Magazine* about saltwater cures?"

"Not yet. You've been hogging it since I bought it."

"The king takes saltwater cures. We might be able to get to him in the sea."

"Not exactly a great place for a discussion."

"We could swim him out to a boat standing offshore."

Corwen's silence spoke volumes.

"Not my best idea, huh?"

"Let me get it straight. You, an increasing lady, may I remind you, intend to kidnap an elderly naked king out of the shallows, shove him into a boat, within sight of the shore and his retainers, and then try and discuss the plight of magic users in general and the rowankind in particular."

"Well, now you put it that way . . . " I sighed. "Since the king rarely goes anywhere without his entourage, I thought they might give him a little space while he was in the sea."

"They wheel him down to the sea in a bathing machine, right?"

"Yes, a very distinctive one—white with blue panels and red cornices, a crown, and a flagpole."

"A flagpole?"

"In case anyone misses the royal coat of arms painted on the front."

"Of course." Corwen's tone was so dry I could almost imagine his words crumbling to dust.

"He gets undressed in the bathing machine," I said. "I don't know whether someone helps him or whether he undresses himself."

"Does a king ever undress himself? Isn't that what all his flunkies are for?"

"Usually, but it's a very small bathing machine, so he can't have more than one attendant. While he's getting undressed, they wheel it down to the water's edge and push it into the waves. The king opens the seaward door and steps, naked, into the water under the supervision of two guides, ladies experienced in the dipping of those who may not even be able to swim. Don't you think it possible for someone who's a strong swimmer to swim under the water and pop up beside the bather?"

"Possibly, but what happens after that? The king's entourage on land would surely have pistols."

"They'd never risk hurting the king. Pistols and muskets are too inaccurate."

"What if they had a sharpshooter with a rifle? Accurate at a distance of four hundred yards."

"Hmmm, all right. You read the article and see if you can come up with a better idea."

Back in our room, I shrugged out of my cloak and threw it on the bed. A meager fire smoldered in the grate. Corwen stirred what was left of the coals with an iron poker and carefully placed two small logs which sizzled and smoked before eventually beginning to flame.

I took the copy of the *Gentleman's Magazine* to the grimy window to catch some daylight and read the article again.

The author, who simply signed himself *A Physician*, strongly recommended full immersion in seawater, combined with taking it as a drink, mixed with milk. Both practices to be done under strict medical supervision, of course, and topped off by a session of bloodletting.

It sounded like the sort of thing designed to line the pockets of the medical profession without offering any benefits to their patients, except perhaps relief when the treatment was over.

Only once had a surgeon recommended bloodletting to me, and it had been the end of a promising professional relationship. I'd seen what losing blood could do to a body. Bleeding after a skirmish or an accident was one thing, but relinquishing blood voluntarily made no sense.

As for drinking seawater . . . I'd drunk it, accidentally, a number of times, and it wasn't something I'd recommend to anyone. When it came to swimming, the warmer waters of the Caribbean were a better prospect than Britain's coastal waters, especially at this time of year. It made me shiver to read the article.

"Look." I handed the magazine to Corwen. "It says here Prince George, apparently, prefers to be dipped at Brighthelmstone, while the king prefers the relative peace of Bognor or Weymouth. The sea at Weymouth apparently cured him of a bilious attack, though it took three months. That's a long time to get over a bilious attack. I bet if he'd stayed in a nice comfy bed, he'd have been cured in three days."

"I would think the king's enthusiasm for Bognor and Weymouth is entirely due to his firstborn's enthusiasm for Brighthelmstone. I can't see the king being enamored of Prinny's set."

Corwen settled down in a chair by the window to read the article for himself. At length, he looked up. "Swimming away with the king is a terrible idea, but what if we were to take the place of his dippers?"

"His dippers are both female," I said.

Corwen raised one eyebrow at me. "Well, you qualify. How long did you pass for a man as Captain Tremayne? I could dress myself in skirts."

"You'd be a powerfully tall woman."

He laughed. "Once in the water, who could tell?" He stared out of the window, looking thoughtful. "I'm not saying it's a bad idea to try and get to him when he visits the coast, but probably not disguised as dippers, especially in your condition."

"My condition? I shouldn't have told you. I've barely missed my first course yet. If I hadn't been sick in the mornings, I wouldn't even have guessed."

"I'm glad you did—tell me, I mean. Though I'd have noticed you throwing up and your breasts."

"What's wrong with my breasts?"

"Nothing. They're lovely." He had a smile on his face. "But definitely more tender than usual and, I do believe, a little heavier."

"Already? No. It's your imagination."

But the smile didn't leave his face. "I won't put you in danger. Let's keep our options open. We need to be able to find out whenever the king leaves London for the country, or maybe even when he's at Windsor. Do we know anyone who might know an insider in the palace?"

"I'll bet the goblins know someone. We could pay a visit in the morning."

"You already owe them a debt. Is it wise to involve them? It might remind them to try and collect."

"Oh, I doubt Mr. Tingle has forgotten. He's an astute businessman."

"Don't tell him about the child."

"I won't tell anyone about the child, at least not until my belly tells them for me."

"Not even my mother?"

"Think how I'd feel if I lost it. I might, you know. It's still very early days. I know how pleased you are, but it's not a sure thing, not yet."

He reached out and took my hand. "You're pleased, too, aren't you?"

I squeezed his fingers. "You know I am."

"Should you see a physician?"

"It's not an illness."

"Talk to the Lady, then."

I smiled at him. "Of course. She probably knows already, and I'll tell Aunt Rosie, too. It's good to have a midwife in the family."

"Even if she's a witch?"

"Especially if she's a witch."

11

Goblins

THE FOLLOWING MORNING, after I'd thrown up again, we took a coach to Whitechapel, to the tailoring establishment of Mr. Tingle, the goblin to whom I was in debt. Not financial debt—that I could have coped with—but a debt of honor, a favor owed for a favor done. It was always dangerous to owe magical creatures a favor, and I'd promised a very open-ended one—unspecified and at the time of Mr. Tingle's own choosing. When I'd rescued Mr. Twomax and a bevy of young goblins, I'd hoped Mr. Tingle would call the debt even, but he said the debt was Twomax's, and that my debt to him was still ongoing.

It was Good Friday, but I guessed it would be business as usual in the clothing trade. Going to church on a working day was a luxury seamstresses couldn't afford. The goblin workshop was in George Yard, a passage connecting Spitalfields and Whitechapel. The dilapidated building looked as if it might come crashing down at any moment if it weren't for the tall buildings on either side of it.

Corwen could see through the glamour, but even though I knew the building was not nearly as bad as it looked, I still felt slightly queasy. We approached what appeared to be a boarded-up doorway. This time I found it easier to link my arm through Corwen's and let him guide me.

He rang the bell and pushed open the door. "Step up," he said.

The toe of my half-boot clicked on the edge of the step and then I was through the doorway and the dizziness faded. Off to the right was a long window into Tingle's workroom where his ladies sat stitching red coats for the army, a very profitable contract for which Deverell's Mill, under the guiding hand of Corwen's sister, Lily, supplied the woolen cloth.

To the right were three doors, one of which was to Mr. Tingle's office.

At the sound of the door, young Barnaby Tingle, Mr. Tingle's grandson, and half-goblin—or maybe even a quarter, I didn't like to ask—appeared from the nearest door and pulled it closed behind him. I thought I heard a girlish giggle in there. When he saw us, he blushed and grinned a somewhat toothy smile. Barnaby had no glamour, so his pale skin, overcrowded teeth, and hawkish nose with slit nostrils was the appearance with which he faced the world. In truth, he wasn't unhandsome when he kept his teeth behind his lips, but I'd stopped thinking of goblins as unusual. What they did was more important than the way they looked, and Mr. Tingle managed his business well, even feeding his workers, both human and goblin, before and during their twelve-hour shifts with needle and thread. I could only wish more manufactory owners would do the same. It would surely help to alleviate some of the poverty in places like Whitechapel.

"Ah, you'll be here to see Uncle Twomax," Barnaby said.

"Actually, we came to see Mr. Tingle," Corwen said.

"Is Mr. Twomax here?" I asked. "I haven't seen him since he left the Okewood. Is he well?"

"Aye, he's very well. Uncle Twomax often pops in for tea."

Twomax was the elderly leader of the goblins we'd rescued from the *Guillaume Tell* alongside Corwen and Freddie. I'd known he was Tingle's cousin, but I hadn't realized they were on regular visiting terms.

"This way," Barnaby said. "I'll bring more cups."

Eating and drinking in a magical creature's lair could put you in their debt, and for this purpose Tingle's place of business counted.

The office was exactly as I remembered it, green walls and a dark wood wainscoting with a rich rug and a merry fire in the hearth. It looked more like a gentleman's den than a place of business. A pair of armchairs were drawn up around the fire.

Mr. Tingle and Mr. Twomax looked more alike than I remembered. I'd never seen them together before. Twomax, under the stress of the escape from the *Guillaume Tell*, had not kept up his glamour consistently. Today, the two goblins looked like a pair of beaming grandfathers, stout of girth, with snowy white periwigs, rosy cheeks, and twinkling eyes. Both goblins stood to greet us.

"Mr. and Mrs. Deverell, as I live and breathe." Mr. Twomax's grin exposed all his pointy teeth. "We were talking about you the other day. I'm glad to see you looking so well, aren't you, Tingle?"

"I am. Come in and welcome." Mr. Tingle's smile was more questioning.

Barnaby carried in more cups, then drew up another pair of chairs. He waved to us to sit and began to pour tea.

I hesitated when he offered me a cup.

"Please, drink without obligation," Mr. Tingle said.

"Thank you." I didn't mention the obligation I already had, and neither did he.

"What can I do for you, today?" Mr. Tingle asked.

"Can't we visit without wanting something?" Corwen asked.

"You can," Mr. Tingle raised an eyebrow, "but I find that generally you don't."

"Then we'll certainly rectify our omission another time," Corwen said.

"Ah, so you do want something."

"Information," I said. "You once told us that since Roman times there were tunnels and cellars under all of this city, and where there are tunnels there are goblins."

He frowned. "I also said we're not sewer goblins anymore."

"You did, and I know you are not, but you have contacts. I'd be very surprised if anything happened in this city without you getting word of it."

"That may be."

"Do you have any contacts within the royal household?"

"I know what's good for me. I steer clear of the royals as much as I steer clear of the Mysterium."

"Ah, a pity," Corwen said.

"What exactly do you want?"

"To know when the king is next likely to venture out of London, maybe to Windsor or Kew, or maybe to Bognor or Weymouth."

Mr. Tingle waved both hands, palm out. "I want nothing to do with spying on the king." But then he looked thoughtful. "Would this be something to do with the Fae and the rowankind, and the Fae's command that you present their ultimatum to the king?"

"Is it common knowledge?"

"Maybe not common. More like uncommon knowledge. Goblins are studious collectors of information that might one day prove useful. We hear things."

"I hope you might hear about the king's excursions."

"In this case . . . no," Tingle said.

"Hold on, Tingle." Twomax turned to us. "I may know someone who knows someone who serves Dr. Cholmondeley, one of the king's physicians. It may be possible to get this information, though . . . "

"Yes?"

"What might it be worth?"

I was about to ask what he wanted in return, but he

didn't leave me time. "Might it cancel out the debt I owe you?"

I was about to say I didn't consider him in debt to me, but I remembered my debt to Tingle. I took a deep breath and tried to look as though I was good at negotiating.

"It might go some way toward canceling it, certainly, though possibly not the whole way." I hedged, waiting to see his reaction before going any further. "It is your life you owe us, and the lives of your young goblins. How many of them were there?"

He cleared his throat uncomfortably.

"Perhaps if your young goblins would be so good as to help get the information to us post-haste, we might also cancel their debt. Receiving the information too late to do anything about it would be as bad as not receiving it at all."

He nodded and held out his hand to seal the bargain, dropping the glamour and appearing as his real self, skinny and pale. The hand he held out had an extra joint on each digit. I took his hand without hesitation, feeling his grasp cool, but as firm as any human hand.

Corwen shook in his turn. "Our thanks to you."

"We hear the king's first minister is in negotiation with Bonaparte to bring about a peace," Tingle said. "Have you any knowledge of what this might entail?"

"There were rumors as far back as Christmas," Corwen said. "Bonaparte is greedy. He wants Europe in his pocket. Peace isn't in his best interests. If Mr. Addington is negotiating a peace, the terms won't be in Britain's favor."

"But even a temporary truce might result in an exchange of prisoners. You know what that would mean."

"Walsingham freed," I breathed.

"If he still lives," Corwen said. "When we sent him unprotected into French waters, he was blind and maimed. He'll not see the low side of fifty again. Surviving in a French prison is not easy even for those who are young and healthy."

"This is Walsingham, we're talking about." I felt as

though my throat had knotted beyond my ability to swallow. "He'd survive on pure willpower if only for the chance to destroy us."

And now that I was carrying Corwen's child, I had another life to protect. Would I have been this afraid if I'd only had myself to look after?

"He is no friend to any magical being," Mr. Tingle said. "I propose we keep each other informed, should the worst happen."

The goblins were in danger now that the Mysterium knew they existed—even though they fitted so well into the city that they were hard to find.

"In addition, the favor you owe me . . . "

I'd been hoping to avoid my debt to Mr. Tingle and the goblins for a little longer, but I'd made a promise and must stick to it.

I saw Corwen start to say something, but I gave a quick shake of my head.

"What is it you need, Mr. Tingle?"

"Nothing onerous. Something that's in your best interests as much as ours. I want the persecution of magical beings ended."

"You're as unrealistic as the Fae if you think we can bring that about."

"Maybe, maybe not. If you are making a case for the protection of the rowankind, it's but a small step to include all magicals."

"And what if it's a step too far?"

"Then my second request is that you put an end to Walsingham. He's a very bad man, with a lot of deaths on his conscience, or he would have if he had a conscience."

I nodded sharply.

"Agreed." Corwen and I said it together, and all four of us shook on it.

❖－－－－❖

Our horses were stabled at an inn on the south bank of the Thames.

Corwen secured a coach to take us from Whitechapel

to our inn room to collect our few belongings, and thence to London Bridge, where the traffic was so thick that we abandoned our coach and made better time on foot.

Dancer whickered when we entered the stable, but Timpani stood aloof as if to ask why we'd left him in this awful place. The Fae couldn't enter big cities because of the stench in the streets and the choking coal smoke. The Fae horses obviously preferred to be out in the country-side, too.

"I'm sorry, boy," Corwen rubbed Timpani's nose gently. "Blame Larien and the Council of Seven for giving us an impossible task."

"I suppose we could simply refuse to do it," I said.

Corwen huffed out a breath. "The Fae would find some way to force us into it. Delivering an ultimatum to the king isn't going to go down well, however we do it. Larien could do it himself, of course."

Larien had proved he could withstand the closeness of towns. He'd spent time in Plymouth in my mother's household. I remembered him, but not well; somehow his presence in the household had made little impact, and that, too, was part of his disguise. He'd been glamoured as a rowankind bondservant, his skin silvered and marked with grain patterns like any rowankind, and his demeanor mild and helpful. Hiding his haughtiness must have been the most difficult part of the whole deception. Surely, if any of the Fae could demand an audience with the king, it was Larien.

Damn the Fae and all their twisted logic. They remembered when my many-times great-grandfather had had the ear of Good Queen Bess, but the family had fallen far since then.

We saddled up and took the road to Richmond, to the gateway into Iaru in the park. From Iaru we could cross through to the Old Maizy Forest.

We kept to an easy pace so as not to attract attention through the Kennington toll gate and along the turnpike, but once through the gate to Iaru, we let the horses have their heads. Corwen was eager to get back. He didn't like leaving Freddie for long, even though the grounds around the cottage were protected by David's barrier.

Corwen had become his brother's keeper.

We traversed the warm green glades of Iaru and emerged through another gate a hundred yards from our cottage.

"Freddie!" Corwen called.

No answer.

"Perhaps he's off hunting," I suggested.

"Or perhaps he's simply sulking."

The latter proved to be the case. Freddie slunk out of the cottage and sat in the middle of the garden path with a where-have-you-been look on his face.

"You know where we've been." Corwen tended to carry on a one-sided conversation, hoping Freddie would understand and at least give a yes or no answer. "We saw the king, and Ross thinks he's magical, or at least he has potential to be so. That's a situation and a half, isn't it? The king having magical powers and not being able to admit it. No wonder the poor fellow's mad."

Freddie growled softly.

"Yes, I know I called you mad once, and I'm sorry for it. But you must admit I had reason. You've been in an impossible situation, but staying in wolf form won't enable you to heal from it. I can petition the Lady to allow you to turn back."

Freddie rose and crossed the garden where he slumped beneath the low branches of the willow, just beginning to burst forth with catkins.

"See." Corwen turned to me. "Sulking."

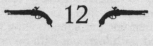 12

Peace

AFTER NINE YEARS of war against France, the church bells rang out across Britain to mark the peace afforded by the Treaty of Amiens, signed only a few days before. Even here, on the borders of the Old Maizy Forest and Iaru, we could hear them.

I should have been overjoyed, but I could only think of the trouble it might bring. Mr. Tingle had reminded us that in the event of peace and the exchange of prisoners, there was every possibility Walsingham might return. He'd been the most secret of secret agents for the Crown, his life dedicated to preventing the release of the rowankind. He took his failure personally and had become my most bitter enemy. I'd had the opportunity to kill him, but I'd not taken it—something I now bitterly regretted. Instead, I'd consigned him to the mercy of a French prison, hoping he'd die without being directly on my conscience, not thinking that less than a year later he might be freed by circumstance.

I sighed.

If Walsingham was freed, it was likely he would make

his way to London, to the Mysterium offices, or even straight to the king. I'd have to trust that the goblins would keep a sharp watch. It was in their best interests to let us know. I couldn't live my life looking over my shoulder to see if Walsingham was behind me. I had a sudden vision of having to protect a baby from Walsingham. Maybe our temporary home in Aunt Rosie's cottage might have to become permanent. How would it be for the child, raised with love, but with no companions her own age? I'd taken to calling our baby "she," but to Corwen, the baby was always a boy. I didn't let myself wonder if he or she would be a wolf or some other kind of shapechanger or if he or she would be a witch. Maybe the child would inherit both capabilities. We'd have our hands full if that was the case, with or without Walsingham.

The cessation of hostilities brought another pressing problem, that of my ship, the *Heart of Oak*, captained by my good friend Hookey Garrity, who had been my family in the days when I had been a lonely widow clinging to the ghost of my dead husband.

The *Heart* was a privateer ship preying on French merchantmen, operating under Letters of Marque from the Crown. She wasn't huge, less than ninety feet from stem to stern, but she was fast, a two-masted tops'l schooner with a fearsome reputation due to the speed of her closing and the ferocity of her crew.

Now the peace had stolen her livelihood, and I wondered whether Hookey, Mr. Sharpner, and Mr. Rafiq could turn their hands, hearts, and minds to the tame trade of cargoes and passengers.

The transition would be difficult.

"We must go to London," I told Corwen.

He was whittling a palm-sized chunk of pine, sitting on an upended log outside the back door of our cottage. It was a peaceful spot with the late afternoon sun shining down. Freddie was lying a few yards away, stretched out in the shade of his favorite willow.

Corwen blew on his carving to clear it of shavings and

looked up, raising one eyebrow and giving me a cool stare.

"Again? We've only been home for two weeks."

"Two weeks and still no word from Mr. Twomax."

"His goblins know where to find us."

"I know London's not safe," I said, "but that's where the *Heart* is heading, and I need to see Hookey. And perhaps Mr. Twomax and Mr. Tingle—"

"Twomax and Tingle will send word when they have news, and as for the *Heart*, you could call her to you anywhere along the coast."

I can summon the *Heart* because of the sliver of magical winterwood spliced into her keel, so if I called her, she would come. The crew long ago learned to follow when she turned contrary to wind and water. I thought about where I might meet up with my ship.

"I'm too well known in Plymouth and South Devonshire. Besides, there are several troops of redcoats stationed along the Dorset coast, and the Royal Navy guards the Bristol Channel."

"How about Bideford?"

North Devonshire. I considered the suggestion. It wasn't a bad idea. Though there was a new Mysterium office in Bideford, the townsfolk had always disliked their interference in town matters. In fact, the reason there was a new office was because the townsfolk burned down the old one.

It would take the *Heart* five days to reach Bideford and add eight days to their journey, but it would only take us one day if we went via Iaru and the Okewood. It would give us a little time to talk to the Lady of the Forests and try to solve the question of Freddie. Corwen thought he was improving, and that it might be time to ask the Lady to allow him to change to human again.

Corwen still felt responsible for him, though I could see a time when Freddie would have to take responsibility for himself.

I didn't know when that would be.

Maybe never.

How was it I could see to the root of Corwen's problems, and Corwen could see to the root of mine, but to our own we were blind?

Corwen had never spent long periods of time as a wolf. Though the Lady had hoped time as a wolf would help Freddie's self-control, I thought he was rapidly turning feral. There was the aging problem as well. He aged seven years for every one year spent in wolf form. He was barely twenty minutes older than Corwen in human time, but already there were flecks of gray around his muzzle.

"If we go via the Okewood, I can talk to the Lady about Freddie while Hartington accompanies you to Bideford."

"I'm perfectly capable of riding to Bideford alone. I'll go in breeches."

In truth, the disguise wasn't as good on land as it was at sea. My sailors had known my gender, of course, and the crews of the ships we engaged usually only saw me in the heat of battle. On land I looked like a young man hardly able to grow a beard, but as long as I didn't attract attention and kept my voice low, I could pass.

"I'd still feel better if—"

"I know. All right, if Hartington is available, I don't mind the company. He may be away on some errand, of course."

Since the Fae had opened the gates of Iaru for the rowankind, some dangerous magical creatures that should never mix with humans had been let loose into the world, and the Lady was directing her people to recapture them and send them back to Iaru, uninjured if possible. Hartington was one of her trusted agents. He was also Corwen's best friend.

"We're going to the Okewood, Freddie." Corwen addressed the wolf. When in wolf form himself, Corwen was perfectly capable of understanding speech and communicating with nods and head shakes as well as the occasional yip. I wasn't sure how much Freddie understood. He hid inside his wolf, letting it take over and relinquishing all responsibility for his actions.

"Are you coming?" Corwen asked.

Freddie didn't so much as flick an ear in Corwen's direction, but there was something about him that told me he'd understood.

"Suit yourself, but you're not staying here," Corwen said. "Do you want me to put a leash around your neck?"

Freddie growled, a low rumble in the back of his throat.

"Fair enough. We travel in an hour. Be ready."

An hour later Freddie was waiting for us. Corwen had saddled Dancer and Timpani. I wore my breeches, a linen shirt and neck cloth, a wine-dark waistcoat which helped to disguise my shape, and a dark blue jacket. A tricorn hat covered my hair which was pulled back in a cue. I fancied I looked like a young gentleman. Corwen's status as a gentleman was in no doubt. He wore buckskin breeches and a dark green coat, but no hat on his silver-gray hair. Most people tended to take him for older than he was, but he'd been born with gray hair, the same silvery shade as his wolf pelt.

"Ready, Freddie?" I asked as the big brown wolf rose from his supine position and trotted to the garden gate.

Dancer and Timpani flared their nostrils, but otherwise ignored him.

I unpicked David's working and the barrier around the cottage fell away.

We crossed into Iaru with no problems.

"Don't go wandering off, Freddie," Corwen said. "If you slip through another gate accidentally, there's no knowing where you might end up."

Freddie couldn't answer, but he stayed close enough to Timpani for the horse to flatten his ears and snake his head around to snap in the wolf's general direction.

"Enough!" Corwen checked the big horse, then he turned to me. "Want to find the gate to the Okewood?"

The Okewood was situated in the real world in Devonshire some ten miles northeast of Plymouth and twenty-five miles south of Bideford. On a map it looked to be twenty-five miles wide and thirty miles from north to south, but inside it seemed endless, maybe not as strange as Iaru, which was a whole world, but definitely one step removed from the rest of Devonshire. There were hamlets within the Okewood, but the inhabitants kept themselves to themselves. I suspected most of them were either magically inclined or not entirely human.

I'd been practicing. Corwen always found the right gate with ease, but he'd had six years of being the Lady's hench-wolf before I ever met him, so he was used to magical byways. I was still learning how to find them, not only the byways themselves, but the right ones to take me where I wanted to go.

I nudged Dancer out in front and let my instinct take over. I'm pretty sure Corwen used his nose to find the right path, but I didn't have the advantage of a wolf sense of smell. Even in human form his nose is keen. Instead of using my nose, I let my eyes and ears take over. My eyesight is good, but my ears are better.

I turned my head this way and that, noting the sound was muted in some directions, the pressure a little different on my eardrums.

"That way," I pointed.

Corwen grinned. "Right first time."

"I'm getting better."

"Yes, you are. Freddie, come back!"

Freddie had passed through the gate from Iaru into the Okewood and was streaking along in front of us.

"I swear I'll put him on a leash, so help me if I don't," Corwen said.

But he hadn't yet, and I knew he was worried about damaging Freddie's already delicate ego. The wolf had not attempted to bite anyone since he'd snapped a few tail hairs from Aileen Reynard. Corwen thought it was progress. I wasn't so sure. We touched our heels to our horses' flanks and set off after our problem brother.

We found Freddie in the glade which Charlotte and Olivia called home. He was rolling on his back, submissively offering his throat to Livvy, while the little girl gently pulled his ears and twined her fingers in his furry ruff. Freddie had always been fond of Livvy. I saw Corwen relax. He swung off Timpani to greet Charlotte.

Charlotte, all rowankind, had been Reverend Purdy's housekeeper in Bigbury, South Devonshire. She'd fallen in love with Henry, the Reverend's son, and they'd married, illegally, of course. Olivia, half-rowankind and half-witch, was the result of that union. Henry had registered as a witch when he turned eighteen, but nothing had come of it until four years ago when redcoats had turned up on his doorstep with papers and he was spirited away to the army without even time to pack a bag.

His family had heard nothing from him since.

Livvy had grown into a self-possessed little girl who had rescued Freddie, or at least saved his soul, when they were both imprisoned by the Mysterium in the *Guillaume Tell*. Had it not been for Livvy, Freddie might have been truly mad by the time we found him. Instead, he was only half-mad.

With much relief, we collected Freddie and retired to the bower which we thought of as ours, though could anyone truly own such a place?

After turning our horses loose to graze—they never appeared to go far, but we suspected they found better grazing in Iaru—Corwen, Freddie, and I retired for the night. It was a little cramped with three, but Corwen didn't trust Freddie enough to let him out of his sight, which was inconvenient as far as our marital bliss was concerned. Instead of anything more intimate, we simply snuggled together, my back against Corwen's chest.

"I asked around. Hartington will be back tomorrow evening," Corwen whispered. "Perhaps he can keep an eye on Freddie for a few hours." I pushed back into him, wriggling against bits of him that were standing to attention. "I do hope so."

In the event, Hartington was late and didn't arrive back until the morning after we'd been expecting him. He'd had some trouble with a troll and had come back for reinforcements.

"He's big," Hartington said as we walked down to the stream together. "Bigger by far than the pair you rescued from the *Guillaume Tell*."

Those two trolls were now happily guarding one of the gateways to Iaru with their own bridge. Once a troll settled beneath a bridge, they were extremely difficult to dislodge. They weren't evil creatures, but they were stubborn, clumsy, and enormous. They could kill without meaning to or injure simply by trying to pick up a human who refused to pay their toll, either in coin or in kind. They loved gold but would happily take a person's only milk cow as fodder or five sheep out of a flock of twenty without realizing the puny humans couldn't afford such losses every time they crossed a bridge.

It was a pleasure to be free of Freddie for an hour or two. We'd left him dozing in the bower with instructions to wait there. There were plenty of people around in the camp, from the Lady's woodland creatures to a few rowankind who didn't want to cross into Iaru.

I left Corwen and Hartington chewing over the methods by which trolls might be separated from their bridges, and wandered upstream, enjoying the mildness of the early spring day.

That's when I heard the snarls and a childish voice high with fear.

Olivia!

And Freddie.

Not in the bower where we'd left him.

I ran.

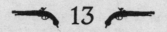

13

Freddie

WHEN YOUR BROTHER-IN-LAW is two hundred pounds of angry wolf, normal rules of family etiquette don't apply.

I pushed Livvy behind me and stared down the big brown wolf, snarls and all.

I knew I should have avoided confrontation, but enough was enough. I checked the dagger at the back of my waist but didn't pull it. It was my last resort, but if it was Freddie or me, I'd damn-well stick him with eight inches of steel. Maybe I'd try and stick it somewhere nonlethal.

Maybe.

I didn't think Freddie would do the same for me. If he lunged, it would be for my throat. I'd seen him do it before, though it had been in the heat of battle.

I put one foot back to brace myself against his charge. A twig snapped beneath my boot heel, sharp in the clear spring morning.

A dappled shape resolved itself among the young silver birches to my left. Hartington flowed smoothly from animal to man.

"Don't move, Ross."

I wasn't about to move. To turn and run would only tempt Freddie to give chase, and his four legs were much faster than my two.

"Corwen's on his way." Hartington kept his voice low.

I didn't have long to resolve this. Corwen loved his brother and would try to make excuses for his bad behavior. I wasn't about to let Freddie get away with snarling at Livvy. The child didn't believe Freddie's wolf would ever harm her, taking risks with him that no one else would ever take, but Freddie had once admitted that humans smelled like food. I knew he loved the girl in his own way, but I wasn't sure that was enough to protect her.

"Look after the child," I said to Hartington. "I'll take care of Freddie."

I snatched off my neck cloth and wrapped it around my left hand and wrist. It wasn't much protection against wolf teeth, but if Freddie came at me, the best defense was to shove something between his teeth before they reached my throat, and that might have to be my hand or forearm. One of the worst mistakes you can make when you get bitten by a dog of any size is to pull away. That's when teeth tear flesh as well as puncture. Of course Freddie wasn't a dog, but the same principle applied.

"Freddie, enough!" Freddie was oblivious to human speech when he was angry. "Back off. Leave Livvy alone. Leave!"

Freddie's snarls had grown in intensity, and his lips were drawn all the way back from his teeth.

I heard Hartington taking the girl gently to one side, not running, but edging back into the shelter of the trees.

Freddie turned his head to follow the child's movement.

"No! Look at me!"

I must have gotten through to him because his eyes snapped back to mine. I expected him to drop eye contact, but he didn't. This was serious.

"Back off, Freddie. You're letting the wolf win."

I stepped to one side. To continue eye contact with me,

he had to move so that Hartington and Livvy were out of his sight line.

"To me, Freddie. Look!"

I snapped it out like an order, and he jerked his stare back to meet mine.

"Back off!"

He dropped into a low crouch, the kind that comes before a spring.

I decided to change tack, though I didn't take my hand from the hidden knife. I laughed and stood upright, relaxing. "You know, Freddie boy, one day someone will take you seriously, and you'll end up in a trophy room or as a wolfskin rug. Better wise up and settle down."

He wasn't coming any closer, but he was still showing a full set of fangs.

"Come on, that's enough. You and I need to come to a better understanding now we're related. Corwen won't like it if you eat his wife. Who else would put up with him?"

I thought the snarl was a little less intense.

"For Corwen's sake we should try to stay friends. Come on, what do you say?"

Even after all these months I didn't expect him to back away, but maybe he realized what he'd almost done to Livvy. I can imagine that would scare anyone in their right mind.

He whined.

"No excuses, Freddie. It's unacceptable to growl, snarl at, or bite any human, especially those under the protection of the Lady."

He whined again.

I didn't let him finish. I stepped in close and booted him under his jaw. He went down like a stunned ox.

"If you ever snap or snarl at Livvy again, I will beat the living daylights out of your mangy hide. Don't think I won't."

"You'd better believe her, brother." Corwen's voice came from behind me.

"How long have you been there?" I asked.

"Long enough. You seem to have my brother under control."

"For now."

"We'll talk about the rest later. Reverend Purdy's arrived. Charlotte's making tea. Our presence is required." He put one arm around me, but as he squired me out of the grove, he spoke over his shoulder, lightly, as if me kicking Freddie was an everyday occurrence. "Come on, Freddie. You have an apology to make."

"What did he do this time?" Corwen said under his breath as we left the grove of trees.

"Snarled at Livvy. I mean seriously snarled."

"Oh." The tone of his voice said it all. "Did he mean it?"

"I'm sure he did. I was truly frightened for her."

I heard the soft padding behind us that told me Freddie was following. By the slump of Corwen's shoulders, I saw he had heard it, too. It appeared Freddie was not yet able to face the world as himself.

"Are you coming to apologize to Livvy?" Corwen asked, but Freddie's only response was to slink away in the direction of our bower.

"I thought for a moment we'd got his attention," I said softly.

Corwen turned and watched until Freddie slunk out of sight, then he huffed out a breath. "I thought he was getting better, but he isn't. I don't know what to do about it."

"Perhaps the Lady can help."

"I'm afraid the Lady might look for a permanent solution."

"She hasn't hurt the kelpie."

"Diana is a killer, but she's also intelligent. She knows how to curb her instincts because she knows the Lady will end her if she looks like a threat to anyone, magical or mundane."

I'd come to an understanding with the kelpie last year when we'd fought the redcoats together in order to bring the rescued magicals to the safety of the Okewood.

"You think the Lady would hurt Freddie?"

"I think she'd put him down like a dog if he attacked Livvy. He's on his final warning after the sprite incident. The Lady has a soft spot for the child. She doesn't say, but it's obvious."

"What can we do?"

Corwen was loyal to the Lady, but Freddie was his brother. And family was family. I didn't want to see Freddie come between Corwen and the Lady, but equally I didn't want to see the Lady put Corwen's loyalty to the test.

Corwen shook his head. He didn't know any more than I did. Here in the Okewood, not all the magical creatures were harmless, but the dangerous ones were kept away from the vulnerable. Maybe Freddie needed to take himself off to the depths of the forest and carve out his own territory, away from anyone he could hurt.

❦

I heard voices through the trees, and we quickened our steps. I felt Corwen straighten beside me, setting aside his worries about Freddie for the time being.

Reverend Purdy's laughter floated on the spring breeze alongside Livvy's giggles. Hartington had delivered the child to her family apparently none the worse for Freddie's threatening behavior. Livvy probably didn't realize how close she'd come to being savaged.

But Charlotte did. She glanced in our direction as we entered the glade, and I saw her expression cloud and her lips purse. She mouthed the word, "Later," and I nodded.

"Mrs. Deverell, Mr. Deverell, how good to see you again," the reverend rose from his carved log seat to greet us.

"Reverend Purdy," I held out my hand. "I'd curtsey, but I don't seem to be dressed for it."

Wearing breeches was so much more practical in the Okewood.

Reverend Purdy laughed. He was used to my odd habits, and knew about Corwen and Freddie's shapechanging, though not, I suspected, about Hartington's. If he thought about it, he might assume Hartington to be a wolf as well, though that seemed strange as Hartington looked like a stag to me, even in human form.

"Tea, Father." Charlotte had only recently begun calling Reverend Purdy father in our presence, and she still sometimes slipped back into calling him Reverend, which was her habit from all the years at Bigbury when her marriage to Henry Purdy had been a secret from everyone.

Reverend Purdy called Charlotte his daughter, even though she was rowankind. He'd presided over their marriage himself, and proudly recorded it—illegally—in the parish register at Bigbury, his previous church. He'd moved parishes to be closer to his family. For the last few months he'd been the vicar of South Brent, on the very edge of the Okewood, an incumbency avoided by most churchmen because of the rumors that the forest was haunted, which, indeed it was, by the Green Man and his Lady, together with their retinue of wild creatures.

"Ross, Corwen, will you take tea with us?" Charlotte had a kettle singing over an open fire and a little table made from a slice cut diagonally from the trunk of a fallen ash. On the table was a teapot and drinking vessels that were a far cry from fine china. They looked organic, fired clay in woodland colors that had definitely never seen a potter's wheel, but they fit the hand comfortably.

I wasn't sure how Charlotte had managed to secure the trappings of gentility in this place. All she lacked was a velvet-covered sofa and a harpsichord.

"What news from the town?" Corwen asked.

"You heard the church bells?" Reverend Purdy asked. "The war is over."

Charlotte looked up. "Does that mean Henry will come home?"

"I hope so, my dear." The reverend reached out and patted Charlotte's forearm.

"Oh, yes!" Livvy jumped up and skipped around her mother and grandfather singing, "Dad-dy's coming ho-ome. Dad-dy's coming ho-ome."

"Now, we didn't say that, Olivia," her grandfather said. "It's still a might-be. We hope he's coming home."

"That's good, isn't it?" the little girl asked.

"Well, it's a little better than it was before, but we still don't know." He patted his knee, and she climbed on it for a whiskery hug.

Charlotte sighed. "In truth, I'm not sure how much she remembers of him. He's been gone so long."

"We could make some enquiries," I said.

"Where would you start?" Reverend Purdy asked.

"The goblins. Mr. Tingle and Mr. Twomax. They seem to know what's going on in the capital." I didn't tell him they were already watching out for Walsingham on our behalf, as well as for an opportunity to talk to the king. "Tailors are always in the know," I said, "or they know a man who is. I suspect the goblins have contacts all over the city and beyond." I certainly hoped so, anyway.

"I can send a message to the goblins via the *Heart*'s crew," I said. "Mr. Rafiq will see it delivered safely."

It wouldn't add to the debt I already owed Mr. Tingle. I liked Tingle and his family. They were magical creatures simply trying to get by in an uncertain world.

Corwen nodded. It was settled.

"Thank you," Charlotte said. "Once more we're in your debt."

The Reverend took his leave, and we made ready to confront Freddie about his temper.

◆────────◆

Freddie looked as miserable as I felt, curled up in our bower as if it was his wolf's den.

He'd stopped snarling now.

"What's to be done with you, Freddie?" Corwen glared down at his brother. "You can't simply remain a wolf and grouch at everyone all the time. Your teeth are too big and your temper too uncertain."

"I'll go and make us all a nice cup of tea." My lightness of tone covered my concern, at least, I hoped it did. Corwen glanced at me. I'm pretty sure he knew I was cutting and running. He knew me better than I knew myself.

I headed back in Charlotte's direction, knowing she wanted a word with Freddie, too.

Now her grandfather had departed, Livvy was chatting away to Hartington, telling him how Freddie had protected her when they were captured by pirates. I don't think anyone had explained to Livvy that it was not pirates, but the Mysterium who had treated the rowankind and the magical creatures so harshly. They were supposed to be the law. Livvy didn't need to know her kind were not protected by law—not yet. She'd discover the harsh realities of life soon enough.

"How long has he been in wolf form?" Charlotte asked.

"Too long. Months. And then there was the time in captivity. He stayed in wolf form then to protect the family. No one knew his identity, so as long as he remained a wolf, they couldn't find out. I think it did something to him."

"He may have forgotten how to be human."

I shook my head, meaning I hoped not rather than I was sure. Staying in wolf form would kill him. Wolves had a comparatively short lifespan, so Freddie would age quickly. Corwen told me it was something he always thought about and tried to keep his wolf-time short.

"It's time the Lady let him change back," Charlotte said, straightening from pouring the boiling water onto the leaves. "You carry the teapot. I'll bring the cups and the sugar. I want a word with that wolf."

"As do we all," I muttered under my breath, but Charlotte heard and gave me a steady look.

"You think he's a danger?" she asked.

"I think he's in danger," I said. "He's been in danger from the first day he changed. Maybe if Corwen had been there to help him . . . " I shrugged.

"Don't let Corwen take the blame for his brother's condition," Charlotte said. "By the time he found out about Freddie's change, it was already far too late. And it's neither Corwen's fault nor yours that the Mysterium shipped the magical folk off to sea, your Freddie and my Livvy along with them. If it hadn't been for you two, they'd still be there, or worse, drowned."

I sighed as I picked up the teapot. "I know, and so does Corwen, but what he knows and what he feels can't easily be reconciled."

"He's got a good heart, your Corwen."

"Yes, he has."

We made our way back to the glade where Freddie was lying with his nose between his forepaws and his ears back, Corwen crouched down on his heels to one side, leaning forward. Freddie wouldn't meet Corwen's eyes.

"Oh, this isn't going well," I said to Charlotte.

"It's hardly surprising, is it?" she said. "Freddie's lost everything—the home he grew up in, the life he tried to make for himself in London. He even feels he's lost his humanity."

And he'd lost the love of his life, too, though that wasn't my truth to tell. Freddie's special friend, Roland, had left London for Gloucestershire. Freddie and Roland had parted on bad terms, an argument that had probably contributed to Freddie's self-destructive final run across Hampstead Heath, straight into a Mysterium catch-net.

Corwen saw us coming and rocked back on his heels. Conversation over.

Freddie looked up as Charlotte plonked the tea tray on the ground, rattling the cups. He whined.

"Is that an apology?" Charlotte leaned over and said something to Freddie, so softly that I couldn't hear.

He whined again.

Charlotte seemed mollified. "I'll leave you to your tea." She bustled away, and I poured.

Freddie whined again and nudged my hand with his nose.

"I accept your apology, Freddie, but will it change anything?"

He settled down again and lay still.

I glanced at Corwen, but he didn't meet my eyes.

Something would have to be done about Freddie if he became a danger to people. I knew the Lady wouldn't hesitate to put him down like a dog if he couldn't be redeemed. She wouldn't do it out of hand, though.

"Talk to the Lady, Corwen."

If we told Freddie his life was in danger, it might make him even worse. There were times when I didn't think he wanted to live as either man or wolf.

Corwen looked up with a world of hurt in his eyes.

"I don't want to leave you now," I said, "but the *Heart* will be in Bideford tomorrow."

"I know. Go. I've asked Hartington to accompany you."

I bit back my protests. Corwen knew full well I could look after myself, but I didn't want to add one more worry to his burden.

"Then I'll wear my riding habit and look like a lady. I'm sure it will amuse the crew."

That brought forth a smile.

"As for you, Freddie, don't give your brother any more trouble while I'm gone."

Freddie blinked and put his nose back on his forepaws, for once contrite.

14

Heart of Oak

HARTINGTON AND I set out for Bideford after breakfast. Dressed in a riding habit that was both serviceable and fashionable without being too extreme, I rode Dancer astride. My split-skirt also served to hide my pistol strapped to my hip, easy to get at through a hidden pocket. I wasn't anticipating trouble, but being prepared never hurt.

Hartington, looking every inch the country gentleman, rode Corwen's Timpani, who had been asked, politely, to accept a new rider. Fae horses have a measure of intelligence and understanding way beyond mortal horses—as well as strength, speed, and endurance—which made our journey much faster than the last time I'd traveled this road.

We reached the outskirts of Bideford just after three in the afternoon by the town clock, then stabled the horses at an inn Corwen and I had used before. We strolled to the quayside, trying to look casual.

Bideford town's twisting, narrow streets were lined with pastel-colored cottages clinging to the hillside above the wide Torridge River, only recently contained by a new embankment. Once a major port in the area, handling cargoes of cotton and tobacco from the New World, Bideford had lost much of its trade to Bristol with the rest curtailed by the war with France. Maybe with the war over, the town would regain some of its former prosperity.

The ships that docked here now were mostly fishing boats and coastal vessels carrying ball clay out and lime in, though if you knew where to look or who to talk to, there were those captains who specialized in the import of certain goods, mostly French, under the noses of the excise men.

We walked the length of the quay looking for the *Heart of Oak*, and there she was, at the seaward end, moored neatly with sails furled. She's a beautiful two-masted tops'l schooner, and she's all mine. I flushed with pride.

"Isn't that the finest ship you've ever seen?" I asked Hartington.

He cleared his throat. "I know very little about ships, Ross. Truly, I'm a land animal in every sense of the word. I can see she's neatly turned out, but she simply looks like a ship to me."

I chuckled, poised to give him a lecture on how her hull was fashioned from the best Bermuda teak and how her clean lines cut the waves like a hot knife through butter, when a roar from on deck interrupted my thoughts. Hookey Garrity was striding down the gangplank—my friend, one-time able seaman, and now captain in my stead. Close behind him at the rail was Daniel Rafiq, our quartermaster, and a gathering crowd of crewmen led by Lazy Billy, Crayfish Jake, Windward, and the Greek. I just had time to wave at them before Hookey swept me up into a bear-hug and whirled me around and around until I thought we should both fall down dizzy.

"Put me down, Hookey." I could barely gasp for laughing. "You wouldn't have done that when I was captain."

"Well, you was captain then, Cap'n. Now you're a lady."

"So you think you can take liberties, eh?"

"Err . . . " I think he actually blushed, though he was so sun-browned and weather-beaten it was hard to tell.

"Only teasing." Hookey and I had been in situations where our gender didn't make a difference. Despite his roughness, well concealed these days, he was the man I trusted most next to Corwen. "Hookey, do you know Hartington?"

"I've heard of you, sir, but I don't think we've ever shaken hands before."

Hookey offered his good right hand, the left being nothing more than a shiny metal hook. Hartington took it.

"Shall I wait here for you, Ross, if you have business to discuss?"

I looked up at the crew. "Mr. Rafiq always manages to brew a fair cup of tea; why don't I introduce you?"

Mr. Rafiq, born into slavery and educated for high office, had escaped from a sultan's palace before they could divest him of his manhood. He was the most cultured person I knew. He was also the most formal. He bowed over my hand and then flashed his white, even-toothed smile at me.

"Mr. Hartington is a friend of Corwen's," I said. "I wonder if you might entertain him while I discuss business with Hookey."

"With pleasure, Captain." Mr. Rafiq was the only person on board who never shortened captain to cap'n, but like all the crew he still used my former title even though Hookey was in charge now.

"And I wonder if you could deliver this note to Mr. Tingle when you get to London. You remember where to find him?"

"I do, and I will. Do you need me to wait for an answer?"

"I don't expect he'll have an answer for me immediately. I've given him an address he can write to."

He took the note and slipped it into the pocket of his immaculate yellow waistcoat.

"Billy, some tea for the cap'n," Hookey called.

Lazy Billy jumped to with a will. "Be right there, Cap'n, and Cap'n."

I chuckled as he raced away. Billy's tea was a concoction that was sometimes more rum than tea. "Things don't change, do they?" I asked.

"Well, now they might have to."

"Aye, Hookey, that's what I've come to talk about."

Hookey led the way down to his cabin, which used to be mine, and before it was mine alone, I'd shared it with Will Tremayne, my late husband. I wondered if any remnant of Will's ghost still lingered here. Will had stayed with me as a specter for three years until finally relinquishing me to Corwen, not that I needed his permission to fall in love again, but I was grateful for his blessing as he passed over the final barrier to a deeper place of rest.

The crew, however, still thought Will's ghost was with them when they entered into a skirmish. They used to ask me, "Is the old cap'n still with us?" and I would tell them, "Yes, he's up front with his cutlass drawn," and they would close with the enemy with a ferocity that sometimes startled even me.

Hookey waved me to the old armchair which had been mine, liberated from a ship we'd taken in the Caribbean in that dismal year after Will's death. The chair both reminded me of my loss and made me smile at the memory of Hookey and Windward huffing and puffing as they manhandled the chair down the narrow companionway and into my cabin, thinking to cheer me up.

Now the chair was Hookey's, but I was glad to sink into its depths once more. We shared pleasantries while Lazy Billy brought us tea, and then we got down to business.

"This damned peace." Hookey scowled. "I daresay they'll be releasing prisoners from France, and you know what that means."

"Are you thinking of Walsingham? If you are, you aren't the first."

"You were too lenient with him."

"Maybe I was, but leaving him a French prisoner of

war didn't feel lenient at the time, especially in his condition."

"It's true enough that we didn't expect peace so soon."

"Do you think it will last?"

He shook his head. "The French are making no effort to pull back their ships from places where they shouldn't be. I think they're using the peace to rebuild their fleet, so it's my guess they're doing the same on land. I don't suppose the British government is doing much different. At best, it's a breathing space. I give it a year, but in the meantime our Letters of Marque are useless because there's no enemy shipping to engage." He took a swig of his tea, laced with rum. "Damn Frenchies."

I sipped my tea cautiously, my nose telling me it was likely to kick like a mule. It was half-tea, half-rum, sweetened with sugar, but not softened with milk.

"The talk is all of Addington having little choice after two failed harvests. I think he signed the peace just in time, before everything fell apart. The bread riots last year were only the start of it. The government isn't going to risk a revolution after what happened in France."

"That's as may be, but what happens to us now?"

"If the peace doesn't last, we need to be ready, but in the meantime, you need to make sure the lads don't starve. I don't want to lay anyone off, but we've too big a crew for a merchantman. It doesn't take sixty men to load grain and cloth, even if we could find the cargoes."

"Ah, lass, I might have inadvertently solved that problem while giving us a new one."

I raised one eyebrow and waited for Hookey to confess to whatever it was that was making him uncomfortable.

He cleared his throat. "We might have taken a French merchantman after the peace was declared. We could hardly be expected to know o'course, but when we made discreet enquiries, the governor in Malta had already stopped paying the bounty on French ships and goods." He looked at me and shrugged. "We could hardly give her back, could we? And 'twould have been such a shame to scupper her."

"What about the crew?"

"Gave in without a fight. We put 'em ashore in Portugal."

"And the ship?"

"A little beauty, A barque. *Le Papillon*. One hundred and twelve feet in length, three masts. She handles well."

"And where is she now?"

"Ah, I thought she might be a bit of an embarrassment, so she's standing off the Isles of Scilly with Mr. Sharpner, Simeon Fairlow, and a skeleton crew. I thought we could send her to Bacalao and reregister her. By rights, she's yours, o'course."

"I was going to ask where Mr. Sharpner was."

"That'd be Cap'n Sharpner, now."

"He deserves his own ship. He's the best sailing master I've ever seen."

"He is, that."

"But I shouldn't be the owner, Hookey. I had nothing to do with the endeavor."

"You own the *Heart*. We couldn't have taken the barque without your ship."

"All right." I nodded. "I'll take a quarter share. You, Mr. Rafiq, and Mr. Sharpner can take a quarter each. Does that seem fair? And sell whatever goods she's carrying, give a bonus to the men, and use the rest to invest in new cargo. Legitimate cargo. It might be a good idea to trade in the Americas for a while until we see whether this peace lasts. Young Sim Fairlow will make a good quartermaster. Mr. Rafiq has trained him well."

"Aye, Mr. Rafiq has trained us all." Hookey waved his hand toward the stack of books on the map table. "Who'd have thought it? I could barely read and write when I first came aboard."

"I'd say Mr. Rafiq had missed his calling, but it seems he's doing more good here than running a sultan's household or schooling the sons of rich gentlefolk. Tell Mr. Sharpner to speak to my man of business at Hillman and Plunkett's Bank. He'll arrange for the paperwork to register the vessel in Bacalao. Call her the *Butterfly*. It's less Frenchified."

"And what of us in the meantime?"

"You're going to London?"

"Aye, to finalize leftover business with the Admiralty, but I fear their clerks have got deep pockets and short arms. We're owed for a ship we brought in before the peace was declared, but I'm guessing they'll try and wriggle out of the obligation."

"See if you can find a legitimate cargo for the *Heart* while you're there. Mr. Rafiq can handle negotiations."

"Legitimate cargo." Hookey didn't quite spit, but his tone of voice said it all.

"Don't give anyone the opportunity to remember this ship was associated with Redbeard Tremayne."

"I won't. Never fear."

"Right, then, I'll be on my way. Nice to see you, Hookey."

"You're riding back in the dark?"

"Yes, indeed, our horses have very good night vision. Don't worry about us. I'll rescue Hartington from Mr. Rafiq before too many unfortunate secrets are spilled."

"Mr. Rafiq is as close-mouthed as they come."

"Aye, but he knows Hartington is a friend. He might be a little more honest with him than I would like. There are some things that even Corwen isn't privy to."

Hookey laughed. "I don't see Corwen Deverell would take offense at whatever you used to get up to."

I sighed. "I'm sure he wouldn't, but a lady has to keep some mysteries."

❖   ❖

Hartington didn't say much on the return journey to the Okewood. We stayed alert. Things could happen on lonely roads under cover of darkness, but my hearing was acute, and the horses would let us know if there was anything ahead that we should worry about. Hartington himself had the senses of a prey animal which told him when it was time for flight. In any event we had a quiet ride back.

"You didn't really need me, did you?" he said.

"I enjoy your company, and it made Corwen feel better. He's acting a little overprotective, and I didn't want to worry him. He has enough to worry about with Freddie."

"Yes, that's a difficult situation."

"I told him to ask the Lady for help, but he doesn't want to draw her attention to Freddie again."

Hartington said nothing, which made me wonder.

"You don't think she'd put Freddie down, do you?"

"If she did, it would be a last resort. I don't think you've reached that stage yet."

"I hope not."

It was after midnight when we arrived at the bower Corwen and I called home. I was exhausted. Parts of my anatomy ached like they'd been in contact with a saddle for twelve hours, which, in fact, they had. The horses, however, seemed as fresh as when we started out.

Corwen came out to meet us.

"Everything all right?"

"Yes, no trouble on the road and the *Heart*'s in fine shape. I've acquired a quarter of a ship. I'll tell you all about it as soon as my backside has stopped aching." I looked around. "Freddie?"

"We reached a compromise, thanks to the Lady."

"Oh, good. I said you should talk to her."

"Well, it's rather a strange compromise. Freddie is still in wolf form, in a cage of his own choosing."

"A cage?"

"Not one of iron bars, a magical one like David created for him back in the Old Maizy. This one is more permanent, an area of woodland where he can run and be himself, but not hurt others. The Lady said she'd give him some time in the wild to think things through. She wants us, all three of us, to go and deal with your troll, Hartington. David has agreed to come, too."

"That's good." I looked forward to seeing David again. "Well, I hope it's good, anyway, and it's not because the

troll is such a monster that it will take four of us to subdue it."

"I think the request was David's. It seems as though
he'd like a break from the Fae."

I could understand that. The Fae were beautiful and
powerful, living in a world which was as magical as they
were, but they were also hidebound by their rules, their
oaths, their traditions, and their high ideals. I wasn't surprised David wanted to get away for a while. He'd inherited all of the power but none of the stuffiness.

Corwen took Timpani's reins from Hartington and
began to unsaddle and rub the horse down. I did the same
for Dancer. No matter how tired I was, my horse always
came first.

"I can do that," Hartington said to Corwen.

"No, it's all right," Corwen said. "He's mine. His wel-
fare is my responsibility. I hope he behaved well for you."

"He never put a foot wrong. You're lucky to have him.
Would I be pushing our friendship too far if I were to let
my mare stray close to him next time she comes into
season?"

Corwen laughed. "You'd better ask him. He's like the
Fae, he gets a little standoffish at times, but if he's not
averse, then your mare has my blessing."

Hartington disappeared back to his own sleeping
quarters with a wave and a casual, "I'll see you in the
morning, early."

After we saw to the horses, we turned them loose,
knowing they would likely cross over into the green pas-
tures of Iaru until we needed them again.

Corwen drew me into the bower which felt almost too
big without Freddie, though it had been too small for the
three of us. The Lady's idea of a bed was springy bracken,
covered over with a linen sheet, and her coverlet was a
quilt stuffed with duck and goose down. I had never seen
the like before, but it was twice as light and twice as warm
as the thickest woolen blankets.

"Oh, that bed looks so wonderful, my bones are aching for it."

"It's also the first time we've had it entirely to ourselves since we brought Freddie back."

Corwen helped me to shrug out of my riding habit and the linen shirt beneath it. He dropped his face to nuzzle my breasts above the confines of my shift and my short stays, then tugged at my laces.

I caught my breath, desire warring with tiredness.

"I've been in the saddle for twelve hours today."

"Then let me take care of you."

My stays and shift fell to the floor and I relaxed into his arms. He lowered me gently to the bed and began to massage my back, my buttocks, and my thighs until I turned to jelly under the warmth of his hands.

"Better?"

"Hmmm."

I was almost asleep, but he turned me over and ran his hands over my belly. His lips touched mine, enquiring gently.

"Oh!"

He touched me there. In the twilight between sleeping and waking, I opened to him readily and let my instincts take over.

15

Trollhunters

LEAVING FREDDIE IN the care of the Lady and the cage of his own choosing, Corwen and I called Timpani and Dancer and saddled up.

I thought wearing my male persona might be the most practical; however, not knowing what we might need, I packed a sensible day dress and my redingote into the magical Fae valise. I strapped it behind Dancer's saddle before we set off for the portal to Iaru, to meet up with David.

The magicals, released unintentionally from Iaru and the Okewood when the Fae opened their gates to let the rowankind return home, had been plaguing the countryside for the last year. Some, like hobs, were quietly tucked away and not causing much trouble; others, like the Cornish pixies, were annoying but not life-threatening. Trolls were not always dangerous, but if they settled themselves beneath a bridge, they could be troublesome. They were big and clumsy, though generally slow to anger. Confrontations could lead to fights, however. I'd never yet seen a human who could best a seven-foot troll, but if the neighborhood was roused to action, a troll couldn't outfight a mob with pitchforks and torches. Both humans and trolls would be injured or even killed.

That was the situation we'd been asked to alleviate. David had volunteered to help round up magicals, but to my knowledge, this was the first time he'd been given dispensation to leave Iaru. Reining in the magicals before the Mysterium took decisive and fatal action against them was one of the tasks the Fae and the forest folk had committed to between them.

David was waiting for us in Iaru.

Timpani and Dancer squealed a welcome to David's mount and then stood nose to nose with her as if they were old friends. They probably were. I hadn't a clue what our horses got up to whenever they crossed back over into Iaru; it was the equivalent of horse heaven. I dismounted and greeted his horse politely before I turned to my brother.

"It's good to know where I stand in the hierarchy," David grinned at me.

"Last but never least." I hugged him.

While most of the Fae couldn't enter our towns and cities because of the industry, which was like poison to them, David, having lived in Plymouth, was relatively immune to the press of people, the smell of the gutters, and the coal smog from the manufactories. He'd volunteered to go where the rest of the Fae couldn't and was obviously pleased to be coming with us.

"Is Annie coming?" I asked. Even if she was staying behind, I was surprised she hadn't come to see us off. She and David were as close as lovebirds.

"What do we know about this troll?" David asked, ignoring my question though I knew he'd heard me.

"Not much about the troll," Corwen said, "but Hartington says the townsfolk of Wakefield are deeply unhappy to have it in residence beneath their Chantry Bridge, charging travelers to cross the Calder. The chapel on the bridge hasn't been used as a place of worship since King Henry destroyed the monasteries. Hartington says it's used as a reading room and a subscription library now. The vicar of Wakefield has sent a request to the Mysterium to have the hindrance removed. I gather no one has named it a troll, but Hartington has seen it, and it most certainly is. It's only a matter of time before a troop of redcoats show up with muskets and swords. The troll hasn't killed anyone yet, but in the event of being faced with either a mob or a troop of soldiers, it isn't likely to give in quietly."

David tightened his horse's girth and swung into the saddle.

"Has something happened between you and Annie?" I asked as I mounted Dancer.

"Oh, no. Annie and I are fine." Something in the way he said it made me even more sure that something was amiss. "She's a sweet girl, don't you think, Ross?"

"I think she's lovely."

I wasn't being polite. I really did think that.

Annie was a rowankind serving girl from an inn in Plymouth. David had become very fond of her when we'd stayed there, and when the rowankind gained their freedom, he'd immediately sought her out. They'd been inseparable ever since. Despite having such long lives the Fae matured early, as did the rowankind. My little brother was only sixteen, but he was easily a young man, not a child.

"My father says Annie's not a suitable marriage prospect, so I should keep her as a concubine and have many fine children with her."

That's how it normally worked between the Fae and their rowankind or human lovers. I can't say I approved, but as far as I knew neither the rowankind not the humans seemed to object to this. There must be hidden advantages.

"Will you love her when she's ninety and you still look seventeen?"

"Of course, Ross. How could I not? Being with Annie is not without precedent. Lord Dax once had a rowankind lover who lived until she was seventy-six years old."

"Did they marry?"

"No, but they stayed together as man and wife all her life."

"Couldn't you do that with Annie?"

"My father has chosen a bride for me, a Fae princess, one of the Merovingian Fae from France. Her name is Calantha, but I don't know anything more about her or the Merovingians. He says it's my duty to bring our two great houses together. Apparently, we've always been wary of them, and they've never much liked us."

"Then Larien should marry her himself." Corwen had been following the conversation.

"He can't. He has a wife already."

"Has he?" I think that shocked me more than anything. "And did Larien have this wife when he was busy seducing our mother in Plymouth?"

"I suppose so. They've been married for three hundred years, but they have no children."

The Fae didn't procreate easily, that was why Fae men often sought human or rowankind partners for the purpose of producing children. Fae women were happy to have an extra person in the household if she brought the benefits of children. Many a human woman had gone "away with the fairies" for the duration of her childbearing years, only to find herself released back into the world twenty years later, puzzled by the time she'd lost, but wealthy with Fae gold. It had happened to my own Aunt Rosie whose daughter, Margann, by Larien's brother, Dantin, still visited whenever she could.

"I don't know how to advise you, David," I said.

"I do," Corwin looked sideways at me. "Don't give up the one you love for anyone or anything."

I felt a little shiver of pleasure run down my spine.

❦

We met Hartington by the Iaru gate as planned. The journey to Wakefield took the four of us through areas of Iaru I'd seen before. We skirted around the spot which most closely connected with Sheffield, blighted by the grime and the smoke from the forges and the steam engines. The bad air from our newly industrialized cities seeped into their equivalent parts of Iaru, causing yet another problem for the Fae.

"Aren't we close to Denby House?" I asked. "Could we visit?"

"I think we should," Corwen said. "As soon as we've dealt with the troll. Wakefield to Denby is only about twelve miles."

"There's a gate in the woodland about three miles south of Wakefield itself," David said. "It's at Chevet, close to a flour mill. If we take the road north from there, it should bring us to the Chantry Bridge."

"How do you know all this?" I asked him. "You were brought up in Plymouth, three hundred miles from Yorkshire."

He raised one eyebrow and shrugged. "It's a Fae thing. There's not one inch of these islands that has not been explored by the Fae, and what one knows, all know. They may have kept their distance over the last two thousand years, but they've always had spies in the human world."

"Well, that's damned useful," Corwen said. "As well as unsettling."

I shivered at the thought.

"It certainly is," David said.

We came out of Iaru on a steep, wooded hillside above a snake-shaped ribbon lake which ended abruptly in a straight dam wall with a road across it and a water-powered mill on the other side. We slithered down the steep hill to the lake and picked up the road to Wakefield by the Dam Inn, a square-fronted hostelry owing much to the local building stone.

Since Hartington was the only one of us not riding a Fae horse, we let him set the pace. The three miles took us less than an hour. We rode past Sandal's substantial church and a ruined castle on a hill before drawing near to Wakefield and the ancient bridge over the Calder. There was a smaller bridge over a new canal before we reached the main bridge. A navigation channel, cut to carry boats past a shallow, rocky stretch of the Calder, meant we were now on a man-made island, long and narrow between the river and the cut. The Calder was navigable from the west as far as an industrial basin that was hemmed in by warehouses. Beyond it, the section that ran under the bridge was wide, but shallow and rocky, with a natural run of rapids below a weir. It might once have been a ford, but it would have been a dangerous crossing when the water ran high, which it did now.

We paused by the river and studied the situation. The bridge itself was old, one of only a few in Britain to accommodate a chantry chapel in the middle of its nine, pointed arches. The ancient building had stood there for four centuries according to Hartington, and though it was now a reading room and library, its ecclesiastical origins were obvious. Some of the windows had been blocked from the inside, but the delicate stone tracery was still in evidence. It must have once been very beautiful. It was two stories tall, part of the bridge's structure. Its foundations rested on an island not much bigger than the chapel itself. The upper level had five impressive arches, four of which were windows, and the fifth, on the north side, a doorway to the bridge's roadway. The frontage was a riot of fantastical carving and tracery, though some of the carvings were badly eroded and the leaded glass showed black where holes had been punched out.

The bridge itself was in good order, even though the old chapel looked rough. I counted five arches on this side of the chapel, and another four on the other. At the far end, again built into the bridge, was a stone house that might once have been the home of the incumbent clergy. It was, however, comparatively plain with none of the glorious carvings that adorned the chapel.

The bank on this side of the river showed signs of having been trampled by cattle coming to drink, but there were none there now. In fact the road was quite deserted. News traveled fast.

Danger. Do not cross.

"No one's using the library now, then," I said.

Hartington shook his head. "The troll has taken up residence in there, though I'm not sure how he fits. The librarian hasn't been seen for a sennight. There was some speculation as to whether he'd died and the terror haunting the bridge was his spirit."

"The locals don't know it's a troll?" I asked.

"They won't let themselves say it out loud."

"Is there another bridge?" Corwen asked.

"To the west where the road to Bretton crosses the new navigation point and the river. The locals have taken to going the long way round."

"I don't blame them." I shuddered. The trolls we'd brought safely off the *Guillaume Tell* alongside the other captured magicals had been almost affable. This troll might prove so intransigent that he provoked a fight. If that happened, he'd lose—I'd seen David's use of fire magic—but the Lady wanted us to give him, or her, the chance to leave the bridge peacefully and migrate to Iaru.

There was a rumble. The stones of the roadbed shook. A lumpen form climbed over the parapet of the bridge and stood to his full height, which made him as tall as the front of the old chapel.

"What will you pay to cross my bridge?"

16

A Mob for a Shilling

"WHY WOULD WE pay to cross your bridge?" Corwen said. "We can cross upriver."

"This is a better bridge," the troll said slowly, his voice rumbling so much that the ground vibrated with it.

"But it has a troll," Corwen said.

"It has books. I like books."

"Do you?" Corwen half-turned and raised one eyebrow at me. A troll that liked books was somewhat unusual.

"Can you read?" I asked.

It shook its head. "Don't need to. Books talk. Words talk. Tell stories."

Did he mean the library was enchanted? I thought enchanted libraries were the stuff of fairy tales.

"Have you got books?" the troll asked.

"Not here," Corwen said. "We have books at home. And there are plenty of books in Iaru."

"Are there?" I asked softly.

"There could be if we needed them," David said. "There are scrolls and histories and records, of course, but not novels."

"He seems like a troll of unusual tastes. Perhaps we could tempt him out with the promise of a library."

The troll waved a hand in dismissal. "Cross upstream if you will. I can feel anyone who steps on my bridge, so don't cross here without you pay a toll."

"What would a suitable toll be?" I asked.

"Books. More books." He turned toward the door. I held my breath, unsure of whether he could squeeze himself through it, but it seemed he could if he hunched down and wriggled sideways. A shape moved behind the glass windows and I thought I could hear something inside.

"Can you hear that?" I asked Corwen. "I thought I heard someone speaking. Has he got someone in there?"

"I didn't hear anything, but I wasn't paying attention. I was wondering whether it might be possible to scale the building. The tower at the northeast corner looks like it has a doorway opening onto the roof."

"If he can feel the vibration from one pair of feet on the bridge, he'll surely feel someone climbing the chapel wall."

"Maybe," was all Corwen would say.

"He doesn't seem particularly violent," David said, "at least not without being provoked. Should we go up into the town and see what the gossip is?"

The other bridge was much farther than we expected because of the river's meanders. We followed the riverbank, with the ruined castle high up on our left, until we came to a pair of new bridges, one over the cut by a lock, and another over the Calder, which was not as wide at this point, but no doubt a lot deeper. We entered Wakefield from the west, along a narrow dirt track, worn wider, we suspected, by the extra pairs of feet walking the long way around. The closer we got to the town, the more David's otherness faded until he looked like a normal young man with no hint of the Fae about him.

We rode past a steep hill which might once have supported a fortification and been a twin to the castle on the other side of the river, though nothing remained now except the shape of it. Wakefield itself, dominated by the somewhat dilapidated spire of All Saints Church, was a town noted for its cloth industry, its market and cattle market, and as a transport hub thanks to the new navigation which linked it not only to Leeds, but also to the Humber and thence to the sea. We'd seen specially built coal wharfs on the river, fed by a wagonway with strong horses drawing tub after tub of coal to fill the barges waiting patiently alongside.

The parish church, hemmed in by a jumble of houses and shops, stood at the high point of the town close to the central bull ring where the three principal streets, Westgate, Kirkgate, and Northgate, converged. Had we been able to cross Chantry Bridge, we would have entered Wakefield town via Kirkgate, so thinking the hostelries closest to the river might be the richest source of gossip, we turned down the hill.

The Old Red Lion looked fairly respectable, or, at least, it didn't look like an inn where we might get ourselves into trouble or start a fight or, worse still, finish one. It didn't smell too stale. All we wanted was a quiet drink and to check the mood of the town, find out what they knew and whether anyone had any plans we should know about. The landlord acknowledged us and served us politely with ale and a bowl of whatever was in the pot, mutton most likely, though it was heavy with potatoes and light on the meat.

We ate in silence, not so much because the food was good, though in truth it wasn't bad, but because Corwen and I were listening to conversations that would have been far too quiet for normal human ears. David and Hartington spoke in hushed tones to give the appearance of normal interaction. If the four of us had eaten in total silence, it might have looked odd.

I focused on a lively group by the doorway. They looked like apprentices, but they'd already been sitting over their ale for way too long, given that this was a working day. Picking up scraps from conversation, I deduced they were normally employed at the Soke Corn Mill, which was on the town side of the bridge, its wheel powered by a mill stream which took water from the Calder above the weir. They were talking about an enterprise with a boat while their hands were idle. From what they said, I took it that Soke Mill was closed until whatever was on the bridge—and even the garrulous apprentices didn't call it a troll—had been chased away. But until then, there was profit to be had by taking foot passengers across by boat from Chalk Mill to Smithson's Coal Staithes. From there it was only a short walk into the town.

The young woman who brought another jug of ale to their table shook her head. "Fine plans, lads, but you should have thought of it a few days ago, Mr. Arnott says the vicar is organizing some of the townsfolk to drive it out, whatever it is." She slapped the jug on the table, slopping its contents over the side. "I don't reckon it's a real man. I ain't never seen a man that tall and with arms as wide as tree trunks."

"What else could it be?" the youngest looking apprentice asked.

"It's the bogie man, my lad." One of the older apprentices loomed over him, waggling his fingers at shoulder height.

"Aww, Benjie, quit teasing. There's no such thing as the bogie man."

He was right, but there were many things worse. I wondered what the vicar was organizing. Maybe it was time to pay a visit to the church.

Corwen didn't have much to add from the conversations he was listening to, except the vicar was proposing to pay a shilling to every man who joined his deputation.

"Not so much a deputation, more of a mob," Corwen said as we left the alehouse and gave a penny to the urchin we'd employed to stay with the horses. They wouldn't have strayed, but it looked more normal to have someone watching them.

It was only a short walk up Kirkgate to the vicarage, an imposing residence built in the old style, which stood in its own grounds at the junction of Wrengate and Vicarage Lane.

"He's not at home," the vicar's housekeeper said. "He's at the church, gathering stout fellows to see to the monster on the bridge. Are you from the Mysterium?" Without giving us the opportunity to reply, she turned all her Yorkshire outspokenness upon us. "It's about time they sent someone. The vicar's been near out of his mind with that ungodly thing threatening the town. If only you'd turned up yesterday, he wouldn't have had to deal with it himself. He's not a young man, you know. He's been vicar here for thirty-eight years."

David stepped forward. "We're not from the Mysterium, Mrs. . . . "

"Bates," she said. "Martha Bates."

"Mrs. Bates." David was using a glamour now. Mrs. Bates' eyes had gone glassy, and the scowl she'd saved up for the Mysterium had mutated into a vacant smile. "You've been the vicar's housekeeper for a long time."

"Twenty-four of his thirty-eight years, ever since I was widowed. My mother was his housekeeper before me."

"So you don't want to see the vicar harmed."

"Isn't that what I've been saying?"

"Then we're here to help, but I need you to let us into the vicar's library. We need to borrow some books."

"Books?"

"It will help to keep him safe, believe me."

She stepped back from the door and waved us into a cozy room at the back of the house which looked as if it served as both library and study. A large breakfront bookcase occupied the center of one wall. David opened the glazed doors and quickly studied the spines.

"Hmm, sermons, sermons, and more sermons. Not many stories here. Oh, wait." He reached up. "*Stories from the Old Testament.* That will do for starters, ah, and this and this." He quickly assembled three piles of books, one for each of us.

"What about you?" I asked him.

"I'm going to collect a shilling from the vicar and join his deputation. You go and reason with the troll."

He turned to the lady before we left. "Thank you, Mrs.

Bates. You've done us a great service today. One more thing . . . I don't suppose you have any lighter reading, maybe a novel or two?"

She was about to shake her head when David smiled at her with all the brightness of the Fae.

"Well, if you don't tell the vicar it was me what gave 'em to you."

"Not a word."

She hurried up the stairs, and I heard her footsteps as she reached the top and then began a second flight to the attic, presumably, to her own room. Then the footsteps in reverse until she arrived, gasping for breath, back down into the hallway. She had five books, quite a collection for a housekeeper.

"Mr. Rackham lets me borrow five at a time on account of me being such a quick reader," she said.

I took the books from her, added them to my own pile, and glanced at the titles quickly: Ben Jonson's *Volpone* and Bunyan's *Pilgrim's Progress* were two I'd read, but right on top of the pile was a *Book of Fairy Tales* by Charles Perrault, translated.

"I know what it is," she said. "I tried to tell the vicar, but he wouldn't believe me. It's a troll, isn't it?"

I nodded. "It is."

"Will you look out for Mr. Rackham, the librarian? No one's seen him since the troll arrived. He's a kindly man, if a little too quiet for his own good."

"I'll do what I can, Mrs. Bates. Thank you."

◆━━◆

We took David's horse while he ran up to the church, and the three of us walked back down to the bridge where a crowd had gathered, some carrying cudgels, others with pitchforks. A couple of enterprising women had gathered an arsenal of kitchen implements, one with a skillet, another a rolling pin. Both looked as if they knew how to wield them in anger.

"You don't want to go across there," one man said. "You won't make it all the way. There's a monster."

"T'vicar's coming to see him off." The woman with the rolling pin said.

"I think we'll be all right," Hartington said. "We've brought him a gift."

"Don't blame us when you get yourself eaten," the first man said.

If we got ourselves eaten, we'd hardly be blaming anyone.

We stepped out onto the bridge to a number of other comments and a general murmur of warning from the crowd. From a distance I could hear the mob on the move in the high part of the town. They were singing a hymn to the tune of "God Save the King."

Come, Thou Almighty King
Help us Thy Name to sing
Help us to praise!
Father all glorious
O'er all victorious
Come and reign over us
Ancient of Days

The speed of their footsteps had changed it into a march.

That couldn't be good. I had to make an effort not to look behind me. They probably weren't even in sight yet. I judged they might still be at the top of Kirkgate, but it wouldn't take them long to march down the hill.

I stepped out in front of Corwen and Hartington. "Come on. We haven't got much time."

Right on cue the troll squeezed himself out of the door of the old chapel and confronted us on the road.

"What will you pay to cross my bridge?"

"Books," I said. "Stories. Lots of stories."

He gave a puzzled grunt and reached out.

I put my whole pile of books, that I'd been carrying in two arms, into the palm of his outstretched, somewhat green-hued, hand.

"You can cross," he said.

"We don't want to cross. We want to talk. We're here to offer you a suggestion. Will you talk with us?"

"Talk?"

"There's a mob on the way."

"I'm stronger than humans."

"Are you stronger than a hundred humans?"

That gave him pause.

From inside the chapel I heard a voice. "Sir Roderick, I think we should reconsider our position."

"Would that be Mr. Rackham?" I dodged around the troll's long reach and made it to the chantry door, then slipped inside, knowing it would take the troll a few minutes to squeeze himself through.

"Mr. Rackham?" I called into the gloom.

"Here I am, and who might you be?"

"Mrs. Bates asked us to look out for you."

"Ah, the vicar's housekeeper. How is she?"

"Worried the troll has eaten you."

"He wouldn't do that."

"How do you know?"

"He's . . . unusual, but beneath that odd exterior there's a gentle soul. He likes books." This last statement seemed to say that if the troll liked books, then nothing else mattered; he was a good person.

"He's imprisoned you."

"Not really . . . well . . . yes, in a way. I chose to stay. He likes books, you see, but he can't read, so I read them to him. He promised me while ever there were new stories, he wouldn't harm any travelers. That's why I told him to ask for books as a fee for crossing the bridge."

"So you're his magic talking book."

"In a way. I'm also teaching him to read for himself."

"That sounds like a worthwhile project, Mr. Rackham, in another time and another place." I cocked my head on one side to listen.

They were still singing, only now there was distinct enthusiasm in their voices as they launched into another verse.

Jesus, our Lord, arise
Scatter our enemies
And make them fall

Let Thine almighty aid
Our sure defense be made
Souls on Thee be stayed
Lord, hear our call.

The Troll—Sir Roderick, Mr. Rackham had called him—was squeezing his way through the door, and I could hear Corwen, stuck on the other side of the obstruction, calling my name. "I'm all right," I shouted back. "Stop the mob if you can. Give me time." I turned back to Mr. Rackham. "The townsfolk are marching down Kirkgate, singing hymns even as we speak. And there's another mob gathering at the north end of the bridge with staves and pitchforks." I didn't mention the rolling pin and the skillet. "They mean your troll harm."

"Sir Roderick," Mr. Rackham addressed the creature as he squeezed through the doorway. "Did you hear what she said?"

I noted with surprise that my true gender had not gone unnoticed.

The troll grunted. He couldn't quite stand up inside the lofty room, so he went down on one knee. "It's my bridge. My books."

"Which is more important, the bridge or the books?" I asked.

The look on his face said both.

"If you want to fight them to the death for the bridge, I can't stop you, but you'll likely die, and so will a lot of them."

"They are only humans."

"But it was humans like them who wrote and printed the books. They made up the stories you love."

"Hmph."

"She's right," Mr. Rackham said. "So very right." He crossed over the floor and reached up to put a slender hand on the troll's shoulders. "You can take your favorite books with you."

"You come, too."

"I think I've taught you enough. With a bit more practice you can read the books for yourself."

"Hmph."

"And we can get you more books," I said. "As many as you can read. Lots of stories."

I could hear voices at the far end of the bridge, now—voices of the mob and Corwen's baritone telling them to stay where they were, reinforced by Hartington.

"Come on. We're out of time. Mr. Rackham, you go first. Seeing you're still alive will give the crowd something to think about."

Rackham gave the troll one last, sad look and stepped into the spring sunshine on the bridge. I followed him out. Behind me, I could hear the troll throwing things around in the dim interior. I hoped it was the sound of him packing.

"No one has been hurt here," Corwen said. "Let us all go in peace and we'll take your problem with us."

"He's called Sir Roderick," Rackham said softly. "He didn't have a name when he came, but he liked that one."

Behind us, a thump which was a sack of books landing in the roadway, followed by the sound of grunting, signaled that the troll was once more squeezing through the chapel door and out into the light.

A roar of awe and horror rippled through the crowd. I supposed it wasn't every day they saw a huge, naked green troll with a sack of books over his shoulder. Some of the women screamed. The one with the skillet shouted, "Get him, lads," and the crowd surged forward around the vicar, clearly visible in their front rank until overtaken by his deputation.

The troll dropped his books and, with a roar, ran at the advancing mob, head lowered and his arms out wide. Those at the front hesitated. Some tried to turn back, but those behind them kept pushing forward. David must be in that mob somewhere, but I couldn't see him. The troll came level with Corwen and Hartington and they all glanced sideways at each other, exchanging understanding glances.

"Wait here," I told the librarian and ran to catch up with the troll, taking my place beside him.

Mr. Rackham ignored my order and followed me. There was a ripple of approval as he appeared to be walking toward the crowd, and then another of disapproval as he allied himself with us and the troll.

"Go on. What are you waiting for? Get him!" someone shouted. Three men, more foolhardy than the rest, ran forward. The troll didn't hesitate. He grabbed one and threw him in an arc over the bridge parapet to the left. A splash followed. The second one he hurled to the right as if he were no more weight than a doll. This one bounced off the parapet and tumbled into the river. It was fast-flowing but shallow, easy enough to drown in if you were unconscious. The third man, seeing what had happened to his two companions, turned and bolted, only to run into a wall of townsfolk inching forward more cautiously, but in a determined manner. The vicar had pushed to the front, and just behind him I saw David.

David didn't seem to have to push at all, but suddenly he was in the front rank of the mob. He beckoned me forward with both hands. I didn't think he wanted me personally, but something he knew I could do. I created a wind, building it from the cool breeze of a spring day to a brisk gale blowing against the advancing crowd. Hats went flying, and some of the people in the front staggered. One enterprising chap called for them to link arms to steady each other. The vicar's cassock billowed like a sail. I sent a cheeky wind to blow it up and over his head, revealing breeches and boots beneath. He staggered backward, fighting his way out of the folds of cloth, losing his balance in the process and falling into the men behind him.

David walked casually across the divide, unaffected by the wind.

"Why not get our friend away across the bridge?" David said to Hartington and Corwen. "We'll hold the mob here."

Corwen glanced at me, so I waved him away with both hands without letting the sharp wind drop. This level of intensity took a lot of energy. I didn't have much spare capacity for conversation. David couldn't give himself away as Fae without angering the Council of Seven, but I was sure he had a plan.

As Corwen, Hartington, and Mr. Rackham pulled the troll away from the front line, David conjured an illusion that all three men and the troll were still standing in their original positions.

"Can you keep this wind up from a distance?" David asked.

"Yes." I sounded more confident than I felt. I didn't tell him how much it would take out of me.

"Strengthen it and back away. Follow the others."

"What about you?"

"I'm Fae."

"You're still my little brother?"

He grinned. And jerked his head in a gesture that said, go! "I'll catch up with you."

I walked backward across the bridge, keeping up the wind. I was feeling distinctly light-headed when Corwen caught me around the waist.

"I thought you'd gone?"

"Without you?"

I relaxed into him. "This takes more out of me than it used to do."

Before I'd freed the rowankind, I'd held an enormous store of wind and weather magic. I'd given most of it back, but still had a small portion of what I used to have. Keeping up this level of wind, however, was a lot more tiring than simply conjuring a steady breeze to fill the *Heart*'s sails.

"I've got you." Corwen whistled for Dancer, scooped me up into his arms, and lifted me into the saddle.

David came trotting across the bridge, leaving behind the illusion that we were all still facing the mob.

"That should hold them for a while. I think we can go now. Ross, one more big push. Scatter them like ninepins, then you can stop."

One more big push might be beyond my capabilities. I was almost at the end of my strength.

I took a deep breath as if I was about to blow the wind

from my own lungs, then I redoubled my efforts and hurled one last enormous gust at the crowd, scattering them backward as if they were paper dolls. The day seemed to dim, and the next thing I knew I'd slid from Dancer's saddle. A small shuffle between David and Corwen and I was now in Corwen's arms, riding on Timpani with Dancer alongside.

"Definitely time to go," said Hartington. "Are you with us, Sir Roderick?"

The troll patted his bag of books. "Where are we going?"

"To the Okewood or to Iaru. You choose," Corwen said.

"Where the books are."

"David said there could be books in Iaru if we needed them."

"Iaru, then," said Corwen.

"Who are you people?" Mr. Rackham stared at David, who had regained some of his Fae luster. I suspected because he'd simply forgotten to tone himself down. I cleared my throat, and David, catching on to my meaning, slowly faded to ordinary again.

"We're no one in particular," my little brother said, adopting his best innocent look.

The troll and Mr. Rackham parted company as friends with a handshake and a few whispered words which I deliberately did not eavesdrop on.

"I'll wait until dark to go back," Rackham said. "Take good care of my literary friend."

"We will," Hartington assured him.

"If you're short of literary friends, you might pay more attention to Mrs. Bates," I told him. "She was most concerned about you."

"She was?"

"She was."

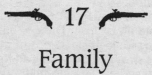 17

Family

WE HURRIED BACK to Chevet, to the gate to Iaru, and there we said farewell to David, Hartington, and Sir Roderick for the time being. By now we'd all begun to use the troll's new name, and it no longer seemed strange to us. Hartington said he'd see Sir Roderick settled, so the three of them headed deeper into Iaru.

"I can ride now," I said, and planted a kiss on Corwen's chin. "But thanks for the lift."

"Sure?"

"Yes, I'm feeling much better. Stronger."

He eased me down to the ground, then dismounted himself and boosted me into Dancer's saddle.

"You shouldn't wear yourself out. What about the baby?"

What about the baby? Did she suffer from me exhausting myself magically? I didn't know, but it was something I should ask Aunt Rosie.

"I'll rest when we get home."

This time I meant Denby House, our other home.

Corwen and I retraced our steps through the gate, coming out into the little wood by Deverell's Mill.

It was late in the afternoon, the sky already darkening to dusk as we turned into the long driveway. Thomas heard us coming and appeared in the stable yard with a lantern, his face crinkled in a smile.

"Mr. Corwen and Mrs. Rossalinde! Good to see you. Let me take your horses."

"Hello, Thomas, thank you." Corwen dismounted and came to help me down from Dancer, but I was already sliding from the saddle. Instead, he unfastened my valise from the saddle straps. "Everything all right?"

"As quiet as can be," Thomas said.

"Good news, indeed."

"That it is, sir. Quiet is how we like it."

Given the recent events, he was right. Quiet was good.

Poppy met us at the front door. She bobbed a formal curtsey to us both and then flung herself into my arms. "Oh, Ross, how wonderful to see you. Did you write? Is Mrs. Deverell expecting you? The ladies are in the dining room. Let me arrange for two more places to be set."

"Thanks, Poppy, good to see you, too, and no, we weren't expected. We found ourselves in the vicinity, so we took the opportunity to call." I looked down at my breeches. "I need to get changed and washed before I'm ready to join anyone for dinner, but I'll be back down in a moment."

"Your room's always kept ready. I'll have Mary bring up some hot water and light a fire to take the chill off."

I gave Corwen a little shove. "You still look respectable enough to say we've been troll-hunting. Go and say hello to your mother and sister while I make myself presentable."

He pecked me on the cheek, and I grabbed the valise from him and stepped smartly up the main stair to the room which had been Corwen's and was now Corwen's and mine.

By the time Mary came up with hot water, I was already out of my breeches and into my shift and short stays.

"Do you need me to do up your laces, madam?" Mary asked after putting down the hot water.

I could manage on my own with a little wriggling, but

it was nice to have someone to tug my lacing into place. I ran my hand down my stomach, still flat. The current fashion for high waistlines would be a boon in another few months. I washed my hands and face and shook my dress out. It was Fae made, and the creases from traveling dropped out of it as if they'd never been. It was a bib-front dress, so I shrugged into the bodice and let Mary pass the strings around me and tie them. Instead of pinning the front, I had tiny buttons to secure it. A cream fichu tucked into the neckline completed the outfit.

"You look very nice, ma'am."

"Thank you, Mary."

"Would you like me to do your hair?"

That was servant speak for your dress is presentable, but your hair's a mess. I'd had it tied in a cue with a hat jammed on top of it all day, so I wasn't surprised.

"Coil it into a knot, Mary, nothing fancy." My belly rumbled, saying I was half-starved.

Mary giggled as if I'd said something funny, and in less than five minutes had my hair looking neat.

I arrived in the dining room to find Corwen already seated with a plate of lamb in front of him. He grinned up at me. "I thought you wouldn't mind if I started without you, since we're eating informally."

"I told him he should wait." Corwen's mother stood to take both of my hands and draw me into a kiss on first one cheek and then the other. "I don't know what kind of manners he has in the Okewood, but when he's here in my house—"

"It's all right, Mama. We don't stand on ceremony much when we're alone together. I really don't mind, as long as he's left some for me."

"There's plenty." Corwen's sister, Lily, all bubbly dark curls and a ready smile was waiting behind his mother to hug me. "I'm pleased to see you looking so well, sister," she said.

I slid into my chair and helped myself to lamb and potatoes with green beans and buttered cabbage. It was a simple meal, but delicious, and I had a second helping. I was eating for two.

Of course, their first question was about Freddie.

"He's well, physically," Corwen said, "but still not . . . "
He paused and waved his fork in the air, searching for the
right word, as if he could stab it. "Stable. He's not stable.
He has outbursts of temper which would be bad enough if
he was a man, but as a wolf he could kill someone."

"Oh, my poor Freddie. I wish I could go to him, comfort him."

"Give him time, Mother."

"I'm not sure I've forgiven him yet." Lily turned to her
mother. "He could have killed you, Mama. If those teeth
had been any closer to an artery . . ."

"But he didn't, and here I am, and I still love him. You
must tell him, Corwen."

"Write it in a letter. I'll take it to him."

"Who does Freddie love, Corwen?" Lily asked. "What
about his friend, the one who went away."

No one ever spoke of Freddie's special friend. His
sexual proclivities were just as likely to get him hanged as
his shapechanging magic. No wonder Freddie was a mess.
Damned twice over in the eyes of the law.

"Roland," I said. "That's Freddie's friend's name. I
believe his family is in Gloucestershire."

"Roland? I don't know about Roland, but there's a letter came for Freddie last week from someone called Betsey, whose return address is close to Stroud. That's in
Gloucestershire, isn't it?"

"Did you open it?"

She shook her head. "I sent it on to your fox-girl, so
you could receive it on Freddie's behalf. Did I do the right
thing?"

"If this Betsey and Roland are connected, we'll see if
it spurs Freddie back to humanity again."

We'd decided it was still too early to tell Corwen's family I was increasing, but after dinner I left Corwen talking
to his mother, and Lily and I sought out Poppy. I'd hardly
had the opportunity to speak with her on our last visit, so
it was good to be able to spend an hour in her company.

She and Stephen Yeardley had converted three small

rooms up in the attics to an apartment with a sitting room, furnished with a hotchpotch of items that might have been in storage for a hundred years or more. Next door there was a bedroom for them and baby Alice, and a tiny alcove room for Robin, who had shot up in height so much that I almost didn't recognize him. Good food and clean air had done the scrawny workhouse boy an immense amount of good.

Alice woke for a feed while Poppy and I were talking, and Stephen brought her in for Poppy to nurse. Afterward, Poppy asked if I'd like to hold the baby. It seemed like a good idea. As I took the thriving five-month-old in my arms I wondered what it would be like to hold my own happy, healthy baby.

Poppy looked at me with Alice, and I knew right away that she'd guessed.

"It's still very early," I said.

"Don't worry, I won't tell a soul." She hugged me.

"We weren't going to tell anyone yet, but do you think it might help Corwen's mother to know?"

"I think it might give her something to hold on to for the future."

"Change of plan, then. I'll talk to Corwen."

I spent the first part of the night alone. After staying up late, talking, Corwen went out for a run with Lily. They rarely got the opportunity to run together, so I didn't begrudge them the time. Corwen was a Yorkshire wolf, and the moors were simply too tempting. He shrugged out of his clothes in the bedroom, and in an instant changed from naked man to a silver-coated wolf. Lily met us on the landing, dressed in a long gown. I walked down to the side door with them and dropped Corwen's father's old banyan on the bench in the porch, so Corwen didn't have to walk through the house naked on his return. Though, I suspected, it wouldn't shock the servants. They had all worked for the family for a long time, and even if they hadn't been let in on the secret officially, they knew better than to ask questions they didn't want answered.

It was well after midnight when I heard Corwen return. He padded up the stairs barefoot and closed the door softly behind him.

"It's all right, no need to creep about. I'm awake."

"Sorry, I didn't want to disturb you."

I raised myself up on one elbow and tossed a witchlight up to the ceiling as Corwen shrugged out of the banyan and stood naked by the bedside.

"You always disturb me. Please don't ever stop."

I never slept when he was out running as a wolf.

What I wanted to say was, *please don't leave me like Will did.* Corwen wasn't as easy to kill as a regular human. He could heal his own injuries by changing from man to wolf and back again, but he couldn't cheat a blade to the heart or a bullet to the brain. I'd thought Will invincible, but he'd been killed by a falling spar, an accident at sea. How senseless a death.

"I've been thinking," I said. "I know we decided against it, but I think we should tell your mother about the baby. Poppy guessed almost immediately, and it doesn't seem fair to keep your mother ignorant, especially since it might give her something to look forward to."

"I thought you said it was still too early."

"There's no need to broadcast it to the world, but your mother can keep a secret."

"Better than anyone I know."

"Then let's tell her before we leave."

❖┄┄┄┄┄❖

Corwen's mother had been quite overcome by the news, but in the nicest possible way. She was already musing over the old nursery furniture that had been relegated to the attic when Lily had grown past it.

She fussed, of course, but that was perfectly normal for an expectant grandmother, and we left her in good spirits for a change.

The visit to Denby House had been a lovely interlude, but I could see Corwen getting more and more on edge as we neared the Okewood. What trouble had Freddie managed to cause while we were away?

"You shouldn't worry," I told him.

"Worry? Am I worried?"

"You're thinking about Freddie. You're always worried about him."

"Am I so obvious?"

"Only to me." I reconsidered. "And probably to the Lady. She's known you a long time."

"The Lady probably saved my life. I wasn't unlike Freddie when I arrived in the Okewood, confused and angry at the world. I was much younger, of course, and being a wolf had altered everything. When I first changed, I reveled in it, and then I realized how much I was losing. I didn't have friends. My family turned down so many invitations on my behalf that I was never invited anywhere. My schooling suffered. Freddie went to Oxford, but poor unreliable Corwen couldn't go. They worried I'd change into a wolf and eat someone. If only they'd realized what was in Freddie's future. Ha! I'd have looked positively tame."

"I suppose they thought they were doing it for the best."

"I think they did, but I didn't appreciate it at the time. Father was embarrassed, and Mother was overprotective. Both things boiled down to insisting I stay at home. No wonder I ran wild when I did get out."

"And so you ran away to the forest."

"I might never have found the Okewood if it hadn't been for Hartington."

"I didn't realize."

Corwen smiled. "It's a long way from Yorkshire to the Okewood, though the Lady has presence wherever there are trees. I found my way first into Sherwood where I guessed there would be plenty of places to hide out and give my wolf his fill of game without anyone noticing. I set my sights too high when I spotted a stag. I thought I could bring him down by myself. Wolves usually hunt in packs for a reason."

"A stag? Hartington? You tried to kill and eat Hartington?"

Corwen grinned ruefully. "I really did, but the old boy has more tricks up his sleeve than I realized. Besides, he knew who I was, or rather what I was, and he'd been sent to bring me to the Lady."

"She knew about you?"

"She'd felt my presence. Hartington led me a merry chase. I thought I'd cleverly trapped him in a cleft in the rock, but that's what he'd intended all along. As I closed in for the kill, he turned into a man again."

"Wasn't that foolhardy?"

"It was, and it wasn't. He had to discover whether I was a mindless killer or not. It turned out I wasn't."

"What if you had been?"

"He had his clothes and a pistol in one of those magical Fae bags strapped around his chest. If I'd gone for his throat, he'd have shot me through the head and walked away. As it was, he invited me to the Okewood, then turned into a stag again and leaped away."

"Did you go immediately?"

"It took me a couple of months to decide and to make the journey through the English shires, but Hartington was there in Exeter when my coach drew in, dressed as a country gentleman and waiting with two horses as if he knew I was coming. Given that the Lady could sense my presence, I suppose he had foreknowledge."

"And you became her watch-wolf."

"I fulfilled a number of roles: her messenger, spy, and, eventually, her ambassador, and sometimes . . . "

"Go on . . . "

"Sometimes the jobs were more difficult than others, either physically or emotionally."

I didn't prompt him. He would tell me if he wanted to.

"A wild boar in the Forest of Dean gored two people—one died. It turned out to be a farmer who'd gone missing a few months before and was irreversibly stuck in animal form."

"You killed him."

Corwen's mouth tightened. "Nothing else for it. The Lady weighed the options and made the decision. I was only grateful he didn't turn human again as he died. That would have been . . . " He shrugged. "I buried him in the forest. Anything else would have been disrespectful. The Lady arranged for her lawyers to send the family a sum of money to help them over their loss, supposedly from a long-lost relative's will."

One fact struck me more than the other. "The Lady has lawyers?"

"Would it surprise you to know that they were weasels?"

"No. Really?"

Some humor returned to Corwen's expression. "No, not really. The size imbalance is too great. It's a question of mass. Human to wolf is barely possible. The fox-girl is very small-boned and only comes up to my shoulder. No, not weasels. The lawyers are sharks."

"Literally?"

He grinned. "Literally. I believe most of the family is in the fishing trade, somewhere near Cromer, but the Basking brothers came up to London to make their fortune. They slip into the Thames after dark and swim out into the estuary to feed."

"If any of the family ever feel like taking up long-distance sailing, I can think of a crew that might welcome them."

"I'll pass that on."

Corwen's brief smile faded, and I knew he was worrying about Freddie again.

I loved Corwen's sister, Lily, like my own, but if I had to liken my feelings about Freddie to my feelings for a brother, it would be Philip who came to mind. David was everything I could hope for in a brother, even though he was Fae, but Philip and I had never been friends. He'd sided with Walsingham against us, and in the end, I'd been forced to kill him. When it came down to a simple choice, I'd killed Philip to save David and Corwen. A hard choice, but I'd made it in a heartbeat. As a summoner I could call the dead, but Philip's shade was one I never wanted to confront.

"Now who's worrying?" Corwen nudged me.

"Not worrying exactly. I was thinking about Philip."

18

Book

WE WERE RELIEVED to find everything peaceful on our return to the Okewood. Freddie had stayed quietly in his own territory and seemed to be content. We visited, and though he stayed in wolf form, so conversation was limited to Corwen reading out his mother's letter and telling him where we'd been, he did seem to listen and there were no snarls.

We were contemplating taking Freddie back to Aunt Rosie's cottage when the Lady called us to her.

We followed one of the sprites to the Lady's grove where she invited us to sit on stools fashioned from upturned logs. Today she was the maiden, looking barely eighteen with ribbons in her hair and high breasts beneath a flowing white gown.

A bevy of lively sprites brought us tiny acorn cups of nectar and morsels of food served on sycamore leaves. The portions may have looked parsimonious, but I'd had the Lady's food before. If you let it, the acorn cup would quench your thirst, and the morsel on the leaf would sustain you for the rest of the day. We ate as she bade us, wondering whether she was about to send us on another journey.

She didn't keep us in suspense for long. She handed me a note. I recognized Aunt Rosie's writing from her notebooks. I opened it up.

Dear Ross and Corwen,

I hope this finds you well. Leo sends his best wishes and hopes you may visit soon, as do I. There are things we need to discuss. The good folk of Summoners Well are very pleased to hear of the peace with France. For my part I have always hated the suffering and privation war brings, and I mourn for the families torn asunder. However, with the cessation of hostilities, I am aware prisoners held in France will be repatriated, including W, who has caused so much grief in the past. I had a Dream in which he returned more powerful than ever, and you know my Dreams are not to be dismissed lightly. If W's notebook is still missing, its contents could be deeply dangerous in the wrong hands. I am very worried as to its whereabouts. Please reassure me if you have the book safely in your possession.

Your Loving
Aunt Rosie

I read it and handed it to Corwen. "She's had a dream. She's worried Walsingham will be released and returned to Britain, more powerful than before."

"As are the goblins." Corwen took the letter and read my aunt's neat handwriting. "It's a perfectly valid worry."

"And Walsingham's notebook?"

"Undoubtedly dangerous."

"I suppose it does contain all his dark spells, but I would think he wrote it in code so that no one else could use it. And he's blind now, so what use will it be to him?"

"If it's in his possession, he'll find a way."

"He surely doesn't have it. If it was on his person when

James Mayo was killed and his ship blown to high heaven, it would have been destroyed in the explosion or soaked in saltwater, its pages no more than a smudgy mess."

"The pirate who pulled him out of the water—"

"Nicholas Thompson, Old Nick," I said. "Cruel even for a pirate. He likes to flay his victims. Walsingham's lucky Old Nick saw more profit in ransom, than pleasure in torture. Even so, I don't expect Nick was gentle. If he saw any profit in the book, he might have kept it."

"Would he have any idea what it was if he had found it on Walsingham's person?"

"I doubt he would have known exactly what it was, and I don't suppose Walsingham would have told him, but he might have recognized it as something valuable. Old Nick always had an eye for profit."

I cast my mind back to those last desperate minutes on the *Black Hawk*, Mayo's flagship. Mayo's fleet had had the *Heart* dead to rights, their guns perfectly positioned to send her to Davy Jones with a single broadside, and so I'd gone to Mayo's flagship to negotiate.

I thought I was in the middle of a spat with a pirate, but Walsingham was on board. I hadn't expected that. He had prepared magic spells the like of which I had never faced before. One spell had me pinned to the deck and another spell had killed James Mayo when he tried to defend me. I'd never given Jim credit for his feelings; however, it seemed he cared for me—enough to get himself killed on my behalf, which I was damn sorry for.

Will's ghost had saved my life, guiding my witchlight to the powder kegs in the ship's magazine. I'd managed to dive over the side barely a minute before the magazine blew, but I was badly injured by the explosion and almost died. I thought Walsingham had died, a just reward for killing Mayo.

Others must have thought him dead, too, because a new Walsingham had been appointed in London, Walsingham being a title rather than a real name. The old Walsingham was officially out of a job, but when he'd returned to London, they'd appointed him to consult on the matter of magical beings loose in the land. That was how he'd come to be on the *Guillaume Tell*, a prison ship for magicals.

So, last year, when Freddie and Corwen had been taken by the Mysterium, there he was—a shadow of his former self, blind and with half his left arm missing, but alive.

Damn, I should have killed him, then his spell book would not have been anything we needed to worry about, but I'd thought him powerless and I didn't have it in me to kill a cripple.

"We could go and visit Aunt Rosie," Corwen said, "but surely we should have heard from the goblins by now. I'm reluctant to take any more time away from the Okewood in case a message arrives."

"I know."

The Lady had been sitting listening to us work through options, and I suddenly felt very rude for not including her. I looked up.

"I'm sorry." I held out the letter, but she waved it away.

"I know your aunt's concerns, and they are very valid. I have felt a stirring in the magical forces that flow through this island. I think your Aunt Rosie is right. Walsingham is back."

"But the Fae want us to take a message to the king and . . . "

"You can't be in two places at once unless you split up."

I nodded, worried that was what she was going to suggest.

"You are two sides of the same coin. Your skills balance each other out. Together, you are more than the sum of your parts. Stay together. Deal with one thing at a time."

"But which is the most important—Walsingham himself, his notebook, or the Fae's ultimatum?" I didn't even have to think about it when I put it that way. The Lady simply smiled at me.

Walsingham would be targeting us. The Fae could target every single human living in the British Isles.

"We'd better get word from the goblins soon," I muttered to Corwen as we walked back to our glade. "This baby's not going to wait."

"Are you feeling quite well?"

"Apart from the mornings I'm fine," I said. And I was. Maybe a little more tired than usual and my breasts were tender. Apart from that I didn't feel any different, but I couldn't deny I had less inclination to take risks, which I supposed was only natural.

<hr />

We couldn't write to Aunt Rosie. If anyone intercepted the letter, they'd be chasing her for the witch she was. We could make it to Summoner's Well and back in a day, and the Lady promised that if the goblins sent a message, she would make sure we got it quickly.

Thus reassured, we called Timpani and Dancer and, dressed as a respectable country gentleman and his lady wife, we dipped in and out of Iaru until we came to the edge of Summoner's Well.

Bullcrest, the house where my mother and Aunt Rosie had grown up until the Mysterium found them, sat on a rise at the edge of the village. It was a fire-blackened ruin, the ground around it still barren after thirty years.

Corwen had never seen it before. I'd come here with David when we'd been looking for Aunt Rosie shortly after my mother died.

"Is that the house?" He pointed up the hill.

"That's it."

"The fire damage looks recent."

"Well, it's thirty years old, but magical. Mother and Aunt Rosie blasted everything within a wide radius."

"Including Walsingham."

"His boss, the previous Walsingham, died along with some of the mob deputized from the nearby town. Our Walsingham was then little more than an apprentice. He was caught in the backlash. Even before he acquired his burn scars from the *Black Hawk* explosion, his face was pockmarked from being sprayed by flying rubble."

"It's no wonder he doesn't love your family."

"It's true. We've done him a great disservice on more than one occasion, though never with the kind of malice he's shown us."

We rode down into the village, a small collection of neat houses, mostly thatched. There was a single street with an additional knot of buildings set back from the road comprising a general store and a tavern with Leo's smithy next door. The smithy consisted of a respectable double-fronted stone cottage with a tiled roof rather than thatched, which I suppose made sense when you considered the fire hazard from upward sparks. The smithy itself was built on the side of the cottage with tall barn doors, opened wide, and a window made up of smaller square panes, somewhat grimy from the smoke. An enormous farm horse was tied up outside and the rump of its twin showed in a shaft of spring sunlight inside the forge.

I could hear Leo's voice carrying on two conversations at once, one with the horse's owner and another with the horse itself which consisted of soft reassuring phrases, "Steady, boy. I think it'll turn wet before the week's out. Whoa-up, you noddy. Give up fidgeting, this'll only take a minute. Aye, you can always tell by the willow. My Rosie always gathers catkins. There, you go, big ninny. Told you it wouldn't hurt."

The smell of charcoal and burning hoof vied with a fresh bread smell from the bake house on the other side of the inn.

"They're at home, then," Corwen said, dismounting.

"It sounds like it." I slithered down from Dancer and into his arms.

"Leo!" Corwen called from the doorway.

"Be with you in a mo—ah, it's you two." He straightened up and grinned at us. "I've nearly finished this pair. Go through into the yard and on into the house. The front door's for guests. Back door for family. Rosie'll be pleased to see you. No doubt she has cake, and the kettle's always on."

We left Timpani and Dancer standing as if tethered to the rings in the outside wall. The powerful heat of the forge struck us as we passed through, nodding politely to Leo's customer, an elderly farmer-type. The back door, also propped open to cool the forge with a through draft, opened up into a yard with a single pony trap resting in the middle of it and a small stable in a separate building with a gray cob's head sticking out over the half door. It whickered hopefully, but when we gave it no attention, it retreated into the gloom of the box.

"Ross! Corwen!" Aunt Rosie emerged from the kitchen, dusting flour from her hands. "Good to see you. You are both looking well." She glanced at my belly, and I knew she'd perceived what was going on in there. I would have told her anyway, but I didn't need to. "And some good news to impart, I see."

"Can't fool you, Aunt Rosie. Not that we'd try."

"Quite right, too, my loves. Come on in."

I knew there were two best rooms at the front of the house, but the kitchen was the heart and hub of the home. A scrubbed wooden table in the center had four spoon-back chairs. A wide bowl, brown-glazed on the outside and cream on the inside, stood on one end with a muslin cover over it.

"You've timed it right. I need to leave the bread to rise for a while." She set the bowl in an alcove next to the fire grate and the cast-iron box oven. The heat from the fire was almost as scorching as Leo's forge.

Aunt Rosie wiped her face with the skirt of her apron. "Can't bake bread without a good hot oven," she said, picking up long tongs and swinging the kettle, dangling from a hinged bar, over the hottest part of the fire. It began to steam almost immediately. She deftly retrieved it using the tongs and a folded cloth and made tea in a sturdy brown teapot. Her china cups were wide-mouthed and copious, decorated with a rose pattern. Each stood in its own deep saucer.

She presided over the making and pouring of tea exactly as my mother used to, though my mother would never have invited visitors into her kitchen. I guessed tea-making had been instilled into both sisters in their girlhood. When I looked at Aunt Rosie, my mother's twin, I saw the person Mother might have been if she hadn't let her hatred of magic sour her. They both had the same features, but where my mother's had been pinched, her lips narrow and creased through a constant expression of disapproval, Rosie's were rounder and softer and she had a ready smile. Her skin, like my mother's, was unblemished, but her eyes had earned their laughter lines. Oh, how I wished I'd been able to bring these twin sisters together again, but my mother had died before I even knew she had a sister. It had taken some ingenuity to find Aunt Rosie. At least I'd been able to reunite her and Leo.

"So is this a social visit or a professional one?" Aunt Rosie asked.

"Professional?"

I didn't quite follow her meaning, but Corwen did. He nudged me and whispered, "Village midwife."

"Oh!" My face grew hot and I think I blushed.

Aunt Rosie laughed. "Twins, is it?"

"What? Oh, my . . . " I hadn't even thought about the possibility, but I should have. Corwen was a twin, and my mother and Rosie were twins.

Aunt Rosie laughed. "Two for the price of one. No reason why they shouldn't both be healthy." She looked at my face. "What's wrong?"

"When Will and I were married, my firstborn came early. He was born on the *Heart*, in the middle of the Atlantic Ocean. He only lived a few days."

"Each confinement is different," she said. "There's no reason for this pregnancy to follow the same pattern as your last. You must take it easy toward the end and send word whenever you need me. Don't expend too much magical energy, or you might draw it from the babies as well. It's likely, with their heritage, that they'll take after one or both of you."

"Thanks, Aunt Rosie. I guess it was a professional visit after all, but really we came to tell you we don't have Walsingham's notebook, though Corwen thinks Walsingham doesn't have it either."

Corwen nodded. "When he was on the *Guillaume Tell* and I was at his mercy, he was inclined to gloat. I think if he'd had the means to make spells, he would have used them."

"So do you know where it might be?"

"I hope it's at the bottom of the sea."

I told her in some detail what had happened on the *Black Hawk*.

"Hmm," she creased her face up and closed her eyes as if looking inward. "I'm not much of a seer, and without having seen the book, I can't locate it or summon it, but I have this scratchy feeling in the back of my mind. I can't explain it, but it's there all the time. I know the book is important. If nothing else, it's important to deny Walsingham and his ilk the use of it."

"If it did come whole out of the sea, it might be in the hands of a pirate called Nicholas Thompson," I said. "Old Nick to his enemies."

"What is he to his friends?"

"He doesn't have any. He used to sail the *Flamingo* with Gentleman Jim's fleet out of Auvienne in the Dark Islands. It wouldn't surprise me if he hadn't taken advantage of the situation and taken over Jim's holdings. With Jim dead, the strongest of his captains would be likely to step in, and that would be whoever had the hardest crew and the greatest firepower."

"Can you send the *Heart* to find out?" Aunt Rosie asked.

"I'm not sure that would be a good idea. Gentleman Jim and Hookey never saw eye to eye, but they weren't likely to kill each other. Hookey and Old Nick are mortal enemies. Nick once skinned a friend of Hookey's—literally."

Rosie shuddered. I didn't blame her.

I thought for a while.

I knew I probably could do it. But whether I should was a different matter. Will's ghost had passed over to a deeper place; to call him back would be unsettling—for both of us. Will had stuck by me for three years after his death. It was only when he let me go, that I realized I needed to let him go as well, to release him. Calling him back now would be cruel.

But there was another ghost more recently deceased.

"I could call the ghost of James Mayo," I said. "Gentleman Jim."

19

Gentleman Jim

I'D DONE IT before, called up ghosts and asked them to investigate things or track things down for me, but usually they were recently-dead specters who meant little to me personally. James Mayo, pirate captain, was my ex-lover. It was only the one time, I swear, well, twice, but both times in one night. I'd been trying to get myself back into the real world after three years of both mourning Will and letting myself believe his ghost was the next best thing to having him with me, warm and alive.

Will had chided me for what he considered my infidelity, and I'd felt somewhat ashamed for using Jim as a man might use a willing woman. Jim had, in fact, been more than willing. I hadn't realized he'd felt more than lust for me until, much later, the moment he'd given his life trying to save mine.

Of course, by that time I'd met Corwen and had to make the difficult choice between my old love and the new. With Will's ghost on one side and Corwen on the other, Jim had never really been in the running, and for leading him on—if I had indeed led him on—I was sorry.

In the end Will had helped me to make that decision himself, and we'd parted company forever.

Now, here I was, with Corwen's child, or maybe children, in my belly, about to ask favors from a one-time lover. I didn't know whether Jim blamed me for his death, or whether his ghost still had some feelings for me. Either way it wasn't going to be an easy encounter.

Here's the thing about ghosts. They're exactly that: ghosts, pale shades of what they once were. They still have an echo of the same feelings as they had when alive, but there's no vitality. And their logic can be muddled. They're no longer focused on the living. Will had loved me, but when my life hung in the balance, he'd urged me to die in order to be with him on the other side.

He couldn't have forced me. Spirits don't have the power to harm, except by suggestion. The biggest danger is that the one who calls them gets drawn over the divide into death. Having someone to anchor you to the real world was a real help. I knew Corwen would anchor me. He'd done it before.

"If I'm going to do it, I'd rather do it here, in safety, with you two," I said.

"Do you need Leo?" Rosie asked.

I shook my head. "I don't want to put him in harm's way."

"Give me a moment," Rosie said. "I'll tell him to pop next door for a flagon of ale. Blacksmithing's thirsty work."

"As long as he doesn't mind being pushed out."

"He won't mind. He knows not to get in the way when I'm working magic, just as I don't get in the way when he's shoeing horses."

"That sounds like a fair accommodation," Corwen said.

Aunt Rosie slipped out of the kitchen door and quickly crossed the yard. I saw her with Leo in the forge doorway, giving each other a peck on the cheek. Aww, I loved the way Rosie and Leo were so perfect for each other.

"What do you need me to do?" Corwen asked.

"Anchor me and don't let me get drawn toward our ghost visitor."

"I won't."

"Jim may think he has a claim on me, but whatever happened was before you and I met."

"I understand." He came to stand behind my chair and dropped a light kiss on top of my head. "Nothing he can say will make me think less of you."

"I hope not."

Aunt Rosie came back in with a smile on her face. "Leo says to let him know when it's safe to come home. I do like being married to an understanding man."

"Me, too." I patted Corwen's hand where it rested on my shoulder.

There's no spell to call up a spirit. It's all about the power of the mind. I took a deep breath to settle my thoughts and concentrated on what I knew of James Mayo, a tall, rangy American with a Virginia drawl and a face more strong than handsome. His complexion was tanned by wind and weather, his hair dark and cut close to his head. His nose had a slight bump as if it had been broken. I expect it had; piracy was a difficult life. The lines around his dark brown eyes showed he was always ready to laugh. There was something flamboyantly gallant about Mayo, which may have been why he'd earned the nickname of Gentleman Jim. The first time we'd met he'd taken my hand and bowed low over it as though I was a queen. When I'd chided him for his extravagant behavior, he'd told me I'd always be a queen in his eyes.

Mayo was fiercely competitive. It seemed he'd set himself a challenge to see if he could wheedle me away from Will, but no amount of wheedling would have separated me from my husband. We spent some time on Auvienne at a pirate and privateer conclave, trying to thrash out equitable rules for dealing with each other. After that, Mayo always seemed to regard me as his, which was somewhat annoying since the only one I ever belonged to was myself. Even Will never aimed to possess me, and Corwen always treated me as an equal. Jim saw me as a woman and therefore property. The competition extended to our ships. If Jim could pluck a target from

under our noses, he did, and Will entered into the spirit
of the game, giving back as good as he got.

After Will's death, Mayo propositioned me a couple of
times, and eventually I'd given in to his not-inconsiderable
charms.

It had been time. Three years a widow, I needed to
prove to myself I was part of the real world once more. I
had proved it spectacularly, but I'd also proved to myself
that James Mayo's charms weren't enough to tempt me
into a lasting relationship. I'd fled his bed and his island
under cover of an attack by British warships.

All this was going through my mind as I stood on the
brink of the spirit world and called.

And called.

Nothing.

I called again.

Still nothing.

My focus slipped. In my mind I took a step forward,
but Corwen's presence kept me anchored.

I thought back to the time I'd had a conversation with
a new-made ghost in Plymouth. How had I called him?
Ah . . . memory coalesced. Will had brought him to me.
My lovely Will.

Ross?

I heard him in my head and didn't need a voice to answer him. *Will?*

How could this be? Will had passed over to that deeper
place. He should have lost all connection with his past
life—with me.

Have you come for me?

How could I tell him that I hadn't? I'd come looking
for the ghost of the man who'd tried to steal me from
him.

Rest in peace, Will.

I felt Corwen's fingers digging into my shoulder. He'd
always been able to see ghosts. Many magicals could.
Corwen and Will had once faced off against each other
when Will's ghost had tried to come between us. Will had
exhibited more jealousy dead than he ever had while

alive. I suppose that while he lived, I had not shown an interest in other men.

Silverwolf, are you still here? Will's ghost turned its attention on Corwen.

"Still here, Tremayne. Now and always."

I opened my eyes. There was Will Tremayne, my first love, my first husband, the man I'd intended to grow old with until a falling spar had turned my world upside down. Other than the fact that I could see through him, he looked much as he had when alive: buckskin breeches, linen shirt, his hair drawn back in a black ribbon. He wore neither coat nor shoes, just as he'd been on the stormy night when he died. It wasn't even the worst storm either of us had seen. We'd run from our cabin and up onto the *Heart*'s deck, but in the dark and the confusion Will had been in the wrong place at the wrong time when a spar came crashing down.

I'd always thought it strange that Will's ghost showed no sign of the head injury that had killed him instantly. It was as if his image had been captured in the moment before his death. Perhaps that's when we are all at our most vital.

"Go back to your rest, Will," I said.

You called me. You must need me. You can't send me back. He was sounding whiny now. Will, in life, had never been whiny, but his ghost had occasionally shown an alarming tendency to self-pity. Even so, I'd loved Will's ghost as fiercely as I'd loved Will himself, and I had clung to him for far too long—to his detriment and mine. *There's something coming, Ross, something bad. I don't know what it is, but the tides in this place are strange. You're going to need me.*

"Rest, Will."

The third time was the charm. Will's ghost faded.

His passing felt like another bereavement.

There was a long silence in Aunt Rosie's kitchen until Corwen whispered, "Are you all right?"

I swallowed a painful lump that had been threatening to form in my throat and patted Corwen's hand, still on my shoulder. "I'm fine. It was . . . the shock of seeing him again. I never expected . . . "

"Handsome devil, wasn't he?" Aunt Rosie said.

"Could you see him as well?"

"Of course, I could. I'm a Sumner, too. Sumner, summoner. It's what our family does. I wonder if you should take note of Will's warning."

"Was it a real warning, or was he only trying to grab my attention?"

"Ah, you know him better than I."

"It's strange that I couldn't summon Gentleman Jim's spirit."

Aunt Rosie huffed out a breath. "Have you considered the possibility that he might not be dead?"

⬦——⬦

I'd seen James Mayo murdered right in front of me, or, at least I'd seen his body slumped on the deck and heard the command to sling his remains overboard. I suppose, if he'd been unconscious rather than dead, the slap of cold water might have brought him round, and if he'd already been in the water and swimming for his life when the *Black Hawk*'s powder magazine blew, he would have stood as much chance as anyone.

Well, good for him.

I smiled to myself.

I might not exactly trust Gentleman Jim, especially when it came to magic and money, but if there was a chance he might be out there, somewhere, that warmed me.

"You liked him, didn't you?" Corwen asked.

"Jim and I were . . . " I searched for the right word. "Complicated." That summed it up. "He was kind to me when he didn't need to be. I think we could have been friends, but he always wanted more. I shouldn't have given it to him. I didn't take his feelings into account. In truth, I didn't credit him with feelings of that sort."

"So now what?" Aunt Rosie said. "We're no nearer to Walsingham's notebook."

"If, indeed, it exists."

She inclined her head in acknowledgment.

Corwen cleared his throat. "If we had no other commitments, a sea voyage might—"

"But we have commitments, thanks to the Fae," I said.

"Ah, delivering your ultimatum to the king," Aunt Rosie said.

"You know about that?"

"Margann told me on her last visit."

"The idea is as mad as the king is supposed to be," I said, "except . . . "

She raised her eyebrows.

"Except the king has magic, or at least the potential for it. They'll never let him admit it, of course, even if they know. It's my theory that he's suppressing magic. His madness is magically induced."

Her mouth formed a perfect O shape, but no words came out.

"So, you see, we have to deliver the message because the king might actually understand it."

"Then whatever you can do to deliver the message, do it swiftly because the more I think about the notebook, the scratchier my feelings get."

I knew better than to disregard Aunt Rosie's scratchy feelings. She was more of a witch than I would ever be.

◆━━━◆

"It's all too much," I said to Corwen as we rode back to the Okewood. "How can we possibly do everything everyone wants us to do? I feel as though I'm rolling with the punches, reacting to things all the time, rather than making my own decisions. The Fae, the Lady, even Aunt Rosie, and Will's vague warning. Go here, do this. All I want to do is settle down and have our baby in peace. Or babies, if Aunt Rosie's right."

"It's been a difficult two years," Corwen said. "You deserve a rest. And our babies deserve the best start in life we can give them."

"Now I feel mean because you've got all the same pressures I've got plus Freddie and your family."

"Ah, life's never simple, is it?" He shrugged. "I always hoped I'd become a father one day, but there were so many obstacles. Too many. Even finding someone to share my life with was something I thought impossible until I met you. And now here we are, in the middle of the most turbulent times, and it's all happening at once." He took a deep breath. "I think we have to decide what the most important thing is and follow it to its logical conclusion. What do you want most of all?"

"To protect my family."

"Define family."

"You, our offspring, David, Aunt Rosie, and Leo." Every time I thought I was coming to the end of my list I opened my arms wider. "Your family, of course, your mother and Lily, and Freddie, too, I suppose, though he's a bit of a horse's arse."

Corwen laughed. "Yes, he is. If he wasn't my brother, I'd have given up on him before now."

I sighed. "And then there's Poppy and her family, and Hookey and the *Heart*'s crew. Damn. I seem to have more family than I'd realized."

"Don't forget the reverend, Charlotte, and Olivia, and— by extension—Henry Purdy, though we've never met him."

"When did my family get so large?"

He reached across and took my hand as we rode. "Life was simpler when I was a single wolf, but it was a lot more lonely."

I squeezed his hand. "I was surrounded by friends, but after Will died, I was lonely, too." Maybe lonely wasn't the right word. "Empty."

"And now?"

I laughed and patted my belly. "Full, I think."

"So, to protect our family, what do we need to do first?"

"Let's take the threats in order. I don't think we have a choice. The threat to magic users is our biggest problem, so first we have to deliver the Fae's message to the king."

Corwen nodded. "I agree. Then we need to investigate Walsingham's notebook."

"Yes, the notebook, definitely. But what about the capture and return of magical creatures to the Okewood and Iaru—"

"That's something we can leave to Hartington with the volunteers from the Okewood and the Fae."

"And Henry Purdy?" I felt guilty about Olivia's father. Although it wasn't, strictly speaking, our problem to deal with, we had volunteered.

"I'm sure Charlotte understands that on the grand scale of things . . . " Corwen's voice trailed off. "Oh, hell, yes, I feel guilty about Henry Purdy, too, but there's not much we can do without knowing where he is. When we get that information, we'll make a decision."

"If we get it." The Mysterium had treated its magicals very badly. I wasn't hopeful the army had done any better by them. I sighed. "We can only do what we can do. Besides, if the king takes notice of the Fae ultimatum, any improvement should help all magicals, including Henry Purdy."

"They're both part of the same overall problem of making the country safe for magicals. We need to bring about a change in the law, but we also need to eliminate the kind of magical threat Walsingham presents. He's proof anyone can learn magic if they have the right teachers and acquire the right spells even though they aren't intrinsically magical themselves. Getting rid of Walsingham won't entirely solve the problem. Getting rid of his notebook at least means no one else can access his dark magic after he's gone."

I nodded. "That's a plan, then. King first, notebook and Walsingham second."

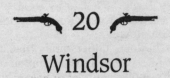

20

Windsor

THE LETTER LILY had spoken about finally caught up with us the day after we arrived back in the Oke-wood. Delivered by Aileen, the fox-girl, it was a slim single sheet folded in on itself and sealed with a wafer.

Corwen read it first, then we went to Freddie's compound, and he waved the letter. "It's for you. It's very personal. It's from someone called Betsey in Gloucestershire. Shall I read it to you?"

Freddie hunkered down while Corwen read it out. It was an apology, a love letter, and an invitation to Gloucestershire.

Without warning, Freddie launched himself into the air, snatched the letter from Corwen's hand, and ran off with it in his teeth.

"Lucky I copied the return address," Corwen said softly. "Maybe we should write to this Betsey person."

"I wonder who she is," I said.

"I suspect she's not a she at all. Betsey's a common nickname in the molly houses."

"Ah, that makes sense. Freddie's lover, Roland."

"That would be my guess."

We penned a letter between us. This was much easier to form than our letter to the king had been.

To Mr. Roland Somerton.

> *Greetings.*
> *And greetings also to Betsey.*
> *I write on behalf of my brother, Freddie, who is currently indisposed and in a troubled state, but I believe would be heartened by a visit from your good self. If you are inclined to accept this invitation, please write back via Mr. Arthur Reynard at the Valiant Soldier in Buckfastleigh, Devonshire, and we will arrange to meet you and conduct you to Freddie in the hope that you might be able to bring him out of his melancholy.*
>
> *Sincerely*
> *Corwen Deverell.*

"He'll either come or he won't," Corwen said. "We have nothing to lose and everything to gain."

"What if he replies while we're away trying to speak to the king?"

"Charlotte will watch for a reply."

The day after that, we got a message from the goblins. The king had gone to Frogmore House, Windsor, to inspect the building works there. Bought as a retreat for Queen Charlotte and the unmarried princesses, the building works had added flanking pavilions and work was now underway on a new dining room and library.

This was our best opportunity. If the king wouldn't meet us willingly, we'd have to use stealth. At Frogmore with his family, King George was at his most informal and least observed.

"Better to catch him in the garden if we can," Corwen said. "Let's get a little help from David. Larien won't allow the Fae to get involved at this stage, so he can't come with us, but he will be able to give us the lay of the land if his Fae talent for geography still holds good."

It took us less than an hour to cross into Iaru and find David. Annie was with him, and I noticed that even when talking to us, David and Annie's hands were not far from touching. I wondered how David and Larien were resolving the impending marriage issue. Surely, David was too young to be tied into a relationship he didn't want. But maybe that was the price that Fae lords paid.

It happened to English nobility, too. Marriages were made to secure support or simply for money. Thank goodness I was too far down the social scale to worry about that. It seemed that there was an unhappy equation—wealth went hand in hand with lack of freedom to marry for love, while those who could marry for love often did so with no hopes of wealth at all.

Corwen and I were lucky.

"You can cross from Iaru to the Windsor Forest," David said, drawing a map in the air. His finger left a line of light. "It's a short sprint from there to Frogmore on horseback. Head for the river. Frogmore is low-lying, hence its name. It's close to the castle, but not too close."

Corwen stared at the map, committing it to memory. "I expect the household servants have all been selected for their common sense and handiness with a weapon."

"That and the Blues, the Royal Horseguards, are now stationed in the new barracks in Clewer Park, three miles away."

Three whole miles. Somehow, that distance didn't give me much confidence. But even without alerting the regiment assigned to protect the king, the royal family would have some kind of protection. All we had to do, or not do, was trigger it.

We didn't waste time; we changed into what I thought of as our real-world clothes. I wore my riding habit, given to me by the Fae, which always looked presentable no matter how I abused it. It was a rich red-brown color with black velvet trim. I wore bloomers for comfort under the divided skirt. I didn't care if bloomers were considered fast. No one was going to see them besides me and Corwen.

Corwen wore a slightly more elegant version of his usual country gentleman style and looked more like a man about town with buckskin breeches and a deep green woolen coat cut in the latest close-fitting style.

"Are we fit to see the king?"

"As fit as we'll ever be."

⬥————⬥

Parts of the Windsor Forest are old. An eerie feeling pervaded the gnarled trunks. The Okewood felt like home, but Windsor's trees felt slightly alien. Herne the Hunter was supposed to abide here, but that was a myth plaited together with stories of the Green Man. I've met him—the Green Man, I mean—a figure of awe, but not cold and alien like the malevolent presence in Windsor.

Corwen shuddered and looked over his shoulder as we passed through the trees.

"Do you feel it, too?" I asked.

"Something," he said, "but I don't know what. I was going to suggest you waited here with the horses while I scouted around Frogmore in wolf form. I can be quick, and I can be sneaky, but . . . " He looked over his shoulder again. "I don't want to leave you here alone."

I didn't want to stay alone, either. Even the horses were uneasy. Dancer tossed his head, and I could feel his whole body stiff and ready to bolt at a moment's notice.

"Let's go down the Long Walk," I suggested. Since Easter, the spring weather had turned mild. The trees were beginning to bud, though they weren't in leaf yet, but there was a double row on each side of the walk, and their trunks would help to keep us from being easily spotted from a distance.

We made a dash for the edge of the forest. The horses needed no urging, and we came out onto the grassy hillside above the Long Walk which led directly to the castle itself, three miles away.

"Impressive," Corwen said.

"It's meant to be."

"Glad the king isn't somewhere in the middle of all those stone walls."

"Frogmore may be as impenetrable."

"Well, we'll have to try."

We walked our horses steadily through the trees bordering the Long Walk. As we left the forest behind, the feeling of oppression gradually lightened. Corwen lost the tendency to keep twitching around to see if we were being followed, and Dancer relaxed.

"Do we have to go back that way?" I asked.

"If we need to make a quick exit."

Presuming we were free to make any kind of exit. How many guards surrounded the king at any one time? Staff, too, and several of them were likely to be military types. The king and his family must be surrounded by people all the time, even when at their most informal.

About two thirds of the way down the Long Walk, Corwen pointed down to the right. "Frogmore, though David says we're as likely to find the king and his family at the Queen's Lodge, that is the Upper Lodge which is the house that protrudes into the Long Walk, not forty yards from the castle walls."

"If the king has come to see the new building at Frogmore and is staying at the Queen's Lodge, perhaps the answer is to find him on the route between the two. Can we shelter somewhere and watch the likely path?"

I breathed a silent thank you to the gardeners who had dotted the environs of the castle with picturesque groves of trees. Thus settled, we observed a party of liveried servants carry basket after basket of what looked like food and drink from the Upper Lodge along the path toward Frogmore.

"Do you think they're planning a picnic in the grounds or a meal within the house itself?" I asked.

"If the house is being renovated, maybe a picnic in the gardens. Let's hope so, anyway."

"If we backtrack the way we came, we could access the gardens from the south side."

"Let's do it."

We waited for the column of servants to march past us. Then, as quietly as we could, we left our grove and re-traced our steps up the Long Walk for maybe a quarter of a mile, then followed a track until we came to the garden wall. It was tall enough to keep out the deer, but not so tall that we couldn't climb it, even with the ditch in front and the trees behind.

Corwen rode up close and peered over. "A good horse could jump that," he said. "What do you think, Timpani?"

The horse huffed out a loud breath.

"Is that a yes or a no?" I asked Corwen.

"It's a yes," he said, sounding more positive than I felt.

It was a huge jump with the width of the ditch and the height of the wall. Misjudging it could bring both horse and rider down with broken bones. I'd spent my child-hood riding small ponies suitable for a girl of my station, that is to say, somewhat docile. My formative years had been on the deck of a ship. I wasn't a bad rider, and my partnership with Dancer had taught me a lot, but it was still a big jump.

I drew in a deep breath and nodded. "After you."

Corwen put Timpani at the wall and soared over. Of course, he'd had the benefit of a country upbringing.

Dancer began to dance. "All right. Here we go." I can-tered in a circle, then turned until the wall was all I could see in front of me. I sat down firmly in the saddle, keeping a good contact with Dancer's mouth, holding him in until he was almost bouncing. Then three strides away from the ditch I gave him his head and pushed him on. One, two, three, and up. Dancer launched himself and I swung forward with him, keeping my center of balance over his. Ditch and wall flew beneath us and then another ditch on the other side which Corwen had conveniently forgotten to warn me about. Dancer's hooves came down, front, rear, with two clumps and his momentum carried us for-ward for a few strides until I gathered him up and circled around to where Corwen was waiting.

"You might have warned me about the second ditch."

Corwen dismissed my complaint with a backward wave of his hand. "You'd only have worried, and the arc of his jump carried you both safely over, which I knew it would."

I harrumphed at him, but he was probably right.

Frogmore's gardens had been laid out to give privacy to an area of lawn trimmed impeccably short, hours of backbreaking work for a team of groundsmen. Toward the boundary wall there was a barrier of hedges and trees and through the middle a serpentine lake, artificially created, no doubt.

We peered out of our tree cover. The first of the servants were carrying tables and chairs onto the lawn, covering the table and setting places.

The house itself had been newly painted a startling white. It was pleasantly proportioned with a colonnaded walkway across the back of the house between two single-story wings. To the right-hand side was a stack of timber and sandstone, the timber mostly covered by a tarpaulin. There were sawhorses and rough-cut planks that looked as though the builders had removed them from the house so that their royal employers could see their progress. That explained why the family intended to take a meal outside.

A group of people stepped out of the house into the colonnade and from there to the garden. They were the first not carrying baskets. It took me a while to recognize the king and to realize this was his family. They were dressed as a normal country family, that is to say, not expensively. Beside the king was a stately lady whom I took to be Queen Charlotte, and four young women. I knew the king had five unmarried daughters, but I didn't recognize them by sight. From this distance it was difficult to guess their ages. It didn't look as though any of the princes were in attendance. Three of the young women linked arms and walked down to the edge of the lake while one remained close by her parents.

Food was served with footmen standing behind each chair to help the diners. My own belly grumbled. "We should have brought a picnic," I whispered to Corwen. "This is going to take forever. How on earth are we going to get the king away from his family?"

"I have an idea," Corwen said as the servants cleared the table and at last left the royal family alone.

I suspected the servants hadn't gone far. They would certainly be within earshot if called. Corwen whispered in Timpani's ear and then sent him out of the bushes into the garden. One of the princesses spotted him first and pointed him out to the others. The king said something and stood. Queen Charlotte put out a restraining arm, but the king patted her hand and stepped toward Timpani.

A riderless horse in an enclosed garden would be a puzzle. Not only that, but the king was famous for his love of horses and riding. Anyone with half an eye could see Timpani was an exceptionally fine horse, and the king had more than half an eye.

One of the princesses, the youngest one, I thought—so that would be Princess Amelia—ran after her father. Timpani's head came up, his nostrils flared, and he took three quick paces backward toward the trees.

"Go back, Emily, dear," the king said. "Don't startle him." Turning back to Timpani, he began to mutter a string of soothing nonsense. "Come on, my boy. There's a boy. What a fine lad you are. Come to Georgie, my boy."

Timpani waited until the king was almost close enough to grab his rein, then sidled away into the bushes. There were enough evergreens to make good cover. Corwen and I held our breath. The king was close. A few feet more would be enough. Timpani stopped, turned his head, and whickered at the king. It was enough. King George, third of his name, stepped into the bushes, right into our waiting arms.

21

Mad King George

"PLEASE DON'T CALL out. We mean you no harm," I said as Corwen swept a deep bow.

I followed with a curtsey. "We've met before—almost," I said. "Maundy Thursday, at Westminster. We shook hands, like this." I held out my hand, willing him to take it.

"You're her," he said, and took my hand.

Our magics met, with a shock and a tingle.

"You remembered."

"I couldn't easily forget."

"Your Majesty—"

The king waved away my formal address. "How did you do that?" His look seemed to cut through me. This man might have had a bout of madness, but he was, undoubtedly the king, used to having everyone around him bow to his wishes.

"I'm a witch, Your Majesty, though not a licensed one. You'll forgive us if we don't give you our names, but the Mysterium would hang us for the talents we were born with." I wasn't specific about Corwen. There was no need.

"It was you who sent the letter . . . the meeting in Richmond Park. My advisers thought it was some plot."

"It was, indeed, us, Majesty," Corwen said. "I'm sorry if it worried you."

"I wasn't worried at all. I was nowhere near the place, but, tell me, how did you get away? My equerry—a good soldier in his day, you know—said you disappeared into thin air? And how did you do this?" He shook his hand as if his fingers still tingled.

"I didn't do anything, Majesty, but the magic in you responds to the magic in me."

For a moment I swear that the king's face was a mask of fear, but he covered it up quickly and adopted a haughty manner. "I have no magic. I am the king of the United Kingdom of Great Britain and Ireland. It would be wholly inappropriate for the king to have magic."

"Yet here we are, and you've not called out yet," Corwen said.

"You do have magic," I said. "Though you may have been trying to tell yourself you haven't for most of your life."

"Young lady, if I had magic, I would know it."

"With the greatest respect, Majesty, you might not. You might have told yourself that what you were feeling was perfectly natural. If you'd never explored your magic, how would you know your capabilities? Some of us can create illusion, some can control the elements to a greater or lesser degree, some can perform magic spells."

"There's a spell book, is there not?"

"A poor thing with limited use. Licensed witches are required to work those spells and no others. It contains small spells only, maybe a concealing spell, or one to make a lady's hair curl, or one to hide a blemish from someone's face—an illusion, you understand, not an actual cure."

"What about love potions?" The king's attitude changed again. I wondered at his capricious nature. Was this part of his affliction? Was he truly cured of the madness which had returned only last year? He seemed to have forgotten we were intruders into his garden. He leaned forward in his eagerness to hear the answer. Love potions! Fairy tale stuff. Always the same question from those who knew nothing.

"Alas, Majesty, though it is possible to sway someone's interest in that direction, it almost never ends well. The person so persuaded may think himself, or herself, enamored, but it can't last, and if certain promises have been made, or certain actions taken that can't be undone, then lives and reputations may be destroyed. Or the spell may go awry, and the subject of the spell may become too enamored, leading to all kinds of inappropriate behavior." I shook my head. "Coercing someone into doing something is a bad use of magic. In some cases, it can be dark magic, so dark it hurts people and twists the soul of the user and the soul of the used."

"Do you practice this dark magic?"

I shook my head. "Magic is a great responsibility. It shouldn't be used to harm people. To use magic to kill or maim or injure would be a grievous thing, and a person would suffer for it. I've defended myself with magic, but I've never deliberately killed with it."

That was no lie. I'd done my killing with a pistol or a sword, but my privateering days were over.

"What can you do? Show me."

I took two deep breaths to center myself and willed light into being. The feeling started in the center of my back, shivered up to my left shoulder and all the way down my arm until a tiny ball of light, no bigger than a pearl, glowed, cool, in my palm. I let it grow until it was half the width of my hand and then I tossed it up into a dense holly tree where it illuminated a little cave within the branches.

"Pretty," the king said.

"And useful on a dark night."

"But you have not registered with the Mysterium. Why not?"

"I intended to, but circumstances conspired against me. I wasn't in the country at the time of my eighteenth birthday, and after that it was too late. The Mysterium would have hanged me."

"For coming forward late? Surely not."

Corwen cleared his throat. "I would suggest, Majesty, they would show no mercy. Even those who register by their eighteenth birthday are not treated well or with respect. Anyone with more power than a hedge-witch is often spirited away and lost to their families. I believe some have been forced to take up positions in the army, using their talents on your behalf. The navy has wind and weather witches, more powerful than any you'd find for public hire in our towns."

"Is it not their duty to use their talents for king and country?"

I shook my head. "Without allowing them to contact their family? Even press-ganged sailors are allowed to escape their fate if their family can pay the smart."

"But it's not only witches, Majesty," Corwen continued. "We've come to talk to you about the rowankind."

I saw by his expression that he knew what we were about to say.

"The rowankind have magic," I said. "They didn't know it until they gained their freedom. It's been suppressed for many long years, but now they know." I didn't tell him my part in the freeing of the rowankind. "They have wind and water magic. Natural magic."

He didn't reply, which confirmed my suspicion that this was not news. Of course, the information would have passed from monarch to monarch via a trusted minister. Each monarch would have inherited a Walsingham.

"You already know, don't you?" I asked.

He spread his hands wide.

"We know about the Walsinghams," Corwen said. "We know Walsingham is not a real name, it's a title. There's been a Walsingham reporting to the monarch about magical threats ever since the first one, Sir Francis Walsingham, was appointed by Queen Elizabeth."

"Is there a current Walsingham?" I asked.

"I don't know what you're talking about."

There was a bead of perspiration on the king's upper lip, and he looked anywhere but directly at me. The king didn't like lying, but lying he was.

I shot Corwen a sideways glance. Yes, he'd picked up on that, too. My heart felt as if it was about to pound its way out of my chest. I pushed down my fear of Walsingham. Now was not the time to let it get the better of me.

"The way this country treats its magical folks is shocking," Corwen said, "and counterproductive. The Mysterium is restrictive. Your magical subjects could use their talents for good—and would if you let them. A volunteer is worth ten pressed men."

"What do you want from me?" The king sounded suddenly wary, as well he might.

Corwen bowed his head slightly. I recognized the gesture. He was trying not to appear dangerous. "We have been asked to bring you a warning, Your Majesty."

"I am the Crown head. I do not respond to threats."

"It's not a threat, truly," I said, "at least not from us. We're only messengers. We bring word from the Fae."

"Fae, fairies. Pah!"

"Majesty, if you know the origins of the rowankind, then you also know that when the Fae refused to help against the Spanish Armada, Queen Bess' summoner did a great working. He drew the rowankind, the Fae's helpmeets, from the forest, and summoned their magic from them so he could destroy Philip of Spain's ships with storms and raging seas. Afterward, the summoner was broken by his own success and couldn't reverse his working to restore the rowankind's magic. The Fae, out of kindness to their former friends, took away their memories of Iaru and magic. Queen Bess placed the rowankind in her subjects' households so that they could be looked after. But people forgot the rowankind's sacrifice—if sacrifice it was and not wanton theft—and so they became servants, and within a few short generations, bonded folk."

"But they're not servants now, are they? Not bonded."

"They have their magic once again. And though these

rowankind are the descendants of those earlier ones, they have a race memory of where they came from. They have free will. Many have already returned to the Fae, but some have made lives here and want to stay. Unfortunately, the Mysterium is now persecuting them. At first it was by rounding them up, throwing them into jails, or shipping them out to sea, which is a terrible cruelty as they die from seasickness, but in Yorkshire they have hanged six rowankind without trial. In other parts of the country, too."

Corwen cleared his throat. "To that end the Fae have charged us with delivering this message: The Mysterium should stop persecuting the rowankind for what they are and should release them all from captivity."

"That, sir, would take an act of Parliament."

Corwen nodded.

"Parliament is much engaged by the peace with France. I doubt it will be possible."

"Majesty, the Fae ask that you make it possible through your ministers."

He sighed. "They're too busy fighting each other to have a care about magicals."

I didn't want to make the threat too overbearing, but I had to warn the king about the wholesale destruction the Fae could create. "We fear that if you don't free the rowankind from persecution, the Fae will take matters into their own hands."

"Great Britain is not afeared of fairies, young lady."

I took a deep breath. "Majesty, you should be. The magic that destroyed the Spanish Armada was rowankind magic. Fae magic is ten—nay—a hundred times more powerful."

"Do you threaten the realm?"

"Personally? No. Our magic is small. All we do is bring you a warning. If you saw a storm out at sea heading in your direction, would you not batten down the hatches and shorten sail? The Fae exist, and they are determined to protect the rowankind. Their honor demands it. The rowankind themselves wish only to be left in peace. They've done nothing to provoke the Fae into this. Please, Majesty, we beg you to stop the Mysterium from arresting and executing rowankind, for all our sakes."

"Go back to your Fae friends and tell them Great Britain does not bow to threats."

Corwen whistled up the horses.

I tried one last time. "I'm sorry, Majesty. I think you'll find the Fae are good friends, but bad enemies. Let us arrange a meeting between the Fae and your ministers to discuss possibilities."

"I have said all I'm going to say on the subject."

Dancer shoved his nose between my shoulder blades and nudged me. I curtseyed to the king and turned to mount. Corwen was already up on Timpani.

"Wait," the king stepped forward and raised one hand. "You can't just come here and—"

"Papa." A female voice called. I could hear light footsteps brushing through the grass. "Did you catch the horse?"

I suddenly had an idea. "How many of your own children are affected, carrying the power and trying to keep it suppressed until it feels like a red-hot coal in their throat. If the Mysterium knew about them, what would happen?"

"Are you saying you would tell them?"

"Never. You can trust me with that secret, but you owe it to your children and your children's children to make this land safe for magicals. You owe it to yourself, before it kills you. Imagine, Majesty, how it might feel to be persecuted for your magic, to be the subject of inhuman experiments. Imagine if your own children were taken forcibly and kept in an iron cage, subject to cruel treatment until they performed magic to order."

"My children will be left out of this."

He spoke so fiercely that I wondered which of his children had demonstrated magical tendencies. They were all over the age of eighteen, and none of them, to my knowledge, had registered with the Mysterium.

"Please think on it, Majesty, and take action."

"Papa? Did you catch the horse? Are you in there?"

I wheeled Dancer alongside Timpani and touched his sides with my heels. He sprang forward, twisting through the trees. We galloped toward the boundary, making the leap to freedom together.

◆━━━◆

As we leaped the wall and ditches, I heard the king's voice yelling, "Intruders. After them. Stop them. Quickly."

We galloped flat out, not bothering to hide ourselves in the trees of the Long Walk, racing for the forest, though neither of us liked it that our fastest way back lay through that haunted place. I turned and looked behind. A number of servants and equerries had come running out. Behind them, half a dozen uniformed riders set their horses into a gallop, chasing us. We had a good head start, but we'd have to slow when we reached the trees. Whatever was in there didn't like us.

Of course, it might not like our pursuers either.

A shot rang out. We had enough of a head start that we were out of range of pistols and only a very lucky shot from a musket could find its target, but if any of those servants on the ground had rifles and could take careful aim, they might be able to hit us. I crouched low and looked back over my shoulder. Dammit, I couldn't tell, but a puff of smoke and a loud crack told me the worst.

"They've got at least one rifleman. Sharpshooter."

We began to weave from side to side to make a more erratic target.

"That wasn't the best meeting we could have hoped for," Corwen said through gritted teeth, and he dropped behind to get between me and the line of fire.

"Don't be an idiot, get up here," I yelled. "Now is not the time to be gallant."

"You go. Fast as you can."

"Not without you."

"I'm right behind you."

We veered to the right and crossed the double bank of trees into the Long Walk to put the trees between us and their sharpshooter, but another half dozen riders were galloping up the Long Walk. At least they wouldn't be able to shoot accurately from horseback. I turned to Corwen only to see his face pale and a spreading stain of dark blood high up on the left breast of his coat.

"Corwen! Why didn't you say?"

"How would it have made a difference?" He coughed, and blood trickled from the corner of his mouth. "Ride, damn you, Ross."

I slapped Timpani across the rump with my hand. "Fast and smooth, boy. Take him home."

I wheeled around and pulled my pistol out of the saddle holster, took a steadying breath, pulled back the doghead, and squeezed off a shot in the direction of our followers. I had no chance of hitting anyone from this distance, but I hoped it might slow them a little if they thought us armed. I clamped my heels to Dancer's flanks and raced to catch up with Timpani and his precious burden. Our Fae horses were fast enough to outpace those behind, but we couldn't lose them altogether until we reached the forest.

We veered left across the foot of Snowden Hill, heading for the thick bank of trees. The feeling of dread that had pervaded the forest rolled toward us like a wave. Our only hope was to find the gate quickly, but I wasn't familiar with this wood, and Corwen was our gate finder.

We crashed through the dense undergrowth at the edge of the forest, to where the lack of light kept the forest floor clear of growth. Last year's leaves carpeted the spaces between the trees. Though the canopy was nothing but bare branches, it still seemed to cut out the daylight as much as fully leaved trees would have done—unless something else was causing the darkness. The horses slowed from a gallop to a canter and thence to a steady jog.

Corwen lay over Timpani's neck, bright blood streaking the gray's shoulder. I could see where the ball had entered to the side of Corwen's left shoulder blade. It had gone right through, doing its damage. He'd already be dead if he was heartshot, but from the blood on his mouth

and Corwen's wheezing, he was lungshot. This was bad.
If I could find him somewhere quiet to hide and he could
change to wolf and back, he could begin to heal, but this
could easily kill him before we found a refuge.

I heard the riders behind us, wading through the undergrowth. So they'd decided to brave the forest. Maybe
whatever it was that felt dark and dangerous to me didn't
affect them. I heard voices as they called to each other,
spreading out through the trees.

"Hold on," I said. "Timpani, find the gate. Go home.
Dancer, you, too."

I tried to close my mind to what was behind and seek
out what was ahead. I was getting better at finding the
gates, but I'd never had to do it entirely on my own, not
when it mattered so much.

A deep bass growl came from somewhere to my left,
and an answering one from the right. We were being
tracked by something. Could whatever it was be following
the smell of blood?

Corwen tried to sit up, but slumped back down, balanced across Timpani's neck. If he were to slide from the
saddle, I doubted I could get him back into it.

The growls came again. Then a shot rang out, splinter-
ing bark from the oak to my left. The bass growls rose to
an unearthly yowl. I still couldn't see anything, but there
was a shadow between us and the riders behind. I heard
one of them shout, "Who's there?" Answered by more
growls. The riders turned and fled.

The growl was closer behind now, but I sensed the gate
ahead.

"Can you hold on?" I asked Corwen.

In answer, he clicked his tongue, and Timpani sprang
forward into a smooth canter.

"Go." I gave Dancer his head and suddenly we were
galloping through the permanent summer of Iaru. I
hoped the thing couldn't follow. Timpani had slithered to
a halt and Corwen had rolled from his back into the
grassy floor.

"Corwen!"

He was trying to turn into a wolf, but his neck cloth would choke him. I flung myself out of the saddle and onto my knees by his side, pulling the knot loose and dragging his coat from his shoulders. His shirt was loose enough, I didn't need to worry about it, but I fumbled the buttons of the fall front on his breeches and dragged each boot off, one after the other. By the time I'd flung the last boot to one side, he was well into the change and paws poked out of his sleeve ends.

"That's it. Change. I'm with you."

He rumbled in his throat.

"I know," I said. "It hurts."

He rumbled again.

I held his paws. "Change back. Heal."

How many times had I done this with him? How many times could he take such an injury and recover completely? Surely it would take its toll eventually.

His paws stretched into fingers and his claws retracted into nails. "Yes, change again."

His snout flattened, and his silver-gray mane became hair.

"Hurts." Was all he managed before he closed his eyes and lapsed into sleep or unconsciousness, but I opened up his shirt and saw the wound on his chest had stopped bleeding.

"Rossalinde, Corwen, how delightful to see you in Iaru." The voice sounded anything but sincere.

I looked up. Dantin, the one Fae I knew was totally unsympathetic to humans loomed above me on horseback, a totally false smile on his lips which didn't reach his eyes.

"Dantin, we need help." I choked down the lump that threatened to cut off my voice. "Please."

A column of riders followed Dantin. One horse, black as a moonless night, detached itself from the column and drew level with Dantin's dark bay. Its rider, dressed in black to match her steed, was eerily perfect.

"What are these creatures?" a musically feminine voice, more contralto than soprano, asked.

I cranked my neck back and found myself looking into the most beautiful face I'd ever seen. Her skin was flawless cream without a hint of color in her cheeks, her eyes a penetrating blue fringed by dark lashes. Her raven hair framed a perfect heart-shaped face. She reached across and put her elegant hand on Dantin's forearm. He brushed his fingers across hers briefly before drawing his hand back.

"My Lady Calantha, nothing you need worry yourself about. My brother's pet humans."

Calantha. Was this the Fae princess David was supposed to marry? I hadn't realized the matter was so pressing.

"Father, would you like me to deal with this matter?" Margann, my Aunt Rosie's daughter, rode up on Dantin's other side.

Dantin gave a short sharp nod, then rode on without a backward glance. A column of ten riders, followed by another column of ten in a livery I didn't recognize, filed past us.

"I'm sorry, Ross." Margann dismounted and knelt by Corwen. "My father can be infuriating when he feels the need to keep up appearances, and Calantha is a princess, literally and figuratively. My father didn't want to be the one in charge of escorting her here, and he's making everyone suffer for his displeasure, except her ladyship, of course, with whom he seems to have something in common."

Margann's voice held little fondness for the princess.

"Is she the one David's been told he has to marry?"

"I'm afraid so."

"She looks a lot older than him."

"Not by much more than two centuries."

"Two centuries!"

"Shh, keep your voice down. It's not that much. In another hundred years no one will notice. Now, how can I help?"

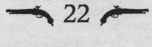

22

Iaru

CORWEN CHANGED BACK to wolf and then back to human, by which time the entry and exit wounds had scabbed over and he'd stopped bleeding from the mouth, but he'd lost a lot of blood and needed complete rest and plenty to drink.

"We should get him back to the Okewood where he can recover," I said, helping him into his breeches, but not bothering to tuck in his shirt.

"The glade is closer," Margann pushed back the lock of hair that had fallen over one eye. "Besides, I'm sure Larien will want to see you both. It looks as though your visit to the king did not go as planned."

"Threatening a monarch never does. I said all along that the Fae should have taken their own message."

She sighed. "My father and Larien disagree on this, but they'll come to an accommodation, I'm sure."

"Here, help me to sit Corwen up. We need to get him onto Timpani. Dantin and Larien never intended us to succeed, did they?"

"I'm sure if you had, it would have been the best solution, but, no, neither of them thought it would work, though Larien hoped it would. My father wanted to bring about a disaster, a great and unnatural storm that would make it clear from the very beginning that the Fae's power was not to be underestimated. Then he wanted to deliver an ultimatum from a position of strength."

She bent forward, and we slid our arms beneath Corwen. He groaned as we eased him into a sitting position, but he didn't fight us.

"And Larien?" I asked Margann.

"Said the humans deserved the opportunity to correct their mistakes without penalty, and that the Fae should not show their hand too soon."

I shook my head. "I'm not sure sending us to ambush the king and deliver a message unofficially was the best way. A king expects ceremony. The Fae could have provided that. He had no reason to trust us, and he didn't—as you can see."

"It's difficult for our people to enter human cities. The stench, the fumes, the dirt, the press of bodies . . . It makes us ill. London is the worst of them all."

"Larien came to Plymouth."

"It took months of purification afterward for him to recover. While he was there, it was all he could do to keep up the illusion of being rowankind. He wasn't able to use his power."

"He seduced my mother. Didn't he use a charm for that?" Did I want to think my mother had not taken him to her bed willingly?

Margann smiled. "That's not our way. If he bedded my aunt, she was willing, believe me. Now, move out of the way and let me lift Corwen up onto his horse."

Margann was no taller than me and slender as a willow, but she scooped up Corwen in her arms as if he were a child and lifted him into Timpani's saddle.

I raised one eyebrow. "You're stronger than you look."

She laughed. "Fae," she said.

We walked alongside Timpani, me on the left and Margann on the right, in case Corwen toppled sideways, but he wasn't that far gone. He managed to stay upright in the saddle. Dancer followed behind.

"I used to wonder"—Margann's voice came from the other side of Timpani, but I couldn't see her—"what it would be like to live in your world. Is it so very different from Iaru? I've only ever crossed over a couple of times."

"The cities are different, obviously, but the countryside is green and beautiful in summer. In winter the trees lose their leaves, the ground sparkles with frost in the mornings, and snow falls like a blanket. It looks lovely, but it's cold and makes travel difficult. Sometimes you have to cancel your journey and sit at home by the fire."

"It sounds cozy."

"Yes. If you have a home and a fire, it's very cozy, but the poor suffer dreadfully in winter."

"My mother taught me about money. We don't use it here."

"Those who have it want to keep it. Those who don't have it want to get it. Mostly, they work for it. Sometimes they beg or rob for it."

"It sounds like a terrible system."

"Yes, except I can't think of anything to replace it."

We arrived at the Fae grove. It was here, in the hall made from hundreds of stately trees meeting over our head, that I had called the magic out of the generations of Sumner children and had given it back to the rowankind.

Margann turned to lift Corwen down from Timpani, but he slithered down by himself, landing on his feet and staying upright by clinging onto the saddle.

"Over here." Annie waved to us from an alcove. "David says he'll come as soon as he can. He's been called to meet her." From the emphasis I knew Annie meant Calantha.

Margann and I walked Corwen slowly to the alcove which had a door of hanging vines, and actual furniture in it, though the design was somewhat fanciful. There was a bed with silken coverlets and a chair.

"I could sleep for a week," Corwen mumbled as he collapsed onto the bed. "Wake me when it's spring."

"You're in Iaru. It's never spring, always summer."

"Hmmm." He made a soft sound halfway between a groan and a sigh. "Wake me in time for Christmas."

And with that he was deeply asleep.

"It's the best thing for him," Margann said. "My mother taught me how to doctor humans. Said it might come in handy one day."

"Your mother's a wisewoman."

"She is, indeed, in more ways than one." Margann departed to attend her father.

Annie brought a meal for me, some kind of thick meaty soup with chunks of fresh bread. She brought broth for Corwen, and though he needed the fluid, I didn't want to wake him. I wasn't even sure I could.

"How are you doing, Annie?" I asked.

"I'm all right, Mrs. Rossalinde."

I sighed inwardly. She rarely called me Ross. Even though I'd asked her to a number of times, she soon slipped back into addressing me more formally.

"I mean . . . really. With David being pushed to marry the princess?"

"It's done." She sighed. "Dantin stood in for David in the court of the Merovingian Fae. They're wed by proxy."

"How can that be? There's got to be a way to undo it."

"Not without losing honor, and David won't let his father down."

A small tear escaped the corner of her eye, but she wiped it with her fingertip when she thought I wasn't looking.

"It's all very well David wanting to please Larien," I said, "but where was Larien when David was being brought up as a bondservant? Obligations go both ways."

She sniffed. "You know David—always trying to do what's right."

I nodded. That's what I liked about him. My late brother, Philip, had been exactly the opposite. Always doing what was best for himself.

"Don't worry, Annie. You know how he feels about you."

"I know it, but it doesn't make it any easier. Those Merovingian Fae have a dark reputation. They're French, you know." She might as well have said they eat babies. The French had been natural enemies of the English since the Normans had tried to unite the two countries and failed miserably. Annie came from Plymouth where the French were counted as bad as Satan and all the demons of Hell. She gave me a meaningful look, gathered up my bowl and spoon with a clatter, and left me to tend Corwen.

As I curled up on the empty side of the bed, with Corwen still deeply asleep, I worried over what I could do to help David and Annie, until I fell into a jumble of weird dreams, none of which I could remember in the morning.

❦

Corwen woke early, hungry, thirsty, and with a desperate need to empty his bladder. All his bodily functions seemed to be working, and there was no sign of infection around the wounds. The ball had passed through cleanly. Or maybe infection wouldn't dare to manifest in Iaru.

Annie and David brought breakfast for us and themselves. Corwen wolfed his porridge down in half the time it normally took him, and he didn't even like porridge that much. Bread and honey next. He ate his own and stared at mine until I broke it in two and gave him the larger piece.

Annie laughed. "I'll get more. I'm not used to feeding wolf-men."

"More for me, too, Annie, please." Well, I was eating for two, or possibly three.

"How are you?" I asked David. "Annie told me about the proxy."

"What's all this about?" Corwen asked.

"David got married while you slept, or, rather, Dantin got married for him and brought his bride home, but it's all right because she's only two hundred years older than he is."

Corwen hissed his disapproval. "Is she as unhappy about it as you are?"

"Calantha? I don't know." David sounded glum. "She's like an ice princess, cool and reserved. We've hardly said two words to each other. We were introduced. I kissed her hand, and that was it."

"Well, don't do more than that," Corwen said.

"What do you mea— Oh."

"Exactly. Once you bed the wench you've lost any argument. She's yours. You're hers."

"I'm not sure I could . . . I mean, she's so unapproachable. I couldn't imagine . . . you know."

"How about Annie?"

David blushed. "She's not unapproachable at all."

I'd forgotten how fast rowankind matured. I still thought of Annie as a child, but she was a young woman now.

"That wasn't what I was asking. I meant what's her status?"

"I don't know. I won't let the Ice Princess treat her like a servant, though."

"Good for you," Corwen said.

Annie returned with more breakfast, this time with cheese and salt pork as well as the bread and honey. We ate with relish. As if to prove what he'd said about Annie not being treated as a servant, David gathered up all our plates and utensils and carried them away with Annie following in his wake.

With a long morning stretching in front of us and, for once, nothing pressing, Corwen took the opportunity to change to wolf and back again, and then rested. I sat in the chair and took a notebook out of my pocket, my notebook this time, into which I'd copied some of the items from Aunt Rosie's that made most sense to me, plus some observations of my own. Some of the things I could do seemed random, but as I continued working, I started to see a thread linking them.

I was still learning about magic. Aunt Rosie's notebooks helped, but I knew I had to find my own way, so I was making my own book. Is this what Walsingham had done? He didn't have his own magic. He'd learned spell-craft, preparing spells in advance to use as weapons when he needed them. Twists of paper that became deadly in his hands. His notebook could be used by anyone skilled enough to decipher its code.

"What are you thinking?"

I hadn't noticed Corwen was awake and watching me.

"About notebooks and magic. About Walsingham."

"That's our next task."

"You need to recover from the damage this task has inflicted," I said. "The Fae could have made this so much easier. With their magic they could have isolated Frogmore House and spoken to the king themselves."

"I think they intend that when they do finally show themselves to humans, they do so in a grand manner and instill enough fear to get their own way instantly."

"A good guess and almost correct."

I jumped and dropped my notebook. Larien bent and picked it up, putting it into my hands.

Corwen swung his legs off the bed, meeting Larien sitting upright. It said a lot about his injury that he was not immediately on his feet.

Larien conjured up another chair out of nowhere and sat facing us both.

"I'm sorry for your hurt," he said to Corwen. "Your king's retinue must be . . . what's your term? Trigger-happy."

"It only takes one sharpshooter with a rifle," I said. "One of the king's equerries, perhaps. They're often from the ranks of the military. The new rifles can be accurate to four hundred yards in the right hands."

"Lucky the ball found its mark in your flesh, wolf-man."

"Exactly what I was thinking," Corwen grimaced. "Though lucky is not the word I'd choose in this instance, but better the shot found me rather than Ross."

"Then we agree."

That obviously ended the matter for Larien. Discussion over.

"So what do you intend next?" I asked.

"Dantin has a plan."

"I'm not sure I like the sound of that. Dantin despises humans. He won't mind if a few die. Hell, he won't mind if a few thousand die. I can't let that happen."

Larien looked at me as if he knew what I'd said was ridiculous. How could one human prevent the Fae from doing exactly as they liked? He had a point, but I wasn't ready to give up.

"Give us another chance, Larien. Let us talk to the king again."

I saw Corwen start to open his mouth to say something, and immediately felt guilty. What was I thinking? He'd almost died. I hadn't asked him if he'd be willing to try again.

"But this time with a little more help," I said. "Fae help."

I tried not to look at Corwen. He needn't come with me.

Corwen leaned forward and put his hand on my arm. "Give her what she wants, Larien," he said.

"And give us David," I said. "He can help to get us a safe audience with the king."

Larien frowned.

"And it will keep him away from his new wife for a little longer and give him a breathing space. Larien, how could you do that to your own son?"

I didn't really expect an answer to the last question. I hadn't meant to mention the marriage, but it slipped out. In the grand scheme of things, one unhappy Fae wasn't important when measured alongside Dantin bringing about some unnatural disaster in the human world.

"The Fae seem powerful to you, and, indeed, we are, but we are not gods. If we move to show the British people what we can do, and perhaps to subdue them, we would be as well to have allies across the channel. The Merovingian Fae have not always looked kindly on those of us from Albion and, in our turn, we have not always looked kindly upon them. They do things differently there. They've not secreted themselves away quite so fully as we have. I believe they even advise Bonaparte on occasions, but they tend to be dark."

"Do you mean they use dark magic?"

"Let's say they are in tune with the darker side of nature."

"I didn't even know there were Fae in France until the matter of David's bride came up."

He laughed.

Why had I never considered it?

"There are Fae everywhere, though we don't make ourselves known very often. Over a thousand years ago, the Merovingian Fae allied themselves with a dynasty that governed the territory now known as France and the low countries. The Merovingians ruled for three hundred years, thanks to the Fae."

"Does Iaru stretch all around the globe?"

"It has different names. Here it's sometimes called Orbisalius, the otherworld. In France it becomes Le Pays Enchanté, the enchanted country. In Ireland it's the Summer Country or Tir na nÓg." He raised one shoulder in a slight shrug. "The Merovingian Fae have, at last, been brought to negotiations and the promise of an alliance."

"Out of all your people, wasn't there someone else suitable? Why did it have to be David?"

"He's my son."

"Does that mean he's not allowed to decide for himself who to marry and where to love?"

"He can love whomever he pleases."

"But not marry?"

"We must all make sacrifices."

"Who has made the sacrifice here, and who has been sacrificed? Can this be undone?"

"Not without losing the alliance."

The matter seemed closed to Larien, but it wasn't closed to me.

Corwen nudged me to remind me Larien had not come to talk about marriage, and said, "Will you let David come with us when we next try to persuade the king to your plan?"

"You think he can make a difference?" Larien asked.

"I know he can," I said. "Besides, if nothing else, he can erect a barrier between us and the king's protectors."

Larien nodded. "Then he can come with you, but he's not to reveal himself as Fae."

I nodded. "I want one more favor."

Larien sighed softly as if he was making a show of disapproval for the sake of it.

"You said there are Fae everywhere."

"That's true."

"Can you talk to them? Pass messages, write letters, or whatever you do?"

"It's not impossible."

"I know you don't really want to wipe out humans, Larien. Dantin might, but you don't."

He tilted his head to one side, thus inviting me to continue.

"When we rescued the magicals and the rowankind from the *Guillaume Tell*, there was an old enemy on board—Walsingham. We left him to the French to imprison, but the peace means he's been released. Even blind and crippled, he's dangerous. He uses dark spellcasting to suppress natural magic."

Larien's mouth turned down when I mentioned spellcasting. It wasn't considered real magic by the Fae, but it got real results.

"Walsingham's spells were written in a notebook. We think—we hope—it was destroyed, but Aunt Rosie fears it may not have been. She has a . . . feeling."

"Rosie has proved remarkably prescient in the past." Larien didn't elaborate. "I wouldn't ignore her warnings."

"Were it not for this business with the king on your behalf, we'd already be sailing for the Caribbean, but Aunt Rosie's premonitions don't extend to where we might begin our search. If the notebook still exists, it seems likely it's passed through the hands of a pirate captain called Nicholas Thompson, otherwise known as Old Nick. Maybe he still has it in his possession. It would be a bad combination if he were to gain access to any of its secrets."

"So what do you want me to do?"

"I want you to talk to the Fae in the Caribbean, in Baccalao and along the coast of the Americas to find out whether they've observed anything unusual, magically, that is, and perhaps if any of them have had sight of Old Nick's ship, the *Flamingo*."

"I'll see what I can do. No promises, though."

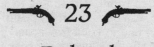

23

Roland

AFTER OUR INTRUSION at Windsor, the king would be surrounded by guards everywhere he went. It was going to be much more difficult to get close to him a second time.

"I'm beginning to think your crazy idea about approaching the king while he's taking a saltwater cure might not be such a bad idea," Corwen said.

We'd been back in the Okewood for four days already, during which time Corwen had recovered completely. Even his scars had faded.

Freddie was still isolating himself. We were hoping for a letter from Roland. A visit might snap Freddie out of his melancholy state, but we were worried that a letter would arrive while we were gone. If the goblins sent word that the king was out and about again, we might have to leave at any time.

We were on tenterhooks, waiting for either one thing or the other and hoping for both . . . but not together.

Neither Corwen nor I were good at waiting. We'd taken to training with sword and pistol each morning, and each afternoon I studied Aunt Rosie's notebooks and continued to compile one of my own.

Then, instead of a letter, Aileen Reynard came with a message.

"Da says please come quick. There's a gent pacing the floor of the coffee room, demanding to see you or Mr. Freddie, and he won't be put off." The girl's sharp vixen features were set in a worried frown, and her ginger hair had escaped the ribbon which tied it back.

"Did he give you a name?" Corwen asked.

"He said Essleborough, and we'd better fetch you quick or there'd be consequences."

"Did he say what it was about?"

"Said it was none of our business."

"Did he have men with him?"

"Not that we saw."

"Go back and tell him I'm on my way," Corwen said.

"Tell him we're on our way," I said.

Corwen glared at me and then nodded.

The fox-girl scurried away while Corwen turned to whistle up Timpani and Dancer. I was dressed in breeches from our morning of sword play, and rather than delay, I grabbed my hat and pulled it down over my head before saddling Dancer and mounting.

We made good time. I doubt we were many minutes behind the fox-girl as we rode into Buckfastleigh. The Valiant Soldier was a squat inn set a little back from its neighboring house and painted creamy white. A rangy brown gelding was tied to one of the rings in the front wall. He had mud up his legs and dried sweat on his neck.

"Our visitor, do you think?" I asked.

"Could be."

The horse pricked up his ears whinnied and as we approached. Dancer responded with a whicker. We needn't tie up our two, but we did for appearances. Aileen Reynard came to meet us on the doorstep.

"He's inside. Da's persuaded him to a glass of port, but he seems anxious."

"Still alone, is he?" I asked.

She nodded. "He's in the coffee room, on your left. Father has kept it private, so you won't be disturbed."

"Thanks, Aileen." Corwen pressed a shilling into her hand. "We appreciate your trouble."

"Thank 'ee, sir." She went ahead of us into the passageway, and we lost sight of her as we turned left.

Our visitor leaped to his feet as we entered the dark, wood-paneled coffee room. His clothes were good, but mud-spattered as if he'd ridden fast and hard. "You're Freddie's brother. I can see the resemblance," he said. "Where's Freddie?"

"Who wants to know?" Corwen advanced cautiously.

"I'm sorry, I forget my manners. Roland Somerton, Viscount Essleborough, at your service, sir."

"Oh, you're Freddie's Roland?" I said.

"I am, indeed, Freddie's Roland." His face, which had been a mask of worry, crinkled into smiles. "Forgive my appearance. I took the mail coach to Exeter and hired a hack from there. The roads are muddy."

Corwen introduced me as Ross Deverell, and I saw Lord Essleborough put two and two together. "Forgive me for staring, Mr. Deverell. Only, it's not mister, is it?"

"It's not," I shrugged, "though I would appreciate it if you didn't say that too loudly."

He lowered his voice. "Are you a wolf, too?"

That answered our unasked question, Roland knew about Freddie, and likely knew about Corwen as well.

"No, I'm not."

"Ah, I thought . . . "

"I'm a witch."

Lord Essleborough stiffened and stepped back.

I gave him my best smile. "Don't worry, I haven't turned anyone into a frog for the longest time."

His eyes widened, and then he got the joke and laughed. "I'm sorry. I don't know why I should be worried about a witch when my friend turns into a wolf."

"He does," Corwen said, "and he has. He's had a somewhat difficult time since you last saw him."

"So I gathered from your letter. What happened?"

"Not here," Corwen looked over his shoulder. "The landlord has reason to be an ally, but this business is private."

"Tell me as we ride. You are taking me to see him, aren't you?"

"Of course, though there are things I should warn you about first."

Roland left a half-guinea on the table and followed us out. He eyed Dancer and Timpani and nodded to his gelding. "I hope we can keep up. I pushed my horse hard to get here."

"We have about seven miles to go. Mr. Reynard can probably hire you a fresh horse." Corwen went back to the inn door and called for Aileen, who skipped off to the back of the inn to alert the ostler that we needed a fresh riding horse and stable space and feed for Lord Essleborough's hack.

Newly mounted on a serviceable bay cob with a docked tail and hogged mane, Lord Essleborough followed us, single file, along a narrow track that led to the Okewood.

Buckfastleigh is on the very edge of the Okewood. There aren't so many stories about hauntings in this part of the forest, and the villagers don't fear going out to gather kindling and blackberries. Maybe because the old abbey, largely ruined down to its foundations since the monasteries were turned over to the Crown, had stood here for centuries and still cast a long shadow.

We rode in silence until the village dropped away behind us and the forest—which is never totally silent—closed in about us. The trees were set wide enough apart for us to ride three abreast. Corwen and I put Lord Essleborough between us.

"Tell me everything," he said.

Corwen shook his head. "There's a lot to take in, and some of it's not ours to tell. How about you tell us what Freddie's already told you, and we'll take it from there."

"That's fair," Lord Essleborough said. "Freddie and I parted badly. Did he tell you?"

"I gather so," Corwen said. "I think that's what started Freddie off on a self-destructive path."

"Oh, please don't say that. I mean, I hope I wasn't to blame."

"I think there's only one person who takes responsibility for Freddie, and that's Freddie himself," I said.

"I understand. He can be quite stubborn." Lord Essleborough swallowed hard. "We met at Oxford and became firm friends."

"If it helps," I said, "we know what kind of firm friends you are."

"And you aren't . . . you don't . . . "

Corwen reined in Timpani. "Lord Essleborough, my brother is a wolf shapechanger. He's got bigger things to worry about than his romantic preferences. For years he tried to hide it from his family, but we all knew, even my mother in the end, though she never spoke of it. She has, however, stopped trying to find suitable unmarried young ladies for him. Though, of course, since he turned into a wolf, marrying him off to some poor unsuspecting virgin would be cruel in the extreme. To the young lady, I mean."

Lord Essleborough huffed out a breath. "If it helps, I love your brother, and I do believe he loves me, even though we argued."

"What did you argue about?" I asked.

"My father, or rather my father's wishes. And marriage. I'm an only child, and my father was keen to have another generation to secure the succession after his death. I'd been summoned to Loriston, our family estate on the edge of the Forest of Dean, to meet a pair of second cousins. I knew what my father had in mind. Their older sister already had five children, so there seemed every likelihood that either one of them would prove fecund. That's all my father was interested in, you understand. I'd determined to go and refuse, once and for all, to be bullied into marriage, but Freddie begged me not to go. He said once there I'd be obliged to fall in with my father's plans."

"That sounds like Freddie's understanding of how a father-son relationship works," Corwen said. "Our own father, until his apoplectic fit, was a hard man to say no to. Though it was always our mother who hatched marriage plans for us."

"My mother died in childbirth when I was eleven years old, and the baby, a daughter, along with her. My father never remarried."

"So you argued about a visit to Gloucestershire," I prompted.

"We did. As it turned out, we needn't have. My father was ill. I didn't realize how ill. I arrived in time to say good-bye. My second cousins had already been packed off home. I can make my own rules now I've come into my inheritance. I'm a wealthy man. I wrote to Freddie to come to Loriston, but he never replied. I thought he was still upset with me. There was a lot of business to take care of. By the time I surfaced from the paperwork and took a trip to London, Freddie had gone from his lodgings."

"What do you know about his wolf?" Corwen asked.

"I was there the first time he changed, and it nearly terrified the life out of me. A hard and brutal thing it was, too. He knew what was happening to him. Before he entirely lost his power of speech, he told me it was a family affliction and asked me to stay with him until he was restored to a man again."

"And you did," I said.

"I did. Not without trepidation. In fact, I was terrified at first."

"But you stayed with him afterward," I asked.

"Love is not love which alters when it alteration finds."

"Well said, Lord Essleborough." I was beginning to like Freddie's lover.

Satisfied that Lord Essleborough knew about Freddie and his own shapechanging, but probably not Lily, and not anything else regarding the state of magic in the kingdom, Corwen began his tale. "After you and Freddie parted on bad terms, Freddie went running across Hampstead Heath. He must have done it several nights in a row and always the same route, because one night the Mysterium was waiting for him."

Lord Essleborough drew in a sharp breath.

"You know, of course, our eldest brother Jonathan died of a burst appendix some seventeen months ago, and our father had an apoplectic seizure at Jonathan's funeral which rendered him unable to move or speak."

"I knew that, yes. Is your father . . . "

"He passed away last December."

"I am so very sorry to hear it."

"Thank you. He was ready to go, trapped inside his own body, a far cry from the vital man he used to be." Corwen took a deep breath. "I knew nothing of Jonathan's death and Father's apoplexy until my sister, Lily, took it upon herself to write in the spring of last year. We, Ross and I, went back to Yorkshire immediately, but Freddie, who should have been taking over the business and the estate, had gone to London—run off to evade his new responsibilities, we all thought—and was not answering correspondence. Ross and I followed him to London, and, like you, found him gone from his lodging. We learned from an acquaintance that a brown wolf had been seen on Hampstead Heath."

The goblins had told us, but Corwen carefully didn't mention them.

"I followed Freddie's trail," Corwen continued. "My change is neither as slow nor as painful as Freddie's, so it made much more sense to use my nose for the hunt. Unfortunately, I was also captured by the Mysterium. Eventually, I was shipped off to sea in what amounted to a prison ship, the *Guillaume Tell*. They already had Freddie there."

"Oh, God! Freddie's terrified of water."

Corwen nodded. "He is. It didn't help. Freddie had kept his wolf form for weeks to hide his identity and protect the family. They thought him a werewolf. Even when he recognized me, he stayed a wolf. If they'd realized we were brothers, our whole family would have come under suspicion."

I picked up the story. "Through the diligence of some friends . . . " I didn't mention goblins either. "I was able to follow. I should explain that I am a ship owner, and my ship happened to be in port, and my crew ready to sail. We caught up with the *Guillaume Tell*. I led a boarding party to rescue Corwen and Freddie. To our surprise we found others imprisoned there. Witches and rowankind."

"Rowankind?"

"When they were freed, their natural magic returned to them," Corwen said.

I nodded. "The Mysterium was trying to discover if their magic could be used in any way. I believe they wanted to use their wind and water affinity on the Royal Navy's behalf, but rowankind get sick on the sea. Some of them died of it before we got there, but we freed a great many."

"Hold on . . . " He turned to me. "You mean you pursued a Navy ship, boarded it, and snatched prisoners away from the Mysterium?"

I raised one eyebrow. "I didn't say it was easy."

"It wasn't easy at all," Corwen said. "The head of the Mysterium countered our rescue attempt with dark magic." Corwen glanced sideways at Lord Essleborough. "Yes, the Mysterium is not above making use of the kind of magic it would hang anyone else for."

"He attacked me with magic," I said. "Freddie came to my rescue. He killed him. Tore out his throat."

Maybe Lord Essleborough was reconsidering wanting to see Freddie.

Corwen continued. "Since then, he's become more uncertain of temper. He's killed twice, and attacked our mother, though luckily only her hands. There have been a couple of near misses, though." I didn't mention the sprite.

"We would understand if you want to turn around and leave the forest and never think of Freddie again," I said. "We won't think less of you for it."

There was an ominous silence before Lord Essleborough drew a deep breath. "I understand, but it sounds as though Freddie needs me now more than ever. Take me to him, please. Let's not waste any more time."

❖————❖

As we entered the glade which was the heart of our small woodland community, I glanced at Lord Essleborough to see if I could gauge what he was thinking. I wondered what it looked like to his eyes. I could see rowankind and sprites going about the business of preparing food for the evening meal. I waved to Charlotte, and she waved back.

I suspected that to Lord Essleborough it looked like a Romany encampment without the wagons. A lord might not take too kindly to being brought into company with traveling folk. He gazed around him, but his expression didn't give away his thoughts.

"You live here?" he asked.

"Visiting." I answered. "We have business. We're waiting for a message, and then we'll probably have to leave for a time."

"To Yorkshire?"

"Sadly not," Corwen said. "Our family is safer if we absent ourselves."

"I understand."

"Come. My brother is this way."

Corwen led the way down to the stream, across on a row of stepping stones and scanned the hillside. Freddie's enclosure was surrounded by an invisible fence, a barrier Freddie couldn't cross without permission, though we could enter as long as we did so between two small piles of loose stones.

"Freddie," Corwen called.

Freddie appeared at the top of the valley side, paused for an instant, tasted the air, and then began to run down the steep slope. Halfway down, he hit a speed faster than his legs could carry him. He rolled, scrabbled to his feet, and rolled again, finally coming to a halt twenty yards distant.

He dropped to his belly and squirmed the rest of the way until Lord Essleborough knelt and put his arms around the dusty wolf.

"Why doesn't he change?" Lord Essleborough asked.

"Because he needs my permission to do so." The Lady was suddenly standing behind us. "I think it's time."

"Thank you," Corwen said.

She inclined her head and left as quietly as she'd come.

The change was on Freddie, but it wasn't going to be easy. Skin showed through his coat which now looked like the worst case of mange I'd ever seen. His nose had begun to retract but seemed to have gotten stuck somewhere between wolf and human. He let out a howl of pain. Fingers poked through the hair surrounding his front feet, but only on one hand, the other remained stubbornly clawed. There was a sickening crunch as the bones in his back legs stretched and twisted, his lower legs shortening to form human feet. Then with another howl, Freddie began to turn back into a full wolf. Had he found the transition too hard?

Corwen went down on his knees and grasped Freddie's half-changed face in his hands. "This is your chance. You can do it, Freddie. You're almost there. Don't give up."

Freddie whined, but his nose retracted further, and his eyes began to look human.

"Let me," Roland said quietly, and Corwen moved aside. Roland looked deep into Freddie's eyes and then planted a kiss on his forehead.

Freddie whined, and I thought the speed of his change began to accelerate. There was more skin now and less wolf pelt. Even so, it took a long time for the change to complete. When it had, Freddie lay gasping. Roland sat by him, one hand on his shoulder. He kept up a string of reassuring words. "I'm here. Here to stay. We can be together. Forever."

He looked up at us. "Can he come with me to Gloucestershire?"

"As long as he's safe and people are safe from him."

"I'll look after him. Guard him, protect him. Whatever is needed."

"You're taking on a lot," Corwen said.

"I have the resources. Whatever Freddie needs, he shall have."

Freddie groaned and rolled to his knees. "I thought you'd gone."

"I'm back now."

The two of them leaned in and clung to each other as if their lives depended on it.

Corwen had a smile on his face as broad as the River Thames.

"Is this what you hoped for?" I asked.

"Hoped, yes. Didn't dare count on." He turned to Freddie. "When you've said your hellos, come back up to the bower."

We walked back up the hill, hand in hand, glad something seemed to be working out.

In the glade, Charlotte was still busy, but Livvy was skipping about here, there, and everywhere. "Mama says Freddie's special friend has arrived."

"Yes," Corwen said. "A very special friend."

"I shall go and say hello."

She turned toward the path, but Corwen caught her with one strong arm around her waist and swept her off her feet, then he swung her high in the air until she giggled. "Let them talk, little Livvy. They haven't seen each other for a long time, and they have a lot of catching up to do."

"Talk? Has Freddie changed?"

"He has."

"Oh." She sounded disappointed. To Livvy, Freddie would always be the big, hairy brown dog who had saved her from the bad men on the *Guillaume Tell*.

It was an hour before Freddie and Lord Essleborough came walking up the hill together. Freddie was wearing Lord Essleborough's shirt while Essleborough had his jacket on over his bare chest. They disengaged hands as they came into our camp. Freddie looked more animated than I'd ever seen him.

Corwen's gaze locked fleetingly with mine, conveying a mixture of satisfaction and hope.

"It's settled," Lord Essleborough said. "Freddie will come to Gloucestershire with me."

Corwen looked from one to the other and nodded. "Should you have any problems—"

"There'll be no problems, brother," Freddie said. "Or at least none we can't overcome. Roland knows me better than I know myself."

"I have dealt with this bad dog before when he's been out of sorts. I think I can do it again, though it may take time and patience." Lord Essleborough looked at Freddie, who nodded. There had been some plain speaking between them, I thought, and Freddie had made some promises. I hoped he would keep them.

"Will you write to Mother?" Corwen asked Freddie.

"I will."

"Maybe she can come and visit," Lord Essleborough said. "You can all come and visit together . . . When the time is right."

"That's very generous of you, Lord Essleborough," Corwen said.

"Please, if we are to be family, and I do believe we are, call me Roland."

"Freddie is my father's heir," Corwen said. "The estate and the mill are his now. There are responsibilities and decisions to be made."

"I leave all that in your capable hands, brother," Freddie said. "You know I never had a head for it. I want nothing from the estate."

"Legally—"

"When we get to Buckfastleigh, I will sign it all over to you."

"Freddie is my family now," Roland said. "I'll provide for him."

Freddie had found his partner for life.

"Just one thing before you go, Freddie," Corwen said.

"What?"

"Your valise is in the bower. Put some clothes on and give Roland his shirt back."

Freddie grinned at us and went to do just that.

It was both a sad and a happy occasion when we escorted Freddie and Roland back to the inn in Buckfastleigh.

Freddie was as good as his word. There was a lawyer in town, an elderly gentleman with rheumy eyes. Despite his somewhat shaky hand, he took Freddie's dictation, added the flowery words to make it legal, and had Roland and Mr. Reynard sign as witnesses.

"There, that should do the trick," Freddie said. "It's all Corwen's. Send it to the family's man of business in London. I'm done with Yorkshire."

Corwen took up more of the man's time and signed ownership of the mill over to Lily in her own right, so the two papers could be sent to London together.

We returned to the inn.

From Buckfastleigh, Freddie and Roland would ride to Plymouth. Rather than take the mail coach, which might put too much of a strain on Freddie's current state of mind, Roland intended to hire a post chaise to take them back to Gloucestershire.

"I'm glad to see you on two legs instead of four," I said to Freddie as he prepared to mount the hired hack.

"For once I'm glad of it, too," he said. "Thank you for my care, and I'm sorry if I did anything inappropriate. It's all a bit of a blur. I'll write, and to Livvy, too, care of Charlotte. I hope you can discover where the army has hidden Henry Purdy. It would be a shame for Livvy to lose her father."

"We'll do our best."

"Farewell, brother, for now at least," Corwen said and embraced Freddie. For once the gesture was returned. Maybe Freddie was recovering. We shook hands with Roland, and the two of them were on their way.

"Was that gentleman the wolf who nearly snapped my tail off?" Aileen Reynard had been watching from the inn doorway.

"He was."

"Don't look so dangerous now, do 'ee?"

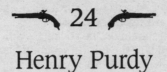 24

Henry Purdy

THOUGH WE'D TRIED all wc could think of, and set the goblins hunting for clues, in the end Henry Purdy saved himself by writing a letter.

His father brought it to the Okewood and placed it in our hands.

"It's taken eleven days to reach me," Reverend Purdy said. "Of course, he doesn't know we've moved. It went to the old parish and was only forwarded on by the kindness of Reverend Patterson. Read it. Read it."

Plymouth Citadel, 5th April

Dearest Father, My Beloved Charlotte, and Darling Olivia.

I am sending this by the kindness of Daniel Davy, a Devonian sergeant who owes me his life due to an illusion I created for him and his troops at Seringapatam.

I hope this finds you all well.

I have been shipped back to England on doctor's orders. India is not kind to weak stomachs. I have been ill with dysentery, and as the army has few witches, we are valued like good horses, but like good horses, kept close in our quarters. We are counted among the cattle rather than the troops as we have neither rank nor official position.

I long to see you all again and will do my utmost to make that happen should the opportunity arise.

Your loving
Henry

"He's in Plymouth," Reverend Purdy said. "So close."

"But in the Citadel," I said. "It's a fortress. Impregnable."

"From the outside," Corwen said. "It's not a prison."

"Have you seen it? Every time the *Heart* sailed under those guns, I felt as though I had a target painted between my shoulder blades. And the landward side has a drawbridge and a dry moat. Its walls are seventy feet high."

"We're not going to storm the walls," Corwen said. "The only way this can work is by stealth and illusion. It sounds as though Henry has some talent in that direction, himself."

He closed his eyes and drew in a deep breath. From the head down a change rippled through his body and he stood there, a perfect redcoat. His face was the same, but his hair was dark brown and his complexion florid, as if he was a heavy drinker. I'd seen him use illusion before, but not often. The Lady had endowed him with the ability when he first became one of her agents. This was as complete an illusion as I'd ever seen him make.

"Oh, perfect," Reverend Purdy said. "I have an idea. I think I can get us inside the fortress if you can find Henry when we get there. There's a chapel within the Citadel precincts, the Royal Chapel of St Katherine-upon-the-Hoe. I might be able to make a visit to the chaplain.

Would that help? I can't stand by and know my son is so close, and I did nothing to help him."

Corwen's illusion flickered and died. He frowned and changed again, but this time the illusion lasted for only a few seconds.

"Damnation!"

"What's wrong?"

"I'm out of practice. It's like any other skill; the more you do it, the easier it becomes."

"How long will it take you—"

He shook his head. "I don't know, but we can't go racing off tomorrow, that's for sure. Maybe if I work on it all day tomorrow, I'll be all right for the day after."

The reverend looked downcast. I could tell he was trying to put on a brave face. "Henry's waited eleven days. He can probably wait a little longer. It will take me a day or two to get an invitation from the chaplain in any case."

Later, when we were alone in our bower, I asked Corwen if two days was long enough for him to recover his power of illusion.

"I don't know. I'll work at it." And he did. He changed into a red-coated soldier again. "Time me."

I counted slowly, reaching a count of forty-seven before the illusion faded.

"Again," he said.

This time I only reached thirty-six.

"Two changes too close together takes too much power," I said. "Don't drain yourself. Wait half an hour and see if that's long enough."

He took out his pocket watch and set it on the bed between us.

Thirty minutes later he lasted for just over a minute.

"Better," he said. "But not good enough."

"How would it be if we stole a uniform and you only had to change your face?"

"That would certainly be easier, but we can't guarantee finding a uniform to steal."

"It's an option, though."

Corwen continued practicing throughout the evening

until his face was gray with tiredness and I persuaded him to stop. His best time so far was two minutes and ten seconds.

"Come to bed."

I'd slipped out of my clothes an hour ago but his determination to work on his redcoat illusion meant that he'd managed to ignore my most seductive pose, half in and half out of the quilt. It was time for direct action. I wriggled closer and put my hand across the front of his breeches. He gasped, and the redcoat soldier disappeared.

"That's better. I thought you'd never notice. It's time to get some sleep."

"I'm never going to get any sleep with you looking at me like that."

I chuckled. "Good."

"Ah, Ross, I'm not sure I can do this."

"What? Make love to me?"

"No, play the perfect redcoat."

"Oh, that." I shrugged. "You'll be better in the morning."

"Do you think so?" His voice dropped to a seductive purr as he nuzzled my neck.

"I know so." I turned my head to catch his lips with mine.

It was all the invitation he needed.

Later, curled in our springy heather bed, I lay in his arms. Our child, or children if Aunt Rosie was right, made me more cautious than I used to be.

I would have been more than happy to sit back and let someone else rescue Henry Purdy, but there was no one in our present company who could pick a lock.

Except me.

Damn.

The next day, and the day after, Corwen continued practicing until he'd increased his time to four and a half minutes.

"Do you think that's enough?" he asked.

"It will have to be."

So we rode over to the reverend's house and made our plans.

The following day dawned bright and sunny for the middle of April, truly springlike after a raw March. We drove through the town and up to Plymouth Citadel in Reverend Purdy's gig. The reverend had the reins, I was dressed as a country miss, or rather, at my age, a country spinster, supposedly his daughter. Corwen lay on the parcel shelf behind the gig, blocking access to the ventilated dog box beneath the seats. I hadn't known he could glamour the wolf as well as the human. He said it took more doing, so rather than a big change, he merely shifted one or two features. It was surprising what a flatter nose, drooped ears and a black patch on the side of his head did to change the silver wolf into a mongrel mutt, albeit a big one. I knew he couldn't keep up the disguise for long, but if he could do it to get in and out of the gates, it would be enough.

I disguised myself as best I could with flour drawn through my hair to create gray streaks. I patted too much rouge on my cheeks and donned a pair of metal-rimmed spectacles, bought a couple of years ago and endowed with magic to enable me to see in the dark. The magic had faded, so I managed to reverse the light spell to remove light from the lenses, creating slightly darkened glass to hide my eyes.

We drove across the Citadel's drawbridge and halted at the imposing baroque gatehouse. It stood twice as high as the walls and was built of Portland stone like the very best London mansions. Above its arch was the date 1670. I stared at the numbers and tried to slow my hammering heart. Reverend Purdy said he was here to see the garrison chaplain and when asked his business, said it was the Lord's. Good answer.

"Shouldn't you keep your dog in the dog box?" one of the guards asked.

"He doesn't like it," the reverend said. "Would you like to argue with him?"

Corwen raised his head and snarled to show his fangs. The guard backed off.

We were ushered through the gates with only the most

cursory of inspections thanks to Corwen's rumbling growl.

As directed, the reverend drove us through the main square of the fortress to the chapel, a small rectangular building with Gothic windows. We'd been told the chaplain was inside. He pulled up the gig close to the chapel wall to give us a shaded area behind which we could change. The docile, dock-tailed cob stretched his neck out and began to doze, lower lip dangling, relaxed.

"I'll discuss err . . . ecclesiastical matters while you two amuse yourselves," the reverend said. "Good luck."

I looked around from the vantage point the gig gave me. Solid star-shaped ramparts surrounded a large compound. I hadn't expected there to be so many separate buildings. Which one housed the barracks, or was there more than one? And was Henry Purdy in the barracks anyway? His letter had said confined to quarters. Hell, couldn't he have given us more of a clue? But of course, he hadn't guessed his mild-mannered father would mount a rescue attempt.

"Ideas, Corwen?" I asked, seeing the mutt resting on the back shelf of the gig now looked more like a big silver wolf with every passing second. He jerked his head into the air, nose first.

"All right. Let's see if your nose gives us a clue." The reverend had given us a pair of gloves that belonged to his son, and though the scent was old, Corwen's wolf nose was exceptionally keen.

Corwen renewed his mutt glamour and jumped down from the gig, bolting across the compound and then appearing to suddenly become interested in a scent.

"Hoy! Whose dog is this?" A red-coated and red-faced sergeant with a parade ground voice yelled to anyone who could hear him.

I held onto my bonnet with one hand and my skirts with the other and ran to Corwen. "I'm sorry, Sergeant Major (it was always good to give them a rank above the one they had). My father's visiting the chaplain, and Bowser here is normally so good. Come here, Bowser, bad boy!" I glared at Corwen who ignored me completely and lifted his leg against the wall. I turned a laugh into a choking sob. "Oh, Bowser, you'll get us into so much trouble." I batted my eyes at the sergeant.

"It's all right, miss. Dumb creatures are sometimes unpredictable."

"He probably smells a cat, Sergeant-Major. He's such a bad boy with cats."

Corwen sniffed at the sergeant's booted feet and then trailed a scent along the wall and sat down. He'd found something.

"Come here, Bowser."

Corwen trotted to my side and made a little whiny noise in the back of his throat. Yes, definitely found something, and he was getting to the end of his ability to maintain "Bowser."

"I'll take him back to the gig, Sergeant-Major, and give him a stern talking to."

"You do that, miss."

I touched my fingers to the lop-eared mongrel's head as we walked across the parade ground straight to the sheltered space between the gig and the chapel wall, whereupon Corwen let Bowser go and turned into the silver wolf I knew and loved.

"Well done. Do you need a moment?"

His tongue lolled out of his mouth, and he panted at me.

"Yes, of course you do. Better not make it a long moment, though. The sergeant has moved away and, for now, there's no one outside that building. You're sure that's where Henry is?"

He gave a little yip.

"Right. Time to join the army."

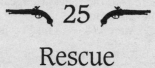

25

Rescue

THE SILVER WOLF reared back on his hind legs and became a naked man, who then became a military man dressed in a red jacket with three stripes on his sleeve and the florid sergeant's face.

"That's good," I said.

"I don't know how long I can keep it up for. Now you."

I took off my bonnet and tied the strings to one of the spindles of the gig seat, and in an instant I, too, looked like a redcoat, this time a younger, smaller one with no stripes to my sleeve.

"I can do something about the way you look, but I can't do anything about the way you walk," Corwen said. "Military bearing, now. Look sharp. We've got two minutes."

I snapped to attention and followed Corwen back across the compound to the stone building which seemed to be our best bet for finding Henry Purdy. At this time of day the barracks should be deserted, but you could never tell. The heavy door wasn't locked. We stepped inside. Corwen let the glamour drop as soon as the door closed behind us. I blinked in the sudden gloom.

The room was long and lined with narrow cots on each side, all neatly made up save for one, on which a soldier sat in his shirt sleeves, playing patience with a dog-eared pack of cards. At the far end of the room was a door.

Corwen ducked back into the shadows and turned himself once more into the redcoat sergeant. It would be a shorter illusion this time.

"Trooper!" Corwen barked in his best imitation of the sergeant's parade ground voice.

"Sir." The soldier leaped to attention scattering cards all over the floor.

"What are you doing in here?"

"Sick, sir."

Corwen's nose twitched. The trooper was probably telling the truth. "It's a fine day. Get outside and get some fresh air."

"But, sir—"

"What didn't you understand, trooper? Get outside, now!"

"Sir. Yes, sir."

I watched the trooper leave.

Corwen immediately let the illusion drop.

"Was he malingering?"

Corwen shook his head. "Got the French pox. I could smell it on him."

"What a boon you would be to the medical profession."

"Only if I could cure the conditions I can detect. Poor bastard. Might as well put a bullet in his brainpan for all the good mercury will do."

He paced down the room toward the door at the end, following his nose. The door was locked. I took my roll of picks out of my dimity pocket.

"Can you do it?" Corwen asked as I probed the lock, trying to get a feel for it.

"Give me a moment."

"We may not have a moment."

"I'm going as fast as I can."

I inserted a flat blade, much ground down, and applied

tension to slightly turn the barrel of the lock, then keeping the tension with my left hand I inserted a second pick, shoved it right to the back of the barrel and yanked it back, feeling the pins bounce. The barrel turned.

"There."

The bolt clicked back.

"You're a genius."

"Lazy Billy would have done it in half the time."

We opened the door cautiously and stepped through, closing it behind us. In front of us were three cells. Each had a heavy iron door with a tiny grill in it at face height, and a wide slot at the bottom big enough for a plate and a taller slot big enough for a jug.

The whole place stank of shit.

Corwen went to the first door. "Henry Purdy?"

"Who wants to know?" The voice had a distinct Scottish twang. Not Henry Purdy.

"Henry Purdy?" Corwen asked again at the second door.

"Next door," the voice said. "If he still lives."

My heart began to race. Had we come through the most heavily fortified fortress in Devon to find a corpse?

"Henry Purdy?" Corwen asked at the third door.

"He's in here," came the reply.

"We've come to take him home."

"Is he sick?" I asked.

"Weak from sickness. I think he's over the worst."

"Can he walk?" Corwen slid back the small trap-door over the grill.

"Barely."

"I can walk," a weak voice said. "If it means getting out of this stinking hole, I can walk."

"Who here is a witch?" I asked.

"All of us except for Angus at the far end," the man sharing a cell with Henry said.

"Nay. Dinna listen to him, lassie. Ahm a witch."

"He's a rapist and a murderer and goes before a firing squad in the morning," the man said.

"If you're all witches, why haven't you broken out?"

"Cold iron. Have you seen these doors?"

Cold iron had never worried me, but I know it affected some magicals more than others. I bent to the lock. "Damn, it's a lever tumbler."

"Can you pick it?" Corwen asked.

"Yes, but it will take longer. Keep a look out."

I bent to the lock and inserted a narrow wrench to apply pressure to the bolt, then I slipped in a finer pick and started feeling for the levers. I had to lift them one at a time until they caught on the bolt's post. Delicate work, and time consuming. This time Corwen didn't interrupt me. I don't know how many minutes passed until I heard the first click.

"Ha!" I breathed.

"Done it?"

"Not yet. Getting there."

The next lever was easier now I had the hang of it. Then the third, but the door still didn't move. "Please don't tell me it has six levers," I mumbled to myself.

The fourth lever clicked for me. "That's it."

Corwen drew back the two heavy bolts on the top and bottom of the door. He dragged it open and coughed at the stench of the open slop bucket.

"Sorry," the voice said. "Pleased to meet you, even though you're a little underdressed. I'm Robert Salt and this is your man, Henry."

"I'm saving the glamour for when I really need it," Corwen said.

I peeped round Corwen's back. Henry Purdy was barely one degree better than a corpse, stick thin and pale as paper, wearing a dirty shirt covered in unnameable stains.

I left Corwen to it. He was capable of getting Henry onto his feet, and I had another door to unlock. I pulled back the slider over the grid, and a brown face stared at me from the other side.

"You're the witch?" I asked.

"Samuel Aloysius Bannerjee at your service, madam."

His face might look Hindoo, but his accent was that of an English gentleman.

"Ahm the witch, lady. My door next," the Scottish voice from the third cell roared out at me.

"Don't believe it, madam. Sammy's your man." Mr. Salt stuck his head round the door. "What o'clock is it?"

"It wants fifteen minutes to noon," Corwen said from inside the cell with Henry.

"Then we must hurry," Mr. Salt said. "They bring us food, such as it is, at noon."

"Leave me," Mr. Bannerjee said. "You're running out of time."

"Not if I can help it." I selected another pick and applied heavy pressure to the bolt, sufficient to stretch all the levers and hold them in place, then I released the pressure gradually, dropping the levers onto the post.

"Whew. That doesn't always work," I said as I drew the bolts on Mr. Bannerjee's door. "Are you alone?"

"I am, and I regret not being fit company, but I am most grateful for the assistance."

"How are we going to do this?" Mr. Salt asked.

"We came in glamoured as a sergeant and a private soldier," Corwen said, "but illusion is not my strength. I'm not even sure I can get us both back across the compound."

"Can you two hold a glamour?" I asked Mr. Salt and Mr. Bannerjee.

"Yes, no problem," Mr. Salt said, and Mr. Bannerjee nodded.

"Corwen, I can make us invisible," I said. "But I can't hold it for long, and I'm likely to need to sleep for a week afterward. You're going to have to get me and Henry across to the gig. If I can put one foot in front of the other, that's all I'll be able to manage."

"I can walk," Henry said, sounding as though he could barely talk.

"I'm sorry, you're on your own from here," Corwen said to Salt and Bannerjee. "We have a space in the gig for Henry, but it's only a dog box. We can't take you two as well."

"You've done us a great service," Mr. Bannerjee bowed. "We can manage from here now there's no cold iron in our way. We have a place we can go. And I think we can help you both to get back to your gig."

We closed and bolted the doors behind us. Corwen half-carried Henry through the barracks room to the door.

"Right. Here we go," I said.

I'd always been able to do this, but I paid such a price for it afterward, that the very idea of it chilled me to the bone. The last time I'd used it I'd fallen unconscious in Hookey's arms and woken up some days later aboard the *Heart*.

Corwen had one shoulder shoved under Henry Purdy's armpit and his right arm around his waist. I slipped my hand into his left and concentrated. The three of us left the building cloaked in invisibility. Corwen was naked. All the glamour in the world didn't make real clothes, but at least he'd be able to change into a wolf instantly if he needed to. All we had to do was cross to the gig soundlessly and without bumping into anyone.

Mr. Bannerjee boosted my invisibility spell.

"Thank you," I said. "Good luck, gentlemen." We set out across the yard with Henry Purdy between us.

Unfortunately, a squad of redcoats had recently been dismissed, and were walking toward us, or rather toward their barracks, some singly, some in groups of two and three, joking and laughing. Corwen staggered right to miss one of the larger groups, and then had to quickly weave left to avoid a soldier walking alone. That took us right into the path of two more soldiers and though Corwen scooted us farther to the right, one of them stumbled over my foot and measured his length on the cobbles.

"What did you do that for?" he said.

"I didn't do nuffink. Must 'ave tripped over yer own lazy arse feet," His pal responded, but stopped to give him a hand up.

"You pushed me." He pushed the other soldier with the flat of his hand.

"Didn't." The second soldier pushed back.

"Did." Push.

"Didn't." Push.

Then they both burst into laughter and continued on their way.

We staggered on. Even with Mr. Bannerjee's help, my feet were definitely out of control. Corwen let go of my hand and put his arm around my waist. I wasn't sure how he managed to get both of us to the gig, but he did. He left me hanging onto the wheel while he bundled Henry into the ventilated dog box beneath the seats. It was big enough to carry two retrievers to and from a shoot. It was a tight fit for a man, but Henry wasn't in any position to argue.

I heard voices inside the chapel. One was Reverend Purdy. I assumed the other was the garrison chaplain. It sounded as though he was escorting the reverend to the door and still chatting about his time serving in India.

I dropped the invisibility. Corwen boosted me into the gig where I sat swaying until I realized I could lean against the spindle back.

The chapel door handle rattled, and the door began to open. I could hear Reverend Purdy quite clearly now, saying, "Oh, good heavens, don't let me interrupt your day any more than I have already. I can see myself out."

"Nonsense, it's no trouble at all. Besides, I'd like to pay my respects to your daughter."

Corwen changed into a wolf and jumped up onto the parcel shelf. I hoped he had enough energy to glamour himself into a mutt again.

Good timing.

The chapel door opened, and Reverend Purdy turned in the doorway to make one more effort to shed the company of the chaplain, but to no avail. In the end he had to introduce us.

"Emma, my dear, please allow me to introduce Captain Jarvis."

"Miss Purdy, delighted to make your acquaintance."

I wasn't sure I could speak without slurring, but I tried to sit up.

"Captain Jarvis." I nodded as prettily as I could, but just that small movement set my head spinning. "I'm sorry, Captain, you don't find me at my best. Papa, may we go home, now?"

"I'm sorry, Emma, I left you alone for too long." He turned to Jarvis. "My daughter's health is frail, sir. I thought the ride in the fresh air might cheer her up."

"Can I help? A drink of water, perhaps?"

I shook my head, leading to another bout of dizziness coming hard upon the first one.

"Thank you, but I should take her home." The reverend shook hands with the captain and climbed up onto the gig.

"I'm sorry to have kept you waiting, daughter," he said as he clicked at the cob and woke her up. She thrust herself into her collar, and the gig rolled forward.

"What's that smell?" Reverend Purdy asked in a quiet voice.

"Say it's the dog if anyone asks. He's been rolling in the midden again."

I heard Corwen growl softly behind me.

I managed to stay upright as we passed through the citadel gates, but as we drove through the town I heaved a great sigh of relief and let my head sink onto the reverend's shoulder.

"Wake me when we get to the Okewood," I said.

⋯⋯◆⋯⋯◆⋯⋯

Henry Purdy's arrival in the Okewood caused a stir. His family, though obviously pleased to see him, were shocked at his condition. Charlotte took charge and, with the reverend's help, got him washed and dressed in borrowed clothes until his own could be laundered. Personally, I thought they were beyond saving, but Charlotte knew best.

We only stopped for long enough to deliver him, and then Corwen picked me up and carried me to our bower. I felt the soft heather mattress beneath me and needed nothing else to fall into a deep sleep.

I awoke to find Corwen sitting next to me.

"How long was I out for this time?"

"Two days. I see why you don't do that very often. How are the babies?"

I immediately felt guilty for using so much magical energy. I put my hand on my belly. Everything felt all right down there.

"All right, I think. How's Henry?"

"Doing splendidly, thanks to the Lady's food and drink."

"The acorn cups and the might-be-mushroom-things?"

"Yes."

"They should do him a world of good. Small enough not to overtax his stomach, but completely satisfying."

"Glad you think so. She sent some for you. Said you need to keep your strength up now."

"Does everyone know I'm increasing?"

"They seem to."

"Oh, well, it saves making an announcement." I took the acorn cup from Corwen and the tiny might-be-a-mushroom, balanced on a leaf plate. It's difficult to eat slowly when you're famished, but I did my best. My stomach felt so much better.

"Ah, that's good. I think I'd like to lie down now."

"You need to sleep again?"

"I do." I put my hands on my stomach.

"You're sure everything's all right?"

"I think so, this time, but Aunt Rosie said not to spend myself magically."

"If there's even the slightest chance that it's harmful . . . "

"I know. I'll be careful."

"Take no more chances."

"What about talking to the king?"

"What about it? We've got David's help now. There should be no need to put yourself in danger."

"That's all right, then." I put my arms around his neck and pulled him down to the bed with me.

26

Weymouth

WITH FREDDIE GONE, life became much simpler. All we had to do was wait around for news from the goblins and be prepared to make haste to wherever our next likely meeting point might be. The weather, which had held mild if damp through the first half of April, turned against us in the third week. The Okewood was shrouded in hoarfrost, its fernlike ice crystals coating every tree and branch. It looked magical, but the magic faded when it nipped at toes and noses. The glade, thanks to the Lady's intervention, didn't freeze, but it was still cold and miserable. I began to think of excuses to visit David in Iaru.

Finally, word came from the goblins.

The king's doctors had recommended he be dipped, and the royal entourage was packing up to head to Gloucester Lodge in Weymouth, the king's own residence. Using the ways through Iaru, blessedly warm, we collected David and headed for the coast.

We left the hoarfrost behind. Weymouth Bay luxuriated in a bright blue sky and cool sunshine. We took lodgings in an unremarkable inn a few streets back from the sea on the north side of the harbor, not far from Customs House Quay. The town had become a fashionable holiday resort thanks to the king's patronage, though the season had not yet begun. I'd read about it in the *Gentleman's Magazine*. It was home to what was described as the giddy and the gay, the kind of place where the gouty peer and the genteel shopkeeper mingled on the beach, though possibly not in April.

The Dorset coast was a well-known danger area to sailors, however. Beyond Portland Harbor, the shifting shingle of Chesil Beach combined with the treacherous currents and undertow had made a graveyard for ships. Six years earlier several British Navy ships had been lost on the same day, and dockside taverns all across the country were rife with stories of over three hundred bodies strewn across the beaches, as the sea gave up her dead.

Corwen and I spent the whole of our first day walking around the town and the harbor to familiarize ourselves with the streets, seeing the Assembly Rooms and the Theater Royal. The only activity at the king's seaside home, Gloucester Lodge, a red brick house built sideways-on to the Esplanade, looked to be a bevy of servants opening up the house. There was a sizable garden, but after our experience at Windsor, approaching the king in his own garden was not a good idea.

Even this early in spring the bathing machines were lined up in the bay. That was where David headed. The king's bathing machine could be seen from a distance. It was hard to miss, painted red, white, and blue with a tall flagpole, and small, wide wheels to cope with the soft sand. It was still the talk of the town that when the king had come to bathe three years earlier, a band had followed his bathing machine to the water's edge, playing "God Save the King", and the bathing women who dipped him wore girdles with GSTK woven through the fabric.

I wondered where those bathing women might be found and how they were selected for the honor of dunking the fat old man, stark naked, in the sea. Asking around, I discovered the dipping ladies were a close-knit bunch who guarded their positions jealously, making it difficult for an outsider to take up the job. It had been my first idea that Corwen and I should pose as dipping ladies and whisk the king away into a boat, but after we met up with David again, another idea developed, one we couldn't undertake without Fae help.

⋯⋯⋯⋯

David returned from his trip to the beach in a state of high excitement. We met him outside the Golden Lion.

"I think I can do it," he said.

"Shh, not here." I drew him into the inn, and we climbed to the first floor. Our room overlooked the street from a large bay window, and a fire had already been lit in the hearth. David looked about ready to burst.

"What have you found?" I asked.

"Remember last year when you summoned me to Yorkshire to rescue the weavers who'd been using magic?"

I nodded, wondering what that had to do with the king.

"You called me through into the mill office because it was a room lined with wood. Wood, not trees."

"I thought it might work because of something Corwen once said to me about the definition of a forest."

"You were right in a way. With the right kind of magic you can make wood remember it was once a tree. I've been to look at the king's bathing machine . . . It's all wood."

He grinned at me and tapped his foot, waiting to see if I made the connection.

"Oh!" I raised my eyebrows and he nodded. "You can make a door into Iaru from the king's bathing machine."

"I can."

"How will that work?" Corwen hadn't been with me when I'd summoned David to the mill last year.

"It was your idea, remember?" I said.

He looked blank.

"We were in bed in the inn—oh, I forget where—and I

said something rude about the Fae and you said hush or they might hear."

"Ah, I remember, now. You said something like how could they hear when we weren't in a forest and—"

"You knocked on the wooden headboard of the bed and said it all depended on how you defined a forest."

"I was joking, I think." Corwen looked bemused.

"Well, joke or not, I believed it, and it worked. You have more insight than you credit yourself with."

He grunted dismissively. "Happy accident."

"Accident or not, I think this will work," David said. "We hide in the bathing machine and when the king enters—"

"Possibly with someone to help him undress," Corwen said.

"We'll deal with that when we have to," I said. "We close the door, David creates a gate, and we walk the king into Iaru. If we can't convince him by showing him the land of the Fae, we'll never be able to convince him, and we might as well let Dantin have his way, though I shudder to think what destruction he could call down."

David grinned. "And when we send the king home again, he won't be able to tell what he's seen because everyone will think he's relapsing into madness."

"That's the plan," I said. "Will it work?"

"We'll need to create an illusion that the bathing machine is empty," Corwen said.

"I can do that," David said, "but there's not much room inside those things, so we'll all have to squash up to one end. An illusion is visual. It won't work if he brushes up against one of us."

"And we have to make sure no one comes in with him to help him with his clothes," Corwen said. "That won't be easy from the inside." He frowned for a moment. "One of us should stay outside."

I started to protest, but he stopped me with a wave. "No, it makes sense. You and David hide in the bathing machine. When the king climbs in, I'll do something outside to distract everyone at the appropriate moment—"

"You mean you'll turn into a wolf."

"Not where they can see me change, but a wolf bounding across the beach should be enough of a distraction. I can get close enough to slam up against the door from the outside, and then I'll be away."

"Where will you change?"

"In the water or, rather, on the water's edge. Men swim naked here. I'll change on the far side of the beach and swim up close, leave the water as a wolf and dash back in as a wolf, then change again."

"And probably get shot at for your trouble."

"It's a chance I'll take. You aren't fast enough on two legs, and if David did it, his Fae magic would light up the beach. Besides he needs to be in the bathing machine to create the gate."

"What then?"

"Talk to the king, then send him back. I'll get the horses and meet you in Iaru."

It was as close to a plan as we could get. I was cautiously hopeful that it might work; however, even if it did and we reached Iaru with the king, we still had to convince him that new legislation for the rowankind and, I hoped, all magicals would be of benefit to the realm.

❦

The king duly arrived in town and, on the first morning, went down early to the sea to be dipped. Unlike his first visit to Weymouth, no band followed to serenade him with "God Save the King." In fact, it was a modest party which accompanied him. The king himself, and his Master of the Robes, plus three royal equerries and a pair of little dogs which seemed to much amuse His Majesty as they dashed about the sand retrieving a stick he threw and threw again. Neither the queen nor any of their daughters accompanied him.

We watched from a distance, my magic-enhanced spyglass giving Corwen and me a good view. David didn't need artificial help. Six uniformed men from the Blues followed at a distance, close enough to step in if needed, but distant enough not to intrude.

We watched again on the second morning. It seemed as though the king was a creature of habit. He emerged from Gloucester Lodge at six-thirty, marched across the road and down the grassy bank to the beach, and across the sand to his bathing machine, accompanied by the same party as the previous day. After some throwing of sticks for the dogs, the king climbed into the machine, his Master of the Robes followed him, and the door closed. The equerries wheeled the machine to the sea and the king emerged from the opposite door, naked into the arms of two stout dipping ladies, already immersed to the waist and wearing girdles over modest chemises. The sea, in April, must have been barely a few degrees above freezing, so the dips were, of necessity, brief, and then the actions were reversed. The king entered the bathing machine and was wheeled back by his equerries. There was a short delay, maybe five minutes, before the king stepped from the machine, fully dressed, with the Master of the Robes carrying the sheet with which the king had been dried.

"The dogs," Corwen said. "I can bolt across the sand, snap at the little dogs, get between the king and his dresser and look as though I've hit the bathing machine door by accident. Then I'll speed back to the sea, change under water, and swim back to my clothes. The rest is up to you two."

"I wish we didn't have to split up like this," I said. "The last time we accosted the king, you took a bullet through the lung."

"I'll be as quick as I can, and I'll jink from side to side to throw off any marksmen."

"It's not just the Blues. The equerries may have pistols."

"Notoriously inaccurate." He waved away my worry. "Couldn't hit a barn if they were standing inside it."

I didn't believe him, of course. We both knew how dangerous a good pistol and a good marksman could be.

They didn't have the range of a rifle, but close up they could be deadly.

The following morning we rose before dawn. Corwen hugged me and told me not to worry before heading off to the north end of the beach. David and I approached the king's bathing machine cautiously in case there was an overnight guard, but all was quiet. I'm sure David could have opened the lock magically, but I had my lock-picks with me. With David as lookout, I dealt with the lock quickly and quietly, then locked it securely with the two of us inside. The machine was not large. Down one side was a wooden bench. David was right; the whole thing was scrubbed plain wood.

"Do you think this is as good as a forest?" I whispered.

"I hope so."

"Can you try it? Test it out?"

"Better not. Trust me, it will be all right when the time comes."

The bathing machine had windows, but they were curtained over. Without twitching the curtains, we couldn't see what was happening out there, but dawn filtered through, and then full daylight. Thankfully, it was another fine day for the time of year.

We heard the dogs yapping and cheery voices urging them on as they chased sticks. The voices came closer until a key scraped in the lock. David and I pressed ourselves to the front wall, as far away from the door as we could get. I felt David cast a glamour to make the interior appear empty. I held my breath, trying hard not to move, to scrape a foot on the floorboards or a sleeve against the wall.

His Majesty huffed and puffed up the steps and stood in the doorway, blocking out the daylight.

"Come on, man," the king said to someone behind him. "Datchet will see to the dogs."

"Coming, Majesty."

Now, Corwen.

I crossed my fingers. He had to time it right.

There was a snarl and a growl worthy of Freddie, and

the two little dogs set up a frenzy of yapping. The open door slammed shut and the king toppled forward. David and I caught an arm each. David put a hand across the king's mouth to prevent him from crying out.

"Make no noise, Majesty, and you'll come to no harm," I hissed in his ear.

"You again." He glared at me when David eased the pressure on his lips.

"Yes, sorry, we have unfinished business." I left the king to David and quickly locked the door.

It sounded as though the two little dogs had stood their ground against the wolf. What Corwen had hoped would become a chase had become a fight. The dresser was shouting, and the equerries were trying to call off the dogs. There was a yelp—Corwen, I thought, though yelping wasn't his style. I hoped he was playacting. The yapping grew fainter as the little dogs chased their quarry along the beach. At least one of the equerries was chasing the dogs, calling their names to bring them back.

There was a scraping of keys, but I'd jammed my lockpick into the mechanism.

"Majesty, the lock seems to be jammed," the equerry shouted. "I'll come around to the front, if you'll unbolt the door." After a few seconds, he shouted, "The front seems to be jammed as well, Majesty."

"Help! Murder! Help!" The king had a good pair of lungs, I'll say that for him. He lunged for the door and rattled it while keeping up the shouting. Fortunately, David's magic meant that no one outside the bathing machine could hear him. Inside, however, was a different matter. The king's face was beetroot red, and I feared he might have an apoplectic fit.

"Majesty, please."

I doubted he could hear me over his own shouts.

I drew moisture out of the air and created a tiny deluge over the king's head. He stopped shouting for a moment to splutter.

"No one can hear you outside," I said. "You are harming your throat and our ears to no avail."

He opened his mouth to shout again and then closed it.

"Thank you. We mean you no harm."

"It's you again!"

"Yes, Majesty. We've already established that. We didn't harm you last time. Please listen to what we have to say."

"Majesty." Someone called and knocked on the door.

"If I can hear him, why can't he hear me?"

David smiled and filled the air with golden sparkles, then let them fade.

"Magic," the king said.

"Very astute, Majesty," I said. "Please allow me to introduce David, who is Fae, though not very fairy-like, I'm afraid."

David gave the king a wicked grin and didn't try to hide his heritage under a human glamour. I was sure Larien would give us hell for exposing David to the king, but we needed an advantage.

"Tell your man you'll undress yourself today," David said.

"I will do no such thing. I am the king and—"

"All right, I'll do it," David said.

"I can climb in through the window, Majesty," the king's man said.

"No, fetch a locksmith, I'll wait." David's impersonation was rather good. When I turned from the door, I saw the reason the king had not cried out again was a magical gag.

I searched my little brother's face. He'd never liked violence and I could see that he was unusually pale.

"Let me watch him," I said. "You do what you have to do to open the gate."

He nodded.

I indicated the king should sit on the bench. "I know it's hard to believe, Majesty, but we really don't wish you any harm. On the other hand, we have to protect ourselves from your people."

The king grunted deep in his throat but wisely didn't try to speak.

Creating a gate wasn't flashy magic, but as David faced the door which gave the king egress to the sea, he placed his palm on the wood and a green shoot sprang forth. He placed his other hand just so, and a second shoot sprang up from it. Where his feet were, grass grew, fresh and green.

David let the magical gag fall away.

The king neither moved nor spoke. Where David's hand hovered over the bench a tiny, perfect woodland orchid grew. The king touched a finger to its drooping head.

"What illusion is this?"

"No illusion, Your Majesty," David said. "Welcome to Iaru."

He pushed open the door at the front of the machine. It should have led out onto a platform about three feet high, from which the king could lower himself to his dipping ladies, but now it was on a level with a grassy path and all around were the stately trunks of trees in the full leaf of summer.

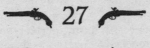

27

Kingnapping

THE KING STOOD, mouth slightly agape, and stepped to the doorway. David skipped out, his face a mask of relief.

"After you, Majesty," I said.

The king took two cautious steps forward, feeling with his foot for the edge of the platform in case it was illusion and the chilly waters of Weymouth Bay were waiting to claim him. When he realized the ground was real, he followed David along the grassy path, and I followed him.

"What is this place?"

"Iaru," I said. "Home of the Fae. Some call it Orbisalius."

"The other world. How can that be?"

"It exists in the same space, but entirely separate from our world. There are places where the two worlds overlap, and that's where it's possible to cross from one to the other."

"How did we get here?"

"David made a gate. If you go out of the door you entered by, you'll be back on Weymouth beach, and, indeed,

I promise we will deliver you back safely once you've listened to what we have to say."

"More threats. Where's the other?"

"Not here, today. David's here, instead. We need to persuade you that this threat is real, Majesty, but it's not a human threat. All I'm doing—all I was trying to do when we approached you in Windsor—was to tell you the Fae take their responsibility to the rowankind seriously. Many of the rowankind have returned to Iaru, but those who have stayed behind need your help. The hangings and abductions are still happening. The Mysterium cites grounds that the rowankind are using magic."

"The Mysterium has my utmost confidence."

"It shouldn't have. In this, the officers are wrong. The rowankind aren't *using* magic, they *are* magic, just as their ancestors were when Martyn the Summoner called them forth from Iaru. Is it right to kill people for what they are rather than what they do?"

He looked as if he was going to cut me off.

I decided to try another tack. I conjured a witchlight, a softly glowing ball in the palm of my hand. "Here, Majesty, hold this."

I held it out.

"Me?"

I put my head on one side and waited.

The king reached out and touched his index finger to the light and then jerked it back again. "It's not hot. I expected—"

"It won't burn you."

He held out his hand, palm upward, and I tipped the witchlight into it. It rolled into the center of his palm and sat there.

"Now, Majesty, you make one in your other hand."

"I can't."

"Yes, you can. Imagine it comes from the core of your being. Take the light inside you and mentally make a ball, like making a snowball. Pat it into a round shape, but without using your hands. When you have the shape in your mind, imagine it's a ball of light. Let it surface from your core, up to your shoulder and down your arm to the palm of your hand."

And there it was, a tiny glowing ball, no bigger than a pearl. I let my light fade.

"You couldn't do that if you didn't have magic, Majesty. That's proof if you needed it. Would it be right if someone decided you should die for what you are rather than what you do?"

"I can't. I truly can't." He closed his hand on the pearl, and his own light died. "Do you know what would happen if the king admitted he had magic? What an uproar there would be in Parliament. Maybe riots in the streets. I can't even begin to think what would happen to the country."

"Magic is no great and terrible thing."

"Yes, it is. It's great and terrible beyond all reckoning. The king must be above all reproach. The best of men. The best of kings."

"And can't you be the best of men if you have magic?"

"The Mysterium—"

"Was created because Good Queen Bess saw what the rowankind magic did to the Spanish Armada and feared that same magic could also be wielded against her. It was a reaction born of fear. Her spymaster, Sir Francis Walsingham, was charged to make sure rowankind magic was never wielded again, and he began to hunt down Martyn the Summoner, who first called forth the rowankind magic. But the Summoner was in hiding, and all his family with him. That didn't stop Walsingham, and all the many successors who inherited his name and his position, from hunting my family down the generations."

"Your family?"

"I'm the last of Martyn the Summoner's direct line." I didn't tell him there might be a new generation soon, or that I'd been the one to return magic to the rowankind. "I put it to you that the Mysterium was created not only to suppress magic, but to make use of the magic they could control."

He didn't deny it. He cleared his throat. "When I first came to the throne, Newcastle led the government. Untrustworthy sort. Never liked him." He shook his head. "But he did me one service, and that was to introduce me to Walsingham and to tell me about the Armada, and the rowankind. It was my duty from then on, to make sure my first ministers knew the whole story, for if I were to die suddenly, or . . . or to lose my reason, the minister's duty would be to pass on the information to my successor."

"You haven't told the Prince of Wales yourself?"

"Good heavens, no. That's not how it's done. Besides . . ." He shrugged. It was an open secret that the king did not get on with his firstborn. "Where was I? Ah . . . Walsingham. There have been three Walsinghams in my reign. Eleven years into my reign my first Walsingham died for his country. The next presented himself to me—a young man with a pockmarked face, who barely looked stout enough to take on the duty. But he served me for thirty years and then disappeared, presumed dead." He shook his head in sorrow. "A new Walsingham came to me. I probably shouldn't have appointed him head of the Mysterium as well, but it was his suggestion. A thruster of a man. It made him a bit too visible. Always best to let the Walsinghams work in the shadows. If he had, he might not have died."

"Did you know he used dark magic? Spells, that is."

"I've never inquired about any of the Walsinghams' magical leanings. Better not to ask, you know. They have always had a free hand to do whatever was needed to fight against magic dangerous to the realm."

"Do I look like a danger to the realm?"

"Well, you have kidnapped your monarch."

"Fair point. You were telling me about Walsingham."

"Yes, by God, the Walsingham I thought dead reappeared after his successor had been appointed. A wreck of a man, but still alive. Couldn't reinstate him, of course—there's only ever one Walsingham at a time—so I appointed him as a special adviser. I swear the man has nine lives. Captured by the French after that, but now he's back again."

My heart skipped a beat. "Surely he has retired with such dreadful injuries."

"You know about his injuries?"

I backtracked quickly. "You said he was a wreck of a man."

"So I did." The king frowned as if trying to remember exactly what he had said. "No, he's too useful to let him go, though he has a man to help him get about. His eyes, you know."

I did know.

Walsingham had lost half an arm and was blind. The king obviously regarded his knowledge highly or he would have been pensioned off.

"You made him your Walsingham again."

"He gave me thirty years' service, I owed him that much. Had he wanted to retire, I would have allowed it, but he didn't."

I knew why. Walsingham had a personal grudge to settle—against me and mine.

"When he returned, I quizzed him about your Fae," the king said.

"You took notice of what we told you at Windsor?"

"Young lady, I wouldn't be much of a monarch if I ignored threats to the realm. Walsingham assured me that Fae magic had faded from the world."

"Did he? Then how do you explain Iaru?" I spread my arms wide to indicate the canopy of trees and the balmy summer breezes.

"A potent illusion, I must admit."

"It's no illusion." David spoke for the first time. He'd let the glamour drop that enabled him to walk around Weymouth like any human, and now he positively glowed.

The king turned to him and narrowed his eyes.

David continued. "The Fae Council of Seven has resolved to protect the rowankind still living in Great Britain." David didn't use the king's title but spoke to him as an equal. "Walsingham is wrong about the Fae and about magic. We have not interfered in the matters of men for millennia." He sounded like his father. I suspected he was drawing on Larien in a way I couldn't begin to perceive. It was as if Larien spoke through David's mouth.

"That was why, when the queen asked for our help against the Armada, we refused. We thought the matter closed, but we should have been more watchful. Martyn the Summoner drew the rowankind, our helpmeets and soulmates from Iaru and sucked the very magic from their bones. We did our best to help them, knowing it would be cruel to return them to Iaru as empty shells. We looked to the Summoner and his family to provide the solution and return the stolen magic."

David was even beginning to look like Larien. He had the same haughty delivery. "Time is not the same for us as it is for you. We live a long time. Our elders were living here in Iaru before your Christ walked the earth. Two hundred years was as the blink of an eye before the Summoner's descendants returned the stolen magic. But we have a duty to protect all the rowankind, even the ones who have chosen not to return to Iaru. We made them from the trees in the forest and our own essence. They are of us."

David shook himself as if awaking from a trance. I raised one eyebrow at him and he cleared his throat, sounding more like himself again. "Dantin, my uncle, lost someone he cared about when the rowankind were stolen away. He has no great love of humans, and he has a loud voice on the council. If you can't change your laws to protect the rowankind, he—and the council—will demonstrate that it's unwise to go against the Fae."

"Your Majesty, you need to take this seriously," I said. "The Fae are powerful. They could reduce London to a smoking ruin as a demonstration of their powers."

"They wouldn't dare."

"I think you'll find we would," David said. "Though there are some of us who would rather not. We don't want to make our presence known, but we will if we have to, and I guarantee you won't like it."

"Majesty, you should return to the bathing machine now," I said. "Talk to Mr. Addington. Persuade him to bring a bill before Parliament to protect the rowankind. That's all the Fae ask. For myself and for all the magicals in the realm, I ask that you include us in the bill. Think of your family. You have magic. It's likely that some of your children have magic, and it will pass down through the generations. Protect them as well. We will meet again, and when we do, the progress you have made will determine what happens next. Let's say six weeks from today, the eighth day of June in Richmond Park, but, please, no traps this time."

I guided the king back toward the open door and into the bathing machine.

"It's been an honor to meet you, Your Majesty." I curtseyed formally. "Please know my magic is at your service and . . . "

"Yes?"

"Your own magic—if you continue to deny it, it could harm you. Your illness could have been caused by fighting it."

"You think magic will drive me mad?"

"I think it might harm your health if it doesn't have an outlet."

"What will be, will be. The king does not use magic."

I couldn't argue. It was his decision, but at least, now, he knew.

I opened the door to the bathing machine. The inside had sprouted vegetation like a glasshouse. It draped from the ceiling, crawled across the floor, and twined up the walls. Blossoms abounded. One of the vines bore grapes, and another branch offered ripe cherries.

The king touched a leaf on his way in. "I should talk to your Fae about farming," he said. "We've had too many poor harvests in the last few years. The people have gone hungry, and that's never a good thing."

I closed the door behind him and heard the other door open and voices expressing relief to find him well and in good spirits, and amazement at the small jungle that someone had obviously taken great pains to decorate the bathing machine with. One asked if he should clear it all away, but as the voices faded, I heard the king say, "No, leave it. I like it."

28

Plymouth

DAVID AND I waited where we were. I reached out with my summoning sense and drew Corwen in the right direction. Three sets of hooves on the track announced his arrival.

I felt a rush of relief. No bullet holes this time.

"Did you get away from the dangerous hounds?" I grinned at him.

"They had no great liking for the sea, and when I changed back to a man in the waves, they got very confused. I felt sorry for them. How did you get on with the king?"

"He seemed less antagonistic. I think Iaru stunned him. I gave him a deadline—six weeks, in Richmond Park. It's up to him now."

"He'll have a hard time convincing his Parliamentarians."

"If he doesn't, the Fae will."

David went still for a moment as if listening. "My father says he has news for you, from the Caribbean."

"The book?"

"It seems likely."

We quickly mounted up and followed David to the grove where Larien was waiting. I flung myself down from Dancer. "Have you news of the book?"

"Not directly," Larien said. "But there's evidence someone is using spell-magic."

"Where?"

"The Dark Islands, centered upon Auvienne."

Gentleman Jim's headquarters. I put two and two together. "Is Nicholas Thompson involved?"

"I can't say. Auvienne is a small island. There are no resident Fae."

"Thank you, Larien. Do you give me your word you'll not move against the king before the six-week deadline we've given him?"

"I doubt I can hold off Dantin and his followers any longer than that. You have six weeks. Don't be late."

"We've done all we can," I said when we were safely back in the Okewood once more. "We have six clear weeks to look for Walsingham's notebook."

"Is six weeks enough to get to the far side of the Atlantic and back again?"

"It is when there's a weather witch on board ship." I grinned at him. "The *Heart*'s off the south coast. I can call her to Plymouth."

"You're a wanted woman in Plymouth."

"So I am, but you didn't say that to me when you wanted my lockpicking skills in the Citadel. Besides, your illusions have proved very effective."

"If brief." He shrugged. "We'll get some sleep and ride at first light."

I wanted to be off immediately, but it made sense to wait until morning.

As we were preparing to ride to Plymouth in the half-light of dawn, Annie appeared in the grove, clutching a bundle to her chest. I looked around for David, but she was on her own.

"Going somewhere?" I asked.

"Back to Plymouth," Annie said. "Anyplace where she's not."

"Has Calantha been bothering you?"

She was about to answer when David hurtled into the grove at a run, causing Timpani and Dancer to throw up their heads in alarm.

"Annie." He sounded out of breath, which was unusual for a Fae. It might have been more distress than exertion.

"I told you, David, I'm letting you get on with your life, and I'll get on with mine."

"Is this about Calantha?" I asked.

David stared down at the ground, not meeting Annie's eyes.

Annie nodded. "She told me in no uncertain terms that there wasn't room for a third person in her marriage, and that I'd better find myself someone else to hang on to, and how could a servant slut like me hope to find favor with a prince."

David winced. "I like my wife less every day. Annie, sweetheart, you mustn't take her to heart."

"She's said the same to you, hasn't she?"

David said nothing which was almost a yes. Then he looked up, and this time he did meet her eyes. "Father said—"

Annie's eyes hardened, and two red spots blossomed on her cheeks. "I don't know what he said to you, but he told me to humor her and stay out of her way." She sniffed and wiped her nose with the back of her hand. "Yes, I know he said you could love where you wanted, but I won't be meeting you in dark corners, waiting for a quick kiss when she's not looking. I'd rather be gone. Make a new life for myself. I'll see if my old job's still open at the Twisted Skein."

"You can't!"

Annie stood as tall as she could, which meant all of five feet. "You can't tell me what to do. You might be a prince and me a servant girl, but I'm no slut and I won't spend my life as the bad smell under somebody's nose. For a while I thought it was going to be a new life in Iaru, and when you said—you know—I was so happy, but I should have known things don't work out like that for girls like me."

David stood, mouth agape. "Annie, I . . . "

"You'll soon forget me. I hope she makes you happy." She set off on the path to the edge of the Okewood.

David looked at me, imploringly. "What do I do?"

I honestly didn't know.

"There's not much you can do," Corwen said, "unless you can appeal against the marriage. You haven't consummated it yet, have you?"

David blushed and shook his head.

"Remember what I told you—don't."

"I wouldn't dare. I told you, she's an ice princess. I'd sooner marry a lump of rock. It would be more comfortable to snuggle up to. I must stop Annie from leaving."

"She'll not thank you for it. Not right now at any rate," Corwen said. "Give her a little time to think about it."

"But . . . she'll be all alone."

"We'll see her safely to Plymouth," I said. "And not to the Twisted Skein. She can go to the Ratcatchers, down by the water. It's not as salubrious as the Skein, but Daniel Fairlow will look after Annie like he was her father, and he knows how to get a message to me if necessary."

"I know the place."

Sometimes I forgot David spent four years looking after my mother—our mother—in Plymouth. He likely knew every inch of the town.

"Are you sure I shouldn't go after her?"

"Sort out the problem here."

"Calantha?"

I nodded. "She's probably lonely and sad to be away from home. Some people put up a front to cover up how nervous they are."

"I don't think Calantha's like that."

"You never know until you talk to her. Maybe she likes this marriage even less than you do, and she might know how to get out of it."

"If I talk to her, aren't I making a commitment?"

"Talking's not your problem."

"I know. I won't do anything else. I swear."

"You don't have to swear to me."

"I know, but it makes me feel better that you know. Tell Annie."

Corwen handed me Dancer's reins and patted David on the back.

"Come on," he said to me. "Let's catch up with Annie before she goes too far."

◆————◆

We caught up with Annie quickly.

She marched along the track, eyes fixed straight ahead. We rode alongside her, Corwen on her right, me on her left. She said nothing, or rather her lack of words spoke volumes. A couple of times I saw her swipe away a tear with the back of her hand.

Eventually, she sniffed and said, "I'm not going back."

"We're not here to take you back," Corwen said.

"In your position, I'd probably get away, too," I admitted. "Though it would tear me apart to do it."

"Yes, well . . . "

"Would you like a ride? It's a long way to Plymouth."

"I know how long it is. When we realized we were free, I walked all the way here, never thinking I'd meet up with . . . I thought he was like me, rowankind. I didn't realize I'd set my cap at a Fae Lord. A prince, no less."

"He grew up thinking he was like you," I said. "Then he discovered his parentage. My mother never told him he was her son, even though he looked after her when she lay dying, as faithful as any son could be. He knew his father was Larien, but he didn't know Larien was Fae. None of us did. Larien lived in our household and came and went as we'd never normally have allowed a servant to do, but no one noticed. We were truly bamboozled by his Fae magic."

"Why would he do that?"

"It was all part of the Fae plan to transfer the stolen power back to the rowankind. He needed a Sumner to do it."

"That was you," Annie said. "And that's when we all woke up to the fact we needn't be bondservants anymore."

"Exactly. So why do you want to go back to the place where you were a bondservant?"

"It's all I know. The missis wasn't too bad, and the master never put himself about with any of us."

"Have you got any money?"

"Ten shillings." She said it proudly. It didn't come from the Fae, they had no use for money. I wondered how long it had taken her to save it when she was a drudge at the inn.

"Don't go back to the Skein. I have a friend who has the Ratcatchers, on Southside, close to Sutton Pool. If I ask him, he'll give you a position and look after you."

"The dockside inns are rough. I won't do more than servant work."

"Of course not. You'll be safe with Daniel."

She nodded. "Maybe I wouldn't mind a ride now, if you're still offering."

"Come up on Timpani with me." Corwen relinquished a stirrup for her to mount and reached down a hand.

⸬————⸬

As we got closer to Plymouth, I began to feel the shiver that told me the *Heart of Oak* was already in the harbor. We'd drop Annie off with Daniel, and leave Dancer and Timpani with him, and then be off across the Atlantic as fast as my weather power could take us. We'd done the crossing to Bacalao in eleven days once. I thought I could beat it.

"Are you sure you'll not be recognized in Plymouth?" Corwen asked.

I'd grown up there and was still wanted for murder. It was a long story, and it was probably justified, but I'd been young and inexperienced in magic, and when faced with redcoats pointing a pistol at Will, I'd panicked. It had been Will who'd put his sword through one of them, but I'd caused a wind to bowl them over like ninepins, contributing to the death of a young lieutenant.

"It's close to a decade ago," I said. "I wouldn't care to draw attention to myself, but if we ride straight to the Ratcatchers and go on foot from there to Sutton Pool, we should be all right. Dan won't give us away."

We rode straight into the inn yard and Dan, hearing horseshoes clattering on his cobbles, came out to meet us. His face creased up when he saw me. "Cap'n, come in, come in. And your friends, too, of course. Let Dicky take your horses. He'll give 'em a good rub down and a feed."

Dancer whickered appreciatively.

"Dan, this is Annie." I put both hands on the girl's shoulders and nudged her forward. "She finds herself in need of a place to stay and a job. She's a good worker, used to the innkeeping trade, and I'd be really obliged if you could treat her as your own."

"Well, I can probably use a little help around the place. Can you cook, Annie?"

"I can keep a pot of stew bubbling until it sticks to your ribs, but I never learned anything fancy. I can scrub pans, though, and light fires, and empty chamber pots, and polish brass, and sweep up."

"Then we shall get on famously." He looked up at Corwen. "Do I remember you, sir?"

I laughed. "You might, Dan. This is Corwen. We weren't on such good terms the last time you saw him."

"I do recall you had him on the wrong end of a pistol." Dan's eyes twinkled with suppressed laughter.

"I did. But he grew on me. We're married."

"Well, congratulations to the both of you. That's worth popping a cork on a bottle of the best."

"Rum," I said to Corwen.

"Aye, and I have a very reliable supplier." Daniel winked as if I should know already.

Oh, no, not the *Heart*. Was she carrying smuggled goods? Had I called her into a port crawling with excise men? Damn! I immediately felt guilty, then indignant. Hookey should know better.

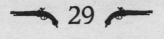

29

New Trade

I WOULD HAVE run to Sutton Pool, but I daren't attract attention, so Corwen and I strolled arm in arm as
if we hadn't a care in the world. Rather than turn us invisible I used a slidey-eye charm. People could see us, but
they didn't take any notice as long as we did nothing to
draw their gaze. I kept getting slightly ahead, but Corwen
gently pulled me back.

"Slow down. What do you think you can do to protect
Hookey from the excise men if they already know there
are smuggled goods on board?"

I shook my head. I didn't know.

"And if they don't know, then a few more minutes
won't hurt."

He was right. I took a deep breath, wondering whether
to congratulate Hookey on his business acumen, or take
him to task for endangering my ship. But at least half the
blame was mine. He'd never have put into Plymouth if I
hadn't called the *Heart*.

We cut through from South Side Street to the New
Quay. The *Heart of Oak* was tied up there. Even after two

years I still felt a pang in my belly to think I was no longer her captain.

Corwen patted the hand I had looped through his arm. "I know what you're going to say. Yes, she is beautiful. I may not know much about the sea and sailing, but even I can appreciate her clean lines." He cleared his throat. "Is it my imagination, or are there more men on deck than usual?"

"More than I would usually put on watch in port."

"They don't look as though they're on watch. Most of them are lolling about."

"Anything else would look suspicious, as if they had something to watch out for."

"Ah, I see. So they have got something on board they don't want the excise men to find."

"It looks like it to me and may look like it to the excise men."

I didn't recognize the crewman next to the gangplank. "Permission to come aboard?" I shouted up.

"State your business."

I couldn't very well tell him who I was. There were too many ears on the dockside. Luckily, I didn't have to. A tall black figure pulled the crewman to one side and said something to him in a low voice that sent him scurrying away.

"Permission granted, ma'am." Mr. Rafiq grinned at me and gave a very proper half-bow to me, and then to Corwen as we reached the top of the gangplank. It wasn't for show, he was always that formal.

"Mr. Rafiq, nice to see you again."

"Captain," he said quietly. "I'm sorry the new crewman didn't know you."

"No problem. I'd much rather they were cautious. Watching out for official visitors, are they?"

He cleared his throat in a manner that said yes.

"I thought so. Is Hookey aboard?"

"I've sent young Lemon to tell him you're here."

"Another new crewman?"

"We let twelve men go when we last docked in Bacalao.

They didn't think they could take to life aboard a merchantman."

"I paid 'em off; no hard feelings." Hookey came up behind me. I'd already heard his boots on the companionway, so it was no surprise.

"They've gone back to pirating," he said. "Likely heading for Auvienne. Come below. Billy! Tea for our guests."

"Aye, Cap'n."

"Auvienne," I said. "Who's in charge there now James Mayo's gone?"

"That bastard Old Nick." Hookey stood back to allow me and Corwen to go down the companionway first. "A bad day for pirating when Gentleman Jim went down to Davy Jones. He was a bastard as well, but not as bad a bastard as Old Nick. At least you knew where you were with Jim. Old Nick's unpredictable. Does things on a whim. No rhyme or reason, and he's cruel. Gives pirating a bad name."

Hookey had been on Jim's crew before joining the *Heart,* and there was no love lost between them. Mayo had never forgiven him for switching his berth.

"I'm sorry to hear it, Hookey."

"Aye, you and me, both."

I'm not saying cruelty was something foreign to either pirates or privateers. It was the occasional act of outrageous cruelty that actually made life easier. Most merchantmen were no match for a pirate ship. They knew if they gave up without a fight they'd lose their goods, maybe even their ship, but they'd escape with their lives. Since most ship captains owned neither their cargo nor their ship, it made sound sense to surrender and live. When the *Heart* had been a privateering vessel, we'd used that ruse many times, only rarely having to resort to violence of the bloody and fatal kind.

But Nicholas Thompson offered safety in return for surrender and then went back on his word, torturing and killing for pleasure. Any captain who knew his crew would receive no quarter would be more likely to fight to the death. I would in their position. A slim chance of escape was better than no chance at all. Thompson—Old Nick—wasn't doing anyone any favors, least of all himself.

We'd reached the captain's cabin, once mine and now Hookey's. He waved me to the sagging armchair I'd liberated from a ship we'd taken the year after Will died. Corwen sat on the edge of the bunk and Hookey perched on a three-legged stool.

Lazy Billy clomped down the stairs and nudged open the door that Hookey had left ajar. "Tea for the cap'n, Cap'n."

He had a tray in a cradle that he could carry one-handed, a blessing on board a ship in rough weather. This wasn't the kind of afternoon tea served up in polite households. This was a hefty brew, devoid of milk but with sugar and a tot of rum. Good rum. The brew tasted as if it had been sitting on the back of the stove since morning. It probably had.

Corwen took a sip and winced. I smiled. The tea tasted like home to me. I'd been seven years aboard the *Heart*, four of them with Will and three as captain.

"So . . . " I looked at my mug. "Rumrunning now, are we?"

"A little private trading," Hookey said. "When the opportunity presents itself. I'd rather not have brought it into Plymouth, though."

"Sorry about that. If I'd known, I would have picked a quiet cove. Smuggling's dangerous, Hookey. If you get caught, you'll have your neck stretched and I'll lose my ship."

"You never objected to a little trade on the side when you were cap'n."

He was right. It hadn't seemed like such a bold step when I was robbing French shipping under Letters of Marque from the king. How far I'd moved on from the person I used to be.

"I don't object to the trade. Smuggling's almost an honest crime—at least no one loses out except the government, and I have no great love for that institution, but

I do care about my ship and my crew. I don't want to see any of you transported or dancing the hempen jig on the gallows."

Hookey pressed his mouth in a line as if trying not to say what was on his mind.

"Out with it, Hookey. What were you going to say?"

"It's not only smuggling." He shrugged. "I meant to write and tell you, but it's not something you can put in a letter. We had a visit from a man who called himself Mr. Singleton. I'm damn sure that wasn't his name, though. Said as how we had one of the best reputations of any of His Majesty's privateers. He wanted to entrust us with a mission." He put one finger to the side of his nose. "A secret mission. He showed me the king's seal. We were to make contact with Lady Henrietta Rothcliffe, a respectable widow from Rye. She had reason to meet up with gentlemen of the smuggling persuasion on account of having a load of wool bound for the French markets where the prices are good for English wool."

"Selling wool to the French is illegal," Corwen said, his clothier's background suddenly jumping to the fore.

"So it is," Hookey said. "But it's profitable. As is bringing good French wine and brandy back to these shores, and maybe a few barrels of the best Jamaica rum, too. Anyhow, at the same time as we make this honest exchange of goods, there might be letters and sealed packets to be delivered, no questions asked, and a fee for doing that."

"Spying for England?" I said.

"I reckon someone else does the spying. All we do is get the results safely delivered to Lady Henrietta who passes them on appropriately. I gather she took over her late husband's task."

"I hope this Mr. Singleton is paying you well. I don't suppose you'll get treated more leniently if you get caught by the excise men."

Hookey shook his head. "Mr. Singleton made it quite clear that if we get caught, he doesn't know us."

"What about Lady Henrietta? Can she be trusted?"

"Oh, yes, stouthearted woman." Hookey smiled, and it was one of those smiles that told me all I needed to know.

"We need to set sail for Auvienne immediately, Hookey," I said.

He frowned. "I'd like to oblige, but how immediate is immediate? Apart from the contraband, I have a package for Etta, and we're not provisioned for a transatlantic crossing."

Damn. We needed to get out of Plymouth quickly. "Where's your drop for Lady Henrietta?"

"Sussex. Camber Sands, close to Romney Marsh. If we can drop the goods and the packet, we could see what provisions might be available in Rye Harbor. I'm sure Etta could help. She has a lot of influence in the area. Her late husband used to be a magistrate. If there's not enough to be had in Rye, we can provision in Portsmouth on the way back."

I noticed Lady Henrietta had become Etta as he spoke of her. I wondered what might be going on between them and tried not to smile to myself.

"Well, if you say you can trust her, I believe you. Get ready for a fast run along the coast."

"Aye." He barely stopped himself from saying *aye, Cap'n,* then he caught my glance, and we both laughed. How easy it was to slip back into old ways.

There was a clatter on the companionway outside. Lazy Billy opened the door. "Excise, Cap'n. Redcoats on the dockside."

Hookey cursed and jumped up. Corwen and I followed.

At the far end of Vauxhall Quay, a troop of redcoats were lined up outside a barque while two officers stepped up the gangplank.

"Go ashore quickly," Hookey propelled me to the gangway with a firm hand.

"It's too late for that," I said. "I presume if they come aboard, there will be something to find."

Hookey's face told me the answer to that.

Corwen swore softly.

"Get all your men below, Hookey. I don't want any movement on deck. You, too, Corwen."

"You're going to do the slidey-eye thing again, aren't you?" Corwen asked.

"I'm going to try, but the *Heart*'s a bit bigger than the things I'm used to diverting attention from."

"I'll be close by at the top of the companionway, keeping my head down. You only need to whistle, and I'll be there."

"I know, now go."

I sauntered to the bottom of the gangway and stood very still, wrapping myself not in invisibility—there was no way I could make the whole ship invisible—but with a bit of luck I could make us less than interesting—so uninteresting that the redcoats would pass by. They were at the next ship, now, once more the troop remaining on the dockside while two officers went aboard. I saw the sergeant in charge of the troop look in our direction, and I increased my efforts.

Nothing to see here. Move to the next ship.

Nothing to see.

I felt as though my head was going to burst.

Nothing to see.

The two officers returned to the dockside and exchanged a few words with each other. My palm was sticky on the rail. My knees ached. I wanted to jiggle from one foot to the other to ease my feet, but I had to hold still.

Nothing to see.

Nothing to see.

Oh, blast! I wanted to sneeze. That would be fatal. I pressed my lips together and concentrated on not sneezing. The troop of redcoats moved toward the *Heart*'s mooring.

Nothing to see.

The officers faltered at the bottom of our gangway. They were less than ten feet away from me. That damn sneeze was going to come whether I wanted it or not. I clenched my chest muscles and squeezed my lips together as hard as I could. The sneeze came, but I held it in tight, making barely a sound. Like a tiny explosion in a sealed container.

One of the lieutenants stiffened and turned toward me.

Nothing to see.

Nothing to see.

Nothing to see.

With a slightly puzzled look on his face, he moved on.

I didn't even let myself breathe until he was safely past and aboard our neighbor. I stayed sentinel until the redcoats had passed to the far end of the quay and then retreated up the gangway to the deck.

"Can we come out now?" Corwen whispered.

"Yes. Let's get underway before they decide they've missed something and come back."

◆━━━━━━◆

I sat on the cargo hatch with Corwen at my side.

"What can I get you?" he asked.

"I'm all right or will be soon. Some of Lazy Billy's tea might help."

"Here you are, Cap'n." Lazy Billy had anticipated my request. "That was a good bit of bamboozling, if I may say so."

"Thanks, Billy, but I don't know how long it will last before they realize they missed us."

"We're casting off now."

I stood up, but my knees were like jelly. Corwen took my elbow, and I sat down again quickly. "Ask Hookey if he needs a breeze. I can manage that from here."

Corwen delivered the message, and Hookey came over.

"If you can manage it, gal. Otherwise, we're going to have to kedge out."

"I can manage a light breeze. Set your tops'ls."

Hookey wasted no time in easing the *Heart* out of Sutton Pool on the tide before the redcoats came back. The next time the *Heart* docked in Plymouth, they would likely be all over her, so she had to be as clean as a new pin.

Until then, she sailed with a hold full of illegal spirits. I would have liked to dump the contraband over the side and make for the Dark Islands immediately, but we couldn't sail without adequate provisions, and the package Hookey had for Lady Henrietta might be of national importance. I would have to work doubly hard to conjure up a wind to take us across the Atlantic in days. At least we didn't have to divert to pick up the trade winds; we could cross to Bacalao and thence to the Dark Islands. Beyond that, I didn't have a plan.

As soon as we cleared Sutton Pool and crossed the harbor bar, I felt the strong seas kick the *Heart* awake. I waited for Hookey's request to conjure a favorable wind, then I sought deep inside myself and connected with the air. It needn't be more than a little blow. It had been a while since I'd used that kind of magic, and it didn't come as easily as it used to before I relinquished a good portion of it back to the rowankind, but I'd recovered enough of its use to help the *Heart* to make good speed along the coast.

It seemed odd to be sailing with such a small crew and, in particular, without Mr. Sharpner on board, but he was doing well, trading in American and Caribbean waters. I couldn't call the *Butterfly* to me like I could call the *Heart of Oak*. Unlike the *Heart*, she had no splice of winterwood in her keel—something I hoped to rectify eventually.

30

Smugglers and Spies

WE MADE GOOD time to Romney Marsh, arriving east of where the River Rother runs into the sea two hours after dusk. I let the breeze die down and heaved a sigh of relief. Corwen came to stand behind me. He wrapped his arms around me and nuzzled my wind-blown hair.

"Mmmm." I relaxed into him.

"If you're so tired after a short run along the coast, how will you manage an Atlantic crossing?"

"I'll manage because it's what's needed."

"Is there anything I can do to help?"

"Be there to pick me up if I fall over."

"Always, though I'd prefer you not to."

Hookey came on deck. "No lights and no more noise than is strictly necessary for the safety of the ship and crew," he ordered, soft-voiced.

The crew passed the order on from one to another.

The anchor dropped with a soft splash.

I straightened up from Corwen's embrace, and he released me to the darkness of the deck.

"How are you supposed to make contact?" I asked Hookey as we stood at the rail looking out toward the shore.

"We signal twenty minutes after midnight. Three long, one short, repeated. Etta signals back exactly five minutes after that: five long flashes, two short, and three long. Anything else, or no signal at all, and we make for open water as fast as we can. Have you got your magic glass?"

"I have." I could call light into the lenses of my spyglass so that the images would be almost as bright as day. "Have you got yours?"

"It's getting a bit dim. Probably needs a top-up."

"Let me take a look."

He passed me the glass I'd given him when I left the *Heart* for good. Sure enough, the image was darker than it had been. I called magic and brightened it. Hookey scanned the shore again.

"Are you taking cargo on board as well as dropping off contraband?"

"Not this time. This is purely a delivery."

"That's good. I wouldn't want you to let down a customer, or the king's spying service."

Hookey chuckled. "You're hardly an inconvenience. The *Heart*'s yours, after all. I was planning a trip to London after this, to tout around the warehouses for a suitable cargo. Mr. Rafiq has a contact there, all lee-git-i-mate." He sounded out every syllable. "But that can wait."

At exactly twenty minutes past midnight by Hookey's pocket watch, with a half-moon on the rise, Hookey nodded to Lazy Billy. "All right, show your light."

Billy slid the lantern's shutter open, closed, open, closed, to give three long and one short flash. Then he repeated it for good measure.

"Now we wait," Hookey said. "Five minutes."

It seemed like a long five minutes, but at last there was an answering signal from the beach—five long, two short and three long.

"Man the boat, lads," Hookey said.

It didn't take long for the *Heart*'s boat to be loaded

with barrels of brandy. Lazy Billy jumped down into it, with Hookey following. I scanned the shoreline with my magic-enhanced glass. I could see a small knot of people and ponies waiting for us in the shadow of the sand dunes. One of them, dressed in buckskin breeches and a frock coat looked a little too rounded to be a man. She was round in all the wrong places, or maybe all the right places if you were a man—a man like Hookey Garrity.

"I think I can see your Lady Henrietta, Hookey," I said over the side. "Does she wear breeches?"

"Aye, that'll be her. She fills her shirt out somewhat generously." He grinned at me, his teeth flashing in the moonlight.

"Hookey, are you smitten?"

"All I said was—"

"It was the way you said it."

He cocked his head on one side.

"Ha! I want to meet this woman."

"Boat's fully crewed," Hookey said, half-heartedly.

"I can row, even though I'm wearing a dress." There wasn't time to change, although I had breeches in my traveling bag.

"Me, too," Corwen said. "What? You think I'm going to waste an excuse to set my feet on dry land for a few moments?"

What he really meant was *I'm coming with you,* but it was as good an excuse as any, so Corwen and I took two places at the oars along with Lazy Billy, Crayfish Jake, Windward, and the Greek, all stalwarts of my old crew, and as good in a skirmish as any who sailed the seven seas.

We pulled for the shore on a rising tide and ran our boat aground on the sand. Damn! I wished I had my breeches on, but Corwen splashed into the ankle-deep water and lifted me out like a fragile doll. I chuckled quietly and kissed his chin, which was the only bit of him I could reach.

An owl hooted. No, it was Lady Henrietta and her men, owlers all. Our men offloaded the barrels which were quickly tied in pairs and slung across the back of the sturdy ponies. As each pony was readied, their handlers led them off into the dunes, each man taking a slightly different direction.

"Captain Garrity." Lady Henrietta's voice was warm and deep for a woman, or maybe she thought her breeches were a good disguise. She looked at me. "Passengers?"

"Not quite," Hookey said. "Lady Henrietta Rothcliffe. Allow me to introduce Mr. Corwen Deverell and Mrs. Rossalinde Deverell. Mrs. Deverell is the *Heart*'s owner."

"Ah, so this is your Ross who wears breeches and climbs the *Heart*'s mast like a boy. I'd curtsey, Mrs. Deverell, but I ain't dressed for it."

"Pleased to meet, you, Lady Henrietta." I held out my hand, and she took it. "You have the advantage over me. Hookey's said very little about you."

"There's not much to know. Rye's a small place. We don't get up to much here."

I suppose she didn't count smuggling and spying.

"Ross, riders coming up the beach at a lick." Corwen had been keeping watch.

"Quick, get the last two ponies away." Lady Henrietta smacked the rump of the nearest pony and sent it trotting into the dunes with a boy hanging onto its lead rein. "Is it excise men?"

"I don't think so," Corwen said. "Or if it is, they're not redcoats."

"Into the boat," Hookey said to Etta and the one man still with her.

"There's no time." She held out her hand for Hookey's glass, grunting in surprise when she put it to her eye and discovered it saw in the dark as if it were daylight. "It's the Snelling gang. Get ready for a fight."

We set our backs against the dunes and bunched up together. Corwen drew his pistol. I had two primed pistols tucked safely away in the pockets tied beneath my skirts, but they were small ones. Though beautifully made by Mr. Bunney of London, they didn't have much range to them.

"Who are they, what do they want?" I asked.

"Joss Snelling and his son George and their gang. Smugglers, cutthroats, thieves." Lady Henrietta said. "They think they own the coast from Kent round to Sussex. Bastards, all of them. My late husband hanged five of them two years ago—not personally, he was a magistrate—so they're not well-disposed toward me and mine. Thank goodness I don't have family, or I'd seriously fear for them."

"Do they know who you are?"

"That's the question, isn't it? My crew are not the only owlers on the marsh."

I saw Corwen shrug out of his jacket and rip off his neck cloth in preparation for changing into a wolf if it should prove advantageous. "Are they likely to shoot first, Lady Henrietta, or are they looking for the goods?"

"Either. Both."

"Billy, Jake, get the boat into the water," Hookey said. "Stand off shore and keep your heads down. If they start shooting, shoot back. Get ready to come in quick if we signal."

"We can escape across the marsh," Lady Henrietta said.

Hookey nodded and modified his instructions to Jake and Billy. "If we go inland, return to the *Heart* and come into Rye Harbor at first light."

They probably couldn't get completely out of pistol-shot range before the gang arrived, but every pull on the oars took them and the boat closer to safety. That left Windward, the Greek, Corwen and me, Hookey, Lady Henrietta, and her one man. Seven of us against a dozen mounted men.

"Into the dunes," I shouted. "Stay together."

I called up a fierce wind and blew sand into the faces of the thugs, but I couldn't call on magic and run at the same time. I felt Corwen at my shoulder, guiding me backward slowly as I kept my face toward the enemy. They'd slowed their gallop and were milling about, trying to turn their backs on the stinging sandstorm, so I swirled the wind around them and caught them coming and going. I felt the firm damp footing turn drier and softer under the soles of my half-boots, and the ground begin to rise. Corwen caught me around the thighs and hoisted me over his shoulder like a sack of potatoes. It meant he could run forward while I looked backward and kept up the wind.

A shot whistled past and then another. Despite the sand in their eyes, they were managing to discharge their pistols in our direction. I heard answering fire from the *Heart*'s boat.

As soon as I lost sight of the gang, I had to let the wind drop since I needed to see my target. Corwen dumped me on my feet, and I gathered my skirts up above my knees.

"This way," Lady Henrietta said, and led us through the soft dunes to where the marsh leveled out behind them.

"If we leave the shelter of the dunes, won't we be sitting targets?" I asked.

"Not if we can get out of their range." Lady Henrietta said. "There's a series of drainage dikes and ditches. It's like a maze unless you know exactly where you're going."

"And you do?"

"Born and raised here. Those bastards are trying to hold all the coastline from Kent round to Sussex, they don't know any one part of it well. Not this well at any rate."

She led us to a wide ditch, steep-sided, deep and waterlogged, bridged by a single plank of wood no wider than a foot. She went across first in the half-moonlight, closely followed by Hookey. I ran across, with Corwen on my heels. The plank dipped in the middle, but it was no more difficult than a gangplank. Windward and the Greek followed, and the manservant came last. He bent and heaved the plank across after him, leaving it on our side. A man might slither down one side, splash across and climb up the other, but not with his pony. That should slow them down.

We ran across the wet grazing of the levels, scattering

a flock of marsh sheep who looked like ground-tied clouds in the half-moon.

A volley of shots rang out. I heard a bleat and then Windward's yelp.

"Are you hurt?"

"No, Cap'n, but one of these sheep is done for. I nearly tripped over it. Shame to waste it." I heard him grunt, and then he was running beside me with a dead sheep over his shoulders, the ewe's head dangling down.

We crossed another two plank bridges, pulling the planks onto our side as we went, until all sounds of pursuit had died away.

"This way," Lady Henrietta led us through a rickety field gate and onto a track, taking care to close the gate after her. "Those are my sheep. I don't want them roaming all the way to Rye."

We trotted up the road for maybe a mile until she turned in through a pair of tall gates. "This is my home. We'll be safe enough here."

"Does Snelling know where to find you?"

"I don't think so. But in any case, it's one thing to take a few shots at anonymous figures in the dark. It's another thing altogether to make trouble for the respectable widow of a local magistrate."

She sounded utterly sure of herself, but I had my doubts. There were several hours of darkness before the dawn.

31

Siege

LADY HENRIETTA'S HOUSE was more than re-spectable. Her late husband must have been a rich man, and since she was not now in a dower house, it seemed likely she had no sons and so was in charge of her own fortune, an enviable position for a woman to be in. She lived in a red-brick manor house, recently built in the classical style. Lanterns burned at the front door, which opened as we all ran up the steps, filing through into the tiled hallway.

A tall, middle-aged butler met us with a lamp and his "M'lady!" was more an expression of surprise as we all trooped past him. Lady Henrietta, her servant, Hookey, me, Corwen, Windward, and the Greek. It wasn't until he moved that I realized he had a crutch tucked into the armpit of his free arm.

"Janie?" the butler asked.

The person I'd taken for a manservant as we'd raced across the levels dragged off his cloak, and it was suddenly obvious in the lamplight that he was a she. "I'm all right, Bartle," she said. "We ran into some trouble, but no one was hurt."

"Only an unfortunate ewe," Windward said. "I left her at the foot o' the steps, but I can draw the carcass if you want me to."

"That won't be necessary," Lady Henrietta said. "Young Cherry can deal with her, Mr. . . . "

"Windward, ma'am. Just Windward. And this here's the Greek. He don't say much on account of bein'—well—Greek, but he understands all right."

"I'm pleased to meet you both, and I thank you for your company tonight. Gentlemen, as you can see, Bartle is temporarily incapacitated . . . "

I looked across at Windward and mouthed, "Lame." He nodded.

"So," she continued, "if you would be so good as to help him in the kitchen, we can all get some food and a warm drink inside us."

"Yus, ma'am, be right glad to," Windward said.

"It's a big enough kitchen table, we'll all come and join you in a few moments. Jane?"

"I'll go and supervise. Yon two big fellows don't look like they're much used to kitchen work."

"If you're not too tired."

"I'll be fine."

Bartle lit a candelabrum and left it on the hall table. Holding his lamp high, he led the foraging party through a door under the stairs.

"Is everyone truly all right?" Lady Henrietta asked. "Please, pile your coats on that chair and come into the breakfast room. There's a good fire burning in the grate, though the room's small. We weren't expecting company."

The breakfast room was, indeed, small, but it was obviously used as a parlor as well, so there were two armchairs and several straight-backed dining chairs which we pulled up to the fire.

Lady Henrietta grinned at us. "Hookey's told me about you both. I didn't expect to meet you on a night such as this."

"I confess, Lady Henrietta—" I said.

"Oh, please, call me Etta."

"Thank you, and you must call me Ross. It was only because of my curiosity that we came ashore in the boat. Hookey doesn't give his admiration easily." I glanced at Hookey who I swear had gone pink, though it could have been the warmth from the roaring fire on his cold cheeks. "I wanted to meet you, though not necessarily under the present circumstances. You've used my trick, wearing breeches. Running across the marsh in a dress isn't to be recommended."

"It certainly isn't. I wish I could get away with breeches in daylight, but I'm a little too well known around here, and not quite the right shape to disguise myself as a man." She looked down at her ample bosom.

Hookey's face went from strawberry to beetroot.

"I'm not sure how I got away with it for so long," I said, knowing my days of dressing in breeches would soon be curtailed by my belly.

"May I offer you all something to drink. We're not short of a bottle or two of spirits."

Hookey looked as if he was about to say yes, but I got up from my chair and peeked between a crack in the drawn shutters. "You have more faith than I have that your position in society will keep you safe," I said. "I'll stand watch while everyone gets some food."

"I'll stand with you," Corwen said.

I nodded. "Then Windward and the Greek can take over."

Etta looked about to protest the necessity, but Hookey touched the back of her hand. "Ross has the right of it. We'll split the night into three watches, I'd be obliged if you'd ask Bartle to stand with me."

"He's barely able to hobble, yet. It was a clean break, but these things take time. I'll stand with you, Hookey. I defer to your sense of danger."

While the others went to the kitchen, Corwen and I took the first watch from the rooms upstairs, the front room a grand parlor and the back a bedroom. With no light behind us, we could see garden-shapes outlined in the silvery half-moonlight. I still had my enhanced glass, so I was able to see partway down the road though some angles were shrouded by trees.

While I had a quiet time, I *summoned* the *Heart*. When my ship turned against the tide, Mr. Rafiq knew that I'd called her. It would tell him that we'd escaped the immediate danger, so he'd bring her into the small harbor at first light.

Hookey joined us barely ten minutes later with a plate of cold meats and a bottle of Burgundy.

"I didn't like to think of you missing out," he said.

"Thanks, Hookey. Have you taken some to Corwen in the back room?"

"I have, but he's getting ready to scout outside. I'll take his watch."

A low yip announced Corwen's presence in wolf form. I ran down the stairs with him and let him out of the front door. "Take care out there," I said, as he bolted out into the night.

"Has someone gone out?" Etta asked as she emerged from the kitchen stair.

"Corwen's gone to see what he can sniff out," I said, not indicating I meant it literally.

Windward and the Greek weren't far behind Etta. Like me, they were wary. "That Joss-man didn't look like one to let anything go," Windward said. "If I were him, I'd be heading here with my gang and loaded pistols. That's the only way to make someone realize you mean business."

"I'm afraid you're right," I said.

"They wouldn't dare." Etta sounded indignant.

"I'm afraid they would, my dear," Hookey said. "I've dealt with their like before. Hells bells, I've been their type. If I were them, I'd be making an example of you this night so that no one else would dare stand against me."

Etta's face paled in the lamplight. "What shall we do?"

"Prepare to repel boarders, I reckon," Hookey said. "What say you, lass?" he turned to me.

"I think you're right. What armaments do we have? I've got two small pistols, a powder flask, and a dozen spare bullets."

"Three pistols and a cutlass," Hookey said. "And spare ammunition."

"Two pistols and a cutlass," Windward said. "Same for the Greek. Both with spare powder and balls."

"What about your own household?" I asked Etta.

"Two fowling pieces, a musket, and my late husband's pistols. There's a pair of swords mounted on the wall over the mantel in Gerald's study."

"That will do for starters," I said. "How many servants do you have?"

"Useful ones? Lucy the cook, Jane and Bartle in the house. Cherry and little Jeremiah have their wits about them, but they sleep in the loft above the stable. The rest are girls who likely don't know one end of a pistol from the other, though now I come to think of it, Julia was an army brat, so she might stand with us."

"I'll go wake them," Jane said. "Bartle's keeping a watch on the back door. He's got a loaded musket by his side."

"Tell him not to take a potshot if he sees a wolf," I told her. "He's on our side."

Etta raised an eyebrow but said nothing.

I kept a watch out of the front room window with my spyglass, and Hookey kept a watch out of the back with his. I wasn't sure how we'd explain the magical light lodged in them. Etta hadn't asked, but she'd definitely noticed.

"I see the wolf," Hookey roared from the back room. "He's coming at a run. Janie, the door."

Downstairs in the hallway, we heard the bolts clang back; Janie squeaked as a large silver wolf streaked by her, up the steps, and into the back room. Corwen emerged less than a minute later, his shirt loose over his breeches.

"There are nine of them, mounted and armed," he said. "Not sure about the other three. Could they have followed your owlers?"

"They might try, but they'll never manage it across the marsh. Everyone has a different destination. The ponies are borrowed from local farms and will be back in their stables before morning."

"In that case there might be another three coming back to join the main gang, but in the meantime, we have nine to deal with."

"The boys in the stable," Etta said. "We need to warn them."

"I'll go," Janie said from halfway up the stair.

"Can you fire a pistol?" Corwen asked her.

"If I have to."

"Good, here's mine. I'll warn your stable lads." He ran down to the kitchen where Bartle was still holding the door. I heard muffled voices and then the scrape of two bolts, the click of the back door, and the firm snick of the bolts sliding back into place.

A short while later I heard a single pony galloping away; the kitchen door opened and closed again. A young man ran up the steps, still tucking his shirt into his breeches. Cherry, I guessed.

"Where's Corwen?" I asked.

"The gentleman sent Jerry off to Rye to call out the militia, ma'am. Said to tell you he's gone to sniff around. Said you'd know what he meant."

I did, indeed, Corwen's wolf was on the loose.

◆──◆

I saw them through the spyglass before they expected to be seen, but I could only count five of them, so I called out to let the others know to watch the back and the sides of the house. Etta sent Cherry down to the kitchen to reinforce Bartle at the door. There was access to the cellars from another door, but it was stout oak and firmly locked and bolted.

The front door was bolted and barred, though the French windows from the dining room to the garden were only shuttered and not sturdy enough to withstand a determined assault. I took Windward and the Greek and stationed myself in the hallway where I could get fast access to all the downstairs rooms. Hookey gave Janie and

Etta the enchanted spyglasses and left them watching from the upstairs rooms, each with a loaded pistol. He stationed himself between them on the upper landing, pistols at the ready.

"Here they come," Hookey yelled. A pistol discharged in a room above my head, and then a second. "Got the bastard."

I heard horses squealing outside and men's voices shouting. Then one man gave a bloodcurdling scream. That would be Corwen causing havoc.

Someone rattled the French windows.

"Right, get ready," I said softly to Windward and the Greek as I unlatched the shutters from the inside. When the French windows flew open, the three men there took five bullets between them from our volley. Two sprawled dead or unconscious amidst broken glass, and one cursed violently as he stumbled away. We slung the bodies outside, slammed the shutters back in place, bolted them, and reloaded while we had the opportunity.

Two pistol shots from belowstairs, a crash of splintered wood, and the clang of steel on steel told us that the gang had broken through in the kitchen. Hookey ran down the stairs, leaped over the banister, and charged through the door, closely followed by the Greek.

"Stay here," I told Windward. "It could be a diversion."

And, indeed, it was. The shutters in the dining room trembled under colossal blows and caved inward. We each fired a pistol, and then a second one. I had one of Etta's husband's swords from the study. It was longer than the one I favored, and not balanced for my hand, but it was three and a half feet of steel and I knew where to shove it. I skewered one smuggler in the belly, though in the age it took me to free my blade from sucking flesh, another had come at me from my right. Windward slashed at his head, and a silver-gray shape launched itself under Windward's flailing cutlass and went straight for the smuggler's ballocks with his teeth. The scream told me he'd found his target.

By the time the militia arrived, it was all over. Of the ten men who'd attacked the house, four lay dead from pistol wounds, including Joss Snelling. His son George was badly wounded, his arm almost torn off, which Etta quickly blamed on one of her hunting dogs who seemed to have run off into the night. I reckoned the young man would be lucky to survive a wound like that if infection set in. Maybe a swift amputation might save his life, but the militia captain seemed reluctant to call out the local surgeon. George Snelling was a dead man walking.

The hunting dog was blamed for the wounds to the unfortunate man who'd had his tender parts mauled.

Two men had run off into the night on foot, including the one I'd skewered in the gut and the militia captain sent men to track them down by the trail of blood.

We let Etta account for the attack to the militia. No, she didn't know why they'd attacked, but it was lucky she had visitors in the house as a poor widow living alone but for a handful of servants would stand no chance against such vicious criminals.

Delighted to catch the Snelling gang, the militia didn't ask too many questions. They sent for a cart and hauled away the dead and wounded. Anyone who survived would be likely to meet his end on a rope.

Hookey was the hero of the hour as far as Etta was concerned, which was fine by us.

Corwen and I took our leave early the following morning after a few hours of sleep, having sent Windward and the Greek to Rye Harbor to meet the *Heart of Oak* as she docked to take on provisions. Hookey would follow later, but I didn't begrudge him some time with his ladylove. It was obvious his feelings were returned.

"However it turns out," I said to Corwen, "Hookey deserves a woman like Etta."

"I always thought he had his eye on you."

"What? No, don't be ridiculous. Hookey's my friend. There's never been anything between us."

"You love each other."

"Well, yes, but not that kind of love. He's family."
Corwen smirked.

◄•————————•►

As it turned out, we couldn't provision completely in Rye
Harbor. It was more acquainted with supplies for fishing
boats and coastal shipping, so our list of requirements
came up sadly lacking.

Mr. Rafiq handed me a list.

600 lbs ship's biscuit
240 lbs salt beef or mutton
120 lbs of salt pork
30 lbs salt cod
90 lbs rice
2 bushels peas
30 lbs butter
60 lbs hard cheese
300 gallons beer
300 gallons fresh water.

We conferred, and on Etta's advice, Mr. Rafiq sent to
Rye itself, which gave Hookey an extra day with Etta and
me a pressing need to complete the Atlantic crossing in
record time.

At length we had everything we needed except a captain, so I sent Windward to fetch Hookey. Etta came
down to the harbor with him, driving them both in a
small, two-wheeled cart behind a contented gray pony.
Jeremiah, the stable boy who'd ridden for help, balanced
on the back of the pony trap and ran to hold the pony's
head when Etta pulled up opposite the *Heart of Oak*.

"I'm glad we've had the opportunity to meet again." Etta
clasped my hand warmly. "I wanted to thank all of you."

"You're welcome," I said, squeezing her hand back.

"I've had a long talk with Hookey, and your secrets are
safe with me."

"Secrets?" I tried to sound nonchalant.

"Sudden sandstorms. Spyglasses that see like daylight
in the darkness, and a wolf who is never around when Mr.
Deverell is present."

"I'm not sure I know what you mean, but it sounds a little weird. I would be extremely grateful if unfounded rumors might be nipped in the bud."

She smiled. "Consider them nipped quite thoroughly."

"Thank you."

"I like your Etta," I said to Hookey as he stood at the helm with Rye Harbor falling behind us fast.

"Is she my Etta?"

"I think she could be if you played your cards right."

He made a sound that might have been taken for contentment.

Once in the Channel, I changed into my breeches and settled down on deck to blow a steady breeze into the *Heart*'s sails, enough to achieve eighteen knots. It was almost like flying. I could keep it up for about four hours before I needed a break. All the time I had to be careful not to pitchpole her, that is to drive her under, nose first, which was what might happen if I only concentrated on the wind and ignored the action of water on the hull. It was a delicate balance, and I achieved it with the help of Hookey and Corwen. Hookey handled the *Heart*. Corwen reminded me to take frequent breaks, and for the eight hours a night that I slept like one dead, he held me close.

We made Elizabethtown, the main port on Bacalao Island, in nine days—a record. I needed to visit Hillman and Plunkett's Bank to make sure my finances were all in order, but first, while Mr. Rafiq resupplied, I slept.

32

The Wreck of James Mayo

I'M DREAMING. I recognize a voice. It's far away and has an American twang to it, a Virginia twang. It's shouting my name, not the name I have now, Rossalinde Deverell, but the name I had when I captained a privateer crew.

"Ross! Ross Tremayne!"

I opened my eyes in the darkness of Hookey's cabin. I'd taken advantage of his kindness and was stretched out on the narrow bunk. The full moon outside the cabin window shone through the salt-frosted glass onto Corwen's silver hair as he slept in the old armchair next to me.

"Ross! Ross Tremayne!"

I recognized the faraway voice, but it was slurred with alcohol and cracked from bellowing.

I heard footsteps coming down the companionway and a knock at the cabin door. I was aware Corwen had passed from sleep to wakefulness in about as much time as it would take for a wolf to do it.

"Ross! You'd better come." Hookey's voice this time.

"What's the matter now?" I intended to call out, but my voice did little more than croak. "How long have we been asleep?" I asked Corwen.

He took out a pocket watch and held the face up to the moonlight. "You've been asleep about seven hours. Me, three or four."

"Why do I feel it's the other way round?"

He grunted. "Try looking from this side of my eyelids."

"Ross?" Hookey again.

"Coming."

I looked down and found I was still fully dressed. Someone, probably Corwen, had taken off my shoes and dropped a blanket over me. I sat up and scrubbed myself awake with the heels of my hands.

"Come on. Whatever it is must be important or Hookey would let us both sleep."

He grunted and heaved himself out of the chair. "After you."

I wobbled slightly as I groped my sleep-fuddled way across the cabin to the door.

"What's the matter, Hookey?" I screwed up my eyes against the light from the lantern.

"Come and see," Hookey said.

We followed him up the companionway to the deck. A knot of sailors, the watch crew and a few more besides, stood around something . . . no . . . someone.

A filthy wretch huddled on the deck. I smelled him before I saw him—shit, piss, vomit, and stale beer in equal proportions.

"Ross Tremayne. There you are. I love you." The man opened his arms, and then, as if the effort were too great, he folded in on himself and began to weep.

I stared, dumbfounded. Was it? No, it couldn't be. He was dead, or was he? Maybe not.

I sank down on my knees in front of him. In the combination of moonlight and lamplight, I stared at the unkempt beard and the shaggy head, dark threaded with gray, trying to find the man I knew behind the bloodshot eyes. He stared up at me, reached out with the index finger of his right hand and touched my chin as if he could hardly believe I was real. At last I knew.

I pulled him into my arms. "It's all right, Jim. I've got you."

James Mayo, Gentleman Jim the pirate, was alive.

⋯⋯ ⋯⋯

I let the filthy pirate weep all over my clean shirt until he'd wept himself out and my knees were stiff from kneeling on the planks of the *Heart*'s deck. After a while the crew, embarrassed by unmanly tears drifted away, though the buzz of conversation followed their retreating backs. I heard snatches . . .

Is that really Gentleman Jim?

I thought he was dead.

Looks like he is.

I thought James Mayo was supposed to be the fiercest pirate in the Dark Islands.

I don't believe it.

The cap'n seems to think it's him.

I heard she once . . .

I was glad I didn't hear the end of that last speculative comment. I had once. I'll give him his due, Mayo waited a decent interval after Will's death before propositioning me, and of course I refused. I refused again the next time we met, but eventually I looked at Mayo, handsome, rakish, not a cruel man, at least, never to me, and I saw someone who might reawaken my senses if not my emotions.

All the while this was going through my head, Gentleman Jim wept gobs of snot and tears into my breast. Though the crew drifted away, Corwen stayed by my side, while Hookey and Mr. Rafiq hovered nearby.

I don't know how long it took, but eventually Jim's sobs subsided to hiccups. Even when they faded, he kept his face turned into my bosom. That was more like the Jim I knew, taking advantage of a situation for as long as he could.

"Can you speak yet?" I asked him.

His nod rubbed his cheek against my nipple. Enough was enough. I pushed him upright.

"I thought you were dead," I said.

"I think I am." His voice sounded cracked, like an old man's. How old was Jim? I'd always thought him to be barely a few years older than Will. With a shock I realized it probably meant he'd turned forty. He cleared his throat. "Strange how much like real life purgatory is," he said. "I thought you'd gone down with my ship."

"I almost did."

If Corwen hadn't pulled me out of the water with my arm opened to the bone and half my ear ripped off, I would have died when the *Black Hawk*'s powder magazine blew.

"I saw you heaved overboard," I said. "How did you survive?"

"Tarpot Robbie. As he was throwing me into the ocean, he realized I was coming round. He managed to kick a square of oiled canvas overboard with me. Did you know that you can trap enough air in oiled canvas to make a float? I began to swim for the nearest vessel. I was far enough away from the *Hawk* when her powder magazine went up. Did you have to sink my ship?"

"It was the only way I could save mine. I'd hoped to kill Walsingham, but I was unsuccessful."

"I know."

"You've seen him since?"

Jim began to laugh, but there was no humor in it, and eventually he subsided into dry sobs again.

◆————◆

"What are we going to do with you?" It was a rhetorical question. I didn't actually expect Gentleman Jim to answer it.

"I'm useless. Give me a few shillings and send me back for a gallon of rum. It'll see me to next week."

I frowned. That didn't sound like Jim. I'm sure he liked his drink, but he'd always been quite sober for a pirate, never giving anyone the chance to get the better of him while in his cups.

Corwen wrinkled his nose. "He smells as though he's been living on rum and not much else."

"Beer when I can't get rum, but rum's the thing. Fierce as an unpaid whore. 'S the only thing that makes me forget."

"Forget what?" I asked.

"Can't remember."

"How long is it since you've been sober?"

He pursed his lips and frowned at me as if trying to remember.

"It doesn't matter. Let's get you cleaned up."

"Just throw me in the harbor."

"That'll make you stink even more."

"Stink? I don't sti—"

"Billy, bring up some buckets of hot water and some lye soap. And a barrel we can dunk him in."

"Aye-aye, Cap'n."

"Jim, you're going to clean yourself up. Then we'll talk again."

"Madam, 'm perfectly clean." He waved Billy away.

I waved him back again. Two more hands brought a barrel.

"Get his clothes off. Take them to the dockside and burn them. Dunk him in the water, all of him. All the way in. Hair and everything. I don't want to see any crawlers on him."

I was beginning to itch myself. I should have thought about lice. "And bring me some washing water down to the cabin."

Dawn was breaking as three crewmembers stripped off Jim's rags. I was shocked at how thin he was as he stood there shivering in the half light. I thought at first it was the filth, but then I realized the marks on Jim's body were scars, long thin stripes where the skin had been peeled away, some still red, others fading to white. I knew for certain then which ship had picked him up out of the water.

"No wonder he's a mess," I said to Corwen. "And I don't just mean his body."

While the men were sluicing down what was left of a once-famous pirate captain, I followed suit in Hookey's cabin. I scrubbed myself down to the skin, washed my hair, and let Corwen check me for lice.

"You're clean," he said, running his warm hands down my flank. "Whether your shirt will ever recover is another matter altogether."

"I'll let Billy boil it," I said as I brushed my hair and tied it back with a thin black ribbon. "I wonder how they're getting on with Jim."

"What did you mean when you said no wonder he's a mess?"

"Did you see his scars?"

"Yes, nasty. I wonder how he got them?"

"Nicholas Thompson, Old Nick. That's who must have picked Jim up out of the sea along with Walsingham. He likes to flay his prisoners, sometimes to death, and sometimes to the point of death, to see how close he can take them while leaving them alive and writhing in pain."

I watched from a distance as Lazy Billy and Windward dunked Gentleman Jim first in one barrel of water and then a second. Billy, quite fastidious for a seaman, sniffed and decided they needed a third barrel. Then he gave Jim a sheet and sat him on the hatchway. At first, I thought he was going to try and comb out the matted mess of his hair and beard, but he obviously decided it was too much of a task and I heard the snip of shears as he cut everything down to stubble, then scrubbed his head and face once more for good measure. Then Windward took him down to the forward hold and strung a hammock for him in the cubicle where Billy did his rough doctoring.

I decided to leave Jim to sleep and get a couple of decent meals inside him. Billy would find him some clothes. I had a few errands to run—the most important of them to Hillman and Plunkett's Bank where I was pleased to see my fortune had increased, thanks to my one-quarter of the profits of the *Butterfly*'s trading. Mr. Sharpner had left a written account with Mr. Plunkett. I recognized Simeon Fairlow's neat hand on the sheet which detailed the figures and Mr. Sharpner's less elegant scrawl on the letter. It seems they'd stuck to legal cargo only, for which I was grateful, and Mr. Sharpner apologized for the empty hold on one run back from Jamaica to Elizabethtown, saying he'd turned down a cargo of livestock when he realized they were human slaves destined for the American enclave on the other side of Bacalao island.

I begged a sheet of paper from Mr. Plunkett and wrote a note to Mr. Sharpner, thanking him for the accounts and telling him I heartily agreed with his decision not to carry slaves.

It was early evening of the same day before Jim climbed the companionway and stood on board deck, his rough hands clutching the deck rail for balance. He was wearing a pair of sailor's slops and a loose shirt. His hair was so short I could see his skull. The day was reasonably springlike, so he wore no waistcoat or jacket. I thought I saw him shuddering as I approached. Corwen had agreed to my suggestion to stay below and let me talk to Jim as an old friend.

"You look more like yourself now." I spoke when I was still some distance off, not wanting to startle him unnecessarily. He jumped anyway and turned to face me.

"I'm not . . . myself, I mean. I might never be again."

"I know you, James Mayo. You've fallen on hard times, but you're still you inside."

"You don't know . . . "

"I saw your scars. Old Nick at a guess. But you survived. You survived the wreck of the *Black Hawk*. I'm sorry about blowing up your ship. I thought you were already dead, and I so dearly wanted to kill Walsingham."

"A pity you didn't."

"Indeed. We bested him when we met again, but he still lives, and he's back in Britain. He's a dangerous man even though he's maimed and blind."

"I know it. I didn't realize it when he first approached me to chase down the *Heart*, but by the time we caught up with you, I knew he was a horse of a different color altogether. Believe me, Ross, I would never have brought him to the *Heart* if I'd known you were on board. That damned box. I knew there was something odd about it."

"You can sense magic."

Jim shrugged. "In a small way. I think that's what intrigued me about you when first we met. You hid it well, but there was something—aside from the way your ship always managed to catch the fairest winds. There had to be something—someone—on board, and I knew it wasn't Tremayne. I figured it was either you or the black fellow, Rafiq, and the more I saw, the more convinced I became that it was you."

"Did you tell your men?"

"What do you take me for?"

I couldn't answer. I had taken Jim to be a dangerous pirate—and he surely had been—but he'd also shown me another side, thoughtful, tender. He didn't expect an answer, so I let him continue.

"After Walsingham tried to kill me, and Robbie gave me a chance, I swam for my life, thinking Robbie helping me was most likely a way of making my death slower. Then I saw a ship in front of me. My elation turned to dread when I realized it was the *Flamingo*."

"Old Nick."

"He sailed with my fleet, but I was never sure of his loyalty. I always thought he had ambitions, but he was deadly and damned good at giving pirates a bad name. It turned out I was right. I should have put Nicholas Thompson down when I had the chance. He kept me chained belowdecks on the *Flamingo*, as good as dead, and took my place as leader of the fleet. And no one stopped him or stood against him. Even Tarpot Robbie works for him now. He's been given his own ship, the *Lady Emma*. I heard that rumor here on the dockside. And my island, lovely Auvienne, is under that bastard's bootheel. He's sleeping in my bed, fucking my whores, killing anyone he thinks is against him. I built Ravenscraig from a tiny fishing village, and now he's pissing on it."

He swiped the heel of his hand across his eyes. "And there's nothing I can do. He's got it all, and I'm . . . broken."

"When you were on Old Nick's ship, did you see Walsingham?"

"Not at first. Nick thought he'd got himself a real prize. Thought he could ransom Walsingham back to the King of England, so he afforded him some care. His sawbones took off Walsingham's left arm when it started to fester. By the time they chained him up in the hold with me, he was beyond dying, so I guess Nick's surgeon saved his life if not his eyes."

"You were chained up with Walsingham. Did he ever speak of his book?"

Jim began to laugh. He laughed so hard his whole body shook, and at length he fell to his knees, still holding on to the deck rail like it was the only thing keeping him in this world. And then his laughter turned to dry sobs.

"What's the matter, Jim? Something about the book?"

"I know about the book. It's the only reason I'm alive. Old Nick took it, but Walsingham wanted it more than anything. He taught me a spell. Invisibility. He had that one in his head. I guess I have a bit of magical talent that I never realized. I was supposed to turn myself invisible and get the book for him. Then he started to teach me one of the codes—there's more than one—said if I could read him the spells, he could get us both out. Get him the book, he said, and he would take me with him. Though I rather think I was supposed to take him with me, since he was blind."

"Did you? Get him the book, I mean."

"I would have tried, even though I knew Walsingham and that damned book were a bad combination, but Nick's answer must have come from the King of England, so Walsingham was dragged away to his freedom. I . . .

was left with Old Nick who wanted to know what was in the book and thought I might be able to tell him. He has ways of being persuasive."

"I saw your scars."

"I knew once I told him everything he'd take enough skin to kill me. I waited until we were close to land, and then I used Walsingham's invisibility spell. It worked. They came to take me up on deck to peel another strip of skin from my body and thought I'd escaped and swum ashore to Jamaica, but I hid and finally made my escape when the ship put into port on the American side of Bacalao. I've been here ever since, dreaming of revenge."

"Looking for it in the bottom of a bottle."

"What if I have?"

"It's not good enough for you. James Mayo. You were one of the finest captains in all of the Dark Islands."

"Was."

"You can be again. You're not that far gone. You've cleaned up pretty well." I might have stretched the truth a little. "You can be the man you once were."

"Ha!"

"We need that book, or we need to destroy it. It's not for the likes of Old Nick, and Walsingham mustn't be allowed to possess it again. No one should have it. It's dangerous. We'll help you get back to Auvienne. Your men will rally to you when they know you're alive."

Jim swiveled round and sat, leaning his face into the deck rail.

"And all you want in return is the book?"

"Yes. The book. Safe in our hands or destroyed."

"It's a good bargain, but . . . "

"But?"

"I might have given Nick the key to translating it—partly, anyway. I didn't give the whole game away. The pain, you know. I'm not proud." His voice shook. "And . . . "

"There's more?"

"Walsingham doesn't need the book for all his spells.

It wasn't just the invisibility spell. He's got some of the other spells memorized."

I felt as though my gut was about to rise up through my throat. I'd had the bastard Walsingham at my mercy and I'd let him go, thinking him harmless without his sight and without his book.

 33

Dockside Ghost

I RELAYED ALL I'd learned from Jim to Corwen, Hookey, and Mr. Rafiq, back in the depths of Hookey's cabin.

"So what do you want us to do next, gal?" Hookey sucked on his teeth and gave nothing away by his expression. "This book is important, right?"

I nodded. "We certainly don't want Walsingham to get it, but if Old Nick learns how to use it, no one is safe from him, including his own crew."

Hookey frowned. "We need to think on this. We can hardly sail right into Ravenscraig under Old Nick's guns, can we? And if we put into any other part of Auvienne, his lookouts will take news back to him within the hour."

Hookey was right, Ravenscraig sat on the southern tip of Auvienne and was as heavily defended as any of His Majesty's Cinque Ports.

If we drew him out onto the ocean, he outgunned and outmanned us. We had only half the crew the *Heart* used to carry in her privateering days, and some of them were new enough that they'd never seen action against another ship. Our eight guns were not enough to go up against any ship Old Nick might send against us. His flagship, the *Flamingo* was equal to a first-rate man o' war. The *Heart* was faster, but broadside for broadside she couldn't compete.

"We have to do this by stealth," I said. "And I think we're going to need Jim to do it, though I'm not sure he's the man he was. He's weak. He needs time to recover properly, but we don't have time."

"You leave Gentleman James Mayo to me," Hookey said. "Give me a couple of days. He hates my guts. I'll put him through his paces—sober him up. There's no way he'll show any weakness if I'm in charge."

"You think so?"

"I know so. Billy can feed him up on the way to Auvienne. We can figure out a plan as we go."

"He said Tarpot Robbie captains his own ship now."

"I'll send Billy to ask around on the dock."

"Robbie might be persuaded to get us into Ravenscraig if we can meet up with him. He sailed with Jim for years. He saved Jim's life."

"Yes, but that was before Old Nick gave Robbie his own ship. His loyalties may have changed."

"It's worth a try if Robbie's anywhere close."

◆————◆

"You must be madder than the English king," James Mayo stared at me in horror and then looked around the cabin to Corwen, Mr. Rafiq, and finally Hookey. "What about you, Garrity? You were never so reckless when you worked for me."

Hookey shrugged. "Reckless? Ha! I never thought I'd hear you call someone else reckless. The Gentleman Jim I used to know would have braved anything to get back what was rightly his."

"It has to be you, Jim," I said. "Your people won't rally to me, but they will rally to you. Old Nick has them in his grip now, but you can't tell me they're loyal to him. They go along with him because they're scared of being the next one he flays alive. Individually, not one of them will stand against him, but collectively, if they have someone to lead them, someone they trust—"

"That's it. They won't trust me anymore. What am I? A dockside ghost, telling his sad story to anyone who'll buy a tot of rum or a jug of ale. Someone who used to be someone but isn't anymore."

"You're still someone, Jim, you've simply forgotten who."

"Maybe that's the best way."

"Then why did you come charging onto the *Heart* yelling for me two nights ago? What did you want?"

"I was drunk. I'm stone-cold sober now, and my head is fit to burst. I go to sleep each night aching for a tot of rum. I wake each morning with my hands shaking and a powerful thirst only spirits will quench. When I'm drunk, I harbor dreams of how it might be in a different world."

"If you leave Old Nick in charge of that book, everything you built on Auvienne will perish. Nick doesn't care about your ships, your men, your whores, or the ordinary folk who make a living from the land or from fishing, carpentry, or growing the crops you eat, or farming enough cattle to make the island self-sufficient. You had a sweet setup. Ravenscraig was a good little community, and it was yours. You cared what happened to it, ran it fairly, kept bastards like Old Nick from doing too much damage."

Jim sank his face into his cupped hands. "It's impossible."

"No, it's not. What if we find Tarpot Robbie? If we can convince him, will you admit the plan might work?"

"And how do you propose to do that? Robbie could be anywhere."

I put my hand up to Jim's ear. He flinched away, and then steadied himself. "That ear stud. Didn't Robbie give it to you?"

"A long time ago. I gave him a matching one."

"I might be able to use it to find him."

Jim scowled in puzzlement.

"I'm a summoner, Jim. This is only one aspect of it. Of

course, if he's not in these immediate waters, it might not work, but if he is, I do believe I can find him."

I could see something akin to hope behind Jim's eyes. Very slowly and deliberately, he removed the ear stud and handed it over. "Find him, and if he's with us, you've got yourself a revolution."

◆━━━◆

We didn't have much time. Whether we found the book or not, we'd have to sail for England by the twenty-seventh of May. Otherwise the king's deadline would go past, and the Fae would take punitive action. That gave us two weeks to find Tarpot Robbie and help Jim oust Old Nick from Ravenscraig, and preferably from life itself. Essentially, we'd be fomenting a minor revolution. If it succeeded, Nicholas Thompson, Old Nick, was too dangerous to leave alive, especially if he'd learned to make use of some of Walsingham's spells.

I thought about the atrocities Old Nick had committed, and I could live with myself even if I was the one to pull the trigger or run him through with a blade.

While Hookey devoted himself to getting Jim ship-shape and hangover-free, I climbed the mast, barefoot, and took Nick Padder's usual place as lookout. I had the ear stud curled in the palm of my hand and everything I remembered about Tarpot Robbie in my mind. We set a course for the Dark Islands.

Corwen was anxious to see me so far above the deck, but I promised him I'd tie on a line, and, indeed I did. Thankfully, now I was past the first three months of my pregnancy, the occasional bouts of morning sickness had abated, and I felt fit and energetic as though I could manage six armed revolutions before breakfast. When I told Corwen, he made a kind of choking sound and said he would try not to be overprotective. I wasn't sure he'd manage it, but I was grateful that he tried.

When I clutched the ear stud tightly in my hand, I thought I felt a slight pull, but as it was more-or-less in the direction we were traveling, I didn't make a big thing out of it. However, as we neared the Dark Islands, I felt a definite tug on my senses. I shouted down a new course to Hookey, climbed down to the deck, and willed a little more wind into our sails.

"You've located him," Corwen said as he came up behind me.

"I believe so, but I can't tell how far away he is or what course he's on."

"Is that you?" Jim looked to where the wind was filling our sails.

I shrugged.

"No wonder we could never catch you unless we had a bit of magical help."

"It's not something for everyday use, Jim. The reason the *Heart* is so fast is because she's a good ship, well sailed."

For two days we followed my seeking sense until, at last, there was a sail on the horizon. Jim climbed the mast after me, and we both sat up aloft, sharing my magic-enhanced spyglass.

"How do you feel now?" I asked.

"Better," he said. "Better than I did a week ago, anyway, but I could murder a tot of rum. Not sure I could stop at one, though, so I'd better not."

We stared out over the ocean in companionable silence.

"I should thank you, Ross. Whatever happens, I don't feel lost anymore."

"You were never lost, Jim, merely a little off course."

"You don't need to be kind. I would gladly have drunk myself to death if I could have found enough coin for it. You saved me."

"Then we're even."

"How can that be?"

"I blew up your ship, I nearly got you killed."

He shook his head. "No, I contacted Walsingham of my own accord. I brought the viper on board. It was my own fault if he bit me. By the time you blew up the *Black Hawk*, I'd lost her anyway. I don't blame you,

Ross." He put out his hand and covered mine. "You know how I feel."

I took my hand away gently. "Can I ask you not to feel it?"

"I don't think you can, but I won't let it complicate matters. Your husband is a fine man, as was Will, but I can't help wishing—"

"I think of you as a very dear friend, Jim. Let's leave it at that, shall we?"

"Of course. If you say so."

"I do." I handed him the spyglass. "Is that the *Lady Emma*?"

"It looks like her to me."

She was a three-masted, ship-rigged frigate carrying twenty-eight long guns on her deck and four carronades on her quarterdeck and fo'c'sle.

"She's a handsome vessel," I said.

"French built. I knew her when Albert Smith had the captaining of her. She could make fourteen knots and fight in the kind of rough weather that would make a ship of the line close gun ports on the lower deck. I wonder what happened to Smith. Death by Old Nick, I shouldn't wonder."

Jim handed me the glass, and as I focused on her, the *Lady Emma* came about and piled on sail.

"She's coming after us, like any pirate would."

"Better raise the parlez flag before she gets us within range of her guns."

"Good idea."

We raised our parlez flag. When she was almost within range, the *Lady Emma* raised hers.

We reefed the mains'l, keeping only enough canvas to hold the *Heart* steady. There was no such thing as still on the ocean. Robbie brought the *Lady Emma* around, and with barely a kiss between the two ships, we moored them together and tied a plank in place with nothing but a line for a steadying rail. There would normally be a bit of jockeying for position between two ships with a stated intent to parlez, but Jim showed himself on the *Heart*'s deck and Tarpot Robbie strode across the planks without so much as a by-your-leave. He gave a cry of joy, and there was some manly hugging and some mutual backslapping before the two men pushed back from each other's embrace and drew breath to ask what had befallen them in the intervening eighteen months.

"It's a long story."

"Not much to tell."

Then they both laughed and backslapped again.

I'd known Tarpot Robbie as long as I'd known Gentleman Jim though I'd never known him as well. We'd never had long, revealing conversations, but his was a familiar face. Now it was dressed up differently. Instead of a tarry pigtail and loose slops, he had light brown hair curling around his ears, and he wore long trousers in the pink of fashion, topped by a peacock-blue waistcoat, snowy linen shirt, and a jacket cut to reveal broad shoulders and narrow hips. His mustache had gone to reveal a clean-shaven face, deeply tanned—not handsome but distinctive.

"Gentlemen." I grabbed their attention. "Much as I hate to cut short this joyous reunion, may we talk below?"

"Of course." Robbie bowed over my hand—something he would never have done before getting his own ship—and followed me down to Hookey's cabin which had been cleared to allow room for enough chairs.

"Robbie, this is Corwen Silverwolf." I didn't use Corwen's real name. "You know Captain Garrity and Mr. Rafiq."

"Cap'n Tremayne, it's good to see you. There's at least two ghosts here today I never expected to see again. I go by Captain Robert Tarr, these days, since good fortune gave me my own ship."

"Your own ship!" Jim said. "How came you by such fortune?"

"Cap'n Thompson—"

"That would be Old Nick," Jim said, rolling the words around his mouth as if they tasted bad.

"Old Nick, aye. He was the only one to benefit from that terrible day. When we saw the smoke coming from the powder magazine, it was every man for himself. Lucky you insisted on us all being able to swim, 'cause we were swimming for our lives. The *Rhodes* picked up survivors, and we headed back to Auvienne, but the weather was boxy. You can't mess with nature without consequences. The witch, Walsingham, had caused that terrible calm, and I reckon the sea and the winds were rebelling. We were blown off course not once, but three times. By the time we reached Ravenscraig, Old Nick had beaten us there by three days. He'd announced your death and had set himself up in your place. No one much liked it, but no one was willing to challenge him over it."

He shrugged. "There was one naysayer who turned up two weeks later. Remember John Jackson, captain of the *Bitter Bird*?"

I'd had a run-in with Jackson once. He was a tough nut. Jim nodded.

Robbie continued. "He challenged Nick. It didn't go well. His skin's still nailed to the mast of the *Flamingo*."

I shuddered.

"So you'd be happy to see Old Nick gone?" Jim asked.

Robbie nodded. "It's not like the old days. Everyone's watching their back all the time. Old Nick might give you a ship one week and flay the skin off you the week after."

"How many can we count on, do you think?"

"After Jackson, there's no one will stand against him, but I reckon there'd be few mourners at his graveside if he were to meet with an accident. He has his own guard, thugs all of them and well paid. Some of them were on the *Flamingo* with him. He's set them up, and he rewards them well. Gold and girls—more than they ever want or need. They're loyal to him while he's paying them, but I don't reckon it goes any deeper than that."

"How many?"

"He's got four land-captains each with twenty or thirty men, and then there's the crew of the *Flamingo* when she's in port."

"Is she in port now?"

"She was when we left, but she was getting ready to

sail. He's named Haggerty as captain. He hasn't sailed himself for many a month. I think he's afraid of losing his grip on Ravenscraig while he's at sea."

"It's a kind of madness," Corwen said. "The more you have, the more afraid you are someone will take it away from you."

"Aye, he's mad all right," Robbie said, "but he's not stupid."

I put my hand on Jim's arm. "Remember, if we help you with this, Ravenscraig's yours, but we want Walsingham's book."

"It's a deal."

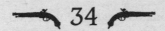 34

Ravenscraig

HOOKEY WANTED TO come with us, of course, but I couldn't allow it. The *Heart* and her crew had to stay safe and out of sight. I could call her to me when I needed to.

The smaller our landing party, the less chance we had of being spotted.

Hookey argued that the trio of Jim, Corwen, and me wasn't enough, and though I agreed with him, I had to balance stealth against firepower. In the end we took Lazy Billy, Windward, and the Greek as well. That made six.

Hookey tried to argue me out of going in the advance party, but as I was the only one who could counter any magic Old Nick might have gleaned from Walsingham's book, I had to go. I wasn't looking forward to it. I was horribly seasick on any vessel other than the *Heart*. The splice of ensorcelled winterwood in the *Heart*'s keel meant that she felt like a floating forest to me.

The six of us crossed to the *Lady Emma*. To balance things out, Robbie ordered six of his crewmen to the

Heart. It made sense. If Robbie's ship sailed in over-manned, the harbormaster might ask questions and news would quickly get to Old Nick.

Three of the *Lady Emma*'s crewmen crossed over without a murmur, but one sailor hesitated.

"I'd rather stay with the *Emma*, Cap'n, if it's all the same to you."

"It isn't, Iverson. You've got your orders."

"But, Cap'n—"

That was as far as he got. Robbie pulled a long-bladed knife from his sash and stuck the unfortunate Iverson in the gut with it.

I gasped and stepped back.

So sudden. So swift. So final.

There were ways to ensure obedience in a crew. Casu-ally murdering them was not one of the ones that gener-ally proved effective.

Robbie stooped forward over his victim, who was gasping like a flounder on the deck. He pulled out the knife with an accompanying sucking sound and then ca-sually swiped it across Iverson's throat, opening a death-smile from ear to ear. The deck ran red with blood. Robbie wiped the knife clean on Iverson's sleeve and then looked up.

"Always suspected he was Old Nick's spy. Anyone else doesn't want to wait it out on board the *Heart*?"

"Cap'n." A fresh-faced young sailor volunteered. "I'd like to go aboard the *Heart*, sir, if I could avoid your knife. You was right about Jackie, there. And . . . " He gulped. "And me, too, but I can't tell anyone anything if I'm not there, an' Old Nick can hardly hold my family to account. I doesn't do it for the money, y'see, but my sister's one o' the girls at the Compass, an' I gotta see her safe."

Robbie jerked his head toward the gangplank. "Off you go, Donny. When this is over, there'll either be Jim or Nick to answer to, but you earned a right to stay out of it with your honesty."

"Beggin', pardon, Cap'n, but it's about time someone did for Old Nick."

"That it is, lad," Robbie said. "Anyone else?"

No one stepped forward, so with everyone where they needed to be, we cast off from the *Heart* and set sail for Auvienne.

Offering to put wind in the *Lady Emma*'s sails would have been a step too far, so I went and sat on the forward hatch and concentrated on not being seasick while searching for any sign of magic. Corwen came and sat with me. Jim leaned against the rail, staring out across the ocean.

"You think there might be a problem?" Corwen asked.

"I don't know what's in Walsingham's book, or how well Old Nick can translate the code. At the very least he might have a warning system set up."

"Will you be able to dismantle it if he has?"

"It depends what it is. There's something in Aunt Rosie's notebook about neutralizing a spell—in effect, scrubbing it clean and washing it away."

"You know how to do it?"

"In theory."

Theory was put to the test soon enough. At the first sight of Auvienne on the far horizon, I felt a tremor. I grabbed Corwen's wrist and squeezed, not having any breath to explain what was happening.

He put his warm hand over my cold one, effectively lending me strength for what I had to do.

I knew of only one method to wash it away. It took precious minutes for me to manipulate the cloud layer and call a downpour as dense as any tropical storm. A satisfying band of rain stretched across our horizon. As the heavens opened, I felt the effects of Old Nick's spell dissipating. I could only hope I'd caught it in time.

Auvienne was a small island, richly wooded on steep slopes leading down to coves with golden beaches and sheltered bays. Ravenscraig, on the southern tip of the island, had been established by buccaneers almost two hundred years ago. They'd taken advantage of its natural deep-water harbor overlooked by a flat-topped hill and had built there. Those first wooden shanties had gradually been replaced, and now there was a long wooden quay and a series of buildings tucked into the foot of the hill, net sheds, fishermen's dwellings, and warehouses.

Above it, the town was fortified. A single street, known as the Stair, zigzagged steeply up to an arched stone gate. The town itself had a stout wooden palisade to the landward side. A promontory outside the walls contained gun emplacements, three batteries of carronade, a mixture of twenty-four and thirty-two pounders. I knew all this from my last visit. Nick might have changed things, but I doubted he'd removed any of the fortifications. He had a reputation for never tapping a small nail with anything less than a sledgehammer.

"Time to go below," I said to Corwen. "We'll have to wait it out until dusk and then make a move."

Our clothes had begun to dry on us and had started to rub in all the wrong places. In the hold, without a fresh breeze, my stomach began to roil.

Jim joined us. "Robbie's going to talk to a few old friends. Or maybe friends is not the right term, but they've certainly no love for Old Nick."

We waited in the depths of the hold as the *Lady Emma* docked, not a moment too soon as far as my gut was concerned. The creak of her timbers, the calls of the sailing master and the responses of the sailors gave way to the sounds of the dockside and the screeches of gulls in search of fish heads. We settled down to wait three hours until darkness allowed us to climb the Stair into town.

The sound of shouts on the dockside and rough voices overhead broke our calm.

Lazy Billy ducked down the aft companionway. "Old Nick's men are searching all newly arrived vessels," he said, and ran back up to the deck.

Our sailors were hiding in plain sight as part of the crew, but Jim and I were easily recognizable and Corwen's silver hair was distinctive enough that he would certainly be recognized on second viewing.

Corwen couldn't hold an illusion for long, especially for three people.

"Get up on deck with the sailors, Corwen," I said. "You can use illusion to blend in."

"Not without you," he said.

"I've got Ross," Jim said. "I can make us both invisible if we're close enough."

I could make us invisible as well, but it always drained me. I needed my wits about me, so I'd have to trust Jim on this.

"Mind how close, close is, pirate." Corwen turned and raced up the companionway after Billy, already looking like a dark-haired Spaniard in sailor's slops.

"I've been looking for an excuse to do this," Jim said and pulled me against the bulkhead, so close to him that I felt the outline of his body, leaving me in no doubt as to what he was thinking.

"If Corwen doesn't call you out for taking liberties with his wife, I might do it myself," I said.

He chuckled softly. "Is it too much like old times?"

"Once, Jim. I came to your bed once, and that was before I knew Corwen."

"Ah, but I've kept it in my memory, and my heart, for a long time."

"I'm sorry. I shouldn't have. If I'd known it meant so much . . . "

"Hush." He put a finger to my lips.

"Let me apologize."

"I mean hush, the search party's coming."

I pressed myself close to Jim and tried to make no sound. I felt his invisibility envelop us and I concentrated on barely breathing as half a dozen men descended into the hold, three down the forward companionway, and three down the aft.

The *Lady Emma*'s main hold was copious, but apart from provisions, which showed she'd been about to begin a voyage, there was no sign of stolen goods. This was a pirate vessel ready for a cruise.

I heard the men searching: tapping full water barrels, punching sacks of flour, and taking the lid off barrels of salt beef. I daren't turn and look. Somehow, I felt as though they wouldn't see me if I kept my eyes shut. Ridiculous, I know. I buried my face in Jim's shoulder. Like me, he was barely breathing.

"You're fully provisioned," a voice said. "Didn't you leave port three days ago? What are you doing back again?"

Robbie responded. "Damned American Navy vessel out there looking for something. I didn't intend to be what they found. Those things usually hunt in pairs."

The questioner gave a noncommittal grunt. "No one else spotted anything."

"It was only this morning. How many vessels have you had come into port today?"

Another noncommittal grunt.

"Be sure and tell Cap'n Thompson. He'll want to know."

We heard feet retreating up the companionway, but we didn't move until Corwen rejoined us.

"They've gone."

Jim released his hold on the invisibility spell before he released his hold on me, leaving Corwen in no doubt as to how close we'd been. I saw the smirk on Jim's face.

Corwen sighed. "Now's not the time, Mayo. Stop playing games."

Jim gave a deep throaty chuckle.

"Shall I call him out, Ross, or would you rather do it yourself?" Corwen asked. "Pistols or rapiers?"

"I'll think about it." I gave Jim a little push and took the hand Corwen offered.

◆━━━━◆

Robbie and ten of his crew went ahead of us into the town. Jim, Corwen, and I waited and left the *Lady Emma* an hour after full dark, hooded and cloaked, walking with half a dozen of Robbie's sailors who appeared intent on finding the nearest tavern. Billy, Windward, and the Greek had sauntered up to the town an hour before us, acting as if they owned the place. Their destination, like ours, was the Golden Compass, once Jim's home on land.

It was the largest of Ravenscraig's many whorehouses and taverns. An unambitious man could have lived well on the profits alone, but Jim had always had ambitions, and so, obviously, did Nicholas Thompson.

Our plan was simple—kill Thompson and let Jim take back Ravenscraig so that we could grab the book and sail back to England.

I was sure Thompson would have more magical wards in place, so we needed caution in our approach.

The Stair was steep and narrow with not a step in it. It was too steep for regular horse-drawn vehicles, though pack mules could make the journey.

A series of staged platforms up the rocky cliff face with wooden cranes offered an alternative way of sending cargoes up and provisions down, using counterweights and a clever system of pulleys. A series of ladders linked the platforms, and I tilted my head back to get a better look, wondering if the ladders might be a potential exit if things went wrong during the takeover.

"That was my idea," Jim said. "The pulleys, I mean. Can you believe they used to bring goods up with slaves?"

I could believe it, but I knew Jim had freed the slaves on Ravenscraig many years ago and, in turn, had acquired loyal free citizens.

As we approached the top of the Stair, the gate, set into a stone archway between two buildings, stood open.

"Wait." I put out a hand to stop Corwen and Jim. "Is there a way around it?"

"What's wrong?" Corwen asked as the rest of our company kept on walking.

"There's some kind of barrier in place."

"What does it do?"

"I don't know whether it's a warning or some kind of active trap."

"Billy, Windward, and the Greek must have gone through," Jim said.

"Or else they're lying dead somewhere."

"We didn't hear any kind of commotion."

The first of our party reached the gate and set off a clanging alarum.

Two soldiers emerged from the door on each side of the gate.

"Weapons, lads," the officer said. "Collect them on the way back down."

We hurried to catch up, and divested ourselves of cutlasses, pistols, and knives.

"You can keep one eating knife each," the officer said. "No blade longer than six inches."

The officer handed our cating knives back to us after we'd passed through the barrier.

"Oh, great," Jim muttered. "I'm going to start a revolution with a single item of cutlery."

"I suppose we have to assume most of the people who don't live here have only one knife, too," I said.

"While Old Nick's guard will have swords, pistols, and probably muskets or rifles, too," Jim said.

"So let's go shopping for more weapons," Corwen said. "Where's the armory?"

We caught up to the sailors from the *Lady Emma*. "Before you go on your way, lads," Jim said, "tell us what's changed since I've been gone. Where do the off-duty guards sleep?"

"The whorehouse that used to be the Blue Ball is now exclusively Captain Faraday's, and the Pineapple is where Captain Buller's men are billeted. The rest are in a new barracks building behind the Compass."

Damn. We hadn't counted on the off-duty guards being so close to the Golden Compass. We really didn't want to kick over a hornets' nest.

"What about the girls who were at the Blue Ball?" Jim asked.

"Oh, they're still there, providing the usual services, only now, I hear, they're not being paid for it."

We let Robbie's lads go on into the town. Their job was to shout loudly for Jim if he managed to oust Old Nick.

"The Blue Ball it is, then," Jim said. "See if we can attract the attention of Kitty Little."

"Who?" I asked.

"She was the Blue Ball's madam. I doubt she'll like her girls not getting paid for services rendered."

"How are we going to get in?"

"We're not. There's a privy behind the building. We'll wait for one of the girls to come out."

"Oh, great," Corwen said. "I've always wanted to hide in a privy."

As it turned out, it was a large communal privy with a long board with four bum-holes cut in it. There was a lantern hanging on a hook, but it burned low and gave off a flickering light. The air came in and went out again through two high holes in the wall set opposite each other, but despite the ventilation and the deep pit beneath the seats, it was still noisome.

We heard footsteps outside, too heavy to be one of the girls. All three of us pulled our knives. A six-inch blade wasn't much, but you could do a lot of damage if you knew where to stick it.

Corwen and Jim each took up their stations, one on either side of the door, while I sat on the far seat. The rough etiquette for using communal privies was that you didn't look too closely at your neighbors while doing whatever you'd come to do. By sitting there quietly I was next to invisible. As the man pulled open the door and stepped through, he already had one hand on the fall-front of his breeches. Jim attacked from behind, wrenching his head around. A satisfying but sickening crunch told us the rest.

I created a small witchlight, brighter than the lantern, and we checked him for weapons. He yielded a pistol, powder and balls, a bayonet for a musket, and a cutlass.

"Not bad for one man," Jim said.

"Did you know him?" I asked.

"No. Might have been from Old Nick's crew. Let's get him down the hole."

Each of the four seats was hinged separately. I lifted the end two and Jim and Corwen tipped the man head-first into the pit. He landed with a squelchy splat and a groan which, since he was definitely dead, must have been escaping air. He also disturbed the contents of the pit which didn't improve the atmosphere at all.

The next person we heard on the path outside came in calling, "Andrew, are you still in there? It's your deal."

This time I stood to one side of the door while Corwen gave a theatrical groan and hunched over his belly, head down in the darkness.

"What's the matter, man, are you ill?"

As the second man stepped through the door, Jim dispatched him with the bayonet from behind. He yielded another pistol, ammunition, a dagger, and a sword, before joining his friend in the pit.

"Let's go before someone else comes out to investigate," I said. "We've got weapons now."

Before we could let ourselves out, lighter footsteps on the path announced the arrival of one of the ladies. I blew out the lantern and we all pressed ourselves to the wall. The woman entered, lifting her skirts. She barely squealed when Corwen grabbed her from behind with one hand over her mouth and nose.

"We mean you no harm. I'll let you go if you promise not to make a sound. Understood?"

She nodded against his hand, so he released her. I brightened the lantern with a witchlight, making it look like a flame.

"You!" She recognized Jim immediately.

"Are you one of Kitty Little's girls?"

"I used to be. Kitty ain't here no more. Ain't no one lookin' out for us except ourselves."

"Where's Kitty?"

"He took her up to the Compass. Heard she hadn't pleased him, so . . . you know."

Yes, we knew. I hoped it had been quick for Kitty Little.

"What's your name?" Jim asked.

"Bella."

"Do I take it you'd prefer to get rid of the guards and Captain Faraday, so you can get back to business as it used to be?"

"I would. We all would. Where is he?"

"Who?"

"Captain Faraday, he came to look for Andrew Bonnett."

"That was Faraday?" Jim shrugged. "He won't be bothering you again."

"Good. He was a right bastard."

"Bella, you would be doing us a service if you went back inside and said Captain Faraday and Mr. Bonnett have gone down the road on business. Make up something that sounds plausible. Say he ordered strong drink all round and get all those guards as drunk as skunks. Lay 'em out with drink until they're useless."

"Are you going up to the Compass?"

"We might be."

"Are you going to do for that bastard Old Nick?"

"Do you expect us to tell you our plans?"

"I want to know if we're safe to get our own back on Faraday's men."

"Get them insensible on strong spirits. By morning, you should know what's safe and what's not."

"Would it be helpful if I got a message to Lucy at the Pineapple? There's a whole troop billeted there."

"If you can do it safely."

"You say Faraday and Bonnett aren't coming back?"

Jim jerked his head toward the privy pit.

She grinned. "Best place for 'em. I'll get a message to the Pineapple, Cap'n. If Old Nick shouts for reinforcements, they won't be coming from down here."

Jim kissed her cheek. "Bella, you deserve a place of your own."

"Don't forget that when you're back in charge."

"I won't."

Armed with two pistols, a sword, a good knife, and a bayonet, we made our way up to the Golden Compass.

Lazy Billy was leaning against the wall beside the door with a tankard of ale, looking as relaxed as you please. He sauntered over the road to meet us.

"We had all our weapons taken at the gate," he said.

"As did we, but we managed to rearm ourselves," I said.

"So did we." He drew aside his coat to reveal a cudgel swinging from his belt on a piece of twine.

"Well done, Billy. What's happening in there?"

"The word is that Old Nick is at home, but he's got six guards in the corridor outside his rooms."

"Good job there's a back way," Jim said. "We'll go in from the kitchen. Billy, when you hear a commotion, come running up like concerned citizens."

I added. "But don't get yourselves shot."

"Understood, Cap'n."

We left Billy to saunter back into the Compass and followed Jim through the yard to the kitchens. The door stood open, which was not unusual. The heat from the fire and the ovens could be unbearable otherwise. Sneaking in was out of the question. We'd have to risk that the kitchen staff were either neutral or friendly.

Jim walked in first. Somewhere inside a pot crashed to the floor, and a voice said. "Don't move if you want to live."

35

Old Nick

"CAP'N JIM!"

"Yes, it's me, Bronwen. Put that skillet down. Are we safe in here?"

"No one's safe these days, but we're as safe as we can be."

I stepped into the kitchen behind Jim. Corwen followed me, pushing the door closed behind him.

A ripple went through the room, from the pot-boy to the scullery maids, nine people in total, three of them rowankind I'd seen on my last visit. The eldest of the rowankind was dressed smartly as a butler. His face lit up in a smile when he saw Jim.

"Captain Mayo, it's good to see you back, sir. Have you come to stay?"

"One way or another, Alfred."

I remembered Jim had told me about finding three very seasick rowankind on a Portuguese vessel that the *Black Hawk* had taken. He'd brought them to Ravenscraig and given them work at the Compass. They couldn't leave again, since going anywhere would involve a sea voyage. I wondered whether they were aware of the freeing of the rowankind in Britain and whether they'd regained any of their wind and weather magic.

"You're going after him, aren't you?" Bronwen, broad and florid, pushed her sleeves up to her elbows.

Jim didn't reply. I knew what he was thinking. His cook, someone he must have trusted not to poison him, was now working for Old Nick.

"I didn't think you'd still be here."

"We weren't given a choice," Bronwen said. "Captain Thompson can be very persuasive."

"I'll bet," I said.

"Why didn't you poison him?" Jim asked.

"Can't you feel it?" The cook gestured toward the air.

"It's a geas," I said. "If they do harm to Nick, they'll suffer the same effects themselves."

"So we've been doing him nothing but good." The cook grinned. "Rich food and plenty of it. Beef, lamb, pork, all served up in fancy sauces. And the best wines. As much port as he can drink, and that's a lot." She sighed. "We're taking bets on whether the flux or the gout gets him first. Too much rich living isn't good for a man."

Jim laughed. "My mother always told me to eat my vegetables."

"I don't think Captain Thompson had a mother. If he did, she didn't know his father."

"What about his guards?"

"There's not much point in poisoning them. There are always more where they came from. You've seen the new barracks?"

"Heard about it. Too dark to see."

"Guards from there can be here in minutes."

"So we need to deal with Nick without raising the alarm."

She nodded.

"Do they know about . . . ?" Jim nodded in the direction of the cellar.

Bronwen shrugged. "I've never seen them use it ,and

they don't guard the entrance. I've never volunteered information that's not asked for."

"Do you cook for the guards in the barracks?" I asked.

She shook her head. "They have a plain cook. He's not
a real artist, so I sometimes send them a treat."

"Could you do that tonight? Laced with a strong lax-
ative?"

She grinned. "I can do better than that. I have ipecac.
It's a strong emetic. Half an hour after they take that,
they'll be casting up their accounts all over the place."

"Have you got syrup of figs as well?" I asked.

She grinned at me.

"You're a wonderful woman, Bronwen Williams." Jim
flashed her a grin. "How long will it take you to deliver
your treat?"

"Give me half an hour to make a respectable sauce
that will disguise the taste. I have a pudding almost ready.
Then half an hour after that it should take effect."

"Did I ever tell you how much I love you?" Jim kissed
her florid cheek and led the way down into the cellar.

"We can wait down here for an hour. We have to go
down in order to go up," he said. "My predecessor was a
cautious man. He had an escape stair that only he had the
key to. That key has been lost."

"How do you know that?" Corwen asked.

"Because it was around my neck when I was thrown
overboard, and it wasn't around my neck when I was
hauled onto the *Flamingo*. You can pick a lock, can't you,
Ross?"

"I can, but not as fast as Lazy Billy, and not silently.
There's always a rattle or a click to give it away for anyone
who cares to listen. Where does the door come out?"

"The paneling in the bedroom."

"Let's hope he hasn't retired early."

We waited for an hour, every minute dragging like ten.

The access to the secret stair was in the ceiling of the
cellar above a stack of barrels. It didn't look like much
from below, but Corwen boosted Jim on his shoulders
and Jim knew exactly how to stick his finger in an un-

likely looking crack in the ceiling, twist and pull. The panel swung down, dislodging plaster and dust, and revealing a cobweb-laden hole barely the width of a man.

Jim went first with only a moderate amount of low cursing, then he reached down a hand for me while Corwen gave me a shove from below. Then Corwen leaped, and together Jim and I drew him up. The hole was exactly that, a hole that had not been used for years. It smelled of old plaster and neglect. There was a small flat area and a stair that was more like a ladder. It was designed for only one person.

"You'll have to be first, Ross," Jim whispered. "It's as tight as a coffin, so it's the only way you can get at the lock."

I had my roll of lockpicks wrapped around my forearm, so I pulled them out from under my jacket before ascending the stair.

My heart pounded in my chest. The higher I climbed, the worse I felt. This was never going to work. Visions of snakes crowded into my head. Were there vipers in this tiny space? I hesitated. Jim tapped my calf impatiently from below. His touch plainly said, "Go on. What are you waiting for?"

I raised my right foot and mounted another step. My head began to pound, and I felt as though the dust was choking me. Left foot. Right foot again. Now I'd lost contact with Jim's hand on my calf. I felt above me. There was another step. The stair was almost vertical now. I reached up and found a small platform, the stair head. Suddenly, I was filled with dread. There was no point in going on. We were doomed to fail, so we should give up now or simply lie down and die. My heart felt as though it was about to explode in my chest or pound its way through my breastbone. My head was full of all the torments that awaited if I climbed right to the top.

Below me, Jim's hand flailed against my ankle, not a firm enquiring touch as before, but a plea for help. It wasn't only me. Jim could feel it as well, and probably Corwen below him, though I had no way of knowing how he fared without shouting down. Right at that moment, if I could have, I would, even though it would have given our presence away. But the feeling had left me mute, my throat dry and choked with fear.

I tried to breathe, but the air I sucked into my lungs seemed to have no sustenance. I was getting dizzy, slowly fading into unconsciousness.

Jim's hand brushed against my calf. He'd managed one more step. Then he touched the back of my knee. He was still managing to climb against the spell.

Spell.

Of course it was a spell, a magical working to sap confidence and even life itself from anyone susceptible. I was the most susceptible of all, attuned as I was to the ebb and flow of magic. This wasn't a trap laid for me, specifically, however; it was a general working surrounding Nick's private apartments, set to attack anyone arriving with ill intent.

Once I recognized it, I began to dismantle the separate elements. First, I sent a witchlight up above me to dispel the darkness. Then I sent another down to Jim and one to Corwen. I could still perform my magic. Good. The spell was one that preyed on the mind, not the body.

Jim's hand steadied on my calf.

I fought the fear element by element. I couldn't remove the spell, but I could negate its effects on me, and I hoped that would negate its effects on Corwen and Jim, too. First of all, breathe. Do not choke. There's no reason to choke, nothing to choke upon. The air is clear.

I used my wind and weather magic to stir up a gentle current of air, bringing the cool, damp cellar air into the still air of the passage. My dizziness began to clear, and with it the pounding in my chest subsided to a manageable level. I climbed another step and then one more, concentrating on gaining the landing one step at a time.

Finally, there were no more steps. I was standing in a small space roughly the size of an upright coffin.

Coffin. Death. Despair.

I knew those feelings were from the spell, so I pushed

them aside and listened for any sounds coming from the other side of the door.

Nothing.

I began to relax.

Then there was a knock. I jumped back, but there was nowhere to go.

Calm down. The knock wasn't on this door, but the outer door of Nick's suite of rooms. Sometimes my hearing was too good.

I heard a voice say, "Come."

Then the voice of the rowankind butler Alfred announced, "Cook sent up some new baked pasties, sir. She thought you might like to try them fresh from the oven."

While there was conversation in the other room, I tried a pick in the lock, found it too big, and tried a narrower one. Holding the pins with one lever, I pushed a second into the lock and felt around.

"Put them over there." Nick sounded annoyed, as though Alfred had disturbed something.

I continued to feel for the sweet spot in the lock.

"Yes, sir. Cook says to eat them hot."

There was a series of clicks as my pick slipped. Dammitalltohell! I'd have to start again. I pushed the first pick into the lock one more time and held the levers back.

"I know how to eat a damn pasty. Get out."

I groped about with the second pick.

"Yes, sir."

And groped.

"Alfred."

And groped.

"Yes, sir?"

And groped.

"I'll have Delia tonight."

A click and the lock yielded.

"Yes, sir. What time?"

I released a breath and pushed the panel an inch. It gave, but with a slight creak and a scrape of wood upon wood.

"Ten of the clock."

I pushed the panel open and stepped out into a bedroom that didn't look substantially different from the last time I'd been in here at Jim's invitation. Nick wasn't one for change . . . except, on a side table was a shallow bowl filled with an assortment of surgical looking knives and a cutthroat razor with a notebook open at a page with a diagram. I started forward, but it was obvious it wasn't Walsingham's book; rather, it was Nick's diagram of muscle layers beneath a flayed face. I swallowed down rising gorge.

"I'll send her up, sir." Alfred's voice was followed by the door clicking closed.

Jim and Corwen crowded behind me, and I saw from the looks on their faces that they were still suffering from the effects of the spell, Jim more than Corwen. With our entry into the room, however, the effects were fading fast. We'd crossed the barrier into Old Nick's inner sanctum.

I heard a curse as Nick bit into a pasty and found it too hot.

"Now," I mouthed. There would never be a better time.

❖————❖

We burst through the door from the bedroom into the living room, again familiar from my visit two years ago, though Nick didn't keep it as neat as Jim used to.

We caught Old Nick bent forward, letting hot jam pasty fall from his lips and reaching for a glass of wine on the table, presumably to cool down his burned mouth.

I dived to the left, going straight for the door, turning the key in the lock and leaving it there. Jim ran straight ahead, a pistol in each hand. Corwen ducked right.

Old Nick barely had time for a curse. He dropped to his knees, thus avoiding Jim's first shot, which shattered the elegant mirror above the mantel, and reached into his pocket.

Oh, I knew that gesture. Walsingham's pockets had

always contained preprepared spells that only had to be tossed at an opponent to take effect. Jim, being the most obvious threat, was the one Nick lobbed a spell at. Time slowed; instead of getting a second shot off immediately, Jim took precious seconds to bring his left hand up, level the second pistol, and fire it at the point where Nick's head had been fully five seconds earlier.

In the meantime, Nick grabbed a cutlass from where it rested by the fireplace and swiped toward Jim's head. Jim had to have seen it coming but caught in the slow-time spell, he couldn't even defend himself. Corwen, however, had not been caught by Nick's spell and as the cutlass swept down, he leaped between Jim and Nick and parried with the sword we'd taken from the dead guard captain.

The guards in the corridor, alerted by the noise, tried the door and found it locked. There was much shouting and kicking of the door panels.

Right boys. Now's the time!

I hoped Lazy Billy, Windward, and the Greek were rushing up the stairs doing their concerned citizen's act and thoroughly confusing matters outside. I heard the thunder of booted feet on the staircase and Lazy Billy yelling, "What's going on? Was that a shot? Do you need help?"

I hurled my small knife at Nick. Had I been an expert at throwing knives, and had the balance of the instrument been better, I might have stuck him with the blade. As it was, I clanged the heavy handle into the bridge of his nose, which was enough of a distraction for him to drop the slow-time spell, which needed concentration from the wielder to keep it working. Jim snapped back into real time and, both pistols spent, flipped the one in his right hand so he was holding it by the barrel and clubbed Old Nick between the eyes.

That would have done for any normal man, but though Nick went down, he wasn't out. He was fighting on pure instinct now, his eyes full of madness but lacking intelligent calculation. He kicked out and swung his cutlass again. Corwen slashed at his sword hand, and the cutlass and three fingers went flying. Jim stamped down hard on Nick's wrist and used the pistol again, smashing hard against Nick's skull—one, two, three times.

It was messy but effective. With half his forehead caved in, Nick writhed on the floor, choking out his last. Everything went quiet.

Then a door panel smashed in, and a loud voice shouted, "Cap'n, are you safe?"

"Quite safe, thank you," Jim shouted. "There's a new captain in town."

"We got 'em covered, Cap'n," Lazy Billy shouted. "And the whole room's cheering downstairs. I don't think Old Nick was any too popular with the locals."

I unlocked the door and let it swing open. Billy, Windward, and the Greek had the six guards sitting in the corridor with their backs against the wall and their hands on their heads.

"What do you want us to do with these?" Windward asked. "Shall I kill 'em?"

Jim stared at the men and scowled at one of them. "Davy Blunt, what are you doing with this scum?"

"Trying to keep from being flayed alive, Cap'n Jim."

"Go to the barracks and tell Robbie and his men to pass the message. There's a pardon for everyone who throws down his weapons and comes out of there naked."

I laughed. Jim certainly had the right idea. Being naked puts you at a distinct disadvantage when you're up against men both armed and clothed, especially when you're still suffering from the effects of ipecac and syrup of figs.

In the end, Jim's rebellion occurred with very little loss of life, though he wasn't inclined to trust the land-captains who'd supported Old Nick. Unsurprisingly, they were from Nick's old crew. He had them all taken down to the *Flamingo* and locked in her hold while he considered what he should do with them. I didn't care. Jim was on his own now, all debts paid.

I called the *Heart* and was pleased to see her sailing into Ravenscraig Harbor ready to take us home. We'd fulfilled our promise, and now Jim had to fulfill his.

We needed Walsingham's book.

36

Atlantic Crossing

THE FIRST THING I checked was the notebook on the table in the bedroom. I'd been correct in my first assumption. This wasn't Walsingham's, but Old Nick had obviously made a copy of some of the pages for his own use and had added notes as well as making his own notes on the flaying of a human. His writing was remarkably neat and his drawings technically correct, but oh so disgusting. Muscles and tendons drawn with the loving accuracy of a surgeon, but not for the purposes of curing the sick.

I was suddenly very glad the man was dead.

I burned the book in the grate, watching it turn to ash. Then I scooped up the ash and tossed it out the window, sending a powerful breeze to spread it on the ocean beyond the harbor.

Jim had Nick's corpse removed to the square outside the inn and tied upright to a post to display—very publicly—that Old Nick was no more and things were about to change. I thought it gruesome. Then I realized Jim knew his townsfolk better than anyone, and if that's what it took to convince them, then who was I to argue?

We searched every drawer and cupboard in Nick's rooms but found nothing except the trappings of Nick's life.

Corwen and I went down to the *Flamingo* to look through everything in the captain's cabin. We found only more flaying knives and a few sheets of what looked like parchment but could have been human skin.

What had Nick done with the book?

He'd obviously been able to access it—or at least some parts of it.

I called the house girls, the kitchen staff, and the rowankind together in the public room downstairs in the Compass. In the cool daylight the room looked sordid. It smelled of old tobacco and yesterday's beer.

"I'm looking for a book," I said. "It's handwritten in some kind of code and may have been wrapped in an oilcloth to keep it dry. Captain Thompson would have set great store by it and would either have kept it with him or put it somewhere very safe. It's not in his strongbox. Neither is it in his apartment or, as far as we know, on the *Flamingo*. There's a reward for anyone who finds it or gives us information which leads to it being found."

"How much of a reward?" one of the whores asked.

"Fifty guineas," Corwen said.

A murmur went around the room.

"Come and see us if you have anything to say." We left people talking.

We hadn't been back in the upstairs apartment for long before Alfred, the rowankind butler, knocked at the door.

"The book," he said.

"Do you know where it is?" I asked.

"I think so, but you're not going to like it."

The pit of my belly suddenly felt chilled. "Tell me."

"A courier ship under Captain Lapenotière arrived from London at the beginning of May under a flag of parlez. Captain Thompson entertained a young gentleman, a passenger, not the captain. An ambassador of some kind, I thought. I don't know what they spoke about, but

I do know that for the next few days, Captain Thompson spent a lot of time alone. Whenever I brought food, I saw him copying from one book to another."

That would be the notebook I'd burned. I thought I knew where this was leading. My scalp tingled, and I felt as if all the blood had drained from my face to my feet.

"And then what happened?"

"A week ago the captain concluded his business with the gentleman. I surmise he'd copied everything he needed. The next time I came in, there was a package wrapped in oilcloth on the table. Shortly after that the young gentleman left with the package. He went straight to his ship. If I'm not mistaken, though all her crew were in ordinary dress, it was a British Navy ship, a Bermuda sloop called the *Pickle*. I'm sure the captain recognized her for what she was, too, and he wouldn't want to start an argument with the British. The book went down, and a box came back up under guard. The kind of box that often contains valuables."

"And the sloop?"

"Sailed with the tide four days ago."

Damn, damn, damn, damn, and damn. So near and yet so far.

Since the Treaty of Amiens, there had been time for Walsingham to impress upon someone from the Mysterium that the notebook was a priority. It didn't sound as though he'd been on the courier vessel himself. I was pretty sure that he wouldn't have risked coming anywhere near Old Nick after his treatment last time. But the young man in charge of the negotiations was either high up in the Mysterium or a Walsingham-in-waiting.

The Walsingham always had a number of young men around to do his bidding and learn from him. My own brother, Philip, had been one of them, in training to become the next Walsingham when the present one fell. It was the way with Walsinghams.

"Did you happen to catch the name of the young gentleman in charge of the negotiations?" I half expected Alfred to say Walsingham, but he didn't.

"Sumner," he said. "Mr. Philip Sumner."

How could it be? My brother Philip was dead. I'd killed him myself to protect Corwen and David. My knees wouldn't hold me. I dropped into a chair.

"Did he look anything like me?"

"Oh, no. He was a skinny fellow, light-boned, with straw-colored hair and pale blue eyes."

I began to breathe again. It was simply someone using Philip's name, quite probably to protect his own, but another sign Walsingham was behind the mission to ransom the book back from Old Nick.

"Thank you, Alfred. By rights you've earned yourself fifty guineas."

"That won't do me any good here on Auvienne. I need a favor instead."

"Such as."

"Your ship, the *Heart of Oak*, she's got winterwood in her keel."

"She has."

"When you leave, please take us with you. We want to go home."

"Across the sea? You might die from seasickness. A lot of rowankind do."

"The three of us survived the crossing on a Portuguese barque. We've done it once. We can do it again if it means going home. A ship blessed with winterwood is our only chance."

"We'll be going all-out to catch the sloop. It's not going to be a pleasant voyage."

"We'll take the risk. And if you'll let us, we can help by providing a favorable wind."

Well, that answered one question. These rowankind knew they had their magic back. I had to sleep sometime, but if the rowankind could call the wind while I slept, we might make the voyage in nine days. We might even catch up with, or overtake, the sloop.

I nodded. "At your own risk, Alfred."

He smiled. "Understood, Cap'n."

◆───◆───◆

We said hasty good-byes to Jim, leaving him to clear up the mess and sort out any who might still fancy the idea of stepping into Old Nick's shoes. I was confident Jim could do it. Each day that passed had seen him growing back into the man, the pirate, he used to be. If there had to be pirates in this world, I was convinced Captain James Mayo was better than a hundred Old Nicks. Pirating was a tough business, but someone had to keep the worst of them in order.

Jim came down to the dock with us. As we prepared to go aboard the *Heart,* he took both my hands and kissed my cheeks. "If you get tired of dry land, you know where to come."

I smiled at him. "I do, but I won't. Though don't think me ungrateful for the offer. Do me a favor, though . . . "

"Anything."

"Ban all your ships from attacking the *Butterfly*. She's trading in American waters, but she's mine."

"Of course. None of our ships will touch her."

I didn't tell him who the other co-owners were, or he might not have agreed so readily.

The three rowankind came hurrying along the quay, possessions in canvas sacks.

"And I see you're stealing my butler and his family."

"We'll do our best to see they get home safely."

"Please do. I confess I'm quite fond of them."

"And they of you, but they need their own kind and their own place."

Hookey shouted an impatient ahoy from the *Heart*'s deck.

"Hookey's ready to cast off, Jim. Have a great life. Stay well and safe."

"And you, my love."

He squeezed my hands once and then let me go. I thought it might be the last time I ever saw him, and I was glad to leave him in such good fettle.

Corwen was waiting for me at the top of the gangplank. As I turned to wave to Jim, he said softly, "It would never have worked, you know."

"What?"

"You and Gentleman James Mayo."

"I know."

"Good." He put one arm around my waist as the *Heart* slipped away from the quay.

❖──────❖

As I predicted, the three rowankind were horribly seasick. I could sympathize. It was a dreadful affliction to have, and they were looking forward to at least nine more days of the relentless roll and heave of the ocean.

"Are you sure you can manage this?" I asked Alfred as he wobbled up onto the deck on the evening of our first day.

"It will take my mind off puking into a bucket," he said. "And the fresh air will do me good."

"Here, lean against the mainmast." I showed him where to sit and how to call the wind and how to work the water. "Take care not to bring the wind on too strong. A few heady gusts into the tops'ls and you could pitchpole her, send her tumbling arse over head to the bottom of the ocean. If you're in any doubt, come and wake me. I'd rather be woken then drowned."

He chuckled, "I won't let it come to that. You've been doing this all day. Get some sleep."

I'd relented and taken up Hookey's offer of using his cabin, and though the bunk was narrow, Corwen and I fitted into it well enough. He was lying in the bunk, waiting for me, as I arrived below.

"Tough day?"

"Relentless, but we're making good time. I've left Alfred on deck filling the *Heart's* sails. I feel mean when he's been so seasick, but he says the distraction will do him good."

"Quite right, too. A little distraction never hurt anyone." He moved over and patted the empty space beside him.

"Ah, that looks good, though I'm not sure I can sleep."

"Who said anything about sleep?"

I shrugged out of my shirt and breeches, the latter getting too tight around my developing belly, so I had left the top buttons unfastened and covered the gap with a sash.

Corwen made appreciative sounds as I snuggled down beside him naked. He cupped my breasts, first one and then the other.

"There's more than there used to be," he said.

"A gentleman wouldn't draw attention to it."

"I like it. I like this, too." He slid his hand down to my belly. "Are our boys comfortable in there?"

"Our girls are very comfortable, thank you, and—oh! Was that you?"

"What?"

"I felt something flutter. It was so light I wasn't sure. I felt it earlier but thought it was indigestion."

"The boys are moving?"

"I think they are."

I felt giddy. For the last few months they'd been silent partners in everything I'd done, but I hadn't allowed myself the luxury of thinking of them as people. Now they were, moving of their own accord inside me.

Corwen raised himself up on one elbow and placed his hand, fingers spread, across my belly, holding still until—

"There!" I said. "Did you feel it?"

"I think I did." I heard the smile in his voice. "Our little miracles."

"Miracles. Yes, they are."

I snuggled closer to Corwen. "I've been cautious about telling people. I didn't even tell Jim, but I'm pretty sure he's guessed."

"Let's plan a visit home as soon as we can and announce it officially. Mother would love to tell everyone, if she hasn't already."

The two of us might soon be four—a real family. Boys or girls, it didn't matter as long as they were healthy. I fell asleep thinking about names.

I woke thinking about breakfast.

Corwen was already up and about. As I finished dressing, he shouldered the cabin door open and brought me a bowl of porridge sweetened with honey.

"I need to go on deck, Alfred must be tired and hungry."

"I couldn't do much about tired," Corwen said, "but I took him porridge as well. He even managed to eat it without throwing up. Maybe using magic is helping with the seasickness."

"I hope so. It's a miserable condition."

Between us, Alfred and I drove the *Heart* like a willing horse into her bridle and made the crossing in nine days. I hadn't really expected to catch up with the Navy sloop, the *Pickle*. Even if we had, short of a miracle we couldn't outgun her, but I hoped we might overtake her and thus be on the dockside when she made port. Of course, if she put into the naval dockyard at Chatham, we had no chance.

Hookey brought us into the Thames estuary and up-river to London where we moored close to Wapping Old Stairs. We scanned the river for signs of the *Pickle*, but we saw nothing. When we made enquiries among the stevedores and the Thames watermen, no one had seen the *Pickle*. Damn, she had to have made port in Chatham, and the notebook could, even now, be in a coach heading for London. We'd never find it in a city this size.

Dammit, we needed the goblins again.

37

Murder

THE GOBLINS WERE rapidly turning into an unofficial magical spy network, but while ever they traded favor for favor, I was always going to be in their debt. I needed a way to gain their cooperation without living in constant fear of owing them something I'd spend the rest of my life trying to repay. Magical debts were much worse than monetary ones. Since the business we were conducting would benefit all magicals, I thought it was about time to give them the rousing speech about cooperation between close cousins all working toward the same common goal.

"Do you think that will work?" Corwen asked as I outlined my ideas. We were rattling along in a hackney coach from Wapping to Whitechapel. I'd abandoned my breeches for a dress and redingote with a respectable bonnet.

"I hope so. The goblins want the same as we do, to be able to live free of persecution from the Mysterium. They keep saying they're not sewer goblins anymore. I think that's really important to them. They're an underground race that wants a share of the sun, or as much sun as they might be able to get in smoggy London. Who knows, they might even aspire to an estate in the country."

"We only know Tingle, Barnaby, and Twomax. What do other goblins aspire to?"

"A good question. Let's find out."

But when we arrived in Whitechapel, we found a great commotion at the entrance to George Yard.

"What's going on?" Corwen asked a young constable standing guard to keep the curious at bay.

"An 'orrible murder, sir. Never seen anyfink like it. Blood up the walls. And rumors of strange sightings."

"We have business with a tailor in the yard. When will we be able to get through?"

"Not ever, sir, I don't fink. It's outside the tailor's premises, an 'orrible corpse what don't even look 'uman."

I felt myself go dizzy. Was it a goblin corpse? I found myself muttering, "Please don't let it be Tingle," under my breath, and then thought it might be Twomax, which was equally as bad, or Barnaby Tingle, Mr. Tingle's grandson.

"We know the tailor and some of his associates," Corwen said. "Do you need someone to identify the body?"

The constable looked interested for the first time and then took a whistle out of his pocket. The ear-splitting screech attracted the attention of a gentleman in a caped coat and bowler. He sent a young lad to ask what the constable needed. When he explained that we might be able to identify the corpse, the lad scurried off, spoke to the cape-coated man, and then ran back, panting an invitation.

"The Bow Street officer asks if you will kindly step this way, sir."

Corwen and I passed the constable while he was still trying to tell us that only Corwen had been asked to come forward.

"John Ward, sir, Bow Street officer." The man in the caped coat offered his hand, saw blood on it, and withdrew it quickly.

"Corwen Deverell, and this is my wife. My family has a mill in Yorkshire. We do business with Mr. Tingle."

"You know him by sight, sir?"

"We both do, and we also know his grandson, Barnaby."

"Then perhaps you wouldn't mind . . . " He nodded toward a shape covered by a large blanket. "Though it's not a sight for a lady."

I inclined my head and let Corwen step forward in front of me, but as Officer Ward raised the blanket from the corpse, I shuffled forward.

"That's not Mr. Tingle," Corwen said, as we both stared down into Tingle's goblin face. His glamour must have faded in the instant of his death, but no one would recognize the pale-faced, slit-nostrilled goblin as the jolly, grandfatherly face Mr. Tingle presented to the world. Though we'd have liked to give a name to this corpse, identifying it as Tingle would expose goblins to the world.

"How did he die?" I asked.

Officer Ward obviously realized I'd not swooned at the sight of a corpse, so he twitched the blanket back a little farther. I gagged and stepped back. Tingle's chest was a mass of ruined meat and bone. Red blood was streaked with the deep green of goblin heart-blood.

"It looks to me like a magical killing," Ward said. "I've never seen this kind of thing before. His heart has exploded."

"You've sent for the Mysterium, I hope," Corwen said.

"Naturally, and I'll be glad to hand the cadaver and the case over."

"I'm sorry we couldn't help with the identification, Officer Ward."

"Corwen, I think I'm going to pass out." I tugged at his sleeve, only overacting by a small margin.

"Excuse us, please. Since we can't help, I think I should take my wife home."

"Certainly, sir. Thank you for trying."

The constable let us out of the alley into the crowd where we found our coach still waiting. We climbed straight in as another coach arrived with the arms of the Mysterium emblazoned on its side.

"Wapping Old Stairs," Corwen told the driver and then fell back onto the seat with me as the coach set off at a fair clip.

"Poor Tingle," I said. "I wonder what happened?"

"How many people do you know who can kill like that?" Corwen answered my question with one of his own.

"Walsingham."

"Or maybe those he's trained."

"The young man who collected the book from Auvienne?"

"There may be more than him."

I glanced out of the coach window. "Hey, this isn't the way to the river. What's happening?"

❖————❖

Corwen pushed open the coach door and leaned out to see the driver.

"It's all right, it's Twomax on the box with the driver," he said.

Relief flooded over me. I'd been preparing to find Walsingham, or the young man calling himself after my brother Philip, or at the very least a Mysterium officer with a guard of redcoats running behind.

The coach trundled on through London's streets. I lost track of where we were until we passed the Palace of Westminster and continued beyond. Eventually, the coach pulled up in a street of houses built close together, but beyond them I could see open land. It looked like the end of London's westward sprawl.

"Quickly, quickly, follow me." Mr. Twomax climbed down from the box and opened the coach door. "Into the house, quick as you can."

I'd barely set both feet to the ground before the coach drove off. We followed Twomax through the front door of an unremarkable house and into a sitting room where Barnaby Tingle sat hunched in a chair.

Barnaby wasn't a full goblin. In most lights he could pass for human—though not a handsome one as his nose was still pointy with slit nostrils and his skin pasty and bloodless. He looked up as we entered.

"It's my fault," he said. "I did it."

"Now, boy, stop talking like that." Twomax balanced on the arm of Barnaby's chair and patted him on the back. "Tell the Deverells what you told me."

Barnaby sniffed and straightened in his chair. "I knew you wanted to get that old bastard Walsingham, so me and the lads—"

"Barnaby has—had—some friends his own age," Twomax said.

He used the past tense. This was getting worse and worse.

"Go on, Barnaby," I said.

"Me and the lads started to ask around. Had anyone seen an old blind bloke with a powerful stink of magic around him? Some of the lads get around . . . underground. I know Grandfather said we weren't sewer goblins anymore, but honestly there's a whole city down there, and it's not all shit. There's underground rivers and overflow drains. Some of it's been there since the Romans."

"Go on, Barnaby. Get to it," Twomax said gently.

"We found something—only not where we expected it to be, and not even when we were underground. We'd decided to have a bit of fun and go to Vauxhall Gardens, it being early in the season. We took a boat across the river, to the Vauxhall Stairs and, getting off the boat, we felt it, smelled it. There was magic happening, and it wasn't good magic."

Barnaby's voice broke like a schoolboy's, and he wiped his nose on his sleeve. Twomax pushed a handkerchief into his hands, but all he did was pull it from one hand to the other repeatedly.

He swallowed and took a deep breath. "We were too afraid to go past it again, so we ran all the way to Westminster Bridge and back over to the north bank. That's when we split up and ran for home. It took me most of the evening to work my way across the city by a roundabout route. I don't know why I went to the workshop instead of home, but I slept in the doorway, waiting for Grandfather. When he came, I told him what had happened, but by that time I was feeling peculiar. My heart was pounding, and I had this feeling that . . . that death was coming for me.

"I've never had much magic. I've never been able to sustain a glamour for more than a couple of minutes on account of me having a human mother, but I've always had a good goblin nose and I could smell something—and it was me. I stank of death. Grandfather could smell it, too. He told me to run and tell the ladies not to come to the workshop today. Then he did something—I don't know what—and suddenly he was the one who smelled like death. He'd taken my death so that I could live. It was my death. I shouted at him then, but he told me it was too late, and to go and do what he'd told me to do, and he'd see me in the next life, and I was to find Uncle Twomax."

Barnaby raised his head and tear tracks marked his face. "I ran. I should have stayed, but I ran. And . . . the others . . . he killed them, too."

I glanced at Twomax. "Barnaby's friends?"

Twomax nodded, clenched his fist over his heart and mimed an explosion, spreading his fingers out. "All three of them. We carried the bodies safely away before anyone reported them."

"Oh, Barnaby." I knelt on the floor in front of him and took his hands, cold and trembling. "Your grandfather loved you. He still loves you. That was what a parent or a grandparent does for their kin. Don't blame yourself. He did it because he wanted to."

"I can't even say thank you."

I glanced at Twomax and raised one eyebrow.

Twomax shrugged. It was up to me.

"Barnaby, would it help to see your grandfather one last time? His spirit, I mean?"

"What? His ghost? Could I?"

"I can call him back, but only for a short time and only once. More than that wouldn't be fair. He has to move on."

"Only for a short time. I understand."

I wondered if he truly did, but I'd offered, and he'd accepted. Now I had to do it.

I used to take my abilities lightly. Calling up spirits seemed almost normal to me. I'd loved Will so much that I kept his spirit with me for three years without realizing how wrong it was. If I called up a spirit now, I did it only out of desperate need and only for a very brief time.

"I don't know what Mr. Tingle's first name was," I said.

"Joshua," Twomax and Barnaby said together.

I rocked back on my heels and sat on the floor at Barnaby's feet, remembering my first visit to Joshua Tingle's tailoring business, his outward appearance as a wholly-human, rotund, rosy-cheeked English grandfather with a periwig and a potbelly accommodated by an excellently tailored suit. Then I remembered being appalled by his goblin countenance. It was my first view of a natural goblin, a white-skinned creature with an emaciated body, a large hairless head, a hooked nose, and slit nostrils. His hands were long and tapered with three joints on each finger. I'd been shocked then, but I'd begun to take it for granted and think of goblins as normal when we'd rescued Twomax and a bunch of youngsters from the *Guillaume Tell*. As goblins went, Tingle was considered handsome.

I concentrated hard on his goblin form, repeating his name over and over again in my head while staring at the random pattern of color on the pegged rug.

"Grandfather!"

The first indication of my success was when Barnaby reacted. I looked up from the rug and a gray, ghostly figure hovered horizontally in the middle of the room. He bent his legs and gradually rotated into an upright position.

"Mr. Tingle. Welcome," I said. "Barnaby needs to see you."

"Ah, Rossalinde Deverell. I wondered who had the power to call me back. Thank you. I need to see Barnaby as well."

"Grandfather, I'm sorry."

"Sorry for what? For being a headstrong, reckless young fool? Yes, yes. We've all been young. With luck, some of us get over it and become headstrong, reckless old fools." He chuckled. "There's no blame attached to you, my boy. The blame is on him who sent the curse." He looked straight at me. "And I'm sure you know who that is."

"Walsingham."

The spirit nodded. "Give me a little time to tell Barnaby things he needs to know about the business, and then I have something else to tell you, Rossalinde."

"Of course."

"Twomax, are you listening?"

"Yes, Tingle. Here I am."

"Barnaby's going to need your help for a year or two."

"Of course. Whatever I can do."

There followed a succession of instructions for Barnaby on which ledgers he needed for which transactions and how he was to pay the workers this much and not a penny less, and to keep up the free breakfasts to help them start the day right. And then it got personal because Tingle said he'd been perfectly aware of the liaison between Barnaby and a certain low-class goblin girl whose family still lived underground, but it was all right because she was a good girl. She had a strong talent for glamour and would help him to keep the business looking the way it ought.

Barnaby sat there and looked stunned. "Well, boy, if there's anything you need to ask me, this is your last chance."

"I . . . err . . . does it hurt?"

"What? Oh. It did, briefly, but not now. I have no regrets, Barnaby. I love you, boy. Be brave and be strong, and don't go looking for black witches."

"I won't. I promise. Never again."

"Rossalinde." Tingle turned his attention to me.

"Yes, sir."

"Your debt to me . . . "

"Kill Walsingham?" I said.

"Yes, that. But also negotiate for the goblins to be a free people under English law, with rights."

"I will. I promise." I saw Corwen wince. I'd made a promise to a magical ghost, which was possibly the most serious promise I could make.

"There's consternation here," Tingle said. "On this side of the divide, I mean. A spirit has been called back across and made corporeal. It wasn't your doing, was it?"

"No, I didn't even know it could be done."

"It can't. It shouldn't be, but it has been. I wondered if it was you because it's your brother."

"Philip?"

Mr. Tingle started to fade. "I've said too much. Do your best, Rossalinde. Barnaby, I love you. Stay out of trouble."

With an audible pop, Joshua Tingle vanished.

We all sat in silence, contemplating Tingle's messages. Things were much more serious than I thought.

If Philip was back, he'd be looking for revenge.

"Whatever you need, the goblins are with you," Twomax said. "Except for Barnaby." He stared at the boy, "Who has promised his grandfather not to go looking for black witches."

Barnaby swallowed whatever he'd been going to say and nodded.

"Walsingham has declared war on the goblins, today. Tingle was a good man, and Barnaby's three friends were loved sons of good families. We can't suffer such losses and allow Walsingham to live. When you're ready to go after him, count us in."

"Thank you."

"I wanted to rouse the goblins with pretty speeches and an appeal to their better nature," I said to Corwen as we left the house and made our way toward the river. "I didn't want to do it over the corpses of Tingle and Barnaby's friends."

"I know." Corwen took my hand and guided me over

the cobbles outside the Palace of Westminster. It was a good thing he did because my eyes were blurry with tears.

◆————◆

Corwen and I reached Westminster Bridge and hired a boat to take us to Wapping Old Stairs where the *Heart of Oak* lay at anchor.

The tide was on the turn. Soon the waters churning beneath London Bridge would be a death trap, but it was slack water, and, for a brief time, the river idled beneath the arches and burbled around the broad, boat-shaped starlings which both protected the bridge piers and narrowed the river flow.

The three rowankind had waited for us on board, recovering from their seasickness and resting up, ready for the journey back to Hull from where they'd been stolen some years ago. We wished them well and gave them the fifty guineas we'd promised for news of the book. Alfred shook our hands, each in turn.

"I'd like to say the fifty guineas is unnecessary," he said, "since we didn't actually find the book for you, but it will get us back home and give us enough to set ourselves up with a little shop."

"If you have any problems, Iaru is still open," Corwen said. "You'll be welcome there."

"We know. We'll remember."

"Don't get caught using magic," I added.

"We won't."

The rowankind clambered down into the boat we'd arrived in. They planned to take the York-bound coach from the Cross Keys in Wood Street. Corwen said softly. "I'm going to miss them. I hope they'll be all right."

"I think Alfred's common sense will guide them through. And the fifty guineas won't hurt. Where did that come from, by the way?"

"Old Nick's coffers. I stood over Jim until he put it into my hand."

I laughed. "He's not going to miss it, is he? He's got a fortune. Several fortunes."

"I hope he lives long enough to spend it all. I don't usually say that about pirates, but after Old Nick, Jim is positively benign. The people of Auvienne are certainly better off with him in charge."

"I'll drink to that."

38

Sundered

THANKS TO BARNABY Tingle, we knew where Walsingham was. We'd found him once before at the White Lion public house close by Vauxhall Stairs. It had been the time we'd rescued Philip. By taking him with us, we'd drawn a viper into our nest.

I wondered why Walsingham would return to a previous location. Mr. Tingle's news, however, about the spirit of my brother being dragged from the afterlife and made flesh carried its own weirdly internal logic.

Walsingham was scarred and maimed. He'd lost one arm and both his eyes, and the explosion on the *Black Hawk* had scarred him all down one side from groin to head. He needed someone to be his eyes, someone he trusted implicitly—and he was not a man to give trust easily. Philip had been his lieutenant, accepting his ideology absolutely. He'd looked to Walsingham as the father figure missing from his childhood.

Our father had been a sea captain, absent on long voyages and then seeming like a visitor in his own house. I was his favorite, and he showed it. I'd been too young to know how unfair it was at the time, but with hindsight I recognized it now. Philip was much younger than me, still a child when Father was lost at sea, but I don't recall any tears other than my own.

For all those reasons and more, Philip was the ideal person to become Walsingham's eyes and hands, and the last place Walsingham had had Philip close to him had been when they'd lodged at the White Lion. Bringing a spirit back from the dead and making him corporeal was a massive undertaking. Walsingham would have needed every advantage, so using the right place for a working might be crucial.

Or Walsingham might have given his spirit another body. Alfred had said the man calling himself Philip Goodliffe looked nothing like me, and I knew that when I dressed as a man, I looked a lot like Philip. So it was possible Philip now inhabited someone else's body. Had that person shared his body with Philip willingly or not? Had he been ripped from his body and left as a sundered spirit?

I could speculate all I wished, but if Walsingham was tied to one place, I knew he would have protected it with every spell in his arsenal.

We needed a magical army.

Luckily, the goblins had offered.

We gathered by Westminster Bridge, ten of the best fighters from the *Heart* and a phalanx of Twomax's goblins. This time Hookey had insisted on being included. Corwen was in wolf form, using his nose to best advantage, and would undoubtedly use his teeth when the time came. Twomax led the goblins, but he looked small compared to the physique of the fighters he'd brought with him, magically savvy as well as strong and quick.

We split into two groups, one to approach by road, one by river. I was in the prow of the *Heart's* boat as we nosed into Vauxhall Stairs. I had Corwen Silverwolf pressed up against my side and Hookey by my shoulder. Billy and Windward handled the oars while the Greek was at the tiller. Our number was enhanced by six strapping sailors.

Twomax led the road party, trying to blend in with merrymakers on their way to Vauxhall Gardens. As we approached Vauxhall Stairs, another boat was disgorging passengers dressed for an evening of revels. We hoped the number of people would mask our intent.

We took our turn and disembarked onto the steps. The stink from the vinegar works, sharp and pungent, overcame the smell of the river. The White Lion fronted onto the lane that led from the river toward the gardens, a low building with two bow windows and a central door. Last time it had been full of customers and lit warmly with lanterns. This time it was dark and deserted, its bow windows like two blind eyes.

Corwen's growl rumbled in his throat. The stink of magic mixed with vinegar was enough to set my eyes watering.

"Where is the bastard?" Hookey asked.

My ears were sharp enough to hear Twomax approaching from the back of the inn.

"We'll soon find out," I said. "In we go."

Exactly as planned, Twomax's goblins burst through the back door as we burst through the front, but instead of an inn full of people the ground floor was deserted except for a couple of broken chairs. Corwen streaked up the steps followed by Hookey and Billy as Twomax checked the cellars.

Nothing.

The bird had flown.

"I can still feel it," I said. "There's dark magic here." I put up a witchlight and saw the flagstone floor covered with symbols, scribed in something dark and sticky.

"Mind where you put your feet," I said. "Someone's done a strong working here."

"What is it?" Twomax curled his nose. "It smells bad."

The last time I'd seen something like this was in an old warehouse in Plymouth where Walsingham had worked blood magic.

"There's something here," I said. "In the center of the working."

"Can't see anything," Hookey said.

Everyone was milling about, now, having ascertained the building was empty.

"Wait." I put out a hand and searched with my magical senses.

I found something small and weak, barely a residual shadow of whatever, whoever it had been.

A sundered spirit, not quite dead, but not alive either.

"Hush," I said. "Keep still. Stand back."

I summoned it.

A shadow appeared in the center of the blood-working, barely a wisp at first, but it slowly coalesced into something human in shape. I called again, and it became clearer, though still not solid. It was, or had been, a young man with fair hair and a slender frame.

"Who are you, shade?" Twomax asked.

The shade sighed. "I don't know who I am now."

"Who were you?" I asked.

"Diccon."

"What brought you here?"

"I was born 'ere."

"Did you die here?"

The shade looked puzzled. "Am I dead?"

"What do you remember?"

"He asked me if I wanted to be a gentleman."

"Who asked you?"

"The man who didn't have a name. Mam used to call him the visitor. Paid good money for the attic rooms but didn't stay all the time. Kept a horse here, well, until the lions got loose from Vauxhall Gardens and tore her up. Bad business."

That would have been the hellhounds Walsingham created to kill me and Corwen on the night we rescued Philip.

"Did the man go away after that?"

"For a long time. Then he came back, though he was maimed. Looked as if he'd been in a battle."

"He asked if you wanted to be a gentleman. And did you?"

"Wouldn't you?"

"Then what?"

The shade frowned. "I was a gentleman, only . . . I wasn't me. Someone else was walking and talking for me, putting on fancy clothes, sleeping in a soft bed. I thought it marvelous at first, but then I started to get smaller and smaller until . . . where am I?"

"The White Lion."

"Where's Mam?"

"There's no one else here."

"She must be here. Mam? Mam!"

"Diccon, the gentleman you became, does he have a different name?"

"Name?"

"Is he called Diccon?"

"No. Not Diccon."

"What is he called?"

"Philip."

I feared as much. Walsingham had brought my brother back and set him in Diccon's body, at first cohabiting, but now Diccon had been cast out completely. Though, while his body still lived, Diccon's spirit was sundered and in limbo.

"Someone find me a bottle with a stopper," I said, while keeping my concentration on Diccon lest he disappear.

"Here, will this do?" Twomax pushed a silver hip flask into my hand. I took out the bung and sniffed. Brandy fumes. That should keep Diccon happy.

"Diccon, I can't promise to put you back, but will you come with us to find your body? I swear I will try my very best to make it right for you."

"I don't know how to do that?"

"It's all right. If you give your permission, I'll carry you in this." I held the hip flask up. "Do you like brandy?"

"I like it fine when I can get it."

"Then I think you'll be very comfortable in here."

With as much gentleness as I could, I summoned Diccon's spirit into the brandy flask and pushed the stopper home.

"Mr. Twomax—" I began.

He sighed. "I know. Set the goblins the task of finding Walsingham."

"And Philip."

"What if they've left London?"

"Do your best, but try not to get anyone killed."

He nodded. "What about you?"

"We'll see the king in a few days' time and find out whether he's been able to set the wheels in motion to disband the Mysterium. If the Mysterium is disbanded, Walsingham will lose both resources and protection."

"That would be a good outcome."

"The best, but I'm not counting on it."

39

Unicorns

WE HAD GIVEN the king until the eighth day of
June to approach his ministers and discuss what
changes might be made to protect the rowankind and the
country's other magicals. So much hung on the king's reply, that I barely slept in the few days leading up to the
meeting.

I knew that Larien wanted this venture to succeed, but
Dantin did not. To that end Larien had sent David to ensure no betrayal at the meeting. David had proved adept
at raising magical barriers that would protect us whatever
happened.

We'd arranged the meeting place in Richmond Park
again, close to the White Lodge where Mr. Addington,
the king's first minister, resided. It was close enough to
the Fae gate that we could make a quick exit if required.
At least this time we would recognize the king and not be
fooled by some substitute in fancy clothing.

We'd arrived in London by sea, without our own
horses. Four days before the meeting, we hired three cobs
and rode to the nearest gate, which happened to be the

Richmond one. Fae gates were scarce around the capital as the industrial blight severely restricted where the Fae were comfortable going.

Mr. Rafiq rode with us to bring the hired hacks back to the capital. Most of the *Heart*'s sailors have little familiarity with good-quality riding horses. Hookey's of the opinion that putting a sailor on a horse is an affront to nature, but Mr. Rafiq looked as elegant on a horse as he did on the deck of a ship. He took our horses in hand and, with a wave, turned for the city.

Unlike our visit in February, Richmond Park was now a patchwork of vibrant green with wooded areas and rolling heath dotted with grazing deer. We hardly noticed the difference when we passed from summer in Richmond to summer in Iaru, except, perhaps, for the smell. Iaru's background smell was spicy with floral undertones. You ceased to notice it after a few breaths, but it was always there.

David met us riding his own horse and leading Timpani and Dancer who had found their way back to Iaru from Plymouth where we had last seen them. I thought my brother looked a little paler than usual.

He scowled at us. "You took Annie to Plymouth," he said.

"I presume you didn't want to let her go off on her own," I said. "She's safe. As to happy, I don't know. What's the situation here?"

"Lady Calantha has found three separate excuses not to talk to me or, indeed, to be in my company, for which I am grateful. My father, however, is not pleased with either of us, and Uncle Dantin has been in a filthy mood for weeks. He scowls and stomps around and won't tell anyone what's bothering him."

"It sounds as though this misalliance has brought misery for everyone. I don't have any suggestions except sitting all parties down together and talking through it, but that doesn't seem like a very Fae thing to do."

He shrugged. "Let's get on with planning to meet the king. If he's managed to persuade his ministers to change the law, the Merovingian alliance may not be so important."

And so we did.

On the morning of the eighth day of June, a Tuesday, we emerged from Iaru on foot and took up a position within sight of the White Lodge. Unlike the last time, there was no steward to erect a canopy. A small group of people set off toward us, with King George in the lead, looking as though he was out for a Sunday stroll. This time I was in female attire. To tell the truth, I was having difficulty accommodating my belly in breeches, but my condition was invisible in my high-waisted day dress.

"That's definitely the king this time," Corwen said.

"I'm surprised he's not surrounded by bodyguards," I said. "Where are the Blues? Or do you think the park is crawling with redcoats again?"

"They'll not get through my shield," David said.

We were in the center of an invisible bubble which no shot could penetrate, and no person could enter unless David allowed it.

As the king approached, Corwen and David bowed low while I curtseyed deeply.

"Yes, yes, it's a little late for that, don't you think?" The king said. He looked a little strained around the mouth. I hoped he wasn't falling ill again.

He waved away his flunkies and stepped forward. He looked at me and David and then at Corwen. "Name yourselves."

"Majesty, names are dangerous for such as us."

"And yet, here I am, your sovereign, asking you a direct question. You can trust me with your names."

Corwen took a deep breath, "Corwen Silverwolf, Majesty, and this is my wife, Rossalinde, and her brother, David Lariensson."

"Thank you. And you are all of the magical persuasion?"

"We are."

"Like you," I said.

The king ignored my comment, but I'm sure it hit home.

"What news, Majesty?" Corwen asked.

The king shook his head. "What you ask is impossible. The Mysterium has protected Britain for two hundred years. Addington tells me it cannot be dissolved without an act of Parliament, and he's not inclined to support a bill while the French question is so prominent."

"And the rowankind, Majesty?" Corwen prompted.

The king took a breath. "There are some things only the reigning monarch and his first minister are privy to. The rowankind question is one of them. It's over two hundred years since Elizabeth, first of her name, found a solution for a very pressing problem. Addington assures me nothing in law makes the rowankind vulnerable to the Mysterium."

"Then why are rowankind being hanged for their magic?" I asked. "The Mysterium is above itself."

"There's nothing I can do without the goodwill of Parliament. I'm sorry."

"So are we," David said softly. "Sorry for what is about to happen."

"Threats?" the king said.

"The Fae don't make threats," David said. "They will offer a demonstration to show you yours is not the only power in the land."

"What kind of demonstration?"

"I can't say."

"Can't, or won't?"

"Can't, Majesty. The Fae Council of Seven will decide."

I had an idea. "Majesty, there always used to be a Fae ambassador at court until the interregnum when Cromwell held the republic. How would it be if you invited the Fae to send an ambassador again? Maybe if one of their own kind were to be at court, they might at least have a better understanding."

"And acknowledge magic is not controlled by the Mysterium?"

"It would certainly indicate that," I said.

He shook his head. "I think what you ask is too much. Magic must be controlled."

"The Mysterium doesn't control magic now," I said. "It drives it underground. There is magic in this country such as the Mysterium has never dreamed of, yet none of it is a threat to the realm. In fact, if allowed their freedom, the magicals could benefit Britain greatly. Your subjects love you, Majesty, including the magical ones. Please, you must help them."

The king looked uncomfortable. I could see he was looking for reasons to refuse. I tried a different tack. "Perhaps you could appoint a royal commission to examine the position of the Mysterium with regard to the rowankind. I do believe the Earl of Stratford might take an active interest if you asked him."

"Stratford. He's not a magical as well, is he?"

"Not at all. In fact, he has a grandson who is a Mysterium officer."

"I'll talk to him. I'm not unsympathetic to your requests, you know, but I am the king, and I must do as a king should. My government is too concerned with war and wheat harvests to pay much heed to magic."

"They may be more inclined to take it seriously, soon, Majesty," David said. "And I'm sorry for it."

◆———◆

We reported back to the Council of Seven who sat in state in the grove. They were ranged in order of age with Lord Dax on the left. I'd not known all their names when we faced them before, but I'd taken David on one side and he'd given me their names and a little of their histories. Lady Iphransia, the elder of the two female council members, sat next to Dax with Tarius next and then Lady Coralie, who looked middle-aged to me. Dantin came next and then Eduran. Larien came last. I was surprised that Larien was the youngest of them, because he seemed to have a potent voice on the council. Age didn't necessarily relate to precedence.

After the council members had all spoken and we had relayed what the king had said, Dantin shot to his feet. "I said we should have acted first and negotiated afterward. This whole matter could have been settled by now. We could have brought the country to its knees already and made the king our vassal."

"And what would be the point of that?" Lord Dax spoke quietly, but as soon as he did, everyone else fell silent. "If we'd wanted to spend time governing the humans, we could have established ourselves millennia ago. I said then and I say again now, we must let them go their own way."

"Not if they are killing rowankind," Dantin stamped his foot for emphasis. "Their king is not fit, and their Parliament is ineffective. I say we destroy their government and let them replace it with something better."

"There's nothing to say that what they replace it with will be better," Larien said. "You know I was skeptical from the very beginning that the king and Parliament could be made to see reason . . . "

That was news to me. Larien had seemed as firmly behind our attempts to see the king as Dantin had, even though he had obviously wanted a better outcome. I filed the information away for later.

Larien continued, "I agree about a demonstration, but let it be nothing too damaging, nothing irreversible. Otherwise, we will only prove to the humans that magic is wicked and that will harden their resolve. They are stubborn beings."

"I don't see why we can't simply order all the rowankind to return to Iaru and let that be an end to it." Lord Eduran spoke up.

"The rowankind aren't exclusively ours anymore," Larien said. "They've lived their own lives for generations."

"With respect . . . " I didn't know whether interrupting the Council of Seven was allowed during a debate, but I couldn't stay quiet any longer. "With respect, it's not only about the rowankind anymore. When you asked me to restore the rowankind magic so that they could leave their bondage, I argued that I would not do it if the rowankind were simply going to return here to be your servants, and you agreed."

"We did," Lady Iphransia said.

"But while the gates to Iaru and the Okewood were open, magical creatures slipped out into the world: pixies and kelpies, trolls and hobs, and probably many more. So the Mysterium is now aware that witchcraft is not the only problem, which endangers us all. We would all like to live free."

"What's this got to do with the rowankind?" Dantin asked.

"Everything. The problem is the Mysterium. Dissolve the Mysterium, and you protect the rowankind, the goblins, the hobs and the trolls, and even the unregistered witches. It will take some time to change the hearts and minds of the people; It's not something that you can do overnight, yet I hope they'll learn to accept their magical neighbors eventually. But you can't expect the people to accept magic if you've used it as a weapon. Show the king and his Parliament wonder, not terror. Show them how magic can be a force for good."

Lord Dax chuckled. "Rossalinde may have the right of it. Give the humans until midsummer before we show them something more serious, but in the meantime, show them wonder."

There was one of those uncanny silences during which I thought the Fae lords might be communicating among themselves, then Larien turned to us. "Ross, Corwen, please return to London and assess the mood of the people if you would be so kind."

Good heavens! Was this Larien asking instead of ordering? We would certainly comply since we were still looking for Walsingham, and—as far as we knew— London was our most likely place to look.

❖———❖

Lord Dax asked for wonder, and wonder he got.

On the tenth day of June, the Horseguards awoke to find

all their steeds had become unicorns overnight. They were the same steeds, gray, black, bay, and brown, but now with a central slender horn protruding from their forehead.

I can only imagine the consternation in the stables. The officers had a choice of not fulfilling their duties as the king's protectors or fulfilling them riding unicorns.

The news didn't become public until rumors started to fly. Three enterprising printers beat the *Times* to the news. They had broadsheets out on the streets within hours, telling of how the colonels had sent to borrow horses from the cavalry, but as soon as those horses set a hoof in the Horseguards' stables, they became endowed with horns also.

It then became apparent that the second magical effect was that the unicorn droppings were silver, smelled of flowers, and sparkled. This news caused great hilarity. The broadsheets were full of it, and urchins quickly began to follow the Horseguards with buckets. Unicorn shit, it turned out, was a salable commodity.

All of London—from the highest members of the ton to the lowest beggar on the streets—was talking about unicorns. The Mysterium, however, was silent on the matter, not being able to name a perpetrator. One of the broadsheets reported that the Mysterium had tried to remove a horn from one of the unicorns, only to discover the beast was well able to protect itself. It impaled two Mysterium officers, one fatally. The unicorn in question then galloped off and was never seen again.

All this we discovered from the broadsheets.

We bundled several editions together and sent them to Lily on the mail coach, and in an accompanying letter asked her to pass on the message to Pomeroy that we had suggested to the king he appoint the Earl of Stratford to head a Royal Commission to look into the treatment of the rowankind.

◆◇◆

Two days after the unicorns, London awoke to a shortage of milk. The dairy herds kept in the parks and enclosures throughout the city and looked after by an army of milkmaids and herdsmen had inexplicably all turned into fat bullocks.

Again the broadsheets picked up the news, although this time the *Times* didn't lag behind, reporting that beef was now so cheap due to the excess of bullocks that even beggars could eat beefsteak.

So far as we knew, these happenings were occurring only in London. That was confirmed when we had a letter back from Lily.

Corwen and I had taken a room at the Town of Ramsgate public house, by Wapping Old Stairs, letting Hookey have his cabin back. Our room was on the upper floor at the back of the building, so we had a view over the river to the *Heart*'s mooring and beyond. It made sense to keep the *Heart* in dock for a while longer until we'd dealt with the Walsingham threat.

Hookey was all in favor of the idea because Lady Henrietta Rothcliffe was in town on some unnamed government business, and he had departed the *Heart*, dressed in his smartest outfit two days before and had not yet returned, though he'd left an address where we could reach him. I noted it was a good address in Mayfair. I wished him and Etta happy for as long as it lasted, and hoped that if their relationship were to end, it wouldn't hurt my friend. Tough as he was with a pistol in his good hand, I didn't think Hookey's heart was armored against rejection.

Lily's letter confirmed all was normal in Yorkshire. No unaccountable unicorns or dairy cows turning into bullocks. They'd had no further trouble from the Mysterium, she said. Also George had written to his grandfather but felt everyone would benefit from disclosure of information. She'd underlined *information* three times for emphasis. We knew what she meant.

Corwen read the letter twice and then passed it over to me. "If we don't test Pomeroy soon, in a controlled situation, Lily's going to give the game away. We should go to Yorkshire."

"What if the goblins get news of Walsingham while we're away?"

He groaned. "I know. We need to be in two places at once."

"We could invite George to come down here."

He frowned, thinking it through. "I suppose it makes sense in a way. If he reacts badly to magic, and, lord knows, I hope he doesn't, arranging an accident might be our only option. It will be easier to arrange when he's a hundred and eighty miles away from Lily and in a large and dangerous city."

I shuddered. "I'm not sure I could do it. I'm getting soft."

"I sincerely hope I don't have to," Corwen said, "but I'll not see Lily endangered. If it's a choice between Pomeroy and my little sister, then I'll not be found wanting."

This was a side of Corwen I didn't see very often; though I knew he would never turn such ruthlessness against me, it still made me shudder.

He wrote back to Lily suggesting Pomeroy might come to London where certain information—underlined three times—might safely be disclosed.

40

Mrs. Pomeroy

WE MIGHT NOT even have noticed the next wonderment from the Fae except that the *Times* reported it. Members of Parliament, both the upper and lower houses, awoke on the morning of the twelfth day of June to find that their left feet had grown to be a full three inches longer than their right. Those keen to undertake their Parliamentary business had wrapped the offending foot in bandages and ventured out, but most had sent for their physicians and remained abed.

What next, we wondered.

On the fourteenth day of June the leaves of every tree in London turned blood red.

"I think the Fae have made their point," Corwen said as we rode Timpani and Dancer around the edge of St James' Park. It seemed like half the population of London was abroad, all ogling the trees in their crimson glory.

We listened to snatches of conversation. There was no sense of fear, rather a sense of wonderment and speculation as to what magic was causing this. Some even sus-

pected the Mysterium of having a hand in it. Some
grumbled at the lack of fresh milk; others laughed at the
predicament of the politicians with their odd-sized feet.
It seemed there was nothing the average Londoner liked
more than the discomfiture of the political classes.

"Do you think the king and Parliament are ready to
listen yet?" I asked.

Corwen shook his head. "I don't know."

On the fifteenth day of June we received a message at
the Town of Ramsgate to say Pomeroy had arrived and
would like to receive us at number thirty-eight Margaret
Street, an address near Cavendish Square.

"It's a good address," I said as we rode through streets
which had become familiar last year when we'd been in
London looking for Freddie.

"Indeed. Well, he did tell us his grandfather was an
earl, but I didn't expect Pomeroy himself to be a gentleman of any great wealth."

We arrived at the correct address, a town house of
substance. As we mounted the steps, the butler opened
the door and called a footman to take our horses. He
showed us upstairs to where Pomeroy was waiting, standing with his back to the fireplace. Next to him stood Lily.

I felt a shock run through Corwen. Lily had come to
town with Pomeroy, and there was no evidence of a chap-
erone. Our own conjugal behavior before we'd married
was one thing, but Lily was Corwen's little sister and a
respectable miss, now much compromised. He took one
step forward in anger, but Lily forestalled him and
jumped between Corwen and Pomeroy, holding out her
left hand to show the gold band on her third finger.

It stopped Corwen in his tracks.

"Don't be angry, brother," Lily said. "Wish us happy."

I saw emotions cross Corwen's face so fast he probably
wasn't aware of them all himself. Rage, frustration, and
then despair. He glared at Pomeroy and then said in a low
voice, "How much does he know?"

Pomeroy took hold of Lily's hand, pulling her to his
side, then faced us.

"I know Mrs. Deverell is a witch," he said. "A powerful one who numbers Fae among her acquaintances. I know there are secrets in the Deverell family, and I swear that nothing you can tell me will make me love Lily any less. Whatever happens, I will protect this family from the Mysterium if it costs me my life to do it."

"See," Lily said. "I told him nothing."

"Then you married him under false pretenses, and I am sorry for it." Corwen's look would have withered grass where it grew, but it slid off Lily in her naiveté.

"Do you have servants in the house besides the butler and footman?" Corwen asked Pomeroy.

"Five, including them," Pomeroy said. "They're my grandfather's. This is one of his houses which he lets me use when I'm in town."

"Send them all out for the afternoon," Corwen said. "What we must discuss needs complete privacy."

Pomeroy nodded and went to give the order. While he was out of the room, Corwen glared at Lily. "You had no right to put him in this position," Corwen said. "If he can't accept what he's about to see, he's a danger not only to us, but to all magicals. I can't let that happen. Do you understand what I'm saying?"

"I . . . you can't . . . I didn't think . . . " She took a deep breath. "Don't hurt him, Corwen. If you do, I'll never forgive you."

"At least you'll be alive and free and will have a choice about forgiving me or not."

"What's all this about forgiveness?" Pomeroy came back into the room.

"A small family disagreement, Mr. Pomeroy," I said. "It will soon be resolved one way or the other."

"Please we're family now. Call me George." He waved us to the elegantly upholstered chairs. "The servants are leaving, so I'm afraid I can't offer you tea. May I offer you a glass of something stronger?" He waved to an array of decanters on the sideboard.

I gave Corwen a sideways glance.

"Maybe later," Corwen said.

Pomeroy sat on the sofa with Lily by his side.

"Let me start," I said. "Mr. Pomeroy . . . George . . . you're right, I am a witch, and not a registered one, either. I expect you already checked the Mysterium's registers to ascertain that. It's a long story as to why I didn't register, but the main reason is that I was out of the country when I turned eighteen. I'm not a regular spell-using witch, though I have some small spells I can work. I'm a summoner. I can summon the spirits of the dead and I can also find things and people and summon them to come to me under certain circumstances. I have an affinity for wind and weather, and I can do this."

I called light into the palm of my hand. I tossed it up and brought it down into the unlit oil lamp on the table. It settled into the glass, giving off a glow like a perfectly normal lamp.

"It's cold light, though. Making it hot enough to turn into fire is much more difficult."

"That's beautiful," George said. "There's nothing frightening in that."

"Yet the Mysterium would hang me for it."

"The Mysterium was formed in 1590 to preserve the country from witchcraft," Corwen said. "I'm sure the intentions of Queen Bess were the best, but power corrupts. You need only look at the history of Matthew Hopkins, who named himself the Witchfinder General. Hundreds of innocents condemned for one man's greed."

"The Mysterium no longer offers a bounty for witches."

"That's one good thing, though with the zeal which some officers pursue witchcraft, one might almost think the days of the Witchfinder General have returned."

George Pomeroy nodded. "Something my grandfather is most concerned about."

"It's not only witchcraft, George," I said. "This country has always had magical beings: goblins, hobs, pixies, trolls, shapechangers, and sprites. Most of them are shy and rarely interact with humans, so they've stayed hidden for centuries." I slipped in the idea of shapechangers along with all the others before we got into specifics.

"And rowankind, too," George said.

"Rowankind are different. They're related to the Fae."

"You didn't mention the Fae in your list of magical beings."

"The Fae are different again. You can't compare a goblin, a hob, or a pixie to a Fae. The Fae are as far above them as humans are to cats. The Fae don't live in our world; they live in a parallel world called Iaru. Some scholars call it Orbisalius, the Otherworld. It exists in the same space as our world, but maybe not in the same time."

I tried to describe it by telling him about two sheets of paper, loosely rolled, that take up the same space as one roll but are still separate. "And where the papers brush up against each other, there are gates where those who know how to use them can travel from one world to the next."

George nodded. All right so far. I glanced at Corwen, and he nodded at me to continue. "So, George, imagine the Fae are all-powerful, and they have their own magical realm, yet for all their power, the one thing they rarely manage is procreation with their own kind. There are very few children born to two Fae parents. Thousands of years ago the Fae solved their problem by creating the rowankind from their own selves and the rowan trees of the forest. The rowankind became Fae servants, and then helpmeets and then lovers and mothers of Fae children."

I told him how Martyn the Summoner, had drawn the rowankind from Iaru with a magical working so huge that he'd never recovered from it. "That's how Queen Bess defeated the Spanish Armada, but the working drove Martyn half mad. He couldn't undo what he'd done, and neither could the Fae, so the Fae did what they thought was best for the rowankind. They took away their memories of Iaru, so they could live in our world without being consumed by sadness for what they'd lost."

"But the rowankind got their magic back suddenly," George said.

"That was Ross," Corwen said. "Martyn the Summoner was her many times great-grandfather, and so it fell to her to restore the magic and the memories to the rowankind, at no small risk to herself, I should add."

"And while you might think the Mysterium is our biggest problem," I said, "it isn't. There's a government appointee so secret that even the Mysterium doesn't know much about him and his followers. The first one was Sir Francis Walsingham, appointed by Queen Bess over two hundred years ago to investigate magical threats to the kingdom. Ever since the first Walsingham, the new appointees have been Walsinghams. It's a position, not a name."

"Sir Francis Walsingham sought Ross' ancestor but couldn't find him," Corwen said. "Successive generations of Walsinghams have sought successive generations of Summoners, or Sumners as they came to be called, until a Walsingham killed all of Ross' family except the twin sisters, Marjorie and Rosie, and died doing it."

"Marjorie was my mother," I said, "and a new Walsingham, the oldest apprentice, arose and continued the quest to wipe out my family to keep us from restoring rowankind power."

"But you did."

"And now he wants his revenge. It's gone beyond his commission from the king. It's personal. Sooner or later, I'll find him, or he'll find me, and we'll finish this thing between us."

"That's the big family secret?" George asked.

"No, that's the background to it," I said. "This is my family secret. I met Corwen while I was trying to solve the problem of the rowankind because he was sent by the Lady of the Forests to watch over me. To be my watch-wolf."

I saw George mouth the words, *watch wolf*, with a puzzled look on his face and then I saw the understanding dawn in his eyes as he remembered the list of magical beings, including "shapechanger." He turned to Corwen. "You're a werewolf."

Corwen raised his eyes to heaven. He's always been markedly annoyed when someone has confused him with a werewolf. "Please, I'm not moon-called. I can control my changes and my bloodlust. I'm a shapechanger."

Lily cleared her throat. "George, my love, I should have told you. It runs in the family."

Lily fell to her knees in front of George and took both his hands in hers.

"I'm sorry. I should have told you before we married, but I was so afraid of losing you."

George said nothing. It was as if the knowledge had turned him into a statue. I'm not even sure he was breathing.

I crossed to the sideboard and poured brandy from a decanter into a glass. Leaning over Lily, I pushed it into George's unresisting hand. "Drink, George."

As if in a dream he downed it all in one gulp and then began to cough. I took the glass from him and refilled it.

"Another?"

"No." His voice cracked. "No, thank you. Lily, I . . . I need time to think."

He walked out of the room, apparently in full command of his emotions, but the instant the door closed behind him, I heard him let out a great shuddering breath. Then the front door slammed behind him as he ran out into the street.

"George!" Lily dashed to the window. "He's gone." She gulped back a sob.

"I should follow him," Corwen said. "If he's heading for the nearest Mysterium office or militia post, we're all dead."

"Don't hurt him!" Lily said.

Corwen simply shook his head, which could have meant anything, and slipped out after Pomeroy.

"For what it's worth, I think George just needs time," I said. "I can't believe that he'd put you in danger." I touched Lily's arm. "He'll be back."

I was sure of that, but I didn't know whether he'd be

returning as part of the family or whether he'd have a Mysterium death squad at his heels.

I watched the minutes tick past on the elegant grandfather clock in the corner. Five became ten. Ten became twenty. Lily began to pace the floor, then she flung herself in a chair for a few minutes before leaping up and pacing again. There was nothing I could say to comfort her, but the longer it went on, the more I thought it unlikely that George had reported us. Surely if he had, we'd have been running from the law by now. I trusted that if George had gone to the Mysterium, Corwen would have been able to come back with a warning and give us time to escape.

It seemed like days, but it was perhaps not much more than an hour before Corwen returned. "He's on his way back," he said. "And he hasn't spoken to anyone. He's simply been walking the streets."

"Oh, thank heavens!" Lily collapsed into a chair with tears running down her cheeks.

I pushed a handkerchief into her hands. "Mop up," I said. "No sniveling, no apologies. Explain all you like, but don't apologize for what you are."

She sniffed and gulped but dried her eyes.

We all tried to look calm when George came back into the room, but Lily's eyes were red-rimmed. He immediately knelt in front of her.

"I'm sorry. I needed to think."

"I'm sorry I didn't find a way to tell you sooner, but . . ." She remembered my words. "I'm not sorry for what I am. I'll try not to let it complicate your life if . . . if you still want me to be your wife."

"Oh, Lily, of course I do."

I glanced over at Corwen with one eyebrow raised, and he shrugged. That was it. George was family now.

I put a second glass of brandy on the small table close to his right hand.

"You'll get used to having a mate who is sometimes human and sometimes not," I said. "Corwen and Lily's changes are beautiful, and they can control them perfectly. When they are in wolf form, they retain human understanding though it meshes with their animal instincts. The advantage is that they have heightened senses of smell and hearing, and in the change, they can heal themselves of wounds."

"And the disadvantage?"

"None at all, unless the Mysterium catches them."

I didn't delve into the story of Corwen and Freddie aboard the *Guillaume Tell*. There was time enough for that detail later.

George groped for the brandy glass and sipped it, as much to give himself thinking time as for the drink itself. He sank into a chair.

Lily stood and pulled the pins from the front of her dress and untied the strings, shrugging out of it and letting waves of muslin fall to the floor.

"Help me with the laces, Ross, if you please."

"Lily . . . " George began.

"No, George, we can talk all we like, but until you see for yourself, you don't know how you'll react."

I undid the laces at the back of Lily's short stays and they followed her dress to the floor along with her chemise.

"Lily's right." Corwen took off his jacket and neck cloth, pulling his shirt over his head. He'd developed the knack of shrugging out of his breeches and boots during the change. Wolf legs are much narrower than human ones.

Corwen and Lily changed at the same time, and two magnificent wolves stood in the middle of George Pomeroy's drawing room—Corwen the larger of the two, silver-gray with a ruff tipped with black, Lily smaller and leggy with a black curly coat.

"I don't need to ask which is which," George said.

"No, you certainly don't."

"Can they understand us?"

"Yes, of course."

Corwen yipped a yes.

Lily put her front paws on George's knees and licked his nose. He laughed, though there was an edge of hysteria in the sound.

"I know it seems strange," I said. "It did to me, at first.

I met Corwen as a wolf, not knowing he was also a man, yet knowing he had intelligence and a sense of humor. Then I met the man, not knowing he was the wolf. It took me a while to realize they were the same person."

Corwen changed back into a naked man and unselfconsciously dressed himself. Lily followed his example, and I quickly dropped her chemise over her head and helped her into her short stays and bib-front dress.

"Say something, George." Lily dropped to her knees in front of him again.

"I . . . don't know what to say." This time, however, he took both her hands in his.

Lily's eyes brimmed with tears. "I didn't think it would be so hard. What a lot there is to tell you."

George swallowed hard. "You're beautiful in both your forms. I'll have to resign from the Mysterium, of course. We can live in Yorkshire, so you have room to . . . change . . . in safety." He frowned and turned to me. "What about . . . children?"

I smiled and ran a hand over my belly, still neatly hidden by the current fashion for high-waisted dresses. "I'll let you know, but if Corwen and Lily's mother raised a brood of shapechangers, I'm sure Lily and I can if that's what fate decrees."

I heard Corwen breathe a sigh of relief. The first hurdle was over.

"Don't resign from the Mysterium, not yet," he said. "You've come to the knowledge of magic at a very difficult time. Having someone inside the Mysterium could be a distinct advantage to us."

"I seem to suddenly be on a different side in all things magical. When I joined the Mysterium, I took an oath to protect this country from dangerous magic. I'll not break that oath."

"Neither should you," Corwen said, "but not all magic is dangerous. The Mysterium, unfortunately, doesn't have enough understanding to differentiate between good and bad."

"What's happening?" George nodded to the window.

"Out there, I mean. Horses turning into unicorns, cows into bullocks, politicians' left feet, blood-red leaves. Is it your doing?"

"We don't have that kind of power," I said. "It's Fae magic—a message to the king and to Parliament. The Fae have issued an ultimatum—protect the rowankind and disband the Mysterium, or else—"

"Or else what?"

"That's the burning question. They could wipe out humanity without blinking, but most of the Fae don't want to. They don't want to govern us, they simply want to get on with their own lives. However, they created the rowankind and feel they have a duty to protect them, even the ones who don't want to return to Iaru. These magical occurrences are a demonstration. If the king and Parliament can't be swayed, things may get more serious."

"You said most of the Fae don't want to destroy us. What about the others?"

"There are some who carry a grudge, but they are in a minority."

"How can we stop them?" George's eyes had gone wide. "Can we stop them?"

"Only the king and Parliament can stop them now, but so far the king has not been able to move his ministers on the matter."

"What if the ministers were to move of their own accord?"

"What do you suggest?"

"My grandfather has the ear of Mr. Pitt."

"Better that he had the ear of the first minister."

"Don't underestimate Mr. Pitt."

"Would your grandfather be willing to speak to us?"

"I'm sure he would."

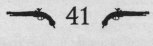

41

Mr. Pitt

ON THE MORNING of the sixteenth day of June, the population awoke to a London with no beer. Every drop of beer in every vat, barrel, bottle, or jug had turned into pure clean water overnight.

A population which had wondered at unicorns and red leaves, and laughed at politicians with oddly-shaped feet, and been mildly disturbed by the lack of fresh milk, was suddenly incensed by the absence of beer.

The *Times* ran a lead article suggesting it was about time the Mysterium dealt with these strange magical occurrences, and if they did not have the resources, then Parliament should perforce give them the resources.

The following day we received a note from George to say he'd arranged a private meeting for us with his grandfather and Mr. Pitt.

"Do you think it's safe?" I read the note and handed it back to Corwen over the breakfast table.

"I don't think anything is safe for us anymore. The more we get into this thing, the more our identity is compromised. When we met the king, we did it as Mr. and

Mrs. Corwen Silverwolf, but George could reveal our identity at any time, even by accident."

"We always have the option of fleeing Britain on the *Heart*. Magicals aren't persecuted on Bacalao."

"Would we take Lily with us? And George? And Freddie and Roland? What about Mother? And Poppy and the servants who have turned a blind eye for us so many times that the Mysterium could hang them all. And then there's the mill and all the rowankind weavers. No, we're too deep into this to ever back out. We have to see it through."

I leaned across the table and kissed him. "I wanted to know we both felt the same."

We took a coach across town. Robert Winter, Earl of Stratford, had a house in Cavendish Square, around the corner from the house where we'd met George and Lily yesterday. We trusted George was not laying any kind of trap for us, but we couldn't be sure about his grandfather or, indeed, Mr. Pitt.

We weren't being entirely reckless. I'd stationed Lazy Billy in the square, dressed as a gentleman. Surprisingly, Billy washed up well and could pass as long as he didn't open his mouth. As our coach pulled up, Billy strolled past and touched his left hand to his forehead in a prearranged signal.

"Billy says it's all clear," I said, taking Corwen's hand as I stepped down from the coach.

George must have been watching for us because the door opened, and he stepped past the butler to usher us inside. Rather than leading us upstairs to the main drawing room, he crossed the hallway. "Grandfather is in his study. Come and meet him."

George's grandfather was a short, rotund man in his midsixties, wearing an impeccably cut jacket and knee breeches. He wore no wig, and his hair, such as it was, was still mostly dark though receding greatly from his forehead.

George cleared his throat, "Grandfather, may I present Mr. and Mrs. Corwen Deverell. Mr. and Mrs. Deverell, my grandfather, the Right Honorable Earl Stratford."

Corwen bowed, and I dipped a respectable curtsey.
"And this is Mr. Pitt."

Pitt had been standing in the shadow by a large break-front bookcase, dressed all in black, save for his white linen neck cloth and shirt. His coat was velveteen, double-breasted and cut away at the front to show a black silk waistcoat. He wore black trousers rather than light colored or buckskin breeches which added to his somber demeanor. I was surprised by his relative youth. For a man with such a political reputation, he was still on the right side of middle age, probably in his early forties, though his hair was gray and tied at the nape of his neck with a black ribbon.

We bowed and curtseyed again and were bowed to in turn, then George ushered us to chairs.

"I've told my grandfather and Mr. Pitt about the Fae and the rowankind," George said. "Anything else you wish to add is entirely up to you."

At last I allowed my eyes to stray downward. Yes, both men had large left feet. Lord Stratford's was accommodated by an enormous slipper, but Mr. Pitt's was encased in bandages.

"Gout." He saw me looking. "And now large gout. I have a personal interest in seeing these magical occurrences are prevented or—better still—reversed. Is that possible?"

"Whatever the Fae can do, they can also undo," I said. I knew they could, but I didn't know whether they would.

"The primary concern of the Fae is the safety of the rowankind," Corwen said, "but they understand that until magic is an everyday part of human life, there will always be problems."

I took up the explanation about the Armada, Martyn the Summoner, Queen Bess, and the Rowankind. Mr. Pitt had been first minister, so he should already know about the rowankind but possibly not about the Fae or the goblins and magical creatures. I paused as Lord Stratford shook his head in disbelief, and Mr. Pitt made a derogatory noise when I mentioned goblins.

"Gentleman, I would be happy to introduce you to a goblin, if you don't believe me," Corwen said. "Or maybe you should ask for a copy of the report of a gruesome murder in Whitechapel which occurred on the first of this month. In particular, read the description of the victim."

I continued. "Goblins are very industrious. They live and work in the capital and in other major cities, pay their taxes, and contribute greatly to the country's economy. Some of the other magical races are more at home in the countryside—hobs and pixies, for instance." There was no need to mention trolls and kelpies.

I became aware both Lord Stratford and Mr. Pitt were looking at me very oddly, and Mr. Pitt's mouth was agape which I'm sure was not something that occurred very often.

"The Mysterium—" Mr. Pitt seemed to gather his thoughts.

"The Mysterium is the problem, not the solution," I said. "They've come to realize that the newly awakened rowankind have magic, and their response is to hang them, even though in law nothing forbids the rowankind from using magic."

Corwen went on to explain how the rowankind at Deverell's Mill had been able to use their magic to power the water wheel. Lily added that there was a mill in Lancashire, where the local Mysterium was compliant, which now powered its machinery by rowankind-created water power.

"Rowankind could be a great benefit to industry," she said.

"Which would also benefit the Fae, as there are parts of Iaru affected by industrial blight seeping through."

George cleared his throat. "I have the figures here from the Mysterium. In the last six months, they've hanged seventy-eight rowankind without trial. Seventy-eight."

I hadn't realized the figure was so high and, by his expression, neither had Corwen. I turned to Lord Stratford and Mr. Pitt. "The Mysterium has neither the resources

nor the knowledge to deal with rowankind or any of the
magical races. The rowankind are gentle people. They're
no threat. As for the other magical races indigenous to
the British Isles, they're self-regulating. The Lady of the
Forests has oversight and will curb any behavior which
threatens humanity."

"The Mysterium is far too fond of its own legend,"
Corwen said. "They're concerned with stamping out any
unregulated witchcraft, but they barely understand it."

"They would hang me in an instant," I said, perceiving
that a demonstration was needed.

I felt the still air in the room and began to move it in a
circle, faster and faster until the paper on Lord Stratford's
desk wafted around the room twice. The trick was set-
tling the paper back down where it had been, but I managed it. Then I made a witchlight and put it up to the
ceiling, brightening the room with magic.

"Parlor tricks, gentleman," I said. "But the Mysterium
would condemn me for them without a trial. You understand what trust I'm placing in you when I admit to my
witchcraft."

George cleared his throat in the direction of his grandfather, who seemed to shake himself back to reality. He
glanced sideways at Mr. Pitt. "Mrs. Deverell, Mr. Deverell,
my grandson has undoubtedly told you I have had severe
misgivings about the power invested in the Mysterium. I
would like to thank you for coming today and assure you
no confidences will be broken. Isn't that right, Pitt?"

"Err, yes, of course." Pitt didn't sound so sure, but
George had assured us his grandfather was a man of his
word.

"Let's get down to business, then," Corwen said. "The
Fae asked us to take a message to the king. They demand
all persecution of the rowankind cease and that the Mysterium be dissolved. The king has told us that Parliament
is too taken up with the French question and the food
shortages to consider legislation they perceive as neither
necessary nor urgent. We have spoken with the Fae and
for the moment persuaded them that they should show

their power without causing irreversible damage. This they have done—so far—but they'll soon do more if the situation isn't resolved."

"What more can they do beyond these parlor tricks writ large?" Mr. Pitt asked.

"They can reduce London to a smoking hole in the ground," I said. "Or they can wipe humanity from this island altogether." I paused to let it sink in. "There's nothing you could do to stop them. You can't fight what you can't find."

"This threat . . . is it real?" Mr. Pitt asked. "How do we know you aren't bamming us, madam?"

"Good question. How would it be if we set up a meeting with the Fae? Would you trust yourselves to us as we have entrusted ourselves to you?"

"They would come to talk to us?"

"I rather think you would have to go and talk to them."

<hr />

The following day we awoke intending to ride to Iaru to secure a meeting with the Fae Council of Seven for Lord Stratford and Mr. Pitt. I threw back the covers and crossed to the window where Corwen was already standing, hands on the sill, looking out over the river.

"Ice," he said, "in June."

"What?" Then I noticed large chunks of gray-white something floating down the river with the outgoing tide.

"It can't be."

But it was. There were people standing on the stair that led down to the river, pointing to a rowboat that was bringing in a large chunk of ice.

"Where's it coming from?" I asked.

Corwen hastily pulled on his clothes and went down-stairs and out to the water's edge. I saw him talking to some of the people there, and then he came back up.

"The river is frozen between Westminster Bridge and London Bridge. Apparently, the ice is so thick that people are already venturing out onto it, and they're talking about holding a frost fair."

"Don't they realize how serious this is? The Thames may freeze in January or February, but never in June." I pushed open the window. "It isn't even cold. If the Fae release the spell, the ice could vanish in an instant, and hundreds of people could drown."

"I doubt we could stop them. Londoners tend to make the best of whatever comes their way. Besides, none of the other Fae changes have reversed themselves suddenly. There's no reason to think the ice will vanish without warning."

I shuddered. "All the same, when we take Lord Stratford and Mr. Pitt to Iaru, let's cross the river by a bridge."

"Of course." He kissed me on the cheek and tied the laces of my short stays which ended above my growing belly.

We collected Timpani and Dancer from their regular stable at the Red Lion and crossed the river by London Bridge. From our vantage point we could see the wide stretch of river frozen on the upstream side. Londoners were already out on the ice, some walking with caution, a few skating, though since the river hadn't frozen for the last seven years, I was surprised to see anyone with skates. A few enterprising souls were already setting up stalls to entice even more people to be bold.

The river was still flowing beneath the ice because from the downstream side water gushed out between the starlings of London Bridge, breaking off great lumps of ice, though more seemed to form almost instantly.

"Can you feel it?" I asked Corwen.

"What?"

"The sun is warm on my back, but cold is rising from the ice. It feels unnatural."

"It is unnatural. The Fae created it."

"Do you think the ice is safe?"

"If it isn't, there's not much we can do about it," he said. "We should ask Larien when we get to Iaru."

Lily had wanted to come, but we'd talked her out of it since we hadn't mentioned her shapechanging abilities to anyone. She could still deny her magic if questioned by the Mysterium. We'd arranged to meet George, Lord Stratford, and Mr. Pitt at the Roehampton Gate to Richmond Park. There was Mr. Pitt's gout to consider and Lord Stratford's age, so they planned to arrive at the rendezvous by coach. The rest of the journey on horseback would be relatively short.

We arrived before they did to check the area for traps and were relieved to find none. The Earl's coach duly arrived, with three mounted grooms each leading a riding horse. George, a competent horseman, mounted first. We watched with some trepidation as Mr. Pitt, complete with gouty foot, was manhandled onto a docile looking cob, his left foot placed in an enlarged stirrup. Lord Stratford, despite his age, mounted without difficulty and looked over to us.

"Lead on," he said and clapped his heels to his horse's sides, urging it into a smart trot.

I thought I heard Mr. Pitt groan slightly, but he made no complaint.

We circumvented the White Lodge and climbed the hill to the west of it, slowing down to access the Fae gate.

George rode up beside me. "How do you know where the gates are?" he asked.

"I don't always, though I'm getting better at finding them. I think Corwen sniffs them out. He's been traversing Iaru on behalf of the Lady of the Forests since he first left home."

"Lily told me he argued with his father and left as soon as he was old enough."

"I never met his father except as an invalid, but there was enough spark in the old man, even then, to suggest a temper. He never forgave Corwen for his wolf, and his attitude to Corwen fixed Freddie's fate."

"Lily has told me about Freddie."

"Let's say he has problems, but we hope he's in a better place now."

"He's dead?"

"Oh, no. I didn't mean that. I meant it literally. He's in Gloucestershire with a friend who has offered him sanctuary, and he intends to stay there. He's renounced his inheritance in favor of Corwen."

"So Corwen owns the estate."

"Only for as long as he and I can stay out of the Mysterium's hands. There's an older sister, Emily, whom I've never met. She's not a shapechanger. Should the Mysterium come for us, as the oldest daughter she's next in line, though when Freddie signed the estate over to Corwen, Corwen, in turn, signed over the mill to Lily. How do you feel about woolen cloth?"

He laughed. "I'm going to have to get used to it. Lily will not be parted from her precious mill."

"She's worked hard for it, and she runs it well. It should be enough to keep you both."

"Ah, about that . . . When I told you that I was a younger son of a younger daughter, without a title, I didn't mean to imply I was penniless. Also, I have a share in the prize money from my years at sea. I can look after Lily, mill or no mill."

I smiled at him. "I'm very pleased to hear that, George."

"Here it is!" Corwen called.

"The gate?" George asked.

"Yes, everyone stay close."

We rode through from summer to summer, but it was as if the sun moved in the sky and the colors all changed. We were still riding through woodland, but among the oaks and beech were trees I couldn't give name to. Birds I didn't recognize flitted from branch to branch, some of them sporting brilliant colors, others with glorious voices. And the smell was once more fresh and green yet somehow spicy.

Lord Stratford pulled up his horse and swiveled in his saddle to see where we'd come from, but the park was gone.

Putting the image of my brother into the front of my mind, I summoned him, not wishing to venture any farther into Iaru with uninvited strangers. The Fae could get very touchy about that.

Almost immediately, I heard the sound of pounding hooves.

"That was quick," I said to Corwen. "I've only just called David."

"It's not David," Corwen said. "Quick, group together. Protect Lord Stratford and Mr. Pitt. No harm must come to them in Iaru or everything is lost."

A troop of Fae warriors, armed with bows and armored in bronze, galloped out of the trees and surrounded us.

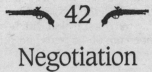

42

Negotiation

CORWEN AND I placed ourselves between the archers and the politicians, and—to give him his due— George Pomeroy joined us. Mr. Pitt exclaimed loudly—something about treachery, but I was too busy trying to shield him from the archers to listen. Lord Stratford said nothing but reached under his coat and drew a pistol.

"Lord Stratford, please, no!" I said. "Mortal weapons don't work the way they should in Iaru. You're as likely to blow your fingers off as shoot someone."

"What's the meaning of this?" Corwen shouted to the captain of the archers. "Take us to Larien."

"Larien no longer holds sway on the Council of Seven."

"Then take us to Lord Dax," I shouted.

"We will take you to Dantin."

"Not what I was hoping for." I kept my voice low.

"What's going on?" Mr. Pitt asked. "Are these Fae?"

I'd been in and out of Iaru for almost two years now, and I was used to the Fae, but I'd forgotten what an effect they'd had on me when I'd first encountered them. Describing them in words made them sound human, but they were as far removed from human as gold is from base metal. Oh, yes, they had human-shaped faces, but they exhibited an unearthly quality, unmarked by life, but all-knowing. Their clothes were woven of the finest thread that shone with the luster of precious metals while remaining as soft as silk. Any dirt that tried to splash them would shrink away in fear.

"Yes, these are Fae, but the Council of Seven seems to have had a shake-up. Larien is on our side. Dantin most definitely is not."

"What about this Lord Dax?"

"He's the oldest Fae I've ever seen and the senior member of the council. I don't know which side he's on, but I trust his wisdom, and he outranks Dantin."

The archers lowered their bows and fell into formation ahead of us and behind. We couldn't break and run anywhere. I suspected that if we'd tried, the magic of Iaru itself would have taken us around in a circle, so we'd end up where we were meant to be.

We passed through a village which seemed to be occupied by rowankind. The houses looked organic, as if grown. They were neither oblong nor rounded, but an asymmetrical mixture of the two. Their timbers were the natural shapes of growing trees and their roofs green turf. No house was taller than a single story with a loft in the apex of the roof, but some of the houses had extra rooms built on. The rowankind came to their doors to see us ride past, but none made comment until we were almost through the village.

A figure ran out of the very last house. "Mr. Corwen," he called, and paced alongside Corwen's horse.

I recognized him instantly—Tommy Topping, the son of the mill's manager and one of the rowankind who had escaped to Iaru with David, seconds ahead of the redcoat troop that had come to arrest them for their use of magic.

"Tommy," Corwen bent low. My ears are good, and I could hear their whispered conversation. "What's going on? What's happened to Larien?"

"Rumor says he's dying. Where are they taking you?"

"I don't know where, but apparently to Dantin. Do you know where David is?"

"With his father, I think."

"Are you well treated here, Tommy?"

"Aye, but I wish we could go home again. This place feels too easy. Know what I mean?"

"I do."

One of the archers rode up alongside Corwen. Without saying anything to Tommy, or harming him by touch or word, the archer nudged him out of the way till he fell back.

"You heard that?" Corwen said to me as I pushed my horse alongside his.

"I did. What can be wrong with Larien? Something natural or foul play? I didn't think the Fae took sick and died of natural causes."

"I don't think they do."

"And what about David? Is he in danger? If this is a political coup, who's behind it?"

"I know who I'd put my money on."

"Dantin."

As I said the name, we arrived in a grove as perfect and beautiful as the one in which the Council of Seven met. The tall tree trunks soared upward and then arched overhead like fan vaulting in a cathedral. The effect was cool and green with the summer sun filtering through the leaves. Two large, thronelike chairs had been placed to one side. Dantin sat in one of them with his daughter, Margann, standing behind and a little to one side. She raised her eyes to meet mine, and for a moment I saw an expression of helplessness. Whatever was happening was outside of her experience and, if I read her face correctly, she didn't much like it.

"Rossalinde and Corwen, welcome," Dantin said. "I see you've brought hostages. How thoughtful."

I heard Mr. Pitt muttering behind me, but he had the good sense not to exclaim out loud.

"What's happening, Dantin?" Corwen asked. "Mr.

Pitt and Lord Stratford are here to talk to the Council of Seven."

"Soon to be a Council of Six, I believe. I invite you all to step down from your horses. I'll have the beasts taken care off." He waved and five rowankind came running to hold our horses. Dancer and Timpani both laid back their ears and looked unhappy. I heard Mr. Pitt let out a breath as his gouty foot hit the floor.

As the rowankind led the horses away, Dantin waved his hand. "Forgive my rudeness. I should have offered you refreshment."

Lord Stratford began to say thank you, but I cut in before he could finish his words. "No, thank you, Dantin. It wouldn't be appropriate." I turned to Lord Stratford and Mr. Pitt. "To accept food or drink in a magical realm puts you under an obligation to the host unless it's offered freely and with no obligation on either side."

"In three days it will be midsummer," Dantin said. "If the king and his ministers have not reached an agreement on the matter of the rowankind by then, all the pretty little illusions we have sent will be as nothing alongside what will happen. I take it these two gentlemen could be instrumental in reaching some kind of agreement."

"An agreement with the Council of Seven first," Corwen said.

"I doubt that can be convened without my brother, Larien. Gentlemen I'm afraid you are in for a long wait. Days, I shouldn't wonder. In the meantime, I guarantee your safety. You are under my protection."

I sent out a thread of summoning to find David. It was important someone knew where we were.

A stir in the trees announced the arrival of a procession. Calantha of the Merovingian Fae, my brother's wife, swept into the clearing, all in black. Her beauty was unparalleled, and she knew how to use it. The half-dozen lesser Fae in her retinue stopped on the edge of the clearing, but Calantha stepped forward and sank into the second thronelike chair next to Dantin, affording him a small, secretive smile.

So that was the way of it.

I cleared my throat softly in Corwen's direction, and he huffed out a breath. Yes, he'd noticed, too.

"If my nose is telling me the truth, and it usually is," Corwen said softly. "Those two are intimate."

"You're sure?"

Of course, he was sure. Corwen's nose didn't lie. Did David know?

"If you won't take any refreshment," Dantin said, "let me offer you somewhere comfortable to wait."

"We'd like to visit with family, if it's all the same to you," I said.

"I'm afraid that won't be possible. Such a busy time right now. Margann will see that you're housed comfortably." He offered his hand to Calantha as they walked out of the grove together. She reached for his hand and put her head next to his. "With Larien incapacitated, we may yet succeed."

Even the Fae underestimated my hearing sometimes. Did she sound pleased about Larien's injuries?

Margann stepped forward. "This way, please."

A few steps outside the first circle of trees, the bronze-armored bowmen stood guard.

"What's going on?" I asked once Dantin and Calantha were far enough away not to hear.

"Hush. Wait a moment."

She led us to a shelter on the edge of the glade, made from woven, living willow. Inside, there were chairs of a somewhat fanciful design, but comfortable enough. The table was a carved dragon with an exaggeratedly flat back. On the table was a carafe of water and some cups.

"I collected the water this morning from your world. It's not of Iaru, but please understand I offer it without any ties of obligation."

"Thanks, Margann. Now, for goodness sake, tell us what's going on."

"Three days ago there was an attack on David, a magical attack, a dark curse. Don't worry. He's all right, but Larien diverted it and took the full blow of the attack on himself . . . and . . . " She took a deep breath. "He hasn't spoken or moved since."

"Do they know who did it?"

"It wasn't my father if that's what you're thinking. I was with him all afternoon, and he was as surprised as I was."

I wondered if Lady Calantha had an alibi.

"But Dantin is taking advantage of it."

Margann nodded. "Oh, yes, fully, and so is she."

Margann jerked her head toward Lady Calantha's retreating back.

Was I doing Lady Calantha a disservice? Had I misinterpreted what I'd heard?

"Surely she's not getting involved in politics already?"

"I think she was born into politics. The Merovingian Fae have always had a reputation for darkness and scheming. Look at her with my father. More importantly, look at him with her. They say there's no fool like an old fool."

"What about David?"

Margann gave me a look as if to say I was being naive. I suppose I was. David had already been told he could keep Annie as a lover, so presumably Lady Calantha was allowed the same leeway. That was no way to begin a marriage, even one not wanted by either party.

"The marriage has not been formalized yet, only the proxy marriage. I think the Lady Calantha is setting her sights higher than David."

"You think she wants to marry your father?"

"I think she'd marry Lord Dax himself if it would give her more power, but my father's the only one on the Council of Seven free to marry. She had plenty of time to charm him while they were traveling back here from France. I saw how she played up to him."

"Surely Dantin can see through her."

"The question is, does he want to?"

"She is very beautiful."

"Yes, she is." Margann pressed her mouth into a thin line.

"Look, Margann, we can't stay here like this. Mr. Pitt

and Lord Stratford will be missed. If Dantin tries to use them as hostages, things could get nasty. At the moment, they are the only allies we have in Parliament, but they have a lot of influence between them, and I truly believe they can help us get what we want without loss of life. They are worth more to us out there, working on our behalf, rather than stuck in here."

"I can't go against my father officially, but I know Lord Dax's granddaughter. I'll see what I can do."

* * *

"I'm sorry, gentlemen," I said to Lord Stratford, Mr. Pitt, and George. "There's been a shift in the balance of power since we were last here, and our biggest ally, Larien, is out of the game—at least for now."

I'd had my differences with Larien, but I didn't want him dead. I sincerely hoped he would recover from whatever damage had been done.

"This Dantin is the one who would like to turn London into a smoking hole in the ground?" asked Mr. Pitt.

"I'm afraid so."

"Can he do it?"

"Whether he has enough power himself is debatable," Corwen said, "but he has enough followers to do it in a combined working."

"Why does he hate us so much?"

"Two hundred years ago, his lover and the rowankind woman who raised him were among those called out of the forest. They never returned and, worse still, they forgot their previous lives—forgot him. But he never forgot them. They are long dead, but Fae live for centuries, and time feels different to them. What happened in 1588 is history to us. To a Fae as long-lived as Dantin, it's yesterday. The wounds are still raw."

"And there are others who think like him?"

"I'm sure there are, but the Council of Seven is wise. Lord Dax may be many thousands of years old, and some of the others may have been living when the Christ-child was born."

Mr. Pitt sucked in his breath with surprise.

Lord Stratford poured himself a cup of water, stared at it and then at me. "You're sure this is safe?"

"Positive, Margann is my cousin, the daughter of my aunt."

"A half-breed?"

"It doesn't work like that. The child of a human or rowankind mother and a Fae are wholly Fae. David is my mother's son, my half-brother. Through his father, Larien, he's a Fae prince. He didn't know his heritage until a couple of years ago, but he's learning fast."

We spent the next couple of hours telling Lord Stratford and Mr. Pitt all we knew about the Fae and about the Green Man, the Lady of the Forests, and the magicals. We even told them about the goblins, though we didn't mention names. This time I included the trolls and the kelpies, and Corwen told the story about the kelpie on Bur Island whom we had been forced to kill because she was eating children.

"That's what I mean about the magicals policing themselves," I said.

We went on to explain how, while we were looking for Corwen's brother, Freddie, we'd discovered the *Guillaume Tell* being used as a prison ship for magicals and how the Mysterium had mistreated the captives.

"Why haven't we heard any of this?" Mr. Pitt asked.

"I've been worried about the power the Mysterium takes for itself," Lord Stratford said. "This shows I was right to worry. I'm for disbanding the Mysterium."

"But what about the magicals?" Mr. Pitt asked.

"They'll be controlled by their own," I said.

There was a commotion outside our shelter. When we peeped out, Dantin's bronze-armored guards were all floating on their backs some six feet in the air. Their weapons were stacked neatly on the ground and Lord Dax was standing in the middle of the glade, a satisfied expression on his face.

"Rossalinde, Corwen," he nodded toward us, face impassive. "You've brought visitors." He bowed to Lord

Stratford and Mr. Pitt and they returned the courtesy. "I hope we don't appear rude. We came as soon as we heard."

Thank you, Margann, I thought.

"Gentlemen, please walk this way. Oh, I'm sorry. I forgot about your feet."

With a single wave of Lord Dax's fingers, Lord Stratford and Mr. Pitt's feet returned to normal and instead of being encased in odd footwear, I saw they were now wearing Fae-made shoes. I knew how comfortable they were, and they'd never wear out. Corwen and I wore our Fae footwear all the time.

"I took care of your little gout problem, Mr. Pitt," Lord Dax said. "I can't guarantee it won't come back, but for now it's gone. Maybe less port wine in your diet. Mr. Pomeroy, I see you are fit and healthy, congratulations, but it never hurts to have the right kind of footwear."

Another wave of Lord Dax's fingers, and George's boots turned into Fae ones.

"Good, now that we are all properly shod, I think we need to hurry." He set off at a run, despite his age. Our feet, Fae shod, followed him at speed. The run didn't seem to take any effort, my heart didn't pound, I wasn't panting and gasping for breath, and I'm sure we were covering the ground as fast as we might have done on horseback. We didn't stop until we reached the grove I recognized. There in the middle was an arc of seven chairs, four of them filled. Lord Dax took the one on the extreme left next to Lady Iphransia, and settled his robes around him, apparently none the worse for several acts of magic and a brisk run.

Five chairs appeared for us. Mr. Pitt dropped into his with much relief, but I saw him stretch out his left foot and wiggle his toes inside his shoe.

"Feel all right?" I asked.

"Amazingly, yes," he said. "If that's magic, I'm all for it."

"I don't promise it's a cure-all, but it can certainly do a lot of good."

Lord Dax clapped his hands and looked at the two

empty chairs. He raised an eyebrow as Dantin stepped into the grove and took up his chair, glaring at us. Margann appeared behind him, standing with the younger Fae squires. Larien's chair remained empty. She looked across at us, and I swear she winked though the dip of one eyelid came and went so quickly I wondered if I'd imagined it.

"We are only six, Lord Dax," Dantin announced.

"You have a gift for the obvious, Lord Dantin," Dax said.

"Should there be a divided vote—"

"Have patience." Dax inclined his head.

David appeared, looking somewhat flustered. He bowed low before Lord Dax, received a gracious nod, and took his father's chair.

Dantin looked thunderous.

Dax's expression never slipped.

David hid it well, but to me he looked terrified.

Lord Dax began, and the words passed around the whole Council of Seven.

"We."

"Convene."

"To."

"Discuss."

"The."

"Human."

"Problem."

Sitting in the seventh chair, I wondered how David would pick up the thread of the sentence, but he barely hesitated before he said his word.

"The humans have done nothing to set right the abuses," Dantin said. "Rowankind are being hanged for their magic. I say we punish the humans and bring all the rowankind home."

"Harsh but fair." Lady Coralie, sitting to Dantin's right, spoke up. If she'd been human, I might have guessed her to be in her forties. Her severe features were emphasized by tightly scraped-back hair topped by a single golden circlet.

"Didn't we give them until midsummer?" Lady

Iphransia, the elder of the two female council members, raised one elegant eyebrow.

"That's less than a week away," Dantin said. "What can they do in that time that they couldn't have done three months ago?"

"I agree with Dantin," Lord Tarius said. That was only what I expected. He always seemed to support Dantin.

Dax turned to us. "Let's ask them."

Mr. Pitt stood, and it was only then I realized why the man had been so successful in Parliament for so long. He seemed to be in complete command of the situation. Maybe he thought he was. There's a saying about ignorance being bliss.

"Permit me to answer," he said. "Our first minister, Mr. Addington, is not fully aware of the situation. In pursuing the country's best interests, he has been concentrating on the peace with France when he should have been sparing a thought for the situation at home. I will speak with the king immediately and offer my support in this matter for a change in the law." He inclined his head to Lord Stratford. "My good friend the Earl of Stratford will speak to the House of Lords."

Lady Coralie leaned forward. "I understand that for something to be made law in your land, your Parliament has to vote on it."

"That is correct," Mr. Pitt replied.

"Are you so sure you can carry that vote?"

"I am."

That was politician speak for *I hope so*, but I admired Mr. Pitt for his gall and hoped his confidence wasn't misplaced.

I stood, and Dax nodded to me to speak.

"When I returned the magic to the rowankind, it was on condition they didn't exchange one servitude for another. You assured me they could choose whether or not to return to Iaru or continue their lives in the world of humans. You all agreed. Lord Dantin suggests they should all be brought into Iaru for their own safety, and I'm sure they could come here, but would they want to? What they need is recognition as equals under the law and the freedom to make their own decisions."

Corwen stood, and I handed over to him. "This should extend not only to rowankind, but to goblins and hobs and all magicals, even kelpies. Any who break the law should be dealt with as criminals, not for what they are, but for what they have done. To that end, the Lady of the Forests and the Green Man should be consulted."

"Quite right, too."

I couldn't see the speaker, but the words echoed around the grove. It sounded like the Lady of the Forests.

At last we were going to get a real conversation.

43

Parliament of All the Magics

LIGHT APPEARED ON the far side of the grove, and the Green Man and his Lady stepped out of it, surrounded by their retinue of sprites, shapechangers, magicals, and woodland creatures. I recognized Hartington in stag form. He dipped his antlers in our direction. Diana, the cream kelpie, walked behind Hartington in human form, her mane and tail hidden beneath her clothing.

Mr. Twomax and a phalanx of goblins came next, for once not sporting any glamour. At the back of the line was the huge troll we had rescued from Chantry Bridge in Wakefield. I blinked twice. He was wearing spectacles and carrying a book, clutched to his chest, a child's ABC primer.

The only ones missing were the rowankind themselves. Ah, no, here they came. Charlotte and the newly restored Henry headed the line with Olivia between them. Following close behind, I saw Mr. Topping, the rowankind manager at the mill, his son Tommy, and Annie, walking by herself.

I saw David's face when he realized Annie was there, but he pressed his lips together and scowled. I suspected he was holding back much more raw emotions. Annie had her eyes downcast. By the time she raised them, David was scowling and looking anywhere but at her. Oh, dear, that wasn't good.

"Welcome."

"Everyone."

"Please."

"Enter."

"And."

"Be."

"Seated."

The Council of Seven welcomed everyone in their usual manner, and then Lord Dax waved a hand and the council's chairs repositioned themselves in an arc around the circumference of the glade. If the glade was a clock face, the council filled the space from ten o'clock to two. Our own chairs formed a separate arc at eight and nine on the clock face, and the Green Man and the Lady of the Forests occupied the space between three and four. At six-of-the-clock chairs appeared for Charlotte, Henry, and Twomax. Everyone else crowded into the center of the circle and sat on the grass. Livvy sat at her parents' feet.

I hadn't seen the rest of the Fae arrive, but they had gathered outside the circle. I saw familiar faces, but none I could put a name to except the Lady Calantha who positioned herself in Dantin's line of sight.

"What is this?" Lord Stratford whispered.

"It's the closest you'll get to a Parliament of all the Magics," Corwen whispered.

"How often does it happen?"

"In my experience, never," I said.

"I heard there was one about three thousand years ago when the Fae decided to retire from the world of humans," Corwen said. "So the answer is almost never."

"What should we do?" Mr. Pitt asked.

"Answer whatever we are asked as truthfully as we

can," Corwen said. "And make sure any promises we make are ones we can keep. The Fae have a way of holding you to your promises. Whatever you say here is like writing in your own heart's blood before the Lord Chief Justice of the land."

Lord Dax called light and let it shine on the rowankind. "We will hear from our friends first."

Charlotte stood. "I am grateful for the offer of a place in Iaru, but I have a husband and daughter, and a father-in-law who would be desolate without his family. My daughter was taken from me by the Mysterium because of her potential to be both rowankind and witch. The Mysterium would have killed her—they tried to feed her to a wolf . . . " There was a rumble of anger at this, but Charlotte continued. "Friends restored her to us and restored her father. We thank them for that. Our dearest wish as a family is to live free in the world of humans."

Mr. Topping stood. "I live in the world of humans. My rowankind wife of eleven years, much loved, died of a fever. I have a good wife now who is not rowankind but is a good mother to all my children whether she bore them or not. I'm a weaver by trade and have a responsible position in Deverell's Mill. Last year the Mysterium issued warrants for some of the mill's rowankind, and it was only thanks to Lord David that they escaped to Iaru. My son was among them. I miss him every day. His family misses him. We want him to come home."

Tommy Topping stood and agreed with his father. One by one, other rowankind told their stories. Finally, it was Annie's turn. She stood, twisting so she was facing Lord Dax and not looking directly at David.

"Like many others when the rowankind awoke, I came to Iaru. I didn't know what I would find here, but my feet seemed to know the way, and I thought it had to be better than skivvying at the Twisted Skein in Plymouth. For a time I was happy. I found love, or thought I did, but the rules here mean we are no freer than we were in the human world. I chose to go back to Plymouth. Don't think

I'm not grateful for the offer to live in Iaru, but it wouldn't suit."

As she finished speaking, she glanced sideways at David, but he had his eyes closed at the wrong moment. I saw her expression tighten as she sat down again.

Lord Dax invited others to speak.

The goblins told of how they had risen from being sewer goblins to having trades and businesses, but always had to wear a glamour to be accepted as human when, in truth, they would rather be accepted for what they were. Twomax told of Mr. Tingle's death at the hands of Walsingham and explained how they had been treated on board the *Guillaume Tell* at the behest of the Mysterium.

Henry Purdy told how he'd followed the letter of the law and registered as a witch only to be ripped from his family and sent into the army to use his magic for the king. "I have used my magic to kill for the Crown," he said. "I don't ever want to be forced to do that again."

Diana the kelpie said that with the help of the Lady of the Forests, she had overcome her true nature and was content not to prey upon humans now or ever. The troll said that he was learning to read, thanks to Mr. Hartington who had persuaded him that he was better off away from humankind, though he admitted that he still had aspirations to occupy a bridge.

Finally, the Lady of the Forest stood. "My mate and I . . . " She indicated that she spoke for the Green Man, too, "claim the deep forests of the human world where magic is strong. We live by nature. My mate oversees the growing things and the flowing streams. I look after the creatures and the people who, by their magic, need refuge from the outside world. My captains are my hands in the human world." She indicated Hartington and inclined her head toward Corwen. "They have investigated cases where magicals have caused problems for humans. And resolved them successfully. I undertake that if the Mysterium is disbanded, which I sincerely hope it will be, the Okewood will remain a haven and that we will continue to watch over and mediate the use of magic which endangers humans."

Lord Dax turned to Mr. Pitt. "How say you?"

"I undertake to put an end to the Mysterium and the persecution of the rowankind. I cannot promise to do it in three days, but it will be my primary concern in Parliament from this day forward. I do not promise that the people of Britain are ready to accept magicals in their everyday lives, but I hope that will come eventually once the law is changed. I hope Britain may call upon the help of the lords of the Fae and the Lady of the Forests should the need arise."

I thought that was as much as any one man could promise, though if anyone could succeed in such an endeavor, Mr. Pitt could. Lord Stratford was nodding in agreement.

Dantin leaped to his feet. "And if this doesn't happen, what then?"

Lord Tarius nodded vigorously. "We should reserve the right to remind the humans there is a cost to ignoring our wishes."

"Not by killing them," David said.

Dantin glared at him.

"He's right. We should not be hasty," Lady Iphransia said. "Humans are stubborn. I have an idea."

The Fae council all went silent, and I suspected Lady Iphransia's idea was being discussed in a way we could never experience.

Lord Dax nodded. "A vote."

I wasn't quite sure what they were voting on, but David, Lady Iphransia, and Lord Eduran voted one way and Dantin, Lord Tarius, and Lady Coralie voted the other, which left Dax himself with the deciding vote.

I held my breath. Dax had always seemed impartial, but he was old and he could have concerns we didn't understand. I didn't know how he would vote.

He looked at each one of us as if weighing up what was in our hearts. I felt his scrutiny. He knew that I'd taken what the Fae had asked me to do for the rowankind and turned it into a wider attempt to better the lives of all magicals. I stood my ground and returned his look. Yes, to be sure, I was self-serving in this, but I was trying to do my best for everyone. If that included my own family, could anyone blame me?

The moment seemed to hang in the air forever.

"I support the motion," he said.

David breathed a sigh of relief.

I wasn't sure exactly what the motion had been, but presumably London would not be turned into a smoking hole on midsummer's day. However, they had something planned. I wondered if David would be allowed to tell me.

Dax turned to Mr. Pitt and Lord Stratford. "We accept your undertaking, gentlemen, but reserve the right to hurry things along."

I wondered what that meant.

❖───────❖

As the meeting broke up, Corwen and I waited for David.

"Where's Annie?" he asked when he arrived.

"She left with the Lady of the Forests. Couldn't you even have smiled at her? Twice she looked at you, and the first time you were frowning and the second you had your eyes closed."

"What? I didn't see."

"No, as I said, eyes closed. You should go after her."

"I can't."

"Can't?"

"Larien needs me. I've been trying to hold his soul into his body, but I'm not such a good summoner as you, Ross. My Sumner half is not as strong as my Fae half. Come and see if you can help him. I'm so afraid he's dying."

"You go, Ross," Corwen said. "I'll look after our visitors. I think they've had an overwhelming amount of new information. I want to make sure they realize the Mysterium is no longer able to deal with the kind of magic there is in the world today, but that's no reason to be afraid. There's no more magic than there always has been. All that's changed is that we all know about it."

I kissed him swiftly on the cheek and followed David through the trees to a bower by a burbling stream. It was idyllic, but for the prone body on the bed inside. A Fae woman perched on a three-legged stool, holding Larien's hand.

"Ross this is Ilona, Larien's wife."

I hadn't even known Larien had a wife until a short while ago. Meeting her took me by surprise. She was one of those women who, had she been human, I would have not been able to guess her age. She looked somewhere between thirty and forty which meant she was easily centuries old, but she was handsome in a way that made age irrelevant. She didn't have wrinkles, but there were worry lines around her eyes and mouth.

"There's no change," she said. "But at least I don't think he's any worse."

"It's a sundering curse, we think," David said. "Designed to separate body and soul."

I knew about sundering. I still had poor Diccon's spirit in the flask in my pocket, drunk as a lord on brandy fumes. Souls didn't always pass over quickly, especially if they had a reason to stay.

"If you can do anything . . . " Ilona's face said it all. Her eyes were wet with tears.

"I'll try, but I'm not sure what I can do."

I took the seat Ilona vacated and touched Larien's hand. It felt cool and oddly lifeless. It was unsettling to see him there, so still, so quiet. He looked like a corpse until I saw the shallow rise and fall of his chest.

"Can you find his spirit and summon it back into his body?" David asked.

"Summon?"

"That's what I was trying to do. There's a thread between body and soul that hasn't yet been broken, though it's stretched almost beyond bearing."

I took Larien's hand more firmly and pictured everything I knew that made him Larien. I remembered him in our household in Plymouth, glamoured to look like a row-ankind, elbows on the kitchen table, eating supper and laughing with Ruth, one of our servants. I remembered him around my mother, always so charming, and then that day when I'd hidden in her bedroom, afraid of getting caught for some minor misdemeanor, only to witness them together beneath the sheets. I was too young to understand what was happening at the time, but later I'd realized what I'd seen and thought if my mother had taken brief comfort from it, then it was no bad thing. Of course, I hadn't known about David until later. She'd done her best to cover up the birth of a bastard who, as far as she knew, was half-rowankind. It was only after I discovered David was my brother that I met Larien in his true form, as a Fae lord.

All these images were Larien. I hadn't thought he'd cared much about David except as an heir, but he'd stepped in front of a deadly spell to save him. Maybe this Fae wasn't such a cold fish as he seemed.

Larien.

I summoned his spirit.

Larien.

I hoped I hadn't gotten this wrong. I didn't want to pull his spirit out of his body. I needed to tempt it back in.

Larien.

The third time was the charm. His spirit didn't come from his body, but toward it. Behind him, holding his hand and trying to draw him in the opposite direction, was a small gray creature, all head, arms, and legs on a tiny body. It looked pinched and malevolent.

I didn't know how old Larien was. I knew he'd been on the Council of Seven for over two hundred years, but I suspected he was a lot older than that. His spirit told me I was right. It wasn't visibly old, but there was something about it that spoke of age and experience.

"Who calls me?"

"Rossalinde."

"Why?"

"To draw you back to your body before it's too late."

"It's already too late." He glanced at the small gray thing and took a step toward where it was trying to pull him.

"No, it isn't. It's not yet your time. Your wife and son are waiting for you."

"I'm sundered."

"Not yet. Not quite."

I leaned forward and put my hand over that of the gray thing to try to pry Larien's hand from the creature's grasp. It pulled its hand free and then tried to yank my hand away from Larien's. I held tight. With my free hand, I pulled on the thread running between Larien and his soul. "See. There's yet a tether."

I pulled again.

Closer.

Again.

The gray thing tugged at Larien's elbow.

I kicked it away. "Begone."

Was it my imagination? Was it getting smaller? It made one more attempt; when I wouldn't let go, it bit my hand. Its teeth were needle-sharp.

"Owww! Enough!" I shook it loose and slapped it on the side of the head before grabbing Larien's hand again.

Now I felt as though Larien's spirit was looking over my shoulder at his own body.

"There's still breath in it," he said.

"It's your breath. Take it."

With a rush that made me dizzy, I felt the spirit and the body rejoin.

Larien gasped a deep breath. His eyes flew open and he sat upright. "I'm back," he said.

I let go of his hand and rubbed my own where blood was oozing from a ring of teeth marks.

Ilona touched Larien's face briefly, then took my hand. "That needs treating immediately," she said. "You mustn't let it fester."

"I can ask the Lady—"

"No. You've done us a great service. Let me help."

Without her calling for anything, a young rowankind brought a bowl of water and some cloths.

"Thank you, Ema." Ilona smiled at the girl. "Please bring the winterwood casket."

Winterwood was ensorcelled wood. The *Heart of Oak* had a sliver in her keel. It wasn't used casually. I wondered what was so precious that Ilona kept it in winterwood. When Ema brought the casket, big enough that she needed to carry it in two hands, I saw a row of small pots. Ilona selected one and opened it.

"This may tingle," she said as she smoothed on a salve with a violet tint. "Don't wash it off for at least a day. I'm afraid the bite may leave a scar."

"What was it—the gray thing?"

She shook her head.

"Something I'm glad you separated me from," Larien said.

44

Freeze

LARIEN DIDN'T QUITE say thank you, though it was obvious he now felt as though he owed me. If I needed a favor, I only had to ask. That was the way it worked with the Fae.

I regarded my bite mark, hot and inflamed, but no longer bleeding. It was beginning to tingle as Ilona had warned. I rejoined Corwen to take George, Lord Stratford, and Mr. Pitt back to their waiting coach by way of Richmond. I was pleased to see their feet didn't grow again when they left Iaru. Lord Dax's reversal of the effect seemed to be permanent.

"How's your gout, Mr. Pitt?"

"Perfectly absent, thank you."

"Do you really think you can persuade Parliament to disband the Mysterium? You weren't simply saying that, were you?"

"I'm not saying it will be as easy as this." He snapped his fingers. "But I'll see the king today, and we'll talk."

"If only we'd met you a few months ago. We had the

devil of a time speaking to the king, and even then it didn't get us anywhere."

"It helps being the former first minister."

I fancied from the way he spoke that he was planning to be the next first minister as well. Good luck to him.

We said good-bye to Lord Stratford, Mr. Pitt, and George at their coach and returned to town in a mood of cautious optimism. When we arrived back, the Thames was still frozen. A huge frost fair was in full swing. Corwen and I looked at each other and took the bridge instead of the ice.

The following day nothing happened.

In its own way it was as stressful as our visit to the Fae or having to tell George Pomeroy his beloved Lily was a part-time wolf. We resisted the temptation to send messages to Lord Stratford or Mr. Pitt, having to trust they were both doing what they said they'd do and let them get on with it.

While Corwen went across to the Red Lion to check on the horses, I took the opportunity to check on Diccon's spirit, languishing in the brandy flask. I hoped he was unaware of the passing of time. I uncorked the flask and poured Diccon out. He grew to his own size and shape, though he was still as insubstantial as morning mist.

"How are you, Diccon?"

"I'm very well, madam." His speech was slurred as if he was literally drunk on the brandy fumes. He couldn't really be drunk. Spirits didn't interact with the real world in such a way, but suggestion and imagination could prove powerful. If Diccon liked to think he was drunk, it might help him to pass the time.

"How far can you range and still come back to me safely?" I asked him.

He looked puzzled.

"For instance, can you see what's happening in the room below?"

"I don't kno—" He knelt and pressed his ghostly head

to the floor, then pushed it through the floorboards. His whole body disappeared after it. I wondered if I'd asked too much of him, but he returned a few moments later.

"Oh, my! There's a lady and a gentleman. She has her skirts up to her waist and he has his trousers down to his knees, and they're . . . " He paused, and I swear his face reddened. "Basket-making, ma'am. Making feet for babies' socks . . . the beast with two backs."

"I get the idea, thank you, Diccon. If you can tear yourself away, can you see what's in the room next to them?"

He disappeared through the floor again. After a few minutes I began to fear I'd lost him, but as I was contemplating disturbing the two lovebirds below to see if Diccon had voyeuristic tendencies, he floated back up through the boards.

"What did you see?"

"Not much. It was over in three thrusts, he paid her, and that was that." I noticed his drunken slur had disappeared.

"I didn't mean that. Did you manage to see the room next door?"

"It was empty. The bar downstairs is doing a rattling trade, though. My mam used to keep a sweet house before he came."

I didn't need to ask who Diccon was talking about.

"Are you ready to go back in your flask?"

He sighed. "Are you still looking for my body and the thief what took it?"

"I am."

Without another word he slid back into the flask.

I hadn't told him the hunt for Walsingham had slipped a little down our priority list in view of the Fae's threat, and that things had taken a very unexpected turn with the involvement of Mr. Pitt.

Corwen, Lily, and I were all dangerously exposed now, and our only safety lay in the Mysterium being disbanded and magic being decriminalized. Did we trust George, Mr. Pitt, and Lord Stratford? The answer was mostly yes, but for that small amount of doubt, we paid our bill at the Town of Ramsgate and signaled for Hookey to send over the *Heart*'s boat. At least we'd have warning if redcoats turned up in force to arrest us. I didn't really think they would, but I wasn't going to risk my life or Corwen's. And Corwen had already taken George to one side and suggested he send Lily to the *Heart*, just in case. If all else failed, we could make a fast exit downriver.

Lily arrived in the afternoon, having taken a boat from below London Bridge. George came with her, although he didn't stay since he'd been pressed to take some invitations to his grandfather's colleagues in the Upper House, inviting them to a meeting.

"Do you know what progress Mr. Pitt has made?" Corwen asked.

"I don't, but I do know he saw the king last night and this morning spoke to both Mr. Addington and Mr. Fox."

I wondered what the results of those meetings were.

"I've never slept in a hammock before," Lily said as I showed her where we three would sleep. I'd refused Hookey's offer of his cabin but had taken up Mr. Rafiq's offer to hang a sail across a corner of the hold. Since our crew was down to thirty, there was much more room in the hold than there used to be in the *Heart*'s privateering days.

It was Lily's first time aboard a sailing ship, so she wanted to know everything and was still asking questions when I helped her into her hammock.

"Remember. Don't try to turn over suddenly."

We finally got some sleep while Hookey organized watches throughout the night, but our worst fears didn't come to pass.

I wondered whether there would be more Fae changes in the night. So far, they'd done something every other day, and it had been two days since the Thames had frozen. What next?

By the time we'd crawled out of our hammocks the following morning, the broadsheets were being shouted from every corner. Calamity had struck. All Kentish hops had withered and died overnight and were discovered at dawn, crumbling and blowing away on the wind. Kent supplied hops to most of the brewers in the country. At a stroke, growers and breweries alike were ruined.

"I suppose we should be glad it's not wheat," Corwen said.

The dire harvest of 1800, which had brought the country to the edge of famine and led to bread riots, was still in recent memory.

"It's not wheat yet," I said. "But it so very easily could be."

With two days to go before midsummer's day, we didn't know what the Fae might visit upon us.

On the 20th with one day to go before midsummer, George arrived by boat and climbed aboard the *Heart* straight into Lily's waiting arms. When he'd had time to extricate himself from her embrace, we retreated to Hookey's cabin.

"How goes everything?" I asked.

"Mr. Pitt has an excellent following in the Commons, though Mr. Addington is not yet convinced. Surprisingly, Mr. Fox and his followers are not dead set against Mr. Pitt in this, though I'm sure it wouldn't take much to make them mortal enemies again, at least in Parliament, so Pitt has to tread carefully."

"What does the bill cover?" Corwen asked.

"It's a bill of two halves. Firstly, there's the disbanding of the Mysterium and an end to the licensing of witches. It also eliminates punishment for the use of non-registered witchcraft."

"That's good for me," I said, "but what about the rowankind and the goblins?"

"In addition, there's the element which gives rights to all magicals, including but not limited to witches, rowankind, goblins, hobs, and shapechangers." He grinned. "I reminded them to add in the last one. It's called the Disbanding of the Mysterium and the Recognition of Magic and Magical Personages Bill. A bit of a mouthful, but Parliament has never been brief."

"Does that cover everything?"

"I hope so. It's been drawn up very hastily. Normally, bills take weeks to get the wording exactly right, but I've read a draft copy and I think it's comprehensive. If this passes through Parliament, magic will no longer be illegal though the bill does say crimes committed by magic are still crimes and will be dealt with as such. The law of the land is still the law of the land."

"Fair enough." I began to feel hope for the first time.

But early in the morning of midsummer's day I woke shivering. It was barely light outside, so it couldn't have been much after four in the morning. Dawn came early and dusk late at this time of year.

"Quick, get up!" I shook Corwen awake.

Lily was already rolling out of her hammock. "Ooh, cold."

"This doesn't feel like June," Corwen said.

I rummaged in the Fae valise and pulled out several layers of winter clothing and a woolen redingote to top them all. A thick rime of frost crunched beneath my boot soles as I climbed the companionway. On deck all was quiet, too quiet.

A spectral scene met my eyes. The *Heart*'s standing rigging was draped with sparkling icicles. The river itself was frozen from shore to shore; all down the river and against the landing stages ship after ship was frozen solid in the ice. The buildings on the river's edge had fared no better. Glass windows had acquired a thick layer of frost, and roofs were white with frost so dense that I thought it was snow until I bent and touched my fingers to the ice crystals on our own deck.

"Smell that," said Corwen, coming up behind me, buttoning his caped coat.

"What?"

"Exactly. This river has a stink of its own—mud, salt, rotten fish, and ordure—now it's so cold there's nothing.

The river's filth is under the ice. I can't even smell soot from the factory chimneys."

"I can't see any movement on shore," Lily leaned over the ship's rail.

"Anyone with any sense will be indoors," Corwen said.

"What about those who don't have a roof over their head?" I said. And then my brain caught up with itself. "Who's on watch?"

I set off for the bow of the ship, skidded on the ice, and took each step a little more cautiously. Sitting on a coil of rope, a frosted blanket wrapped around his shoulders, Windward looked like a statue. I knelt beside him, fearing the worst, but he seemed to be asleep. I shook him, and he muttered but didn't move. I shook him again, and he opened his eyes, but they were wild and staring. He didn't seem to know me.

"Lily, ring the ship's bell, wake everyone. Corwen, give me a hand with Windward. He's not even shivering. This is bad."

Swearing, Hookey staggered up on deck, saw what we were about with Windward and came to help.

"Get him into my cabin," he yelled. "Billy!"

"Aye, Cap'n."

"Warm some blankets as best you can and bring hot water. Make sure everyone's awake and well wrapped up."

"Aye, Cap'n."

The Greek had arrived on deck at the first stroke of the bell. He helped us carry Windward to Hookey's cabin, wrap him in what dry blankets we had, then chafe his hands and arms, legs and feet to get his blood flowing. Billy arrived with blankets and a warm fire-clay brick which had been on the back of the stove. We wrapped it in a blanket, so it didn't burn him and placed his arms round it for him to hug to his chest.

"Need warm," the Greek said. "Bunk. Huddle."

This was a major speech for the Greek, but we followed his meaning. The Greek climbed into the narrow bunk, and we manhandled Windward into his arms so that the two were lying like spoons. The Greek put his burly arms around Windward, pulling the fire-clay brick closer. We piled extra blankets around them both. If that didn't help, nothing would. Extreme cold was a killer.

"Is everyone up and mobile?" I asked.

"Cold and shivering, but up and awake," Hookey said. "Billy's cooking porridge, and there's water boiling for tea."

"No rum in it, today," I said. "Alcohol makes you feel warm, but it doesn't warm you in these temperatures."

I'd seen two crewmen die after one fell overboard in cold seas and the other jumped in to bring him out. Neither survived the cold though we got them both out of the water alive.

Our warning bell had roused other ships nearby, and their own bells were passing the warning down the river.

"This is more serious than turning leaves red or turning horses into unicorns," I said. "It's midsummer. This is the Fae's reminder. I wonder how far it extends. If it spreads into the country and affects the wheat harvest, we're going to have wholesale famine."

"It's time to go to Cavendish Square," Corwen said. "Even though we risk ourselves, we may be able to help persuade members of Parliament before the vote."

"Yes. It's time for us to stand and be counted. No more hiding."

"No more hiding."

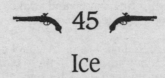

45

Ice

MUFFLED UP WITH gloves and scarves and wearing layers of the warmest clothing we had, the three of us crossed to Wapping Old Stairs on the ice. I didn't trust it to take our weight at first, but it was as solid as stone. I worried that the pressure of the ice might damage the *Heart*'s hull, but there wasn't much I could do about it except wish that I'd sent Hookey away from London days ago.

The ice was treacherous and the steps slippery, but we made it to the Town of Ramsgate without incident. At this time in the morning it was all locked up, but I could see flickering flames reflected on the frosted window glass. The landlady was obviously stoking the fire in the public room, trying to keep out the cold.

"How will Timpani and Dancer fare in this?" I asked.

"They're Fae," Corwen said. "They should be all right."

"I'm sure it's getting colder," I said. "My lungs hurt every time I breathe."

"It's my eyes I'm worried about," Lily said. "Every

time I blink, I'm sure I can feel ice cracking on my eye-balls."

We had to hammer on the door of the Red Lion to get any service, but finally the landlord came and drew the bolts.

"What do you want?"

"Our horses and one extra," Corwen said. "We have to get across London and there's not a coach to be had."

"Are you surprised? Go home, stay warm."

I shook my head, my teeth chattering so much I could hardly speak. "Horses, now."

"What my wife means is we're happy to pay you well for the hire of the horse."

The landlord sniffed and held out his hand for coins. "You'll need to shout for young Luke. He sleeps in the loft."

It being obvious the landlord wasn't going to come out with us, we made our way around the back of the inn where there was stabling. Corwen tried the door, and it swung open.

"Who's there? What does yer want?"

"Our horses, and one more, paid for," Corwen shouted.

"In this weather?"

We found Luke in one of the stalls pressed up against a stocky dray horse for warmth, his fingers twined in the horse's mane, a blanket around his shoulders. His cheeks looked pinched and pale, and his lips had a slight blue tinge.

"Are you all right?" I asked.

"Does it look like I'm all right?"

"Haven't you got a stove in your loft?"

"Aye, but ain't got no coals."

"Why not?"

"It's summer."

Right. That made sense.

"Saddle a hardy cob for the young lady and then get yourself over to the Town of Ramsgate for a beefsteak breakfast." Corwen tipped him two shillings. "The land-lady's got a fire roaring up the chimney."

"Thanks, mister."

Timpani and Dancer didn't seem to notice the cold. Luke saddled a gray cob and draped an extra blanket over her hindquarters since she was in her summer coat. I hoped Luke got his beefsteak breakfast, but we didn't hang around to check.

We weren't the only ones on the road, but London was much quieter than usual. We rode parallel to the river, through the jumble of streets at St. Catherine's and around the glutinous boggy moat, now frozen solid, and the forbidding stone walls of the Tower. From the Tower, we struck north to Cheapside and then followed it to High Holborn, Broad Street, and finally Oxford Street. Margaret Street was two streets north close to Cavendish Square. Our destination was firstly Margaret Street to collect George and then on to Cavendish Square to his grandfather's house.

We saw our first corpse, frozen to death in the mouth of an alley, before we reached the Tower. By the time we reached Oxford Street, we'd seen seven, two of them children, huddled together, but quite cold, their faces glassy with frost. Those vagrants sleeping in the streets, crouched in alleyways and shop doorways, had not fared well. We stopped for the first one, and for the children, but we were obviously too late, so we rode past the rest and tried not to look.

It was still wanting a few minutes before nine of the clock when we arrived at Margaret Street. Lily rang the front door bell and then pounded on the door panel with the flat of her hand.

A footman came out to take our horses round to the stable in the mews behind the house. He didn't look any too pleased to be out in such a frost, but at least he was wrapped up warmly in a caped coat.

Lily practically sprinted through the front door, and Corwen and I followed her into the relative warmth of the house.

George stepped onto the first-floor landing. "Good God in His heaven, but it's cold."

"Try riding across London in it," Lily said.

George came downstairs to the morning room. It was small, with a sofa, a couple of chairs, and a breakfast table set for one. A fire blazed in the grate.

We divested ourselves of outer garments and George asked the footman to bring more breakfast rolls, hot chocolate, and coffee.

"Oooh, George, no wonder Lily loves you," I said. "If I were free, I'd marry you for hot chocolate right now."

He laughed and poured me a cup.

Corwen helped himself to coffee and a warm bread roll.

"So is this what the Fae meant by saying they might try to hurry us along?" George asked.

"I'm guessing so," Corwen said. "We need to know how far the freeze has spread. If it's limited to London, it's bad but not a grand-scale disaster. If it's spread farther out to the wheat fields . . . "

"Crop failure, famine, more bread riots, civil unrest," George said.

We nodded.

"So we'll do whatever we can to help resolve this quickly," I said. "If that means doing party tricks for politicians to show them the extent of magic, then I'll do it."

"Wrap up warm, George," Corwen said. "Let's go and see your grandfather."

"You are not keeping me out of things this time," Lily said. "I'm coming, too."

George looked as though he'd like to protest but, wisely, didn't.

We left our horses in George's mews stable, tucked away behind the house, where they would be warm enough, and walked around the corner to Lord Stratford's house. He was already working on correspondence in his office and didn't stand on ceremony, receiving us there.

He listened to what we had to say and nodded sagely. "We have support in both houses, but I'm not sure we have enough to carry the bill with a secure majority.

However, I think today's weather proves we must move quickly. I've already had reports from Surrey and Hampshire. They are suffering the same low temperatures. Crops will fail, and we don't have reserves after the last few poor harvests." He frowned. "You realize I can't offer you safety from the Mysterium if you make yourselves known."

"We hope, sir, if the bill passes, that the Mysterium will be taken care of," Corwen said.

"And if it doesn't?"

"Pray that it does."

⬦⸺⬦

We traveled in Lord Stratford's coach, entering the Palace of Westminster through a columned portico. We followed him through the building to a smallish room where he asked us to wait while he sent his secretary in search of Mr. Pitt and the first minister himself, Mr. Addington.

I heard them speaking in the corridor as they approached. From what Mr. Addington said, the king had, indeed, asked him to deal with the rowankind question, but the forthcoming election and the peace with France had wholly occupied him.

"Of course, there's no question of dissolving Parliament at the end of this month if the country's facing famine," I heard Mr. Pitt saying as they approached our room. "The general election will have to be postponed."

I didn't quite catch Mr. Addington's answer before the door opened.

Mr. Pitt and Mr. Addington were easy in each other's company, so I took it that rather than being political rivals, they were, in fact, colleagues. Mr. Addington had taken over as first minister when Mr. Pitt had resigned over the Irish Catholic question, but I got the impression Mr. Addington still deferred to Mr. Pitt in some matters.

Introductions were made, and in our presence Mr. Pitt apprised Mr. Addington of his visit to the Fae. If Mr. Addington's eyebrows could have risen any higher, I swear they would have disappeared into his hair.

Lord Stratford supported all Mr. Pitt said, and then it was our turn.

Corwen began. "Mr. Addington, you don't need us to tell you about the power of the Fae. You've had the proof of it already with the unicorns, the dairy cattle, the red leaves, the beer turned to water. Indeed, I see you are standing on it." Mr. Addington sported one foot three inches longer than the other. "You will note," Corwen continued, "both Mr. Pitt and Lord Stratford have been cured of that affliction."

I took over. "The Fae are now reminding us they have the power to cause conditions so against nature that they could endanger the lives of all the population of these islands. They don't want to rule us, they simply want to remind us that magic is endemic, and our treatment of magicals, including the rowankind, is abhorrent and must be changed."

"I'm an officer of the Mysterium," George added, "I can testify that rowankind have been hanged for their magic, despite their status as non-persons according to all the statutes, meaning that they are outside the parameters of the Mysterium Act of 1590."

Mr. Addington looked worried. "We can't lose the wheat crop. The country is one bad harvest away from famine and revolution." He looked at Mr. Pitt. "What do you advise? If we dissolve the Mysterium and recognize the right of magicals as persons within the law, will the Fae leave us alone?"

Mr. Pitt looked at me.

"I'm sure they will," I said, hoping they would.

"So it only remains for us to convince the members of both houses," Mr. Pitt said.

"Could we help with that?" I created a witchlight and tossed it into the air. Catching it with a tiny gust of wind, I blew it around the room. "What would it take to convince them?"

Lily took the bag she'd been carrying and requested a room to change. She returned a short while later wearing a belted dressing robe.

"Gentlemen, would this help to convince the honorable members of both houses?" she asked. Then she turned her back to everyone, unfastened the robe, and sank to the floor. Within seconds she stood there as a large black wolf. She wasn't as big as Corwen, but she was still impressive.

"Is that an illusion?" Mr. Addington asked.

"No, sir," George responded. "That's my wife. Isn't she beautiful?"

I dropped the robe over Lily, and she turned back without showing so much as an inch of flesh. A lively conversation followed and resulted in Mr. Pitt, Mr. Addington, and Lord Stratford summoning their colleagues to meet the magicals in advance of a debate and a vote.

For the next two hours I thought I knew what animals in a zoo felt like. I talked myself hoarse, answering question both sensible and inane. Corwen and Lily changed countless times, and I produced lights and winds and even a tiny rainstorm for one gentleman who tried to remain unimpressed.

At length, Mr. Addington marshaled the Commons, and Lord Stratford departed likewise to speak to the Lords.

Corwen, Lily, George, and I crept into the public gallery at the west end of the House to listen to the debate. Since ladies were not allowed to view the deliberations of the House, Corwen glamoured Lily and me until we were all safely installed and George guarded our backs lest one of the stewards should ask us to leave. Ladies or not, neither Lily nor I were going to miss this. The gallery held over a hundred people and was more than half full already. I heard Corwen chuckle.

"Goblins," he said. "Every last one of them. All glamoured."

One of them turned around on hearing Corwen's voice, and I realized it was Mr. Twomax. He winked at me and then turned back to the proceedings.

A short while later a contingent of rowankind arrived. The House itself was very grand. Formerly a chapel, there were benches down both sides, each row raised higher than the one in front of it. Facing down the middle was a huge thronelike chair with the king's arms on top of it. This, Corwen said, was the Speaker's chair. The Speaker himself, dressed all in black, wore a full wig. In front of him was a table at which sat three clerks, also dressed in black, whose purpose was to read the bills and to record all that passed. On the table lay the Speaker's mace, a huge gilded thing, itself a symbol of authority.

Mr. Addington and Mr. Pitt sat on the front bench to the Speaker's right surrounded by their supporters, and a florid man with a large belly encased in a tightly buttoned waistcoat occupied the bench opposite with his supporters. Mr. Fox, I supposed. Good job he wasn't a fox shapechanger. He'd make the biggest fox ever seen. I tried to hide my smile at the thought.

The bill was read. Mr. Pitt stood and spoke most eloquently about how the Mysterium had been formed to serve a need of the day but now, two hundred and eleven years later, had become something it was never intended to be. Someone on Mr. Fox's bench replied that the Mysterium was Britain's only protection from the threat of unlicensed magic. Mr. Addington responded, though not in such an authoritative way as Mr. Pitt, that licensed or unlicensed, the Mysterium was incapable of preventing the use of magic, only punishing it after the fact, and those punishments were only meted out to lesser magic users who had not the power to protect themselves. Greater magic users were hard to expose and even harder to bring to justice. The Mysterium cost a lot to maintain and achieved comparatively little. He bandied some figures about and then handed back to Mr. Pitt.

Mr. Pitt read from several witness statements about hangings without trial, including the case of the rowankind, and the imprisonment of magicals aboard the *Guillaume Tell*. When Mr. Fox spoke in favor of the bill from the opposition benches, it looked as if we'd reached a turning point in the debate.

Since this was a bill of two parts, they also had to discuss the other races and magicals. One young fellow on the third bench behind Mr. Pitt said he didn't believe magicals lived among us, and goblins were a child's fairy tale. At that, such a hubbub went up from the public gallery that it drew everyone's attention. Immediately, the goblins all dropped their glamour, and seventy paleskinned, bulgy-eyed, slit-nostriled goblins politely stood to attention, bowed, and cried as one, "God save the king!" before adopting their glamour once more and coming to order.

The uproar in the House of Commons took a little longer to die away; the Speaker had to call for order three times.

"Gentlemen," Mr. Pitt said. "I would guess each and every one of you has at some time dealt with a goblin whether you know it or not. Many of them are in the tailoring business. Who here has never been measured for a suit of clothes?"

The debate continued.

I was surprised when a gentleman entered the gallery wearing no finery, but a many-caped coat. I recognized him instantly.

"Majesty." I began to curtsey, but he waved me upright again.

"I'm not here," he said. "You haven't seen me."

"Of course not, Majesty." I gestured for Lily and George to turn back to watch the proceedings. "Can I assume that you will give royal assent if the bills are passed in both houses?"

"You can, young lady. We cannot risk a famine. Your Fae have won. Are you happy now?"

"What would make me truly happy, Majesty, is if you allowed your own magic to reveal itself. I do believe its suppression will continue to have an adverse effect on Your Majesty's health."

"That, I regret to say, is not possible." He sighed. "I'm the king, you know."

And that was that.

The adoption of the Disbanding of the Mysterium and the Recognition of Magic and Magical Personages Bill required only one courteous reading each in the Lords and Commons to pass into law with royal assent. They pushed the bill through both houses on the same day, an unprecedented occurrence. The Mysterium was no more. I felt weak at the knees. All my life the Mysterium had loomed over me. I grabbed Corwen's hand.

"I don't know whether to laugh or cry."

46

Fae Trial

THE KING DEPARTED as quietly as he'd come. As we left Parliament in the company of Lord Stratford, surrounded by members of both houses, we ran into a wall of goblins and rowankind, all grinning and shaking hands with each other.

A shiver in the air that might have been a fanfare, felt but not heard, announced the arrival of the Fae. They came two by two, riding through the Old Palace Yard in a procession, with Lord Dax at their head. Larien and Dantin were immediately behind him. Larien looked as well as I'd ever seen him. The whole parade emanated a soft glow of golden light. None of the Fae was muffled up in winter garb, but they all looked perfectly comfortable, as though the frost didn't touch them. No one who saw them doubted who or what they were.

"They could have saved this whole mess if they'd ridden in like that six months ago," Corwen whispered.

Dantin turned his head slightly and glared at him as if he'd heard the remark.

"Well, it's true," I said, as much to Dantin as Corwen.

The parade stopped. The Council of Seven, each mounted on a magnificent Fae steed, rode forward and halted in a line in front of their honor guard.

"Have."

"You."

"Come."

"To."

"The."

"Correct."

"Decision?"

They passed the question between them.

Someone must have run for Mr. Addington, for that gentleman stepped forward from the crowd and said. "We are disbanding the Mysterium. There will be no more hangings. We have recognized the magical people of this island as equal under the law."

"Do you speak for the king?" Lord Dax asked. Although he spoke at normal volume, his voice could be heard throughout Westminster. I wouldn't have been surprised if it hadn't been heard across London.

"I speak for Parliament which makes the laws."

Lord Dax nodded, spread the fingers of one hand, and all the members of Parliament hopped about as their feet returned to normal size.

"I thought the Fae couldn't enter human cities because of the smog and smoke and filth," I whispered to Corwen.

"I think it's the cold," he said. "The filth is trapped under the ice."

"We will bring back summer," Lord Dax said. "Your wheat crops will prosper." I noticed he didn't say anything about Kentish hops. I assumed they were lost.

"What about the beer?" someone shouted from the crowd.

"And the unicorns," someone else shouted.

"And the dairy herds . . . "

"Don't presume on our benevolence," Dax said. "For we have none."

A shiver traveled down my spine. He was right. Benevolence wasn't one of their traits. I looked at the crowd.

They'd stopped asking questions and started to look uncomfortable. Even the rowankind and the goblins who were the beneficiaries of today's vote stood silent.

"Corwen, Rossalinde," Dax turned to us. "Your presence is required in Iaru."

What now?

From somewhere toward the back of the honor guard, Dancer and Timpani came trotting toward us, saddled and bridled. I wasn't sure how they'd escaped from George's stable, and I wasn't going to ask. Corwen boosted me into the saddle and mounted Timpani. With a nod to Lily and George, we fell in behind the Council of Seven, with the honor guard behind us. Riding west, parallel to the river, we soon left London's streets behind. I felt my scalp tingle as we passed through a gate which I'm sure had been created specially and would melt away with the frost. Iaru was blessedly warm and I soon came to regret my winter garments. I unbuttoned my redingote as we rode and saw Corwen had done the same with his caped coat.

Back at the Fae grove we were able to shrug out of our coats at last. I wondered where David was. Margann was absent, too. The Council of Seven dismounted and crossed to their chairs. Court was obviously in session.

"I hope they haven't any more insane tasks for us," I said to Corwen. "I want to go home and have our babies in peace."

"Home sounds good. There's nothing to stop us going back to Yorkshire."

"George and Lily, too. Now he's out of a job, Lily will be able to introduce him to the delights of being a clothier."

Corwen shuddered, "And jolly good luck to him. I can't think of anything worse."

The grove gradually filled up with Fae around the circumference, three and four deep and their gentle chatter filled the air, until suddenly it ceased as if someone had rung a bell. The Council of Seven was ready to begin.

"Calantha."

"Of."

"The."

"Merovingian."

"Fae."

"Stand."

"Forward."

A small disturbance in the crowd allowed Calantha to enter, head held high. David and Margann flanked her. For a moment I thought they were going to make David go through with solemnizing the marriage, but this looked more like a trial.

Lord Dax said, "Calantha, you are charged with using a sundering curse upon Larien. That it didn't kill him is thanks only to the fast action of his son, David, and the intervention of Rossalinde, a summoner of exceptional skill for a human. How do you answer?"

"I did not intend to hurt Larien."

The Fae don't lie, though they can dissemble and allow people to misinterpret their words. I was sure Calantha hadn't intended the curse for Larien. She'd intended it for David, the husband she didn't want.

"Isn't it true the curse was aimed at David?" Dax asked.

"I didn't hurt David."

"That's true, you did not." Dax nodded. "Rossalinde. Please bear witness. Is it true that you restored Larien's soul to his body?"

"I did."

"Was his soul subject to a sundering curse?"

"When I found Larien's soul, it was still connected to his body by the finest thread, stretched so thin I thought it might part at any time and then I would have lost him. A small gray creature was trying to lead him away by the hand."

"How did you free him from it?"

"I took his hand and held on, even though the thing bit me."

"Bit?"

"I still have the mark."

I held up my hand to show the perfect half-circle of teeth marks on the edge of my palm.

"Describe the creature."

"Gray, about half the height of a man, all arms and legs with a very small body, a large round head, and needle-sharp teeth."

The Council of Seven stilled as if they were discussing something no one else could hear. After a couple of minutes during which no one tried to fill the silence, Dax seemed to come back into himself.

"Lady Calantha, daughter of the Merovingian Fae, the sundering curse used was of Merovingian design. No one here could have executed the curse in quite the same way. What have you to say for yourself?"

Calantha gave away nothing. Her expression remained calm, serene, even. "I did not intend to kill Larien, and I did not harm David."

"So you have said, and we believe you. However, please answer yes or no to this question. Did you create the sundering curse?"

She swallowed hard. "Yes."

"And was David the intended victim of your curse?"

"I did not hurt—"

"Please answer the question, yes or no. Was David the intended victim of your curse?"

"Yes."

No one showed signs of surprise. I watched Dantin, suspecting he might have known all along that Calantha was guilty.

There was another one of those silences. Again, I watched Dantin because it seemed to me that whatever was being discussed involved him. I simply couldn't tell what was going on though I was sure something was. Had Dantin planned this with Calantha? Surely, if he had, he would have warned her that a Merovingian sundering curse would be recognizably different from a Britannic one.

I thought he might have discovered what she'd done after the event and made use of Larien's incapacity. I didn't actually think he would have instigated anything that would harm his own brother, but he was Fae. What did I know?

Dax came into himself again, but the whole Council of Seven delivered the verdict. It went around the council three times.

"Calantha."

"Of."

"The."

"Merovingian."

"Fae."

"You."

"Are."

"Hereby."

"Found."

"Guilty."

"Your."

"Marriage."

"Is."

"Officially."

"Dissolved."

"You."

"Will."

"Be."

"Escorted."

"Home."

"Forthwith."

Marriage dissolved. I looked at David. Was that worth almost getting cursed to death for? I saw that it was. Though he looked as though he was trying to retain an impassive expression, a small smile played around his mouth.

◆────◆

After the council had ended and Calantha had been taken away, David bounced up to me with a big grin on his face. "I'm free again, Ross. I can marry Annie."

"If she'll have you," I said. "She was feeling pretty badly treated when we took her to Plymouth."

"Yes, but she must have come back to testify at the Parliament of all the Magics. I bet she's still in the Okewood. I must go to her straight away."

I sighed. "Normally, I'd suggest you are both too young to know your own mind, but if you remain unwed, there's every chance the Fae will arrange something else for you."

David shuddered.

"Don't rush in like a puppy," I said. "Annie needs to know you mean it, and that nothing your father can do will make you set her aside."

"Does the new act mean it's legal for rowankind to marry in church."

"I suppose it does."

"Then that's what we'll do. Perhaps your Reverend Purdy will do the honors."

"You'll need a license. You're both underage, so you'll have to obtain consent of a parent or guardian."

"Annie doesn't have anyone. Her parents are both dead, and she doesn't have a guardian, and Larien—"

"Leave Larien to me," I said. "He owes me."

"We could probably get a signature from her previous employer at the Twisted Skein," Corwen said. "You can leave that to me."

I found Larien in his bower, apparently resting.

"Forgive the intrusion. Are you quite well, Larien?" I asked.

"Oh, yes, merely a little tired. I've decided to leave it up to Dantin to restore Calantha to her people."

I thought he must be mightily tired to even admit that much.

"Is that wise? Dantin and Calantha—"

He waved away my protest. "My brother knows where his loyalties lie."

"Will it cause a rift with the Merovingians?"

He sighed. "We were not on good terms before, and we won't be on good terms after, but even the Merovingians must admit that trying to kill your intended spouse is unacceptable behavior. It's a storm we can weather."

"I came to talk about intended spouses."

I explained what I wanted, and why.

He eventually gave his consent, in writing, though it was obvious he didn't want to. However, he owed me a favor, and I was glad to use it up for David's sake. "He's got a long life ahead of him, Larien," I said. "Annie will live for—what?—another eighty years if she's lucky. In a hundred years' time, when he's gotten over his grief, you can suggest that David might want to remarry for dynastic reasons. Neither Corwen nor I will be around to object." I laughed. "Though I don't guarantee our great-grandchildren won't take an interest."

With Larien's written permission safely in Corwen's pocket, Corwen, David, and I rode to the Okewood.

Charlotte, Henry, and Livvy were packing up some of their possessions and giving away others to friends.

"We're going home." Livvy bounced up to us as soon as we arrived in the grove. "Not to our old home, but to Grandfather's new parish. Isn't that fine?"

"Very fine," I assured her, and turned to Charlotte. "Have you seen Annie?"

"Not since the day before yesterday. She went back to Plymouth. Said she had a job to go to."

"Did someone take her?" David asked.

"Not that I know of. Said she could easily walk it in a day."

David turned to me. "I've got to go after her."

"She should be in Plymouth by now," I said. "Probably safe at the Ratcatchers with Dan."

David stilled for a moment and took a deep, steadying breath. "Yes, of course. She's perfectly capable of looking after herself. I'll go and pay court to her there." He paused, suddenly looking unsure. "Do you think she'll forgive me?"

"Calantha was hardly your fault."

"I could have handled it better."

"You've got another chance."

"Yes." He smiled. "Yes, I have."

47

Decommissioning

WITH LOOSE ENDS to tie up and still no idea about where Walsingham might be, or whether he had his notebook back, we returned to London.

The deep frost had thawed. The weather was balmy and warm. London's houses must have been empty and all the people abroad in the streets to judge by the crush across London Bridge. With the warmth, the stink of the city had returned. The locals were inured to it, though Corwen's sensitive nose may not have been so happy.

We spotted several goblins walking about freely without their glamour, and though they drew comments, there were no major upsets evident. Then we saw, nailed to a board, a notice that told the people about the new law in simple terms and announced that the Mysterium, from the twenty-first day of June, was no more and that the King's Commission for the Integration of Magical Personages would be setting up offices all over the country.

"It's going to take more than that," Corwen said. "People are going to be afraid of their new neighbors."

"Even though they've been living next to them for decades?"

He nodded. "It's all about perceptions. Getting people to accept magic and magical beings is going to be a long process, but we've started it now. The rest is up to the magicals themselves . . . and their neighbors."

We visited George and Lily, first to tell them we were back and then to find out the practical implications of the new laws.

Two well-dressed gentlemen were leaving as we arrived at the house in Margaret Street and surrendered our horses to the footman.

"Well, that's an about turn!" George said as we entered the house. "I seem to have a new position."

He still looked a little bemused, but Lily was grinning. "It helps to be the grandson of the King's Commissioner," she said. "George is to oversee the disbanding of the Mysterium and the integration of magic across the whole West Riding of Yorkshire, which means he gets to make his office in Wakefield, not twelve miles from home."

"How very convenient," Corwen said. "Congratulations, George."

"Thank you . . . I think. I'm still not quite sure what the job entails, but I shall very much enjoy putting the officers from the Mysterium in Sheffield out of work. Once that's done, I'm not quite sure how to go about the rest. I daresay there may be some feeling of fear that will need to be overcome, but I will have the power to call out the redcoats in support of the magicals if there is any trouble. That makes a change. Everyone, magical or not, will have recourse to the law. I shall appoint rowankind and goblins to my staff, and maybe a witch or two."

"I hope the rowankind who fled to Iaru will return," Lily said. "As soon as we get home, I'm going to talk to the rowankind about using their water magic to keep the mill wheel turning. It would mean we'd have no need to consider a pumping engine, so no dirty smoke and steam. Of course, we'd pay them for their work now that it's legal."

"Pumping water out of mine workings could save a lot of lives," Corwen said. "I wonder if the rowankind might be persuaded to use their talents to power all manner of manufactories. It might even ease the problem of the blight bleeding through into Iaru from industrial areas."

Lily grinned. "Rowankind power would be so much safer than steam power. There are so many industries it could be used for. And, of course, the rowankind would be in high demand, so they'd be well-treated and well paid." Her eyes widened. "And witch-power, too. How many witches can make light like you can, Ross?"

I shrugged, not knowing. "It's one of the easier magics, so probably a lot."

"Then our streets could be lit at night as if it were day. Just think, what a boon. Assembly halls and private houses could run on witchlight."

I laughed. "Steady on, Lily. You'll have the whole country running on magic."

"Why not?" she said. "It may not answer every need, but surely inventors and engineers will use what's available. I read about Mr. Trevithick's road locomotive powered by steam. What if it were to be powered by magic?"

I suppose I shouldn't have been surprised. Suddenly, we were living in a new age. The government had been shocked into a reversal of two hundred years of law and persecution, and anything was possible.

"There's more," George said. "Mr. Addington has stepped down, and Mr. Pitt is, even now, seeing the king. We confidently expect that before nightfall he'll be the first minister again."

"That is good news," Corwen said.

"You know, Mr. Pitt told my grandfather there was a seat in Parliament for someone such as yourself."

Corwen raised one eyebrow. "I don't know much about politics."

"But you have a great deal of common sense and a wealth of knowledge about the magical world, not to mention a direct connection with the Fae, should it be required. Mr. Pitt believes we shall soon be at war with France again. Boney is using the peace to rebuild his armies—and we are doing the same."

I stored that nugget of information away for Hookey. War with France meant a return to privateering for the *Heart*. Much as I didn't wish for war in general terms, if it was inevitable, Hookey might as well make the most of it.

"I'll think about it," Corwen said. "Do you suppose there would be room for a new constituency of the Okewood?"

He laughed at the notion, but I suddenly saw a whole new life for us. Corwen could either be the country squire in Yorkshire, or he could make a real difference to the magicals here in London. Dammit, if they'd let women into Parliament, I'd do it myself, but that was a struggle for another time.

"Before we settle the future, there's one more matter we need to take care of," I said. "Walsingham is still free. We don't know whether he's been reunited with his notebook, but it seems likely. As first minister, Mr. Pitt would have known about Walsingham. Maybe he can give us a lead as to where he is."

"I'll see if Grandfather can arrange an appointment."

"Thank you."

We collected our horses and the hired hack we'd left behind during the freeze and rode to Wapping where we settled Timpani and Dancer into the stables at the Red Lion and left strict instructions for their care with the young ostler, who seemed to have recovered from nearly freezing to death.

We called in at the Town of Ramsgate and reserved our old room for the next few days, then walked down the passage to Wapping Old Stairs and the river.

The *Heart of Oak* was at her mooring across from the steps. Hookey and Mr. Rafiq, with a couple of seamen at the oars, were closely inspecting the ship's planking on the waterline. I hoped the ice hadn't damaged her. I put my fingers to my mouth and gave a most unladylike whistle. Hookey turned, saw me, and waved.

"How has the *Heart* fared?" I asked as Corwen and I stepped off the stair into the ship's boat.

"I feared she might be damaged," Hookey said, "but she's sound. I've been all over her, inside and out."

"And Windward?"

"Took him a while to come round, but he's chirpy now. I put him on light duties, which means he's sitting on deck soaking up the sunshine."

"I'm very pleased to hear it."

"I've seen the notices," Hookey said. "It seems you got what you wanted."

"What the Fae wanted, Hookey."

"Aye, I know what you did. Took what the Fae wanted and turned it to the benefit of all magicals. Seems like you should be in Parliament."

"Only if they'd let me in wearing breeches, and I think they might suspect something was amiss when my belly bulged out of them." I grinned. "Though Corwen's had an offer."

"Aye, well, maybe it's about time there was someone in Parliament with honest intentions."

Corwen said nothing. I could tell he was still thinking about it.

<hr/>

The following morning we got a note from George, delivered by a footman to the Town of Ramsgate. Mr. Pitt would spare us fifteen minutes at three o'clock that same afternoon at number ten Downing Street where, it seemed, he was in the process of moving in, having removed from there when he gave up the first ministry to Mr. Addington.

I was surprised to find that what looked like a normal London house from the outside opened to reveal a vast number of rooms on the inside, running sideways into numbers eleven and twelve, but also backward into a mansion with a terrace which had a view of the park.

We arrived to find the place in chaos. Mr. Addington's servants were moving boxes out as Mr. Pitt's servants were moving boxes in. The footman led us through several rooms and along a corridor to a small, comfortable library where Mr. Pitt had made an oasis of calm in the midst of chaos.

"Come in, my friends, come in," he called, waving us into the room when the footman announced us. "My apologies for all the upset. This is a vast, awkward house, but I confess I have made it my home for so long that I found leaving a wrench and returning again a pleasure, even in this state of transition."

He waved us to seats, addressing himself to Corwen. I understood that Mr. Pitt, though charming, was more comfortable in the company of men. "What can I do for you?" he asked. "Do you have more messages from our Fae friends?"

"No, nothing," Corwen said. "I fancy that's the last you'll see of them for a while unless anything goes awry with the plans to remove the Mysterium."

"Good. Good." He left a gap for us to fill.

I filled it. "As first minister, you must have been conversant with the man known as Walsingham who reported directly to the Crown," I said.

"Aware of the office of Walsingham, but not entirely aware of the man himself. He operated in secret, even from me most of the time. He brought us his results. He was, of course, charged with seeking out magic which might prove a danger to the Crown."

"He was supposed to prevent the freeing of the rowankind."

"He was. He . . . We . . . feared it would destabilize the economy and lead to riots if the rowankind turned against their former masters."

"Which didn't happen."

"It did not."

I didn't elaborate. "Did you know that Walsingham's methods included the use of very nasty blood magic, and he was not above torturing victims for information and killing them when he'd done with them?"

Mr. Pitt drew in a breath. "With hindsight, we should have looked deeper. We didn't ask about his methods, merely authorized his requests for resources."

"Such as the use of the *Guillaume Tell*."

"I confess I authorized that, but it was for a new Walsingham after the old one failed to return from a mission. I agreed with his idea to make the new Walsingham responsible for the Mysterium, thinking it would make him more accountable. It didn't work, unfortunately. We no sooner had the new Walsingham in place than the old one turned up, maimed and full of righteous anger. And then the new Walsingham was killed in a hideous manner."

"By a wolf he'd tortured for weeks," Corwen said.

"Not you, then."

"No, not me and not my sister," Corwen said.

"I had wondered."

"That wolf is far from London, in the country, healing in mind and spirit and looked after by a good friend. He's no danger to anyone now."

Mr. Pitt nodded.

"It's the old Walsingham we need to find," I said, trying to keep on track. We only had fifteen minutes of Mr. Pitt's time.

"As do we. He made contact briefly when he was released from a French prison ship. I can't think how he ended up in French hands."

I knew, but I wasn't saying.

Mr. Pitt shrugged. "We've stopped his funds, and we will tell him the office of Walsingham is no more. We no longer need someone in that role. We'll offer him a pension, of course."

"Walsingham bears a deep grudge against me and mine. He's a dangerous man. I will feel a lot better when he's out of a job. Can I take it, now the new act is law, that anyone using magic to commit illegal acts can be stopped by the magical community?"

Mr. Pitt hesitated, but finally he nodded. "He no longer has the protection of his job."

"Good."

To be fair, I had murder in my heart, but I'd be willing to leave Walsingham alone if he was willing to leave me and mine alone. Somehow, though, if he'd gone to so much trouble to get his notebook back, I doubted he was finished with us. And now I had babies to protect, so I wouldn't feel safe until we'd resolved this—sooner rather than later.

"Mr. Pitt," Corwen said. "Do you have a list of the resources you've granted Walsingham in the past? Safe houses where he might stay? A place for his apprentices? Buildings where he might be isolated enough to perform his magic?"

"Walsingham's finances always came out of a War Office fund used for private affairs."

Ha! A spy fund, I fancied.

"Is there no record?" Corwen asked.

"There's always a record, but it may be buried deep. Give me a few days and I'll send whatever I can find to George Pomeroy."

We thanked the first minister, left him to his busy schedule, and returned to Wapping, still not sure where to start.

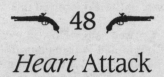 48

Heart Attack

THE FIRST I knew of the attack was a roaring sound outside our window in the middle of the night. I sprang from our bed in a panic, not knowing what was wrong, but knowing something was. I yanked back the curtain and saw a sheet of flame where the *Heart* used to be.

"Corwen!"

I needn't have shouted; he was already out of bed and at my side.

He uttered some very succinct curses while I stood frozen with fear. I had nothing in my arsenal of spells that could combat this. A small ship moored downwind from the *Heart* had caught fire in three places from the sparks, and I could see her crew battling the blazes with buckets, while four of them struggled to get a pump set up.

I could see nothing of the *Heart* except fire.

Corwen was dressed now and turning the handle of the bedroom door.

"Wait for me," I called.

"No. Wait here, unless the building catches fire. Keep our children safe. There's nothing you can do."

"Then what are you doing?"

"Going to pull any survivors out of the river if I can."

A crowd had gathered on the steps. The tide was low, and there was a small beach of river mud and shingle at their base, illuminated now by flames.

I dragged on my clothes, not wanting to tear my eyes away any more than I had to. If the *Heart* was burning—if my crew, my friends, were dying—then the very least I could do was bear witness.

I heard a sob. It was mine.

Hookey was more of a father to me than my own had ever been.

Mr. Rafiq had escaped a life of slavery to end up roasting to death on the Thames.

Windward, who'd so narrowly escaped death from cold, shouldn't now die in an inferno.

The Greek, who said so little, but was always there when needed.

Lazy Billy, cook, doctor, picklock, friend.

I went through the whole crew by name, even the ones who were new since my time as captain. They were still my crew.

The other ships and boats on the crowded river were moving away as far as they could, tugged out of the danger zone by their own crews.

The twins were turning somersaults in my belly, reminding me why I was up here while Corwen was out there.

I touched the window glass; it was hot. Then, just as I was wondering whether this was the safest place to be, a splatter of water hit the glass and two of the panes cracked with a sharp ping. There was a pump down on the muddy beach operated by two men and aimed by a third. They were playing water over the back of the building to prevent the clapboard siding from catching a spark.

I couldn't stay here any longer. I primed my pistol and ran down the steps to the bar.

A magical attack of this magnitude must have the attacker somewhere close. Walsingham. It had to be Walsingham. If he was close, I could kill him. I didn't care that he was blind and maimed. I would shoot him at point blank range if I could. I'd be happy to turn his head to ruined meat.

The bar was full of gawkers, not stupid enough to stand right next to the back window, but standing halfway down the room, eerily silent, their speech sapped by the magnitude of the disaster unfolding before their eyes. A side door opened into the narrow passage that led from Wapping High Street to the river.

Walsingham would not be on the steps. Corwen would have seen him. A blind man with one arm wouldn't be difficult to spot. I turned the other way. On the High Street, with a row of buildings between me and the river, I could see the sky in the east was lightening to that deep, ethereal blue which only shows itself at dawn, never at dusk. It must be close to four in the morning. It still didn't give me enough light to see by. There were people moving about already, going to early morning jobs, or returning home from carousing. Any one of them could be Walsingham. He wouldn't be on his own, though. He'd need someone to be his eyes. I wondered whether he still had Philip with him, masquerading as the unfortunate Diccon, whose spirit still resided in the brandy flask I had tucked away in my pocket.

A great cry went up from the riverside as the fire glow subsided. Did that mean the *Heart* was under water and the flames extinguished? I turned back to look. A hackney coach rolled past the end of the alleyway, surprising me by its speed. I looked up to see a face peering out of the window. I didn't recognize it at first because I'd only ever seen it as an insubstantial ghost. Diccon!

Or, rather, Philip.

I ran back to Wapping High Street, but the coachman had sprung his horses and they were already disappearing into the darkness heading west.

I turned back to the river to see if any survivors had

swum ashore. *Please let some of them have survived. Please.* I didn't know whether I was praying or not.

On the river, in the deep blue of early dawn stood the *Heart of Oak*, untouched by fire.

I felt dizzy and leaned against the side wall of the alley, which was where Corwen found me, laughing and crying in equal measures.

"Thank you, Aunt Rosie."

It was Aunt Rosie who saved the *Heart*, or rather her notebook from which I learned her protection spell.

❦

I was shaking so much I could barely hold the glass of brandy Corwen pressed into my hands.

"Drink," he said, sliding into the chair on the other side of the table.

The Town of Ramsgate had opened early and was doing great trade over the bar with most of the conversation tending toward the did-you-see variety, with the occasional what-caused-that and only one voice saying, "They shouldn't have disbanded the Mysterium, that's what!"

I sipped the brandy, feeling it score a sharp line down my gullet. This wasn't Hookey's good stuff. I coughed.

"Drink," Corwen said again.

I wiped my eyes on the back of my hand and did as I was told. The twins had settled down in my belly.

A commotion in the alley spilled into the bar through the side door. Mr. Rafiq, impeccably dressed, pushed a wave of curious folk in front of him.

"Yes, we are all fine. No we don't know what it was. Excuse me, a little privacy, gentleman and ladies."

They let him leave them, and Mr. Rafiq came to sit at our table, placing his tricorn hat on the side and accepting a tankard of ale from a serving girl.

"Captain Garrity sends his regards. He's still checking over the ship for damage but has so far found none. He wanted you to know that apart from Jeb Woodhead passing out in a dead faint and hitting his head on the deck, no one has sustained any kind of injury. It wasn't even particularly warm. It was as if there was an invisible dome over us. The flames couldn't penetrate."

I reached out and took his hand. "Please tell Hookey I'm so sorry."

"Do you have anything to be sorry for, Captain?"

"For not killing that bastard Walsingham when I had the chance, but I'll remedy that, Mr. Rafiq. I promise."

"It's a promise from both of us," Corwen said.

"I'll come aboard later this morning and renew the protection spell," I said. "Then I think the *Heart* would be safer at sea."

"I'm sure Captain Garrity will want to stay and help if you are hunting Walsingham," Mr. Rafiq said. "But I'll give him your message."

I renewed the protection spell on the *Heart* and placed one on the Town of Ramsgate. For good measure, I put one on the stable at the Red Lion when we went to collect Dancer and Timpani, and when we arrived at George and Lily's house, I put one on that as well.

Mr. Pitt, as good as his word, had sent a list of potential places which Walsingham had used in the past. It wasn't a long list, only eight addresses, but they were all over London. This was a job for the goblins.

49

Narrowing Options

"**I** CAN TELL you where he isn't," Mr. Twomax said when we met him for the second time in two days, this time at a busy coaching inn on Fleet Street, where so many people passed through that no one would notice three people drinking coffee together.

Mr. Twomax was glamoured to further reduce the risk of being noticed. "We've eliminated all but two of the addresses."

"What about the two you haven't eliminated?" Corwen asked.

"Inconclusive, both of them. One is an old warehouse in Southwark, on Bankside. It's been designated for demolition for a new bridge across the Thames, but there's a cluster of ancient buildings, and it's so deeply embedded in them that it's almost impossible to be sure we've covered every access and egress point."

"And the other?" I asked.

"Another riverside warehouse, this time on the Isle of Dogs."

"We'll have to try both," Corwen said.

It made no sense to confront Walsingham unarmed. He would certainly have resources if he had his notebook and the help of my brother, Philip, returned from the dead.

"How are we going to do this?" I asked Corwen. "A magical duel doesn't seem like a good idea."

"I suppose sneaking in, killing him, and sneaking out again would be too easy."

I shuddered. I never liked the idea of murder for its own sake, even if Walsingham had a lot more murders on his conscience—presuming he had a conscience. I should think of this more as an execution. When men had been hanged for the simple crime of theft, someone like Walsingham should have been justly done away with years ago, but it seemed that the bigger the crime, the more difficult it was to punish. The law couldn't touch Walsingham. I doubted a prison could hold him. The new act said magical crimes could be policed by fellow magicals. We were about to put that to the test.

"I wonder if . . . " Last year I hadn't hesitated to call on a recently deceased spirit to spy for us, but I was becoming more aware of how unfair it was on those who had departed. However, I had another alternative. I patted my pocket. "Diccon," I said.

"Can you send him to spy for us?" Corwen asked.

"He's a lost soul. He wants his body back." I looked around at the busy inn room to make sure no one was listening. "He can't stay in limbo forever."

"You mean—"

I nodded. "If we can't reunite him with his body . . . " I looked up. "He's got to move on."

"We'll try the first warehouse tonight," Corwen said.

"If it's not the right one, we should go to the second immediately," I said. "He might have some warning system set up, and we don't want to give him time to prepare."

"It's a pity we can't go to both at the same time," Twomax said.

"Split our resources?" I asked.

Corwen looked thoughtful. "With the goblins and Hookey's sailors, we've got a goodly company of scrappers."

"But only one witch and only one sundered spirit," I said.

"Sadly, yes. Let's do it tonight," Corwen said. "Southwark first and then the Isle of Dogs."

Twomax nodded. It was as good a plan as any.

How many did we need to tackle Walsingham? Twomax had already offered a company of his fiercest goblins, and Hookey insisted on bringing half the crew of the *Heart*, volunteers all.

"I won't see you go after that bastard on your own," Hookey said, when we met him in the Town of Ramsgate's public bar. "I'll have the crew ready whenever you need us. In the meantime, I'll send two men to each establishment to watch for activity."

"Tell them not to get too close," I said. "Walsingham's dangerous. They should watch from a safe distance."

"If he's not in Southwark, we'll need to get to the Isle of Dogs as quickly as we can," Corwen said.

"By river, then," Hookey said. "On an outgoing tide. How many goblins?"

"Sixteen including Twomax."

"We'll need four boats, and four good crews to row them if we're to shoot London Bridge in the dark."

"Oh, wonderful." Corwen pulled a face.

We'd done it once before when Walsingham's hellhounds had been chasing us, and we'd almost capsized in the maelstrom.

"Leave it to me," Hookey said. "I'll get enough boats and proper watermen to man 'em. The tide will be on the turn around eleven, so we need to be west of London Bridge by then."

We left the arrangements to Hookey.

He sent two spies to each location in the afternoon. Goblins and sailors met at London Bridge soon after ten. They eyed each other for a few minutes, then decided that since their objective was the same, they could work together. Hookey and Twomax shook hands in a silent pact.

Hookey sent the watermen and their boats down to Horseshoe Stairs to wait for us and we made our way on foot to Southwark.

The long summer dusk still offered enough residual light that we could see where to put our feet. Some of the houses along the road already had lanterns at their doors. We found our way to the jumble of buildings Twomax had described. He was right about the Southwark warehouse. It was old and rickety. Newer buildings had been built onto it and around it. Everything was in shadow. Even the shadows had shadows. I shivered. I would very much like the comfort of a witchlight or a lantern, but until we knew whether Walsingham was inside, I couldn't risk either.

Corwen walked next to me, brushing his knuckles against mine. The touch steadied me.

"Where are your men, Hookey?" I whispered.

"Should be here."

"Who did you send?"

"Nick Padder and Crayfish Jake."

It wasn't like either of them to be slack in their duties, but they could easily be around the other side of the warehouse in the maze of alleyways.

"Two of our crewmen should be here," I whispered to Twomax. "Ask your men to keep a watch for them, please."

Twomax nodded.

One of the goblins went ahead, perhaps the one who'd scouted this location earlier. He stopped, so we all stopped. Then he pointed left and right, and the goblins silently peeled away from our company to surround the building and cover any other potential entrances and exits.

In front of us was a tall doorway with heavy double doors. I heard a few clicks as people pulled the dogheads of their pistols back. It was time for Diccon to earn his keep. I took the flask out of my jacket pocket. Diccon emerged from the flask, looking serious. He had a slight luminescence about him, though it didn't cast a glow. I'd warned him earlier about what I might ask him to do. If he wanted his body back, he needed to scout ahead for us. I pointed him to the warehouse and he oozed through the locked door. It didn't take long for him to reappear.

"Empty," he said. "Not a living soul . . . but he's been in there. There's . . . evidence." I thought if a spirit could retch, that might be what he would do next. I held up the flask, and he bolted into it as if it was a sanctuary.

"Billy."

I motioned Lazy Billy forward. He picked the lock in less time than it would have taken me to unroll my lock-picks. Corwen pushed open one of the large double doors and Billy the other.

The stench made me gag. Something or someone had died in here.

I made a witchlight and sent it up into the rafters. That was a mistake. I saw immediately what was causing the stench. Inscribed in the middle of the floor, in a channel two inches deep, was a large circle inset with a long, narrow triangle. Whether it was the right way up or upside down depended on where you stood, Hanging from ceiling joists by their feet were two naked and very dead bodies.

Recognition came slowly because I didn't want to believe it, and because their faces had been carved into bloody masks.

Nick Padder.

Crayfish Jake.

"That ain't right," Windward said.

Someone else cursed, and the angry muttering rose to a crescendo.

Nick had been on my crew since he was ten. He'd been a pageboy at my wedding to Will, and a guest at my wedding to Corwen. He was not even twenty, and he was dead.

"We'll get the bastards what did this, Cap'n, won't we?" Windward asked.

"We will," I said. Or die trying.

Crayfish Jake had joined the crew after Will died. He'd been an old comrade of Hookey's and Hookey had vouched for him. His time on the *Heart* had led to this.

They'd obviously been alive when they'd been hung there because they were gagged and secured, not only by their feet but by a rope around their wrists and necks tied to a spike hammered into the floor. They wouldn't have been able to swing or spin or struggle in any way while they bled to death. They'd died slowly by the state of their bodies. Rather than a single slice across the throat, which might, in certain circumstances, have been a mercy, they'd bled out from a series of shallow cuts to head, arms, torso, belly, and genitals.

Their blood had been channeled into the circle, and from the circle into the triangle. In the center of the triangle was ash from a fire, and directly above the fire, the pantiles from the roof had been removed, or maybe blown to pieces.

"Bad men," the Greek said, and then he said something else in Greek, which from the inflection was a string of curses.

"Cut them down, Hookey, please." I heard my voice rise. I wanted to scream around the hard knot in my throat, but instead I turned to Corwen and buried my face in his shoulder. He held me without trying to say anything to make it better. There was nothing he could say. Walsingham was a bastard. This was a deliberate act of provocation because the working they bled into was old.

How did I know that?

I took a deep breath and turned back to the scene, putting my knowledge and my instincts to good use.

"This is the fire-working that they used to try and burn the *Heart*," I said. "You can see where the fire shot up through the roof." Damn, my voice was shaking. I took another deep breath. "But that was before Jake and Nick came here."

I didn't watch the team of goblins and sailors taking down the bodies together. We didn't have anything to cover them with, but the goblins laid them gently by the far wall. Mr. Twomax took a handkerchief and laid it gently over Nick Padder's face. Hookey surprised me by having a handkerchief of his own, and this he used to cover Crayfish Jake's face. I heard him say something softly and thought he might have made a promise to an old friend.

I took a deep breath and stepped out of the protection of Corwen's embrace. I needed to take charge. I swallowed hard and looked at the evidence for the working. "Walsingham must have been here." I pointed to the triangle. "Philip was stationed closer to the *Heart* to direct the flames."

Hookey delivered a stream of invective which might have made me blush under other circumstances, but this time I agreed with him wholeheartedly.

"We should send the bodies back to the *Heart*," he said. "Give them a proper burial."

"Not now. We'll come back later. I think this was meant either to delay us or discourage us. We mustn't let it."

"Over here." One of the goblins called from the back of the warehouse. As we got closer, he lifted some old sacking. "I thought I might find something to cover your crewmen, but the sacking had already been put to use."

A body had been dumped carelessly. By the state of her, I guessed she was the source of the blood for the magical fire-working. I wondered who she was. We might never find out. There were always people on the street for someone like Walsingham to prey on. If we survived this night, we would give her a decent burial along with Nick and Jake.

We backed away, and Billy secured the doors again.

"To the Isle of Dogs, then," Corwen said. "Do you think Walsingham left any kind of warning spell. Might he know we found this place?"

"I think it highly likely. He'll know we've been here, but he won't know where we're going next."

"He'll be watching out for us, though."

"Oh, yes. Killing Nick and Jake was his way of sending an invitation. He wants to finish it. He wants to finish us."

The boats were waiting for us at Horseshoe Alley Stairs, four of them big enough to take ten passengers each and crewed by experienced Thames watermen. We piled in, Corwen and I behind Hookey and Lazy Billy with Windward and the Greek behind us. I held onto the planking of my seat as we sped downriver toward the gaps between the piers of London Bridge. The fat starlings which protected the bridge also narrowed the gap to such a degree that water gushed through, creating a maelstrom. Many lives had been lost here, so cautious passengers often disembarked before the bridge and rejoined their boat below it. There was one wider arch, however, where the water was swift but not as dangerous. Last time we'd shot the bridge, we'd deliberately chosen one of the narrow arches, trying to drown our hellhound pursuers. This time, we took the wide arch, splashing through without incident, though I felt as if my heart was in my mouth as we swooshed through safely to the other side.

Corwen pried my fingers from the edge of the seat and gave them a squeeze. I squeezed back.

He put his head close to mine. "I love you."

It took my breath away. I knew that he did. It was in everything we did and said together. I loved him, too. Why say it now unless he knew that, if we found Walsingham, there was a likelihood that one or both of us would not survive? The twins turned somersaults in my belly. I was responsible for more lives than my own. I told myself that the fear was natural and no different from the fear I squashed down each time I led a boarding party from the *Heart*, but I knew that this time I wasn't simply afraid for myself.

Yet if I didn't try and end this conflict with Walsingham, our children would always be in danger. And much as he would have liked to do this without me, Corwen knew he couldn't. It would take magic to fight magic.

If only the Fae . . .

But they wouldn't get involved in this. We were on our own.

Well, not quite on our own. We had the *Heart*'s crew out for revenge, and a squad of goblins with a grudge. Surely that would be enough.

❖——————❖

The river carried us swiftly through London in the darkness. Our boats drew in at Mill Wall Stairs, below the massive basins and buildings for the new West India Docks and the City Canal.

I heard the chink of coins changing hands, then Hookey said, "Wait two hours. If there's been no word, you can leave."

"Right you are, guv," the lead waterman said.

Two hours. We'd be back sooner than that if Walsingham wasn't here. If he was here . . . I let my thoughts trail off. It would all be over in two hours, one way or another.

The blustery wind hit us as we climbed to land. It buffeted my ears and took my breath away. Someone lost a tricorn hat which swirled above us and vanished into the night. We jogged down the Deptford Road, helped along by the half-moon rising in the sky, but bedeviled by the crosswind. To our right, between the road and the river, there were ship breakers' yards, rope makers, and timber merchants, but here there was a deal of space between them, unlike the buildings of Bankside which were almost on top of one another. Land here must be as cheap as it was dismal. You could tell it had a natural inclination toward swamp, and if the river-wall was ever breached, the Isle of Dogs would be the Isle of Frogs, or even the Isle of Fish.

On the left of the road it was all open countryside, low-lying and intersected by drainage ditches. Something was growing; barley, I thought, by the way the wind set it rippling in the moonlight.

An iron foundry was working through the night. Through its open doors we could see the lava-flow glow of molten metal poured from a crucible, and an oily, burned smell drifted across on the wind. Farther down the road, we passed a warehouse, dark save for a couple of lanterns, probably carried by night watchmen.

Whereas Blackwall, along the river, was known for shipbuilding, here on the isle of Dogs, ships came to die and to be broken up. We passed a dry dock with the remains of a hulk in it. Farther along, a lonely windmill turned, its sails buffeted by the wind.

We pulled up sharply as one of Twomax's goblins pointed out a large building of weathered wood, bleached gray in the moonlight. The outline was irregular as if one corner had sunk into the soft clay and peat. It looked drunk.

"Is that it?" I whispered.

The goblin nodded and then scurried to his friends.

Hookey had sent two men here as well, Abe Bennett and Saul Bunyan, but there was no sign of them. *Please, God, don't let them be bleeding to death in the warehouse.*

As I had that thought, two figures emerged from the ditch on the far side of the road. I heaved a sigh of relief.

"Cap'n." Abe spoke for both of them. "Two coves, one of 'em being led by the other, went into the warehouse about three hours ago. There's been neither sight nor sound since."

Time for Diccon to earn his brandy fumes. I took the flask from my jacket pocket and uncorked it. Diccon oozed out.

"Over there," I told him. "We need to know whether Walsingham's in that building."

"I can feel it." He gave a low moan.

"What?"

"Me. My body. It's in there." He appeared to take a deep breath, though I doubted whether he had actual functioning lungs. He swayed toward the warehouse as if drawn by deep desire.

"I think the answer is yes," Corwen said. "If Philip's in there, Walsingham will be as well. No sense in putting the little chap in any more danger than he is already, and no sense in risking Walsingham learning we're here."

"He may know already."

"Possibly, but if there's any chance we have surprise on our side, we should use it."

I held the flask up. "In you go, Diccon. Not long, now."

"But I can feel it. So close. So close." He swirled round, broke away from us, and sped over the ground like an arrow released from a bow.

"Diccon," I hissed his name, and then I tried summoning his spirit, but he was deaf to me, fixated on what he'd lost.

"He's going to get himself sundered permanently," I said. "No time to waste. Come on. Keep your heads down until you're sure there's no magic flying."

Corwen stripped off his clothes in next to no time and bundled them into the magic bag.

We split into two parties. Twomax, some of his goblins, and half our crewmen went looking for a back way into the building. Corwen and I with Hookey, Windward, and the Greek, plus seven determined-looking goblins raced in a direct charge toward the front door. Corwen, still human, set up an illusion to run in front of us. It was the most complex I'd ever seen him produce, a dozen pirates, armed to the teeth; the leaders looked remarkably like Nick Padder and Crayfish Jake.

I primed my pistols, my navy piece and a smaller one, half of the pair that had been made for me by Mr. Bunney of London. I pulled back the dogheads, then I gathered my weather powers about me and harnessed the buffeting wind. With an explosive crack I blew the warehouse's double doors inward, ripping one off its hinges.

Corwen's illusion saved us. Walsingham's first blow was aimed at the nonexistent pirates and not at us. Two of the foremost goblins leaped for the rafters. Corwen rolled to the right and changed into a wolf. I slid to the left, Hookey close behind me. A huge crash announced the doors resealing themselves with Windward, the Greek, and most of the goblins still on the outside.

Damn and double damn.

50

Brother Philip

I ROSE TO my knees and sent five witchlights at once into the rafters, though not close to where the two goblins crouched on a high beam. The warehouse wasn't entirely empty. Along the near wall was a bank of wooden crates, and along the far wall were barrels stacked two high and two deep. Walsingham sat on a wooden crate in the middle of the floor. Philip, wearing Diccon's body, stood next to him, one hand on his shoulder. I followed up with a gale-force gust of wind across the floor that pushed the packing crate back a few feet. It detached Philip from Walsingham and bowled him over completely.

Hookey leaped to his feet and fired both his pistols before ducking down again. I found it hard to believe he'd missed, but no one fell.

Corwen hurtled forward and leaped at Walsingham but hit an invisible barrier and was flung off to one side, landing in a heap by the barrels.

"Stay down." Walsingham flung a crumpled paper in his general direction and the spell exploded, tumbling barrels around and throwing Corwen against the wall. I heard the sickening crunch of bones.

Everything pulled at my senses. I needed to go to Corwen, now! But that would be fatal.

While Walsingham was distracted, I fired my Navy pistol and ducked back behind the crates. I was a good shot. I knew I hadn't missed. Dammit, Hookey hadn't missed either, but Walsingham sat there, uninjured. I couldn't work out what had happened until he waved his good right hand in front of his head as if searching for something.

"Ah, there it is." He picked my bullet out of the air where it had stuck as if frozen in time. "You might have guessed I would have protection."

"You didn't guess the *Heart* was protected."

I moved, keeping a bank of packing cases between me and Walsingham. If he aimed something toward the sound of my voice, I was no longer where he expected me to be.

"Consider that my calling card. An invitation. And you accepted. How kind. We have business to settle."

Blind, he needed no light, but I heard Philip tell Walsingham the building was illuminated as bright as day.

"It doesn't signify," Walsingham waved his hand dismissively. "I wondered how long it would take you to find us, Ross Tremayne," he still used my previous name. "Have you come to see your brother? Say hello to your big sister, Philip."

Diccon's body stood and bowed to me, somewhat unsteadily.

"Is that . . . ?" Hookey asked.

"Philip," I said. "In Diccon's body."

Somewhere above me, I heard Diccon howl.

"Sister, you don't know how much I've been looking forward to seeing you again," Philip said.

The last time I saw him was when I shot and killed him, so I was pretty sure I did know. Philip's was the last spirit I'd ever wanted to summon, so to see him made flesh again was my worst nightmare. I didn't know whether it was fear or guilt. I'd shot him to save Corwen and David—before David had come into his Fae powers—but could I have found another way? Had I pulled the trigger because I'd never liked Philip? He'd been a brat as a child, and no better as a man. But he was my brother, and no matter how much I disliked him, he was family. I would have died for him, but when it came down to it, I discovered I would kill for Corwen and David.

I didn't say anything to give away my new position. If he'd actually looked like Philip, I might have cracked completely, but Diccon's face was a reminder that Philip was prepared to kill an innocent and steal his body.

Philip pulled a pistol from his belt and drew the doghead back ready to fire.

Corwen, lying still as death, was not out of the game. He produced an illusion of me, and had it step out from behind a crate some ten feet away from where I was hidden. Philip took a shot. Did he have another loaded pistol, or would he have to stop to reload? I had my third pistol in my hand, primed and ready.

"Philip, what's happening?" Walsingham snapped out.

"I shot an illusion."

"Come here, boy."

Philip had never liked being addressed as "boy" even when he was one. I took scant pleasure in the fact that Walsingham would have as much trouble with him as everyone else had. Philip never did anything that wasn't ultimately for the good of Philip.

A montage of memories flashed past almost faster than I could catch them. Only once had we bonded as siblings, and that was when mother had gone traveling—to give birth to David, though we didn't know that at the time—and left us in the care of an over-strict governess against whom we had immediately united. Why remember that, now? I had felt affection for him and I think, he for me—briefly.

He was my baby brother, yet I had killed him.

Corwen yipped as if he knew what I was thinking. He knew me well enough by now. He squirmed to hide himself behind the barrels and then changed into a man. Then immediately back to wolf again. He'd be healing broken bones with each change.

In the shadows overhead, the two goblins inched along the rafters. I didn't know if they had a plan, but it seemed as though Philip had forgotten them, and Walsingham had never seen them. I looked away so as not to draw attention.

There was no way I could win a magical duel against Walsingham without being sneaky. I needed a little time to prepare. I jerked my head toward Walsingham.

Corwen rolled over and stood up, snarling, enough to take attention from me, though wisely he didn't spring. He dropped down behind the crates again to change.

I stepped out from behind my crates and fired my second pistol, this time at Philip, aiming for his legs. I didn't want to kill Diccon's body, just get him out of it. I heard Philip yell and saw him crumple to the ground clutching his thigh. Yes!

At the same time I sent a whirlwind around both Walsingham and Philip, sucking the breathable air away from them. They should be unconscious in little more than a minute.

Damn! Walsingham seemed untouched by the wind. Philip, visibly gasping, crawled toward Walsingham, leaving a smear of blood on the floor. As he got his head close to the crate, he sucked in deep breaths.

Ah, now I understood. Walsingham's protection spell was centered on the crate he was sitting on. Like I had protected the *Heart*, Walsingham had bespelled the crate with a bubble of protection.

Damn and double damn!

"My leg. She shot me in the blasted leg." Philip's voice shook.

"Stupid boy. I told you to stay close." Walsingham took a crumpled paper from his pocket and held it out for Philip to take. Philip snatched it and pressed it against the wound on his thigh, his face a mask of agony, but the spell did its job. He flopped back against the side of the crate, his complexion gray with pain, but the blood had stopped welling from the wound. Using the corner of the crate, he hauled himself upright and tested his weight on the leg. It held.

He said something to Walsingham that I didn't catch. Walsingham nodded. I hoped he wasn't telling him about the two goblins who were silently advancing overhead in the rafters. The back of my neck prickled. If I had hackles, they'd be rising. I could feel Philip was building a summoning. The ability ran in the family. What or who was he summoning?

No. Please, no.

But it was too late. The specter of my first husband, Will, appeared in the air between us.

Will!

Hello, love. Will's ghost and I had been together for three years. We didn't need to speak out loud to each other. *What's going on?*

Philip.

Little bastard! Will said with great vehemence.

Before he and I had run off together, Will had been a regular visitor to our house, so he'd known Philip as a boy and had never been fond of him. My mother had never spotted Philip's sly tricks, but Will had seen everything.

Walsingham took another paper twist out of his pocket and passed it to Philip. "Don't waste the blood, boy."

Philip looked at it. A cruel smile twisted his mouth. He held up his hand red from his own blood and began to read silently from the twist of paper.

Oh! Oh, no. Will's ghost began to twist in the air and spin toward Corwen, still in wolf form. *I'm not going into that thing. I'm not!*

"Philip! In God's name, what do you think you're doing?" I screamed as Will slid inexorably toward Corwen, who was still only half-healed.

"Getting rid of your wolf-man and giving you your husband back, only he doesn't have the skill to change back into a man, so I destroy the only two men you ever loved with one blow. How do you like that?"

"Not one little bit."

I felt the disturbance in the spirit world. There would be hell to pay for this, possibly literally, or something close to it. The balance had already been damaged, and this new indignity would rip a hole in the fabric of that plane.

Will was screaming now, but Corwen seemed calm. His spirit was still firmly lodged in his own body, and he wasn't going to give it up to Will or anybody. At the very last minute, he flopped to the ground, changed back to human, and pulled Will's spirit into himself. Then quick as a flash changed back into a wolf.

Philip scowled at the sudden change but seemed satisfied when everything ended up where he'd expected. "Your wolf-man has gone, Ross. Hello, Will, how do you like four legs instead of two?"

He didn't get an answer. He didn't expect one.

I could hear what was going on because I was still attuned to Will. There was a very strange conversation taking place between Will and Corwen, trapped together in one body.

What's happened?

Shut up, Tremayne, let me think.

Think all you like. God's ballocks, what is that stench?

That's what the world smells like to a wolf.

Shit!

And sweat, and blood, and wood, and grass, and the river.

The wolf that was now half-Corwen and half-Will Tremayne stood up, wobbled as if he didn't know what to do with his legs, and sank to the floor again.

Philip laughed.

What are you doing wolf-man? Will asked.

Convincing Philip that we're no threat.

We aren't.

Don't you believe it.

I'm a wolf.

No, we're a wolf. Both of us in one body. For now.

For now? Are you going somewhere?

Philip thinks I've gone, but he didn't check. You're the one who's going. Ross will put this right, and you can go back to your rest.

Corwen had such faith in me. I hoped I could right the wrong, for both Will and Diccon.

What if I don't want to?

Then you'll be as bad as Philip.

Point taken. So what do we do now?

We wait for an opportunity.

51

Walsingham

WALSINGHAM HAD HAD enough of Philip's games. He rolled another spell toward me and Hookey, remarkably accurate since he was locating us by ear. Pressure knocked me flat. Out of the corner of my eye, I saw Hookey down on the ground, struggling to breathe. It was the same spell he'd used on James Mayo on board the *Black Hawk*. It hadn't killed Mayo, so it probably wouldn't kill us—I hoped. I curled around my belly to protect the twins. They'd been turning somersaults, but now they were ominously still.

No no no. Come on, babies, get moving. Stay with me. We can do this.

The air thickened around me where I lay. It felt as though I'd landed in a tub of molasses that was rapidly solidifying. Every movement I tried to make, I had to push against something which pushed me back. I had one more shot left, the second of my small pistols, tucked into my sash. I managed to reach it, but I didn't dare fire. It would either explode in my hand, or the bullet would simply grind to a halt in midair. I mustn't waste my last shot.

"Where's the wolf?" Walsingham asked.

"Over by the wall, immobile," Philip said.

It took some time for me to turn my head and see what looked like a heap of silver-gray fur. An ear twitched. Slowly, but it twitched, and a low rumble emanated from Will-Corwen's throat.

Phillip left the shelter of Walsingham's protective bubble. From my position on the floor I had a good view of his booted feet as he walked toward me. Quality boots, not footwear Diccon would have been able to afford, so he had turned Diccon into a gentleman after all—his body, anyway.

He checked on Hookey and casually kicked him in the ribs. I heard a grunt, reassuring me that Hookey wasn't dead. Then he took out a pistol, drew back the doghead, and put it to my temple.

"I owe you, sister." Philip squatted so his face was close to mine. The bullet wound didn't seem to be troubling him, though his breeches were rent and covered in blood. "Or, should I say, you owe me." He lowered his voice to barely a whisper. "I see there's a way you might be able to repay the debt."

I saw him glance at my belly. I went hot and cold in turn. My babies. What did he intend?

He touched his face. "I can't stay in here forever. An unformed mind would be much easier to handle and grow into. How would you feel about becoming my mother?"

I heard Corwen growl. He'd realized what Philip meant before I did. He intended to take over my unborn child and live his life again. He didn't know there were two unborns, and I wasn't going to tell him.

"You'd trust yourself to me, Philip? Newborn and defenseless? Look what I did to you last time."

"You'd never harm your own child. You'd always wonder whether there was something of him still in there."

"Or her. Do you fancy being born a girl?"

I saw a fleeting look of surprise cross Philip's face. He hadn't considered that.

"Philip, I need you here." Walsingham rapped out an

order. Surprise turned to annoyance at the peremptory tone. So it wasn't all sweetness and light between them.

"Better go to your master, Philip."

He rose, but as he did so, the damaged leg gave way beneath him, and he staggered before steadying himself. He turned and aimed his pistol at Hookey.

I wanted to tell him no, but that would only make him more certain to shoot. He pulled the trigger. There was a thunderous crack and a cry from Hookey. I swiveled my head with difficulty to see that Philip had shot Hookey in the thigh, in the exact same place I'd shot Philip. Hookey was barely able to move, but I saw he'd clamped his hand over the wound to slow the bleeding.

Philip smirked at me, enjoying my distress.

As he crossed back over to Walsingham, his gait was uneven. I wondered whether Diccon's body was letting him down.

"What did you say to her?" Walsingham asked.

"Greetings of brotherly affection," Philip said.

"Come, read me the book. We need to take care of what's outside our doors before we deal with your sister. I thought they'd bring the Fae boy, not an army of goblins. Page twenty-two."

Philip took a slim notebook from his jacket pocket.

The spell book.

Damnation!

"He said he wanted to take over my baby's existence," I shouted to Walsingham. "He said he'd be reborn as my son. Where would that leave you? You'd lose your eyes and the only other person who has the key to your scribblings."

"Philip?" Walsingham's head swiveled toward where Philip had been the last time he spoke, though Philip was now several paces away.

"You can't trust him, Walsingham. I'm his sister, and I could never trust him. He's always seeking the best opportunity for himself. He'll only stay with you as long as it suits him."

A short yip from Will-Corwen, attracted my attention.

I saw where his gaze was turned. Floating in the rafters of the building was a faint luminescent glow, Diccon's sundered spirit, hovering between the two aerial goblins. I blinked to show him I'd taken notice. I needed to get Philip's spirit out of that body and Diccon's back into it.

Unable to move, I used all my willpower to summon Philip's spirit. I didn't know how secure he was in Diccon, but he couldn't be as secure as someone who had been born into that body and who had grown up in it.

My head began to ache, but I kept on pulling.

Philip knew full well what was happening, but he was using every ounce of his energy to fight me and had no spare capacity for his body or his speech. He dropped to his knees.

Will-Corwen moved. I heard Corwen say, *Leave the wolf to me, Tremayne. You store up some righteous anger and use it*, and then the silver wolf dashed across the warehouse floor. He pounced on Philip, but instead of tearing his throat out, which he could so easily do, he bowled him over, grabbed him by the shoulder, and shook him hard.

Philip twisted and kicked out, but Corwen's grip didn't falter. If once he let go, then Philip might be able to produce one of those damned spells.

"What's happening?" Walsingham's voice rose a couple of tones. "Philip! What's happening?"

"Damned wolf. Tremayne. Let go!"

He hadn't realized Corwen was still in charge of the wolf. Will's determination was shoring up Corwen's damaged body. Corwen hadn't had enough time or done enough changes to heal fully.

The goblins dropped down from the rafters and began to beat Philip around the head with their fists.

Philip's concentration wavered.

I pulled again, and his spirit began to detach from Diccon's body until his hold became tenuous.

"Philip, what's happening?" Walsingham's voice held an edge of panic.

I yanked; Philip's spirit slithered free. The body he'd

been inhabiting collapsed. Corwen and the goblins held onto it but stopped the shaking and hitting.

I let Philip's spirit go and pulled on Diccon's, bundling it up and shoving it back into its own body.

"Oww! Owww!" There was no doubt; Diccon was back where he belonged. Will-Corwen released the boy, who rolled away. The goblins grabbed him by the arms, pulled him to the far side of the warehouse, and shoved him down to the floor.

"Stay down if you want to live."

Diccon stayed.

The wolf grabbed Walsingham's spell book from where it had dropped from Philip's hand. He brought it to me, but I was still pinned down by Walsingham's spell.

"Good," I said. "Don't lose it."

The wolf turned into a man, naked except for the bag over his shoulder. He shoved the book in the bag and began to change back.

No wait. This body. I like it. That was Will speaking. He jiggled up and down and then put his hands to his groin. *It's a long time since I've felt—*

Corwen flipped back to wolf form.

Grow up, Tremayne.

It's all right for you.

No, it's not.

Philip's spirit, now free, spun, fueled by anger. He tried to get close to me, but I wouldn't let him near.

"Go back where you came from, Philip. You've been here too long."

"Philip? What's happening?" Walsingham called.

"Philip doesn't have a tongue anymore," I said, "Or a body. I'm sending him back to the spirit world."

"No!"

"No!"

Philip and Walsingham spoke at once, but I wasn't sure Walsingham could hear Philip.

"Philip, come to me," Walsingham said.

I'm sure he didn't mean it literally—at least I don't think he did, but Philip was in a panic now, taking any chance to retain his hold on the world. He shot toward Walsingham.

"Philip, no!" I put as much command in my voice as I could, but Walsingham's spell still had me trapped on the floor.

I saw Philip's spirit begin to batter the fringes of Walsingham's personality.

Walsingham flinched, and I felt his immobility spell weaken. I rolled over with great difficulty, and sat up, feeling as if a ton weight was pressing me down to the ground. "Philip!"

But Philip was deaf to my call. I saw him sink his spirit hands into Walsingham's flesh. Walsingham jerked upright on his box. His back arched and he clawed at his face with his good hand.

I saw their spirits merge.

For a tense moment nothing happened, then Walsingham began to laugh. "I can see through his eyes! I can see." He turned his head this way and that. I saw Philip's eyes looking out of Walsingham's ruined ones. "And my arm—I can feel it." He waved the stump of his left arm in the air, and I swear I could see a phantom arm and hand. "Oh, I'd have done this sooner if I'd known!"

He stood and faced us.

"Philip is mine. He's my eyes, my hand. His power is my power."

Walsingham seemed to swell. He reached out his phantom hand. "My book. Where is my book? Give it to me."

I felt the pull. He had acquired Philip's power to summon. The book was safe in Corwen's Fae bag. I didn't know how Walsingham could wrest it from him. In effect, it was in another world while ever Corwen was in wolf form. Surely Walsingham-Philip couldn't summon it all the way from Iaru.

Walsingham stood, his eyes glittering with a feverish energy. He turned his attention to the wolf. What Philip knew, Walsingham knew. That worked in reverse. What Philip didn't know was also important. Philip hadn't realized both Will and Corwen were sharing one body. He thought the wolf was Will and therefore didn't expect that the wolf could regain humanity.

When Corwen changed back to naked man, it surprised him, but Walsingham still thought he was confronting Will. "Give me the book, Tremayne."

The bag in which the book was stored lifted free of Corwen's side and, as if drawn by a lodestone, strained toward Walsingham. Corwen threw his weight against the strap that held the bag but was being drawn inexorably closer.

We ... must ... change. That was Corwen.

No. Stay human. Better chance. That was Will.

Will didn't appreciate the devastating importance of the book. If Corwen could change back to wolf, then the book would be inaccessible to Walsingham, but Will was fighting him—fighting the change.

Suddenly, one of the goblins who had helped Diccon to the side of the warehouse sprang into action and flung himself at Corwen's bag, crashing it and Will-Corwen down to the ground.

Corwen took the opportunity to quickly change back to wolf. There was an echo of, *Damn you, wolf-man,* from Will.

Walsingham roared his disappointment.

Keep the book safe, Tremayne. Whatever happens to us, Walsingham mustn't get it.

The goblin rolled sideways, away from the wolf. Walsingham flung a twist of paper into the air and a glowing ball of energy formed in an instant. It swooped down on the unfortunate goblin, exploding inside him so that he was, for an instant, illuminated like the sun, then suddenly reduced to a pile of ash.

It was pure frustration that Walsingham vented against the goblin. He daren't destroy Corwen like that because he might also destroy the book.

I concentrated on Walsingham-Philip, unsure if I should try to separate them. Together, they were enormously powerful, but one of those entities was Philip, and he'd never worked well with others.

I summoned Philip experimentally and found him deeply entrenched within Walsingham and hanging on for dear life. That gave me an idea. Instead of summoning Philip, I summoned Walsingham's spirit, trying to dislodge it from its own body.

Philip immediately caught onto the idea.

"What? No!" Walsingham said that to the Philip inside him. "You need me. You need me!"

I could no longer hear Philip, but I knew what was going on. Walsingham was being pushed back and back, out of his own consciousness. He was being sundered. Philip had had the practice.

And with each reduction in Walsingham's tenure of his own body, I regained more and more movement. I managed to get to my knees and then stumble to my feet. Drawing my last loaded pistol from my sash, I pulled back the doghead and shot Walsingham or, maybe now, Philip smack between the eyes.

Then I sank to my knees and wept.

The doors crashed open. Goblins and sailors poured in from the front and back of the building, led by Twomax from one direction and Windward from the other. Will-Corwen changed back to human and stepped aside to quickly drag on breeches and a shirt.

"Ross!" He knelt beside me.

I flung myself into his arms, not caring, for the moment, whether it was Will or Corwen. He kissed me.

"Will!"

"Ah, my love, I have missed you. I want to stay with you forever. I'll share this body with your wolf-man and love you as he does. I don't think so, Tremayne. This was a temporary alliance born out of necessity. Say your good-byes and let's get it over with."

Hearing them arguing with each other in the same voice shocked me back to reality.

"You can't stay, Will."

"Why not? Do you love him more than me?"

"It's not a question you should ask, now or ever. I loved you with all my heart, but you died. I have a new life now, a new love. I will always love you, Will, but by all the laws of the universe, you must return to your rest and surrender Corwen's body."

Corwen, wisely, said nothing.

For a time, neither did Will. I could almost hear him thinking.

At length he sighed. "I know. Thank you, wolf-man, for giving me the chance to say good-bye. Set me free, sweet Rossalinde, and I'll lead these two damned souls so deep into the nether-world that not even you will be able to call them back."

"You're a free spirit, Will. You always have been and always will be."

I didn't even have to pull very hard. I drew Will's spirit from Corwen's body and watched him round up both Philip and Walsingham and drag them away.

I was left in Corwen's arms.

52

The Book

THE GOBLINS TOOK charge of Walsingham's corpse, burning it to ash on a pyre of packing crates on the bank of the Thames. He couldn't come back from that and neither could Philip. I would deal with my feelings later. If it was possible to kill someone who was already dead, I'd killed my brother not once, but twice.

I bound Hookey's leg with a brandy-soaked bandage, thankful that the bullet had gone straight through without hitting a spurting blood vessel.

Despite being in pain, Hookey had sent Lazy Billy to ask the watermen to wait and had then taken charge of Diccon. Diccon's leg wound was sore, but after the spell that Walsingham had used, it hadn't opened up again. Just like Hookey's wound, the bullet had gone right through without snagging anything vital. He would recover, physically at least.

Hookey offered him a place on the *Heart*'s crew, but he declined, saying he needed to find his mother. I hoped he succeeded. I wasn't going to get involved. It was over now. All we had to do was dispose of the book.

"Have you still got it?" I asked Corwen quietly.

"I have."

"Have you read it?"

"I have not. Nor do I want to."

"How do we destroy it?"

"Your Aunt Rosie will know."

Dawn was streaking the eastern sky with lavender fingers, and the wind had dropped as the crew carried Hookey back to the boats on a board. I was exempt from carrying duties. The twins had begun to wake again and carrying them was all the exercise I needed. We said our good-byes to Mr. Twomax and the goblins at Mill Wall Stairs. They were going upriver as far as Westminster, while we were going back to Wapping.

Back to the *Heart of Oak*.

Hookey grumbled at us for making a fuss but didn't object when we sent for Lady Henrietta. She arrived before breakfast and carried him off to her London house, promising to send for her own surgeon to tend him. I gave him a hug as he departed, and Lady Henrietta grinned at me. "I'll take good care of him."

"I know you will."

Mr. Rafiq, who had been, all this time, guarding the *Heart* with the other half of her crew, took charge. We all dined on Lazy Billy's breakfast of porridge with bacon and hunks of fresh bread, still warm from the bakery.

By midmorning, we'd received a message from Lady Henrietta that the surgeon had declared himself satisfied that the wound was clean, and Hookey was sleeping, aided by a dose of laudanum strong enough to fell an ox.

Mr. Rafiq smiled. "We've time for one more cargo of wool to France and brandy back to Sussex before the war against Boney resumes. I can handle that. Let Captain Garrity spend some time with his Etta before we sail again."

I had a feeling that Hookey might find a string of excuses to keep returning to Rye Harbor. I heartily approved.

"What about when the war starts again? I'm not insisting that you sail into danger."

"I think you'll find we've had enough of peace time."

"You'll go back to Bacalao?"

"With our Letters of Marque for the *Heart* and the *Butterfly*."

"Give my regards to Captain Sharpner."

He smiled. "I will, and I'll look after your investment."

"I know you will."

Corwen and I spent one last night in the Town of Ramsgate and woke the following morning long after the *Heart* had sailed. I didn't like dockside good-byes.

"You'll always miss that part of your life," Corwen said. "But it's not as if you'll never see them again."

"I know," I patted my belly. "Besides, I'm going to be busy for a while. These little monsters have been dancing on my bladder all night, and it's only going to get worse between now and November."

He put one warm hand on the small of my back and rubbed my ever-increasing belly with the other, then bent and kissed it through my nightgown.

"No more breeches for a while," he said.

"I'm afraid not."

"Don't sound so rueful."

"I'm not. Really I'm not." I almost believed myself.

We dressed, breakfasted, and then collected Timpani and Dancer from the Red Lion stables. On the way out of London, we called at Margaret Street to catch up with Lily and George and let them know that the Walsingham problem had been solved.

Lily hugged us both for a long time without saying anything. And then made us tell everything in the minutest of detail.

We disclosed everything except Philip's threat to take up residence in one of our babies. I thought that might upset her too much, especially if she was contemplating motherhood herself.

George said they would see us back in Yorkshire four days from now. They had an appointment with an architect to talk about drawing up plans for a new house on the hillside above the mill.

"We'll need a place of our own if you two are going to fill Denby House with children," Lily said. "And it will be close enough to visit. I thought we might include an apartment for Mother, so she can spend some time with us."

"I'm sure she'll like that," Corwen said.

"My grandfather asked me to remind you about the place in Parliament," George said. "He says the suggestion comes from Mr. Pitt himself. There's no rush, but he asks you to think about it once you've settled yourselves in Yorkshire."

Corwen promised he would consider it carefully, and we left Lily and George to their plans.

Our way to Aunt Rosie's led us through Iaru, so we stopped off to see David, pleased to find that Annie was with him again.

"Father has given in gracefully," David said. "And Annie has consented to marry me. We're going to do it twice, a handfasting here and a church wedding with Reverend Purdy officiating. We'd like you to come, of course."

"We'd be delighted." I hugged him, and then I hugged Annie for good measure. "Are you happy?" I whispered.

Her broad grin told me everything I wanted to know.

"It's good to see everything coming right for everyone," I said. "We've had Walsingham and the Mysterium hanging over our heads for too long. It will be good to please ourselves and not be pushed this way and that by the Fae."

"Though you know you're their first port of call if they want anything from the human world," David said. "It almost seems worth Corwen taking that seat in Parliament."

"I wasn't fobbing him off when I told George I'd think about it," Corwen said.

"I know," I said. "I recognized the signs, but let's have our babies first."

"Of course."

We made our way to Summoner's Well and found Leo in the forge, without customers for once, blowing air through the fire with bellows.

"What are you making?" I asked, looking around to see if there was anything half-made.

"Nothing. Rosie said you'd be coming today and I was to get the fire nice and hot as you'd have something to burn."

"Ah, it sounds as though Aunt Rosie is ahead of us."

"Ahead of you and fully behind you." Aunt Rosie came into the forge, dusting off her hands on her apron. "You've got it, then?"

"We have, and Walsingham is no more." We'd tell her the whole story, including the way I'd had to kill my own brother for the second time, once we'd disposed of the book.

"I had Leo make this." From the bench at the side of the forge, Rosie took a contraption that consisted of two hinged iron frames, roughly book-sized, with a short handle that flattened out. "Put the book in here."

Corwen took it out of his pocket and offered it to her. "No, you've touched it. You put it in the iron. I don't want to handle it."

"Aren't you a little bit curious to know what's in it," I said.

"No," Rosie answered. "You didn't peep, did you?"

I shook my head.

"You?" she asked Corwen.

"No."

"Good." She turned around. "Leo, will you do the honors?"

Leo latched the hinges, sealing the book inside, picked it up with a huge pair of iron tongs, and shoved it into the white-hot heart of the fire. It smoked and then burst into flames with an ear-splitting shriek. Then instead of powdering to ash, it began to melt, oozing blood which boiled and spat in the flames and then burned with oily black smoke and a whimpering sound. At last the whole lot was consumed until only the iron was left.

"You know what to do?" Rosie asked.

"Aye," Leo said. "Break the iron up and bury it deep

in four separate places, here, the Old Maizy, Iaru, and the Okewood."

"Right," Aunt Rosie said. "I think we could all do with a nice cup of tea and a piece of cake."

Tea and cake. Medicine for whatever ails you.

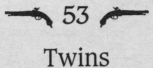# 53

Twins

ON THE LAST day of October Aunt Rosie arrived at Denby House with her midwife's bag and a reassuring smile.

"I thought we'd have to send for you when it was time," I said as I eased myself into a chair in the drawing room.

"It's time," Aunt Rosie said. "Or it will be tomorrow."

"Oh! I've been feeling as big as a house side for weeks now. I've been hoping it would be today, and today and today. I thought I must have got my dates wrong."

Aunt Rosie laughed. "I've been keeping track."

She looked at me and Corwen. "Have you two been keeping up your marital relations?"

"What? Aunt Rosie, I have a bump the size of a small mountain."

"That's no excuse. Tonight. It'll remind those two how they got in there and tell them it's time to come out. It may be an old wives' tale, but it works, trust me. Have you been taking your raspberry leaf tea?"

"Every day."

"Well, then, what can go wrong?"

"I love your Aunt Rosie, she's so down to earth," Corwen said as we climbed the stairs after supper. "Have you two been keeping up your marital relations?" He did a passable imitation of her voice and set me off giggling.

"Come on." We reached our door. "Marital relations coming up as ordered."

"Do you need an order?"

"No, I simply need permission. You've been so uncomfortable these last few weeks. I thought you'd appreciate a back rub more than anything."

"Is my belly too gross?"

"It's not gross at all, it's beautiful. You're beautiful."

He kissed me.

I believe I may have kissed him back.

"Even if you do block out the sun."

I aimed a lazy blow at his chin, but he caught my hand and kissed it. "I don't want you to get too conceited."

He helped me out of my dress and my short stays—there may have been more kisses involved—and knelt in front of me with his ear to my enormous belly. "They're lazy. I swear I can hear them snoring in there."

He undid the ribbon on my chemise. It slid off my shoulders and pooled on the floor around my ankles.

"Oh, look at that. I think it's even bigger today than it was yesterday." He stroked my belly. "Tight as a drum. You, my love, are ripe and ready for plucking."

"Plucking?"

"That's what I said. Plucking."

"Just checking."

He picked me up, groaning overdramatically under my weight and deposited me gently on the counterpane, kissing my lips and letting his kisses wander down to my throat and my breasts, also tight and fulsome. I wriggled with the pleasure of it and then made a moue when he stopped for a moment. It didn't take him long to rid himself of his breeches and shirt.

"What about my stockings," I said. "They seem to be all that's between me and debauchery."

"Well, we can't have anything in our way, can we?"

He addressed the problem of my stockings very thoroughly with more stroking and kissing until I melted into an incoherent blob.

"How are you doing in there?"

"I'm fine."

"I was speaking to the children."

"Corwen!"

"Yes, my love?"

I reached for him and found him ready. "Get on with it."

We both collapsed into laughter, and he drew me close, with my back to his belly, making good use of his hands as he found his way home.

We dozed off in each other's arms only to come around later. We were shivering because the fire was dying, and we'd completely forgotten to get under the covers. Corwen made up the fire and pulled the covers into place, but then—well—we were both awake again, so . . .

"I love you so much," he said afterward. "You know that, don't you?"

"I think you may have proved it a few times. You know I love you, too, don't you?"

"I do."

"I want you to remember that when I'm cursing your name and screaming like a fishwife." I felt my belly tighten. "It's starting."

"Shall I get Aunt Rosie?"

"No, not yet. Let's lie here for a while."

Within a couple of hours lying down was worse than walking around the bedroom. Corwen walked me up and down, up and down. He rubbed my back and rubbed my belly.

"Ah." The pains were closer now and sharper, and longer, and this time my knees gave way.

"I'll get Aunt Rosie."

"I think it's time."

I don't remember too much about the next part. I suppose that's nature's way of making sure women don't say never again. I have flashes of memory. Aunt Rosie, of course. Poppy wiping my face with a damp cloth soaked in lemon juice. Screaming so loud that the women couldn't keep Corwen out of the room any longer, though they made him sit by my head and hold my hand.

I don't think I cursed him for putting in my belly what was struggling to get out, but when he put his head to mine and said, "It's a boy. What did I tell you?" I simply gritted my teeth and hoped the second one would be a girl.

She was.

And when Corwen helped me to sit up and put our beautiful pink-faced healthy babies into my arms, I think he was crying as much as I was.

It was June 1803. We'd spent a whole year in Yorkshire without the shadow of Walsingham or the Mysterium. I'd had reports that the *Heart of Oak* and the *Butterfly* were doing good trade by causing chaos among French merchant shipping. My own private fortune was comfortable enough that I was in the process of investing in another ship, the *Montague*, which would carry sixteen guns and be captained by Mr. Rafiq once she was fitted out for the privateering trade.

Corwen was still considering whether to become the first magical member of Parliament for the Okewood constituency, but he hadn't made up his mind yet. There was no rush to do so with the war with France being the most pressing Parliamentary matter. Truth to tell, he was enjoying the estate, picking up where his older brother Jonathan had left off. And we were all, Timpani and Dancer included, anxiously awaiting the arrival of four foals, the first, as far as we knew, magical cross-breeds.

The day was blue-sky perfection. I suggested a gentle stroll down to the lake. It had to be a gentle stroll because Lily was so advanced in her pregnancy that she claimed she hadn't seen her feet for months. I was expecting Aunt Rosie to turn up on the doorstep any day now. The new house, Mill House, was almost complete, but George and

Lily wouldn't be moving in until after the birth and the churching.

Poppy was quick to accept our invitation to walk in the sunshine since Alice was now on leading strings and loved being outside. Robin, her adopted son, the ex-workhouse boy, was given a reprieve from conjugating Latin verbs. Maybe it was Latin that drove children mad because he couldn't manage a gentle stroll and galloped down to the lake, screaming for the joy of it, and then flopped down on the grass to await our arrival.

I hadn't expected Mama to join us, but I was delighted when she said she would. She'd been withdrawn and melancholy over the winter months, still missing her husband, but I thought at last she might be coming out of the long dark tunnel.

Stephen Yeardley, Poppy's husband, who had looked after Mr. Deverell in his last illness, had grown into the post of estate steward. He had decided to award himself an afternoon off, and walked behind us, carrying a blanket and a basket of refreshments. He was just as much part of the extended family as Poppy was.

The other new addition to our family was Liza, our rowankind nurserymaid who was Mr. Topping's third-oldest daughter, and worth her weight in gold. Twins were such hard work. Liza carried Hugh, and I carried Emma, who at the age of eight months was a substantial weight.

Stephen spread a large blanket, and Liza and I plonked the babies in the middle of it, giving them a selection of rattles and wooden blocks. They soon worked out that the most entertaining game was throwing things as far as they could and watching Robin retrieving them. Emma, particularly, had picked up the idea that teasing Robin was great sport.

I could see Corwen striding toward us from the direction of the stables. He looked like a country squire, wearing breeches, top boots, and an open-necked shirt, his sleeves rolled up to the elbow. There was a spring in his step. He looked happy. In truth, we were all happy. It was a moment of grace. Whatever life threw at us in future, we could cope with because we were family.

I turned away from the twins for a moment to wave to Corwen and heard a gasp from Liza. Emma had had enough of rattles and teasing and had decided to explore the blanket by squirming forward. That was when it happened. Instead of a baby, there was a brindle wolf cub struggling to wriggle out of a tangle of baby garments.

"Oh, sweetheart," I picked her up and held her close. "Going to take after your father, I see."

She licked my nose and yipped.

Not to be outdone, Hugh started to roll over and his little hands flexed into pads. By the time I scooped him up he was a snowy white cub.

I hugged them both and began to laugh.

Jacey Bedford

The Psi-Tech Novels

"Space opera isn't dead; instead, delightfully, it has grown up."　—Jaine Fenn,
　　　　author of *Principles of Angels*

"A well-defined and intriguing tale set in the not-too-distant future.... Everything is undeniably creative and colorful, from the technology to foreign planets to the human (and humanoid) characters."
　—*RT Book Reviews*

"Bedford mixes romance and intrigue in this promising debut.... Readers who crave high adventure and tense plots will enjoy this voyage into the future."
　—*Publishers Weekly*

Empire of Dust
978-0-7564-1016-2

Crossways
978-0-7564-1017-9

Nimbus
978-0-7564-1189-3

To Order Call: 1-800-788-6262
www.dawbooks.com